Pashtun

Books by Ron Lealos

Don't Mean Nuthin'

No Merci

No Direction Home

Saigon Redux

Jaws of the Traitor

The Sixth Man

www.ronlealosbooks.com

Pashtun

A Military Thriller

Ron Lealos

Skyhorse Publishing

Library of Congress Cataloging-in-Publication Data is available on file.

Cover design by Ashley Lau
Front cover photograph: Thinkstock

ISBN: 978-1-5107-1200-3
Ebook ISBN: 978-1-62914-151-0
Previous ISBN: 978-1-62873-781-3

Printed in the United States of America

This book is dedicated to the master, Tom Spanbauer, who taught me there is no such thing as a boring story. Only boring writing. I've tried to live up to that and many of the gems of wisdom he imparted. Thanks, Tom.

So simple. Just breathe. Inhale. Exhale. The migraine came from sucking, like someone just took me off the ventilator. They said I'd get used to it. Swallow the pills. Even Viagra helped, if you could get it. And I was sick of looking at brown rocks and mountains. And Pashtuns. But what I really wanted was to breathe air thick enough to hold more than just a hint of oxygen. Where a match stays lit. Maybe the artillery in my temples would go away. And I wouldn't hate the dirt garden of Afghanistan like I did.

It hadn't been my plan to come over to this desolation to hate. Looking at my reflection in the shallows of a clear Afghan mountain lake, I could still see the face of a smalltown Kansas boy. Not a killer. But the lines on my forehead and around my eyes were increasing. The high altitude made me hallucinate.

Six months and they had sent me even deeper into Tora Bora. More of the hadjis needed killing. It was my job. A Jayhawk dispatched to the Company for one purpose—and only because I knew the difference between *ddeemokraasi* and democracy. Sometimes, I cursed my *Zhebe,* tongue, for its unwanted skill in wrapping itself around a language of too many vowels. But, all the CIA training couldn't teach me to get over the smell. I'd learned that, while on an op, I could smear Vicks Vaporub in my nose, just like the cops before they fish out an overripe corpse from the dumpster. Water around these parts wasn't wasted on bathing, and my victims usually voided themselves in the death rattle.

I was just kidding myself. It wasn't the smell. Or the air so thin we could be on a lunar desert. It was the eyes. Those big, black eyes that followed me like I was the anti-Muhammad every time I came near a Pashtu. Haunting, beautiful eyes that make the cover of *National Geographic*. When I close my own, other eyes are imprinted on my lids. The eyes of the dead.

None of the gung-ho stuff scared me. I wasn't any kind of macho, mindless patriotic machine. It's not that. Friends, family, and the support system of a small Kansas community groomed me in the ethic of the Plains. I've learned to compartmentalize the terror. What kept sleep away was doubt. The fear and knowledge that those eyes were truly innocent, not the bearded mujahedeen madmen described by every drill sergeant and CIA instructor. And I had been ordered over and over to send them on their journey to meet Allah on the word of a desk jockey sifting through a spreadsheet. The intel around there was infamously wrong. And the attitude was a big yawn. One fewer suicide bomber in the making. I could have been sent out on the word of a Pashtu who felt his daughter had been dishonored by the neighbor's glance.

In the field, I had been accused of being reckless. It's a love-hate thing. If my actions raised the body count and no one but a local was greased, I'd get "atta-boys." Of course, nothing went in my file back in Langley unless a friendly became collateral damage. That event might have even brought the ire of the *New York Times*. The reckless part of me grew. The new me was a personality who had seen enough and understood retribution was approaching. And it would be an eternal bitch.

Fate. It was near, and I was afraid of the debt, not the doing. Not scared of looking up to the cliffs when AK rounds chipped the rocks beside my head. Nor the sound of an RPG shooshing by. Or the smoking hulk of an APC on the side of a mountain road, medics rushing in to pull out bodies before skin peeled off like the outside of a burnt marshmallow. No, it was the fucking mines.

Dead was better than a legless plane ride home to weeping relatives. I hoped my karma wasn't that bad. Mahoney was always on the winning side when we played a lazy afternoon game of touch football back at the base. He could out-jump every other spook in the barracks. You just had to throw the ball high enough. Now the only thing he'll be leaping for is his disability check from a wheelchair. I want to keep my legs.

Even the smiling little village girls with shawls over their heads, begging for chocolate, couldn't get me to return their grins. The spectacular purple flowers that sprung out of the rocks in the most unlikely places only made me wonder what was fertilizing their growth in this dry landscape. Sure, I could see some of the highest mountains in the world out the window of the chopper. But then, I looked down. Everywhere, brown ugly rocks. The Discovery Channel might show pictures that made this wasteland seem spectacular. Colorful tribesmen with toothless smiles. Green valleys with gentle steams irrigating lush farms. You know, that rugged, wild look. But the photographer got to go home. He didn't live to wake up in the morning to a diet of boulders and blood. He got escorted around with a squad of jarheads who didn't take him into areas that hadn't been swept. Maybe, if the reporter got lucky, some insane Pashtu would take a shot at the convoy, giving him lots to talk about over his glass of Chablis back at the Kabul Hilton. *Exotic. Primitive. Serene. Raw beauty.* All words and pictures to fantasize about from the couch. Me, it's life. And it sure ain't beautiful.

Home to me was this tent. The people I worked for weren't really military. They came from a long line of killers made notorious in Vietnam. Wild Bill Donovan was our daddy. His spawn, the Phoenix Program. The skills I was taught are just a refinement of the methods my ancestors learned when they snuck up on Victor Charley asleep in his hootch and put a silenced bullet in his brain. Now, it's Harry or Helen Hadji. Same story. Same old men in their Brooks Brothers suits writing the death warrants. Same Generals with their spit-shine aides wiping their asses and ordering me into Khewa to grease a suspected al-Qaeda sympathizer. There were no courts here. Suspect was enough to get you dead.

The shrinks might say people don't change, even though, if there is no hope, there's no reason for anyone to see fuckin' therapist. I didn't used to swear. Wouldn't think of calling anyone a *dune coon* or a *dung shit*. I used to get a time-out and fined twenty-five cents from my allowance if I used *fuck*. So, it was better to say *damn*. It only cost a nickel. My vocabulary increased every day. Before, I never knew that horse cock was Spam. Or that a nutsack was a 100-round ammo holder on an M249 Automatic Weapon.

We went to church, too, like most everyone else in Millard, Kansas. None of my friends were terrorists. Sure, we dropped rotten pumpkins on Mrs. Devlin's porch and turned her underwear inside out on the clothesline.

But it was harmless. We never called her a fuckin' skank raghead bitch. Not even Timmy Russet, the real town outlaw and my best friend. Now, Timmy's finishing up an accelerated doctoral program in particle physics at Michigan State. But he used to throw M1 fire crackers with extended fuses. He built them from wound paper and glue. We tossed the homemade fireworks at the cop cars parked in front of Swindley's Donuts. Timmy got busted and grounded for a week. No gangs. No crack. No AIDS. Now, I'm in the toughest gang of all. The CIA. Headquartered in the meanest place on Earth outside Baghdad. Jalalabad, Afghanistan.

Nothing much of note after leaving the corn fields of Millard. Four years of study at Kansas State. Visiting parents lots of weekends. A girlfriend off to New York City to find her voice in the publishing world. The usual tailgate parties on Fall Saturdays. Middle American college fun with classes the only distraction. Easy. Aimless. No one died. Then 9/11. In the dorm, I watched the smoke billow from the World Trade Center, and I was angry. Not just at the horror. At myself. I was contributing nothing but a few more dollars to the Coors piggy bank.

For a young man who'd never been west of Denver or east of Louisville, a magic wand had been passed over my tongue. Languages slid off as easy as the fifth tequila shooter went down. If I heard a group of foreign students chatting outside the library, I could pick up the words, and a screen in my brain gave them life. It wasn't as if I translated verbatim, but the cadences, clicks, rolls, and grunts weren't alien. And, if I chose, I could get a book, a tape, or go on the web and join the group the next day, at least able to communicate. Luis, the Hispanic who mowed our neighbor's lawn at home, couldn't call Mrs. LaPlante a *vaca gorda puta* because I knew he meant she was a fat cow whore. And she didn't weigh an ounce more than two-hundred. When I enlisted and after basic and more advanced training, I was sent to the Defense Language Institute in Monterey. Master Sergeant Gomez had noticed it wasn't just Spanish that slid off my tongue. That's where the Company found me. My career as a patriotic semi-Pashto-speaking killer was launched.

Last night, an MH-6 Little Bird helicopter dropped us just south of Shahi Kowt. Intel said a mud hut outside the town was a meeting place for al-Qaeda operatives. But there was no reason to believe the sources were more right this time than any of the other clusterfucks.

Moonbeams danced off the peaks of twenty-thousand-foot mountains. In the valley below, an occasional muted orange came from a kerosene lamp inside a hut. From miles away, a few passing cars or jeeps bounced on the hardscrabble trails, the glow from their headlights jumping wildly with each pothole or rock. Sheep grazed lazily, searching for anything that resembled food, their silhouettes dark against the slopes. We were running naked, the lights off and the sound suppressors on, the Little Bird painted black and unmarked. I followed the twisting lines of a river, fed by snowmelt in the Hindukush, and wondered if the next twenty-four hours would keep me awake like the last three missions. Or find me fertilizing one of a trillion rocks.

Not even waiting for us to touch down, the Little Bird pulled away. Thorsten and I jumped to the pebbled ground and quickly dashed for the nearest cover. We still had to hump a few klicks east and wouldn't be considered friendlies in this neighborhood, where every man carried a rifle and had an arsenal stashed in the well. The ATN Cougar 2I Night Vision Goggles strapped around our heads gave a clear view for 150 yards. It was easy to pick out one boulder from the next and, after a while, the moon gave us enough light to put away the goggles. Sweat ran down our faces as though we were in a rainstorm in a land where anything over twelve inches in a year is a monsoon.

The CIA had made sure we were outfitted in the best technology corporate America could supply for efficient stealth killing. When we arrived at our hidey hole, we could watch for movement in the dark through the ATN Thermal Eye 225Ds in our Blackhawk X-1 Backpacks with the silent zipper pulls in case anyone was near enough to hear us reach for a HOOAH! Chocolate Crisp Energy Bar or slurp from our HydraStorm Hydration System tubes. If we needed to call in a Drone and spread the shit of a tribe of Pashtuns around on the gravel, we could guide the missiles with an L-3 TruTrak GPS so accurate it would trim the beard of the targeted enemy before it slammed into the ground. The black earpiece and the mike in front of our mouths let us stay in communication with each other and the minders back at the ops base on the FS 5000 Spy Radio. But all these gadgets were nothing compared to the arsenal on our backs, stuffed in the pockets of our night camo fatigues, or in our hands.

We could blow up a suburb of Kabul if it all detonated at once. My favorite, the old trusty standby, was the .22 Hush Puppy silenced pistol, made notorious in Vietnam by my mentors from Phoenix. I wasn't going to shoot any dogs. Success in these kinds of ops really meant getting in quietly and out even more quietly. If we had to use the armory on our backs, we were in a world of shit. That was the point of not just phoning in an air strike and blasting the targets further into the Stone Age. We needed intel. Or so I was told. And to leave a few bodies as a reminder if we found hostiles.

The old woman stood by the stone well, looking down. She tried to turn the bucket lift, but it was stuck on the dog. I only knew she was old because the Steiner 8 x 30 binoculars brought her stoop and the wrinkles into focus from nearly three hundred yards. Up close, she could have been fifteen. Now, I thought "old" seemed right, even though she might not have been a year past my twenty-five. Afghanistan aged women harshly. And men. If they lived.

Two small boys kicked a crushed can and chased each other in the dusty courtyard, screaming *"barj ra-histah,"* catch me, in the morning sun. The old woman yelled *"aram."* Quiet. I could hear the boys shriek and the old woman's commands through the DetectEar Parabolic Microphone headset. With all the techno widgets, I felt like Luke Skywalker in a desert of dinosaurs.

The old woman went back to fiddling with the rope, every few seconds glancing below the wooden support beams, leaning on the rough-edged rocks. No one, it seemed, had missed the dog. During the late night, before we placed the listening devices, the dog yelped to warn of intruders. He had that mongrel third-world look, though taller than most and skinny enough to be a meal only for the starving. His milky eyes shone in the darkness and he growled as Thorsten's silenced .22 bullet went into his brain. Thorsten knew I wouldn't shoot a dog. A Taliban probably, but I drew the line at animals. He pulled the trigger and winked at me. There was no place to hide the carcass, so we dropped it down the well and scuffed the blood stains with our desert boots. Now, the only thing that marked our trail was the flies.

They might come in daylight if the meeting was urgent. It was more likely we would have to wait into the night, hunkered behind boulders the size of Humvees. We had the camo blankets over us, and even a sheep would start to nibble on our feet before he knew we were there. At least we had the hydration bottles and hoses so we could drink without movement in the afternoon heat. Pissing was a problem, but having my dick in the gravel was the least of my worries.

It was supposed to be a summit of local Taliban chieftains, certainly supporters of al-Qaeda if they were. They wouldn't come alone to this place. Not their style. It would be in teams of at least six, probably more. And the women better not be visible. Their duty was to be unseen. Any respectable Taliban man knew women were seducers and only distracted from Allah's work.

If intel was right, and we had to phone for the Predator Drones, the women wouldn't be whipped again, and the children would never kick another can in the dust. They'd be red blood smears on the brown rocks. But, I wasn't going to let that annihilation happen. Too many eyes would appear in my nightmares.

Our job was supposed to be simple—listen and report. With my smattering of Pashto, I was a thousand klicks ahead of anyone else with an Anglo face around this part of Tora Bora. If I heard the devil's name, Osama, come through my headset or picked up any hint of evil intent, it was time for the bandits to shoot their Hellfire missiles and make tomato soup spiced with clay. If it was more innocent, take a few snaps with the LIVAR 400 long-range surveillance camera, adding to the rows of mug shots pinned to the corkboard at HQ or filling the Windows Vista picture files labeled Suspected al-Qaeda.

Tired. Not from the lack of real air or the times I woke in the middle of night thinking I was drowning—only to find out I was in my cot and it was just another attack of altitude sickness. Or from the ten-klick humps up and down the hardscrabble bleakness. It was the killing.

The RPGs didn't choose between women, children, and enemy. They just did their job, blowing body parts into the clear blue sky. The darkness didn't veil the last wide-eyed look of a target if he awoke before I put a round through his forehead. But his shock invaded my dreams. The visions always asked "why?" And I couldn't answer.

I was in this fucked-up place because of a belief I was resolving guilt issues. And a patriotic debt. And I was actually only feeling guiltier.

I was helping make sure the oil pipeline from Central Asia to the Arabian Sea was completed. Anyone getting in the way pissed off the petroleum lobby, Haliburton, and its subsidizer, the Pentagon, and all the politicians with oil greasing their veins. And the funding was helped by the world's largest suppliers of heroin, the Taliban. Tonight's op was just another reminder. If Osama's name came up, I was ordered to have the voices silenced with four hundred pounds of high explosives, not captured so the interrogators at the base could gather intel. I now feared no one wanted Osama found. He was the face splashed around the globe to justify any and all atrocities.

Thorsten was a believer, though. It was easier that way. Turn off the conscience and do your duty. Focus on the planes burrowing into the Twin Towers like a drill bit into a bonanza oil field. It used to be "kill a commie for Christ." Now, it was "murder a Mujahideen for more oil." Thorsten didn't think that way, nor did most of the grunts at the base. Those thoughts could drive you crazy. Or get you dead. He carried out his orders, and the list of corpses always kept the good guys ahead in the body count. Now, he was a problem. I wasn't killing anyone else unless they had "Terrorist" tattooed below their turbans.

Movement on a far hill. Within seconds, the profiles of five men, walking slowly across the horizon. Sky framing their steps behind the rocks. Flowing pants, sleeveless orders, and fleece-lined jackets, beards, turbans, and AK74Ms.

Two of the men had Soviet-made RGD5 grenades on criss-crossed bandoleers strapped to their chests. A black-and-white spotted dog loped along in front of the men. As they came down the rocky hillside, their grayness blended with the terrain. It was only the change in the shadows that allowed us to track them. They were early.

The old woman looked up, staring at the men, and covered her face with a black shawl. Still running in the gravel, the boys hadn't noticed the arrivals. "*Stana*," she barked. Inside. "*Ak-nun*." Now. The boys stopped, stood still, and followed the old woman's gaze to the approaching men. No further hesitation. They moved toward a tent near the baked mud hut, opened the flaps, and disappeared.

A nudge from Thorsten. I followed his stare a hundred meters left of the descending men. Coming over the ridge, six more in identical uniforms. Just as well-armed and cautiously moving. Something had to be important. Men like them rarely moved about during daylight. They would be easy targets for any soldiers from a dozen countries keeping peace in a land that had never lost a war.

Within minutes, they were exchanging bear hugs and cheek kisses in the open area in front of the hut, Kalashnikovs dangling from shoulder straps. Our headsets were filled with "*khudai de mal sha*." May God be with you.

Not even the ever-present vultures were circling overhead. The sheep had stopped grazing. A silent messenger must have told every living thing in this kill zone that violence was near. The dog nestled against the wall of the hut, panting shallowly and watching. Nothing but the men moved. The constant, low howl of the mountain wind through the valley ended, and the only noise came from the hissing under our earplugs. It was deathly silent.

The turbaned men went into the hut; one man stayed outside with his AK, scanning the hillsides. We switched from the parabolics to the ASB1200 listening-device receivers. Thorsten wouldn't know what he was hearing, only alert to the name "Osama."

The voices were clear, and I heard them easily. They spoke quietly of lost comrades and past campaigns. Soldier's stories. Mostly, talk was about their glorious victory over the Russian heathens. Much of it I understood, but there were words beyond my Pashto vocabulary. Even if anything came out of their mouths that would give the intel guys a boner, I knew I wasn't going to pass it on, especially now that a young man had made his way down the mountainside, leading a flock of sheep thin enough to hear their ribs creak. He bowed to the guard and went inside the tent.

Thorsten kept glancing at me, a question on his face. He wanted to know if it was time to phone home. Or if we should just crawl up and lob a few M67 grenades into the hut, followed by a shitstorm from the Heckler & Koch G36 semi-automatics. I kept shaking my head, acting as if nothing worthy of an execution was being said.

Even this high in the lower Safed Koh Mountains, the rising sun made it uncomfortable to lay out in the open while covered by a camo blanket. Behind, and much higher, the land was filled with pine, larch, and yew. Here, it was even more barren than the Mojave. Not even bushes. The earth only grew rocks in these parts. Earthquakes regularly hit the area, but we weren't in danger of being crushed by falling building material. Only boulders. The smell of burning meat came from a cooking fire, the smoke disappearing in the breeze as soon as it escaped the tent's vent. The dry chalky scent of the earth coated my nostrils and made me want to sneeze. Thorsten was getting itchy; he was a bigger problem than the ants that had found their way into my crotch.

The military feasted on men like Thorsten. Men who found killing a suspected enemy to be as carefree as snuffing a dog. While there were others like me, wondering whether Hamid Karzai's job with Unocal—before being named puppet President of Afghanistan—had anything to do with our lying in the dust, rocks poking into our balls, ready to waste more threats to the oil supply. Sometimes, a few of us would get together for a bull session. Now that the Pentagon seemed to be run by an arm of the Church of Pat Robertson, these gatherings felt more like those of Jews secretly huddling in Nazi Germany. I was only invited to the séance because Snyder heard me question a Captain about his command to "waste a few ragheads today. And keep it off CNN." I was only a guest among grunts. Since my first landing at the base, a hundred years ago, I had become someone the CIA wouldn't want talking to the media—or defending the motherland and its greed for a full fuel tank with a load of smack in the arm.

What I saw of the Taliban and their insanity—not the visions of 9/11 or the threat of court marshal—kept me going out on these ops every day.

As the noose tightened again, especially in the south, girls were killed for going to school. Teachers and anyone hinting at intellectual or artistic pursuits were being murdered. If you weren't part of the Taliban tribe, it was better to stay behind mud walls. If you were female, to go out was tempting death.

While I didn't want to kill anymore just so Aunt Margaret could drive her old Cadillac to Wal-mart, something had to be done to stop the evil of the Taliban. And their bloody brothers, the al-Qaeda. But I couldn't kill any more innocents, especially in a land where guilt was easy to prove when the judge's sentence had already been given. Picking a guilty party in this death dance was nearly impossible for me.

I tightened my earplugs and listened to the sucking sounds that come from men passing a hookah and the slurps of Kahva green tea.

Nothing more sinister than the gathering of a clan. A heavily armed one. "*Hawaa*," weather, was the most used word after "Allah." This reunion could have been in front of the fireplace back in Kansas, chatting about the latest blizzard, if it weren't for the Kalashnikovs. In Millard, they were Smith & Wessons.

Beside me, Thorsten was becoming more anxious. Could be the Dexedrine he swallowed for performance enhancement, aggravated by the urge to put another notch on his Heckler & Koch. The medics handed the little tablets out like white M&Ms and called them "go-pills," the opposite of the red "no-go pills" that let sleep come when the nightmares kept you awake, but that never stopped the daymares. In a lecture back at Camp Perry, a suit from the Pentagon's Defense Advanced Research Projects Agency (DARPA), explained: "In short, the capability to operate effectively, without sleep, is no less than a twenty-first century revolution in military affairs that results in operational dominance across the whole range of potential US military employments." So, boys, go out and butcher. You'll rule the world without feeling tired or losing focus. Back at base, we'll keep the dreams away with better sleep through chemistry.

Thorsten's twitches could've also been a product of blood lust, the mantra of "kill" lingering from his days of bayoneting turbaned dummies at boot camp. The cocktail of uppers and brainwashing made him the perfect mindless killer. No conscience to weight his stoned soul. No hesitation when a target of opportunity was available. No self-doubt to cloud a murderous perspective. He stared at me, a vein in his neck pulsing to the beat of a mind aching to waste a few al-Qaeda.

"You fuckin' ready yet?" Thorsten asked. "Or you gonna let 'em call a camel and ride on outta here, candyass?" He jabbed me in the shoulder with the butt of his H & K.

Just then, one of the voices from inside the mud hut, loudly said "Osama." Thorsten's head snapped toward the hovel, dislodging his earpiece. *Osama* was one of the few words or names from Arabic or Pashto he knew, other than "*Khra oghaya*," go fuck a donkey. That greeting was used often when he strolled though a village and legless beggars, victims of Russian land mines, held out their hands.

"You hear that?" he asked. "Time to call in the Drones." He reached for the transmit button on his FS 5000 radio.

I grabbed his hand and squeezed.

"Not yet," I said. "Lots of Osamas here. Could be an uncle." I gripped harder as Thorsten tried to pull his fingers away. "Let me listen a little longer."

"Fuck you, Morgan," he said. "You know these hadjis are plannin' to grease somebody. And I ain't gonna let 'em." He jerked his hand free, trying again to get to his transmitter.

The silenced .22 Hush Puppy was on the rocks close to me. It was never far away. Early on in-country, I'd learned the value of quiet rather than the use of overwhelming weapons superiority to perform my job. An M67 grenade or a burst from an H & K wasn't quiet. All the Indians in the vicinity immediately knew my location. The soft *phhuuuppp* of the Hush Puppy didn't even wake the babies. I pushed the muzzle into Thorsten's side.

"Not just yet, pardner," I said. "I'd hate to have to leave you bleedin' for the locals. They like to slowly cut off body parts before layin' you out for the vultures." I shoved the pistol harder. "Just be patient. Besides, as the Fobbits say, 'I'm in command.'"

Thorsten made a move for his Ka-Bar knife, his most trusted tool. I pressed the Hush Puppy until I felt Thorsten's Kevlar vest firm against his ribs and he softly groaned. "Don't think for a heartbeat you can get that Ka-Bar out quicker than it takes a .22 slug to reach your lungs," I said.

Hatred. The look Thorsten gave me could have been reserved for the grunt who mailed Thorsten's mother pictures of him holding a lifeless, bloody mujahedeen by his turban, grinning. Thorsten found that soldier and set fire to his bunk using a teaspoonful of C-4 and a remote detonator. While the grunt was in it.

"Don't," I said. "We're not phonin' for the Predators 'til we've got something solid. I'm not gonna have more dead kids' eyes keepin' me awake, even if I don't care as much about the men in the hut. Those Hellfire missiles don't discriminate by age."

Not the time or place for this argument. And I knew Thorsten would make sure that, no matter whether these hadjis and their children were vaporized, my traitorous chickenshit attitudes were punished.

Stand-off. Thorsten continued to stare, knowing I was one glance away from his chance to transmit the "go" signal to the Drones. And he was absolutely sure I wouldn't shoot him. He smiled. And reached for the call button.

"Echo 16," he said into the mic. "This is Regestan 1. Confirm coordinates and begin descent. Out."

We both knew the Drones were circling overhead, waiting for just those words to rain death from the safety of their cockpits. It was all in the ops plan. Thorsten was the radioman and designated to call in the airstrike. We had already taken pictures of those doomed hadjis earlier through the long-range lens of the LIVAR 400. Intel would certainly be able to match them up to blurred shots of other bad guys, adding to the body count of terrorists, even if this party was just a celebration of a cousin's birthday.

"Roger, Regestan 1," Echo 16 said. "Site 94. We'll be there in 30. Keep your heads behind a rock. Out."

Thirty seconds and the mud hut, tent, dogs, goats, women, children, and soon-to-be-designated-dead terrorists would be staining the high desert with their blood.

I jumped to my feet and screamed toward the hut, "*Dzghelem.* American *alwateka. Dzghelem.*" Run. American airplane. Run.

I could hear the Drones in the distance. I yelled again. The outside guard was pointing his Kalashnikov in my direction, trying to sight my profile in the darkness. The door opened, and armed men ran out, the guard pointing in my general area.

Thorsten pulled hard at my leg. "Get down," he hissed. "Even if the hadjis don't shoot you, the Hellfires'll splatter your shit."

The men below were all raising their rifles. The first bullet hit in the dirt ten yards to my right. The next was closer. Splinters of rock stung my arm, and I dropped to the ground.

The Drones arrived.

A *whush* and, a nanosecond later, the world turned orange.

The mountains were white-capped dragons in the moonlight, shadowed peaks threatening like columns of frozen gargoyles. Winds and high altitude made the Little Bird buck and dip as if we were on the Tilt-a-Whirl at the Millard County Fair. Orion was bright and clear, a perfect constellation for two hunters on a night ride back to base. It was cold, and I shivered in the back seat of the Bird, not knowing if I would be on the way to the nearest detention facility, a court martial on my docket. Probably not, though. Today, I was only "assigned" to Special Forces Afghanistan and not really a grunt. The people I worked for would rather shoot traitors than have any kind of public trial. Easy to arrange an "accident" in a country littered with Russian butterfly landmines disguised as pieces of candy and IEDs planted wherever infidel Americans traveled.

Thorsten was buckled in next to me, all the high-tech gear making his shoulder straps squeal with each dive of the chopper. We hadn't spoken much since the Drones sanitized the hut. Not our job to pick through the rubble. That was the duty of intelligence forensics. But they made us hang around through most of the night. We were to bring home the proof these hadjis were truly worthy of evaporation. Make another dot on the computer-generated map, displaying where the bad guys had been terminated. Tell the *Washington Post* of another small victory against evil without civilian or coalition casualties.

I didn't want any part of it. And Thorsten knew.

Still, this didn't make *him* a target. At least a sentence to some remote CIA outpost far from this war would mean I wouldn't have to creep up on more victims in the night. Or snuff Thorsten while he slept on his cot to keep him from spreading the news his teammate had gone over to the turban side.

Inside the concertina wire of the compound, Thorsten led me toward the Special Forces de-briefing tent like this was the Inquisition. He was the judge. Me, the already-condemned heretic. The verdict was completely in the hands of Thorsten. Bad guys had been blown to oblivion, and the mission's success had surely been designated "achieved by command."

Early morning sunlight crept over the Salang Mountains, soon to warm the brown rocks of the desert plain below. Choppers, in from night ops, rotors turning in the breeze, were wheeled into the mechanic's area for servicing. Uniformed grunts walked toward the mess tent, rubbing sleep from their eyes. As always, white-backed vultures circled overhead, awaiting delivery of delicacies to the base dump. The crystalline air smelled of diesel, jet fuel, grease, and pancakes. A dry wind sucked moisture out of anything liquid that dared exist in this arid land. And I trailed behind my escort, wondering if it was the last time for a long while I would be walking without handcuffs, if I was upright at all.

Inside the debriefing tent, light from computers and desk lamps cast shadows on the dark-green walls. Hatless men hunkered over screens and sipped from coffee mugs; no one paid us any attention. Thorsten sat at one end of a portable conference table, his helmet on the floor next to him. He stripped off the rest of his gear and gently created a pile. It was SOP to immediately report here after a mission, but no one seemed in any hurry to begin the interrogation. I sat two chairs away from Thorsten, not bothering to remove my helmet or anything else. The closest soldier other than him was ten yards away.

"Don't worry, spook," Thorsten whispered. "All I'm gonna tell 'em is we smoked a nest of al-Qaeda, just like we were ordered. But, you owe me, cowboy. And I got a little somethin' I need help with. You're gonna be mine 'til I set you free." He grinned. "Alright with you?"

Not much of a decision. For now. I nodded my head.

"You do have a brain, Morgan," Thorsten said. "I was havin' my doubts. We'll rap later."

Two men moved toward us, one with Captain's bars, the other in civilian clothes. The one with tan slacks and a white Oxford shirt was Dunne, a hydraulic engineer in Afghanistan to help the locals with water-supply issues. At least, that's what his papers read. Reality was CIA sector chief for Central and Southern Afghanistan and the spook that had sent me out with Thorsten. War in Afghanistan had brought an unparalleled cooperative spirit between the Company and the military. They used each other like petroleum giants joined together to fight the terror of electric fuel cells. CIA operatives did much of the up-close wet work and groomed Afghan assets. If the mission called for more firepower or an operative needed assistance, the Army was recruited.

No cuddling. No foreplay.

"What did you hear out there?" Dunne asked, standing across the table, a clipboard in his hands. Dunne's hair was even shorter than the Captain's beside him. The sector chief was fit and filled his button-down as if he'd spent many of his forty-plus years in the Langley weight room. It was hard for the Company potbellies to get respect from Army robots; Dunne's physique was part of what brought him this delicate assignment whoring with the military.

Unless I hacked into the Company network, something well beyond my level of computerese, intel on superiors like Dunne was limited to gossip among the ghosts of the spook world. There was little making the camp rounds about Dunne except the extent of his professional focus and lack of a sense of humor. My interactions with the station head were limited and strictly on purpose. Geo-political discussions were rare, and I knew very little about Dunne's history. The topic was primarily who needed killing and how it would be accomplished. While I understood he was doing his job, something about the cold secretiveness of his responses bothered me.

This camp sector was Special Operations Group. None of the cripples in the regular Army were allowed to bring down the testosterone level. Only, and reluctantly, quasi-civilians like me and Dunne. Thorsten was part of the tribe of brotherly killers trained to be the Army's assassins, and he drew waves of congratulations from any of his soul mates who walked by. He ignored Dunne's question and leaned back in his chair, an "I just killed me a wild Injun" grin on his face.

"They were mostly discussing last winter's blizzards and hoping it didn't get as bad this year," I said. "One of 'em did use the name 'Osama,' and Thorsten thought that was enough to call in the drones."

No use denying anything. It wasn't my voice on the recording talking to the Drones. I stared at Dunne, waiting to hear where, if anyplace, the questions were headed.

I didn't need to worry. The hot wash was minimal. Surprisingly, Dunne's interrogation wasn't up to the in-depth level common to his normal debriefings. I figured it was because there were too many other missions still on the board to bother with one that had already been accomplished. Now, all I had to do was deal with Thorsten.

We were released after fifteen minutes and handed over our cameras and much of the wizard gear.

As usual, the base was jumping like there was a war on. Jeeps dodged soldiers and news cameramen while sentries manned towers framed by distant mountain tops, everything engulfed in a background of piercing blue sky. Choppers offloaded tired grunts, ground crews waved their arms. Overhead, an unmanned Predator circled, sending back real-time data to base command and making sure the hostiles were asleep in their caves. In a far corner, the elephant cage sprouted stalks of antenna arrays surrounded by a circular chain-link fence, and an engineer was adjusting one of the dishes. Probably trying to tune in FOX News so the ops center would know what was really happening. Thorsten walked beside me toward the Green Beret tents, the last bit of a superior smile on his lips.

"Let's head to the gedunk and get us a treat after we stow our gear," Thorsten said. "I'm jones'n for some a' those red sprinkles on vanilla ice cream."

Cute. He thought he had my ass and all he had to do was twitch to make me quiver.

"I don't want ice cream," I said. "And I'm not your bitch. What do you want?"

The smile got bigger, and Thorsten turned toward me, doing a little shuffle with his desert boots.

"That's where you're wrong, Morgan," he said. "With all that ed-u-ca-tion, you're sure a dumb fuck. You *are* my bitch. And tonight, me and my buddies are gonna gang bang your ass."

Faking a stumble, I dropped to one knee, head down like I was about to faint.

Thorsten bent over to help, a hand on my shoulder. He believed he was quicker and more accurate than me with his Ka-Bar, but the end of my knife was in his groin before he could finish asking "What's the matter with you?" The blade was hidden by his baggy pants and my camo-fatigued arms. Our little waltz was unremarkable in a place like this, where incoming mortars weren't cause for agitation unless they fell within fifty yards. I pressed just hard enough to cut through the fabric and touch skin.

"Listen up, troop," I hissed. "You know what I do for a living. You'll be cold and dead with just a little drop of blood on your forehead in the morning. None of your buddies will hear a thing or know how it happened. You won't be answerin' reveille."

Thorsten tried to stand, but I pushed the tip until I knew it was drawing blood. He froze.

One thing about all that training—I was good. Even if Thorsten outweighed me by forty pounds and was much stronger, I knew I could take him. Too many Special Forces muscle heads had tried before, grinning all the way until their faces hit the ground. And with a knife, no one was better. If I wanted, my next posting could be in the woods at Camp Perry, giving hand-to-hand instructions and doing tricks with a Ka-Bar.

"That's twice today you've threatened me, Morgan, "Thorsten said. "You're gonna have to make good soon, or you'll be the one in the body bag flyin' home to momma." But he didn't move — just snarled like Saddam in his hidey hole.

I held the pressure on the knife, wiggling it gently.

"If I move this Ka-Bar even an inch," I said, "you'll need a sex change. I just want it clear where we stand. You told your story back at the ops center. Kinda' hard ta go back now. They might wonder which one of your versions is the truth. You've got nuthin' on me. That means we can still be friends. Doesn't it, Thorsten?" Another wiggle.

A jeep stopped next to us. Two soldiers, one with a medic armband, sat in the front.

"Need any help?" the medic asked.

I turned toward the jeep, leaving the knife right where it was. Thorsten didn't look at them, a concerned grimace on his face.

"No thanks, doc," I said. "Just a touch of altitude sickness. I'll be alright in a minute." I smiled.

The medic gave a little wave, and they drove off.

Thorsten still hadn't moved.

"Alright," he said. "We're straight. For now. I wasn't gonna rat you out to the guppies anyway. I was gonna save it for all your mates who don't wanna live with a traitor spoilin' the party. Maybe we'll get a chance to settle this for good later, Morgan."

Morgan. Not my real name. My real name was buried back in a file at Langley. I was the first and only since Vietnam to be given this handle. It was legend. No one after Frank Morgan had passed though CIA training with more distinction than me. It was expected I would live up to the celebrity of the most deadly assassin in the Company's history. Of course *assassin* was a description never used. I was just another Company asset. Even if Frank Morgan's tour ended under a cloud, no one had brought fear to the hootches of Vietnam like "*gan con ran,*" the Night Snake. The bounty on his head surpassed the budget of a battalion of NVA. No Viet Cong knew what he looked like. They only knew of his calling card: a cobra carved from shrapnel and available at trinket stands throughout 'Nam. I wasn't into the theatrics of psychological warfare and hoped my legend never approached the Night Snake's. But, at the moment, I didn't mind any comparisons made between me and my namesake.

The knife was back in its sheath before I stood up. A spot of red was growing on Thorsten's crotch.

"No," I said. "If I hear even the slightest bit of talk about what went down today, you won't have a chance for salvation. Best you forget."

Stalemate. I was one of the spooks even the most hardened Special Forces troops feared. Their training was well known and established, while we were always veiled in secrecy and magic, a reputation the Company had groomed from the early days. What they did know was this: anyone who crossed us was disappeared. Usually, in the night.

Thorsten nodded with that crooked grin on his face, letting me know it wasn't over. We walked toward our tents.

As we approached his compound, Thorsten put his arm over my shoulder and squeezed hard enough to make the bones rub together.

"After you get done stickin' pins in dolls and sacrificin' one a' those mangy camp cats, come on over and join us real soldiers for a beer," Thorsten said.

The spooks, me included, didn't bunk with the military. We had our own sector. Separate and divided by a cloud of mythology, we didn't mix often unless it was orders. There weren't that many of us, and the Army personnel rarely even dared to look in our direction, fearing some kind of spell would surely steal their souls. I was just a corn-fed Kansas boy, but I would never convince those outside our compound I was anything less than the anti-Christ.

Twisting gently away from Thorsten's grip, I walked away.

We probably wouldn't meet alive again. Not after last night.

The stars winked in the clear night sky so close I thought I could reach out, take hold, and put them in my pocket. Below, one of the normal power outages. The dimmed light came from campfires and lanterns. Another post-midnight Bird ride. The cabin was in near-total darkness. This time, it was a CIA Bird and we were flying as silent as technology allowed.

"Urgent," I was told. And classified as too sensitive even for the Pentagon to know about this mission. The target was a local shopkeeper in Jalalabad. I was dressed in baggy trousers, a white Nehru collared shirt, a sleeveless jacket, and a turban. The three days of growth on my chin hopefully gave me enough cover to pass as a local in the dark. Insertion was in the suburbs of the city, and I would have to make my way alone. Curfew would make this even more difficult, but I had done it several times. Before I killed the shopkeeper, Badam Chinar, I would persuade him to tell me who his Army contacts were. Intel said he was the ringleader of a Taliban cell supporting arms acquisition with the fruit of the poppy fields and marketing the heroin through US Army personnel. The reports were verified by numerous informants and convincing enough to set aside any doubts. Intel even had recordings of cell phone messages discussing pricing with a man speaking American English in a northeastern drawl and using military speak.

Ten minutes to drop off.

Ten minutes to think.

Near the end of his time in 'Nam, my namesake, Frank Morgan, had become disillusioned like so many in-country. Surprisingly, his post-tour questioning didn't taint him with the spook management team, who cherished results over attitude. We were on the same career path. Being on a "need to know" basis didn't keep information from filtering into my brain. Ultimately, I understood I was in Afghanistan to protect America's ability to gas up at its leisure and continue to allow petroleum-industry executives on the golf courses of their private clubs. Somehow, on the path of discovery, I had realized heroin was in the mix.

The foreign media had reported the connection between the puppet leader of Afghanistan and Unocal. As with other stories that tarnished industries so clearly enmeshed in the supposed security interests of the United States, the articles had a short shelf-life in America and were buried in the back pages. Not much was made of Taliban visits to Houston to negotiate a deal to complete a pipeline from the oil fields of the Caspian Sea, nor of the CIA escort of oil engineers to the region the pipeline would cross. Nor the naming by the Bush administration of another former Unocal advisor and Taliban cheerleader, Zalmay Khalilzad, as US envoy to Afghanistan. Oil interests needed a stable government to complete construction, so they orchestrated the ascension of a little-known Unocal consultant, Hamid Karzai, to the presidency of Afghanistan. In the Afghan war against the Russians, Karzai had been an asset of the CIA and in personal contact with the US President, George Bush. In past lives, Karzai had also been a Taliban supporter. After moving to the United States as a reward for his hard work on big oil's behalf, he was even asked to be the Taliban ambassador to the United Nations. He refused, seeing a more lucrative path as a butt boy of the US administration and the oil industry. These were just a fraction of the facts roiling in my brain as I was sent out to secure the pipeline—a cause we'd spent billions of dollars on that we couldn't abandon just because of a war or the atrocities committed against women and non-Taliban.

While this picture was supported only by so-called hatemongers, government bashers, and traitors, I knew it to be the truth. There was no way the Company could keep this information from me as they justified another killing under the guise of "national security." For a boy from the Republican stronghold of Kansas, believing he was fighting the good fight for all the right reasons, it took an incredible amount of data to convince me I had been deceived. And so had the American people. But I was stuck. And the Taliban were still evil. And heroin was reaching the arms of Americans by way of the Taliban and the US Army. So here I was.

It was widely reported that Afghanistan was the producer of more than 90 percent of the world's heroin. The warlords and Taliban who control the country make sure this situation continues. And its stability is maintained and assisted, often unknowingly, by the US military. Supply routes of raw opium and processed heroin use US-made and -improved roads to Uzbekistan and Turkey. Drug convoys are protected by US troops with the assistance, and at the request of, the Afghan military leader, General Abdul Rashid Dostum. The connections go on and on. The intrigues and high-level power plays are beyond me. Tonight, it's my job to do just a little to slow the flow of smack reaching the shores of Manhattan.

The short ride from the CIA-built Tora Bora military camp near Jalalabad ended in a compound on the outskirts of town. In the darkness, the tops of palm trees sagged in the stillness over the razor-wired walls. Rockets and mortars had blown holes in the sides of the buildings, and a man dressed in jeans and a t-shirt backlit by a muted lantern waved me toward an open door.

The Bird didn't hesitate and was airborne as I crossed the courtyard, sand and pebbles skittering off my back. The unmarked chopper was gone in seconds, the noise replaced by the barking of a neighborhood dog. Inside the door, I was led into a room filled with maps stuck to dried-mud walls and very little furniture. Only my greeter was present. No guards. They were hidden outside and patrolling the walls. This piece of real estate was one of the most hazardous on Earth, its existence well known. No one got within blocks without proper identification and the day's password. This was the CIA base in Jalalabad, and my host was Finnen, an Irishman with more scars than skin. We'd collaborated several times, but a nod and a smile substituted for a hug. He was lean, and freckles dotted his face; his forehead creased as he examined a map of Kandahar. Finnen motioned me to a hard-backed wooden chair.

"*Pikheyr,* Morgan," he said. Welcome. He was one of the few who had gone beyond "*ho,*" yes, and "*ya,*" no, in the local dialect. Or "*mrakedal,* raghead." Die. I was fluent compared to Finnen's limited Pashto vocabulary, though.

The chair grunted with fatigue and old age when I sat. No weapons to stow, I took the turban off and sat it on a table filled with coffee mugs and a black-screened laptop.

Finnen rested his Heckler & Koch against another chair and sat.

"Would offer you a Guinness," Finnen said, "but the delivery truck got roasted by an IED."

The room smelled like moldy sand, cigars, kerosene, and flame-broiled goat kebabs, a remnant from its former life as a kitchen hand. Smoke from the lantern cast shadows on the walls, the designs dancing gently in the slight breeze from the partially open door. The red eyes of a rat peeked from a small hole in the corner, but they quickly disappeared. Not the usual hangout for Company men. I leaned back, and the chair squealed.

"Not thirsty," I said. "How is this going down? Not a lot of night left."

The time for banter was always after the operation. Finnen was a professional and knew this, but his Irish blarney controlled his mouth.

"You'd never be accused of talkin' the teeth out of a saw, Morgan," he said. "But what would I expect out of a pig but a grunt?" He slapped his hand on his jeans and cackled.

I didn't give him the pleasure of a grin; I just stared.

"When you're finished," I said, "maybe we can get to it."

"Ah, Morgan," Finnen said, "when Allah made time, he made plenty of it." But he reached for a map on the table and scooted his chair closer. He pointed to a mark on the printout.

"We're here," he said. "I'll take you through the tunnel that'll bring you out here." He moved his finger. "Chinar lives there, behind his shop at 16 *Angur* Street." Grape. "Whatever business you've got, I'm not supposed ta' know. I'm just to give you directions. There's lots of chatter on the Company frequency about this hadji. Care to give me an update?"

I studied the map for a second and twisted to Finnen.

"You'll never plow a field by turnin' it over in your mind," I said.

That got another hoot from Finnen.

"Why I'll be gawd damned," he said. "You coulda' just said no. Seems a touch of the Irish is slitherin' into your soul. But never give cherries to a pig or advice to a fool, Morgan. Let's get moving. It's no use boilin' your cabbage twice."

Finnen was too long between these mud walls, surrounded by hostiles and rock deserts with nobody to talk to, listening to coded messages and lies. It was too obvious he missed the shores of his ancestors, but I knew he was one of the best minders the Company had. We both stood, and he picked up his G36, letting it droop from his hand.

"Follow me," he said. "Keep your head down. There's hardly enough room for a fairy."

The turban was already wound, and I put it on my head, the .22 Hush Puppy snug against my waist, and followed the glow of Finnen's lantern through a short door in the back of the now-dark room.

We both had to stoop as we made our way through the tunnel. There were no intersecting shafts, and sometimes it was so narrow, the rough clay rubbed against my arms. No hieroglyphs decorated the walls. Only a few occasional Arabic words painted in white or scratched into the brown sides of the tunnel. The smell was musty. Old. The passageway had been dug a long time before Americans came to keep the peace. Mostly, we went in a straight line with very few turns, the pitch slightly downward. No conversation. After five minutes, Finnen stopped at a metal ladder. He pointed up toward a wooden trap door with an iron ring attached in the middle.

"Through there'll take you into the courtyard of one the local mullahs on our payroll," Finnen whispers. "He won't be around. Go through the gate to your right, and you'll be in a small olive garden. It'll give you some protection. It's always watched, and you'll be clear 'til you make *Zerghun* Street." Green. "You know the way from there. I'll be waiting here in three hours. Don't be late." He stepped aside.

I slid past and started to climb the ladder.

From below, Finnen said, "May God protect you better than his only son."

I hoped he was right.

Moonlight sliced between the branches of the olive trees and provided the only light in a town under a midnight curfew and a shortage of electricity. The dog still barked, but now the sound was much further away. A breeze, barely more than a breath, rustled the leaves above me. If there were watchers, they were well hidden. Shadows would be easy to follow. They were everywhere. I stayed in the dimmest areas and moved slowly toward *Zerghun* Street.

As I got closer to Chinar's home, the lack of noise behind any of the closed doors made my surroundings feel like a city of the dead. Last night's cooking fires gave the scent of burning charcoal and wood. The holes made by the frequent mortar rounds couldn't be called windows, nor the pockmarks from bullets called decoration. Most of the shops had roll-down steel doors, secured tight to the ground with large, antique padlocks. Glass was non-existent when bomb concussions, AK rounds, and earthquakes made them impossible to keep unshattered. I could see the door to Number 16 across the road. Nothing moved.

Ten minutes later, I opened the old lock with just a few twists of a CIA burglar tool, and I was inside another courtyard, hoping there were no dogs. They were the biggest job hazard. And I hated killing them, preferring the old trick of hamburger laced with fast-acting barbiturates. Sometimes that took too long, and I had to use the .22 Hush Puppy.

No dogs. No guards. Just the rhythm of sleep.

I stayed against the wall and made my way to a door at the far end.

One of the reasons I had been given Frank Morgan's name was that I lived up to his level of stealth. After Morgan, no one came through training with his ability to creep into a room and leave without being seen or heard—until me. Tonight, I would have to use all my skills if I wanted to sort out the men, women, and children surely sleeping inside and trade Irish insults with Finnen again.

The door opened with just the slightest squeak. No moonlight. Complete darkness. I let my eyes adjust for a few seconds, listening to the sounds of the hundred-year-old mud house. I was in the entry room, lined with couches, rugs on the floor. Doors led off in two directions, and I could see through to what had to be the kitchen. I picked the door to the left. And got lucky.

On a floor mat covered with pillows, a man softly snored. He was on his back. Alone. Not surprising. If his wife was in the house, she would be with the children, not allowed to disturb the master after providing whatever service he demanded.

Lessons. A model Frank Morgan established was to get the target's attention first. Let him know the seriousness of the nightmare he was in. Hush Puppy out and silencer screwed tight, I crept across the room to make sure this man matched the picture Dunne had shown me back at Tora Bora. It was him. Fifties and fat. Beard and a scar across his forehead. A mole on the left side of his hooked nose sprouted hairs just like in the photo.

Careful to avoid an artery, I shot him in the knee, covering his mouth with my hand and pressing his head firmly into the pillow. I held the tip of the pistol against the wound, knowing from the cell phone recordings he spoke English. He would want to talk, if only to try and save his life. Any twist of the barrel, and Chinar would be reminded this wasn't a dream.

"Who's your American Army contact?" I said. "Names. Now."

Chinar was protected. His contacts went to the highest level of both the Afghan government and military. The Company was unwilling to just bring him in and use a water board. Too many would know. That's why I was here. And he knew it. Usually, the Company turned a blind eye to the drug lords. They had their uses. But trading dope through US forces was beyond even CIA morality.

I lifted my hand just enough so he could talk. His eyes were wide, and I could hear him mumbling prayers. He wasn't squirming, just staring, unwilling to say anything yet. Without moving the Hush Puppy, I shot him again. A muffled *phuuup,* and his leg jumped. I clamped tight, waiting for his breathing to slow and his eyes to open.

"Names," I said. "Or I move on to the other leg."

Panic now. His eyelids were about to disappear into his forehead.

"Washington," he said.

For a split second, I was confused. It couldn't be this evil went all the way back to the Potomac.

"Lieutenant Washington," he said.

I took some of the force off the barrel, just to let him know I had a heart.

"Who else?" I asked.

"I only talk to Washington," he said.

"You're lying. Who else?"

"Only Washington. I never met anyone else."

"What does he look like?"

"A *tor sodar.*" Black pig.

"Stationed at Tora Bora?"

"Yes."

"He gives you money. You give him heroin?"

"Yes. And no. He picks up the heroin later."

"Where does he get the dope?"

Nothing. He would give up any infidel if it could possibly keep him alive, but he was scared shitless of the Taliban. There had to be guards around somewhere, and we both knew I didn't have much more time.

Sweat broke out on his brow, and he began to shake. He mumbled prayers again, and I feared he would soon go into shock.

I moved the pistol to his other knee and covered his mouth. I shot him, letting the bounce of his body settle before I asked again.

"Where? And who does he get the dope from?"

This time, I didn't keep the pistol on the wound. I pushed the tip into his balls. He gasped.

"Sheik Wahidi," he said.

"Is he in Jalalabad?"

"No. In the mountains."

"Taliban?"

"Yes."

A noise outside the door, and Chinar began to struggle and grunt. With my hand over his mouth, I shot him between the eyes and left him to find his seventy-two *houris* in heaven. And the twenty-six young boys the Muslims seemed to not mention.

I was behind the door as it slowly opened. A bearded, turban-less man stepped through and looked at Chinar. He must have sensed something was wrong and started to walk toward Chinar's now lifeless body. Softly closing the door with my foot, I shot him at the base of the skull, the barrel pointed up so the bullet would go into his brain. As he slumped, I held him around the waist and eased his body to the floor. Within seconds, I was in the street and on my way back to the tunnel and Finnen.

A small tent in the magic kingdom. Flaps down, guards outside, U2 playing for distortion. The Army had some of the same bugging equipment and parabolics as the Company, like the Orbitar One, that could pick up voices inside a house from a hundred yards. No one got close enough to plant a listening device with the heavily armed sentries walking the beat in Spookville. The Army knuckle draggers who patrolled the base weren't welcome. Nor were their commanders. This was the Company, and dangers like bugs were always taken seriously, even with the chances of our being overheard about the same as the possibility of rain this month.

Though I'd closed the contract on Chinar, there was the question of how to use the intel he'd given up, especially with the Army connection. Dunne, the station master, sat across from me, squeezing a rubber ball.

"Dead check?" Dunne asked.

The morning sun was blasting the canvas of the tent, and it was already warm enough inside to bake a few sheets of *naan*. I was stripped down to one of those drab, green military t-shirts and drinking a cold Dasani water, courtesy of Coca Cola and Haliburton.

"Didn't bring back Chinar's meat tag," I said. "But he stopped fingering his prayer beads."

Dunne was no perfumed prince. One of the few rumors about him had it he was too hot to stay in Iraq any longer. The insurgents didn't believe his cover as a benevolent USAID engineer since he rarely left the base, and there were too many unfortunate accidents on his watch.

The Outfit didn't have all the grooming rules of the Army. Both Dunne and I were getting to look more like mujahedeen every day, beards covering our chins. Dunne scratched his, and I wondered why he bothered with the stubble since he was a desk jockey.

"Collateral?" he asked.

"A guard," I said. "It was painless. He didn't see me. Nobody else."

"Intel?" Dunne asked.

No Irish homilies. No preaching. No soul sharing. Dunne was a professional, and there wasn't time or a desire to get to know me. Just a job. He watched something on the computer screen and waited.

Without any color commentary, I told him about Lieutenant Washington and Sheik Wahidi. There would be delicacy required. The Army didn't want to know, or have the *New York Times* hear, that one of theirs was trading with the Taliban for dope. Probably exchanged for dollars, thermobaric grenades, RPGs, and H & K semi-automatics. The Army would want the traitors disappeared with prejudice. That would be the Company's role.

"Lieutenant Washington," Dunne said. He typed something into the laptop in front of him and leaned back.

Nothing much in the tent but computers, a boom box, a small refrigerator, and a few cots for the night crew. On the support post, someone had taped a picture of a smiling woman holding two blond-haired boys. A bulldog sat at attention next to them, his tongue hanging out the side of his face. I didn't think it was Dunne's family, since it was hard to imagine how he could have spawned children. There wouldn't be time, and it wasn't in his job description. Styrofoam coffee cups were scattered around the room, and it smelled like everything else around here: dry, hot sand, old rocks, and sweat.

None of this was shocking. Since warfare had first begun, there had always been someone greedy enough to trade with the enemy. The Romans of Hannibal's day used to tie legionnaires caught doing business with their rivals between elephants and play tug-of-war. The question nagging at me like the sand grinding in my crotch was the method of transport used to extract large quantities of heroin out of this rock pile. Someone was getting protection from higher up the command chain than the Lieutenant level.

The lifeline I was given certainly included finding out more. Dunne would trace Washington in seconds, and I would be dispatched to gather intel. No more missions to hadjiville to grease suspects for now. Concentrate on good, old American criminals and local mullahs. And I had a suspicion Thorsten was a member of the gang.

The muscles flexed in Dunne's arms, and he looked up.

"Washington's MOS is Squad Leader of Special Forces Insertion Team Alpha," Dunne said. "Does a lot of the wet work for the weenies. Kinda reads like your bio, Morgan."

It was scary when Dunne smiled. His teeth were too white. And big. Made him look like a wolf with a good orthodontist.

"He's stationed at Gardez," Dunne said. "But he's a utility man. Gets around, by the looks of his file."

Of course, Dunne would be reading the most secure information the Army had on record. The Company, in its newfound cooperative spirit, would still be peeking, just to make sure they had all the latest updates.

A fucking sand fly landed on my arm. I swatted it. These monsters were responsible for leishmaniasis—a.k.a. the Kabul Krud. In Iraq, it was the Baghdad Boil. Ugly, weeping skin sores on the face caused by the bite of this tiny parasite. Fatal if untreated. The bugs lived on garbage and blood. Plenty of both in these parts.

"Anything there on a Delta named Thorsten?" I asked.

Dunne typed a few letters and waited.

"Why?" he asked.

A speck of blood on my arm. I rubbed it in.

"Just coincidence," I said. "Had a slight disagreement with Thorsten the other day. He mentioned a chat with him and a few buddies for something hush-hush. They needed a little help. Didn't tell me anything else. Wondering if maybe Washington could be one of his friends and why Thorsten could need a hand from the Company. Can you see if they might have been partnered?"

If Dunne was interested in the "disagreement," he didn't show it. Washington wouldn't be working solo. Too many logistical problems trading money and guns for heroin.

"They went through training together," Dunne said. "Both Deltas. They certainly know each other. You think Thorsten could be mixed up in this?" Dunne asked the question with his typical on-task look, as if he already knew the answer.

"Not as any kind of brain," I said. "Not enough cells remaining. Plenty of muscle."

"What do you think's going on?" Dunne asked.

The sand-fly bite was itching. I scratched, taking my time to answer.

"Just a guess," I said. "Rumor command's been saying for a while that new gear is getting to the tribal leaders and the Taliban. Drugs and money don't ever seem to be far behind. Opium's the only currency the mujahedeen have. If it's not Washington, it's somebody else. Thorsten's a possible. From what little I know about him, he's capable. I don't know anything about Sheik Wahidi, but I'll bet that laptop does." I nodded toward the computer in front of Dunne.

Some of the Afghans had blue eyes as clear and bottomless as a Himalayan lake. Like Dunne's. Made it seem even more likely that he was about to start howling at the moon. He tapped keys and waited.

"We know him." Dunne said, a minute later. "But he's been a friendly. Nothing here links him to the Taliban except he's a tribal leader in Afghanistan. That'd be the way it needed to get done. Low-profile American supporter while he's their quartermaster."

"What are you gonna do?" I asked.

"I think we should talk to Washington," Dunne said. "Of course, this is on a 'need to know' with the Army, and there's not a need or even a want to know from them. Even Langley will want it that way, especially if we can get to Wahidi. Anything we might do will have to be kept close."

"I'm still wondering about the drug part," I said. "How would a grunt get all that dope out of here? And where would it go? Can't just board a Northwest flight to LaGuardia."

The statistics on the poppy economy of Afghanistan were well known. When the Taliban took over the country in 1998, Afghan farmers were responsible for 41 percent of the world's heroin. The poppy crop was almost completely eliminated by the Taliban, but with the entrance of the United States and the Allies, poppy production in Afghanistan was greater now than ever. Today, some estimates put it at supply of 93 percent of the world's smack. Opium trade was thought to be close to 60 percent of the gross national product of Afghanistan.

Weapons disappeared all the time. There were too many of them around here to give an absolute accounting. The GAO projected the military had no idea where nearly 10 percent of all the munitions were at any given time. Even worse in a war zone. And that amount could arm several battalions of Taliban. A stroll through a bazaar in Afghanistan gave the opportunity to buy almost any of the arms used by US forces. These weren't just scavenged off bodies but a mainstay of Afghan trade just below opium.

There was too much money to be made to be surprised that there were Americans in-country willing to supply half the formula, money, guns, and explosives. The other half, filling the world demand for escape through a needle, was the Taliban contribution.

Metals mined in the mountains of Afghanistan and sold in Mesopotamia created the first trade route more than five thousand years ago. It was called the Tin Road and followed some of the same trails still used to transport opium and heroin through Iran and into Turkey, home of the world's largest heroin refineries. Until now. The Afghans had decided to keep that part of the profit and boil the poppies themselves. Only the product had changed.

None of this was classified information. I knew it as part of the classes back at Langley that explored the geo-political and historical roots of terrorism. For thousands of years, border guards made their living letting contraband pass. Nowadays, an Afghan guard who might make twenty thousand Afghanis' salary per month could get a hundred thousand Afghanis by turning his head as a truckload of heroin passed by.

Simple economics. And I couldn't shake the feeling that something bigger than just this equation was in play.

Dunne was giving me a lot of time to mull it over. He was probably not fixated on the Tin Road or the impact of the poppy crop on rural Afghan agriculture. He was operations, and plotting was what curled his lips into a rare smile. He grinned, and it was creepy.

"You're going to Gardez," he said. "The weenies across the street will send you out alone with Washington. According to his file, he's done plenty of these ops, so he shouldn't suspect anything. I won't tell them what it's about." He leaned forward and opened a file next to the laptop. "We'll have to give you a different name. If Thorsten's involved, Washington might already know yours."

Two itches. The bite on my arm and the sand in my crotch. The rash never seemed to go away. I scratched like Roger Clemens.

"Donovan," I said. "I love being named after our father."

The founder of the Office of Strategic Services, the forerunner of the CIA, Wild Bill Donovan had led the World War II espionage and sabotage campaign across Europe, inventing some of the dirty tricks used today. Many in Langley still worshipped at his altar, even though he died in 1959.

"Okay, Donovan," Dunne said. "I'll have you on the flight schedule for the morning. Be ready at 0600. You'll be riding a Bird."

D awn. The white-backed vultures were out for breakfast. Against the crystal blue background, a lone Imperial eagle dove between them, winning the first snack of the day from the camp dump. The bird's reddish-brown back contrasted with the white of the other scavengers, and his wing span rivaled the vultures'. But the eagle was a lot quicker to the garbage feast. On the base, the usual busyness as soldiers, photographers, reporters, and spooks processed the morning's coffee. A jeep raced past, probably carrying doughnuts for the command tent. The smell of scrambled eggs mixed with the nose-coating stench of diesel. Across the valley, snow-capped twenty-thousand-foot-plus mountains dominated the horizon over the razor wire. I waited while the pilot did his preflight check, circling the chopper and thumping in places to show he knew exactly if the bird was airworthy. A "thumbs up" and we boarded.

The operation Dunne outlined earlier was to rendezvous with Washington outside the Camp Lightning compound and take him to a safe house in Gardez city under the guise of a joint assassination of an al-Qaeda cell leader. Finnen would be waiting for us. The Irishman was getting a little R & R from his assignment in the suburbs of Jalalabad. Washington would be "debriefed" without water boards or hoods. The method would be one refined by Kim Philby: convince Washington he had been betrayed and we had a use for him. Kind of true, even if truth in these situations was as hard to give as receive. I'd play bad guy and Finnen the jolly good guy. Still undecided was whether Washington would live. His future was dependent on the level of cooperation and how the Company could use him. After he left Afghanistan, all bets were off.

In the daylight, the marked Bird wasn't attempting stealth. We flew down the Shah-i-Kot Valley, a small stream dividing the ridges on both sides. Spindly trees stood out like a tuft of grass in the desert, lining the newly paved road leading to the city. Vehicle traffic was mostly military and small Korean, Indonesian, and Japanese pickups—transportation of choice throughout Afghanistan. The men wore either turbans or helmets, and the few women were covered head to toe in burqas of various colors, mostly black. Many carried baskets on their heads, and children danced circles around them, pointing and throwing rocks as we passed overhead.

Brown. Even the water in the stream was chocolate-colored. Trees that should have been green were coated in dust that blew in the ceaseless wind. No vegetation beyond a hundred yards of the creek, only rocks. It looked like the world had been drawn with non-fat latte crayons. Old CIA hands spoke about the assault of green in 'Nam. The suffocating sense of humidity, decay, and lush color. It was the opposite here. Arid. So dry, snot wouldn't harden in my nose. It just got sucked away in the breeze.

Closer to Gardez, we flew over the refugee camps. Seemingly endless scatterings of tents with people walking aimlessly between. Trucks with the UN logos and white vans with Red Crosses painted on the top were parked on the dirt paths. Ditches lined the perimeter, sewage darkening the clay. Smoke rose from cooking fires, and the smell of crowded, dirt-poor humanity reached even as high as the Bird.

A few klicks outside Gardez, the Special Operations Group base was surrounded by sandbags and razor wire. Compared to the randomness of the refugee camps, the base was an example of modern military planning: tents in rows, all leading to a central administration compound, housing the command center. Heavily armed Rangers walked between the wide aisles, and a detachment surrounded the Bird's landing area. The base was under constant threat of mortar attack from the caves and crags of the nearby mountains.

Two grunts led me toward the operations tent. Nothing cried out I was a Company man, but the Rangers knew I was from Spookville. The old cliché of heightened awareness in a combat zone was true for these grunts. I was outfitted pretty much just like them. Semi-automatic H & K, ammunition belt, helmet, and drab brown uniform. No grab-assing or jive talk. No smiles. Just "Follow me, sir" from the leader.

The tent could have been any one of thousands around Afghanistan. Folding tables and chairs with computers and documents. Charts covering all the walls. Helmetless buzz-cut soldiers with headsets talking, scanning monitors, or adding pins to maps. The constant low-level chatter of radios and the smell of coffee and sweat. We walked through the ordered disorder into a side room with one large map of Paktia Province on the far wall, a large conference table, and a half-dozen chairs.

A smooth-faced black Ranger the size of Mike Tyson sprawled in one of the seats, helmet on the table and H & K resting against his thigh. Even in a slouch, he was as graceful, strong, and as athletic as an NBA star. Hooded eyes didn't hide an attitude of intelligence and suspicion. He had probably graduated head of his class at John Wayne High School in Fort Bragg. Rangers never liked working with spooks. The missions too often ended with litter cases being loaded on the evac chopper. Or stories that were more secret than ears-only classification. He just stared lazily, seemingly confident that he was smarter, tougher, and, certainly, better looking than the other guys in the room.

My escort left without any farewells, and I sat across from the SF soldier who had to be Washington. No nametag stitched to his chest, which was threatening to bust the seams on his camo top. No salute. No exchange of greetings or friendly banter. Not even a nod. The gaze of a man who had four aces in his hand. Or a sniper with an open target in his laser sight at fifty yards. Washington was trying to show he was in control, knowing full well he was dispatched as a grunt on this mission and was under my orders. I took off my helmet and set it on the table across from his.

"Donovan," I said. "And you must be Washington." I waited for his acknowledgment.

His eyes opened only fractionally wider, but he didn't straighten up. Like he was awakened from dreamland and only wanted to get back to sleep.

"Lieutenant Washington, 3rd Special Forces Group," he said. "MAIN 3415778. Wanna see my ID card, spook?"

A smirk. The more he chuffed me, the easier this would be.

"Nah, troop," I said. "I don't want to get to know you. We're just gonna be buddies for the day. Any problem with that?"

Washington slowly unwound, stretching lazily, stressing the buttons on his shirt. He sat forward, eyes now fully open.

"Every time I go out on one of these ops, somebody dies," he said. "I wanna make sure it's not me. And I won't do anything that puts me in harm's way before you, Donovan. You're no brother of mine."

Getting simpler by the second. I smiled.

"A man can't be too careful with his choice of enemies, Washington," I said. "An old Irish saying that has great meaning in this rock pile."

"Did you read the book *How to Rent a Negro*?" Washington asked.

I shook my head.

"Well, I didn't write it," he said. "And I sure as shit ain't for rent."

"How about a short-term lease?" I asked. "And don't worry. No Company voodoo. You'll be back in your cot by lights-out without a curse on your ass."

"As long as they're not stuffing my parts in a body bag," Washington said. "It appears I ain't got no say in the matter anyway. Just wanna make sure you know where I stand on the issues. It's you before me."

"If it gets to that," I said, "I'm sure I'll make the appropriate command decision."

Across Afghanistan, soldiers were beginning to rebel. With the Pentagon's "stop-loss" directive, grunts didn't know when or if they were going home after their tours were involuntarily extended to cover a shortage of troops. Not yet as bad as 'Nam, where lieutenants were as likely to be killed by a grenade from their own personnel as the enemy, but angry soldiers were refusing to go into the caves at the whim of the Fobbits. No officer murders had been publicly reported, but I had access to more intel than even Seymour Hersh. The Army's response: Prozac. It could be why Washington, still seemingly relaxed, was sending out veiled threat vibes.

"Ten four, boss man," Washington said, leaning back. The chair squealed in agony.

No paperwork. No map. Just an anonymous picture given to me earlier by Dunne. The snapshot looked like a million other Pashtu males in man-jammies. I handed the photo to Washington.

"Atal Ghazan," I said. "We're headed to his house in the city. You can guess why. For certain, not to share a hookah. Just know, he's a bad guy."

Washington held the picture in his hand, shaking his head.

"Sure it's not another clusterfuck?" he asked. "Been on enough of those to fill a comic book."

He handed the photo back, and I shoved it in my pocket.

"No guarantees," I said. "You know who I'm working for."

Washington, and thousands like him, had been ordered out on ops that were not only dangerous but also seemingly stupid and unproductive. When the intel was paid for and came from locals who would laugh at American blood, it was hard to trust. The one sure thing—someone was very likely to die, innocent or not.

"We're part of the morning convoy," I said. "We'll slip away from a patrol when we get to Ghazan's neighborhood. We've got a place to hide out 'til night. Then, we'll give Ghazan Allah's greetings." I stood, picking up my helmet.

"Let's saddle up," I said. "The transports're waiting."

Washington pushed back his chair and put his helmet on, letting the H & K droop easily from his hand. He followed me out of the tent into another blue-sky day.

No kids playing soccer in the roads or legless beggars in doorways. No one headed to the market or the relief trucks for food. The street telegraph had told everyone of our presence, and the civilians had retreated behind mud walls, knowing the appearance of a heavily armed infidel patrol was often the target of insurgents. No telling when violence would break out or a *langarei,* mortar, would cloud the street in red. Washington and I were on drag, making sure no eyes followed us onto 28 Asman Street. The squad leader knew his only job today was escort, and he expected us to go missing. He just didn't know where or when it'd happen.

We walked a few doors beyond 28 and stopped, checking all perimeters for watchers. No one about. I gave Washington a hand sign, and we stepped back to number 28, slipping inside the unlocked wood door.

RON LEALOS

A walled courtyard with a well in the middle. Buckets sat below the hand crank. The ground was swept, hardened clay. Everything was an off-white color—the motif most favored by Afghan designers. Flower pots, their stalks unwatered and spindly, withered under an archway. Blue sky and the bright sun cast silhouettes off the overhangs. Two crows were silent sentries perched on top the far wall above a carved doorway. Everything tidy and in order. Washington followed me toward the back, his eyes scanning, never idle to possible danger.

Inside, a kerosene lantern on a table. No windows. A man sitting at a desk turned, a Browning automatic pistol in his hand.

"Top'a the mornin' to you fellas," Finnen said, pointing the barrel toward us.

Closing the thin door, I immediately pushed the nose of the .22 Hush Puppy into Washington's neck and grabbed the H & K in my other hand. With the silenced pistol as guide, I directed Washington to the chair. He was grinning and didn't appear frightened in the least. Or surprised. Even if he tried some Special Ops martial-arts move, the pressure of the gun and Finnen's Browning aimed at his face made it obvious he would be dead before he could twirl and strike.

As he began to sit, I kicked the chair away.

"On your stomach," I said. "Now." I pushed the Hush Puppy harder into the top of his spine.

In a slight crouch, he began to turn. I lowered the .22 and shot him in the back. The Kevlar vest wouldn't let the bullet penetrate, but the force put Washington on the clay floor, groaning.

Finnen stood and walked the few steps across the room. He bent over and took off Washington's helmet and then patted him down, gathering grenades, a Ka-Bar, and a sissy little Colt pistol strapped to his ankle. He loosened Washington's ammo belt and threw it in the corner.

"A traitor is a man hangin' by his fingernails over chaos," Finnen said, standing up.

Washington was struggling to get his breath, the thin air coming in gasps.

Even in this compromised position, a man as highly trained as Washington was still as dangerous as a wounded grizzly. Finnen and I stepped back, the

42

pistols never wavering from the target that was Washington's head. We waited for a minute until Washington's breathing settled. I didn't want him to have a panic attack. Not yet.

"Get the handcuffs," I said to Finnen.

He grinned and pulled the restraints out of his pocket.

The Company favored the plastic cuffs. As strong as steel, but much lighter. And we didn't need a key. Just had to cut them off.

Finnen rolled Washington over and grabbed his arms. He steered Washington's hands above and behind his head and snapped two pairs of handcuffs on his wrists.

"Just in case," Finnen said. "He's as strong as a gale off the Irish Sea."

Smoke from the lantern did a belly dance on the walls. A rug hung on one side, colorful checked patterns woven in the wool. No human figures or lettering. Islam forbade that heresy. Above, wooden beams supported the mud roof. The room felt unused and ancient.

Washington began to thrash, trying to get his arms comfortable.

"Settle down," Finnen said. "'Tis better to be a coward for a minute than dead the rest of your life."

No hurry. We had lots of time to decide Washington's fate, and I wanted him to wonder about his current situation.

Finnen began to hum an old sea shanty, knowing as much as I did about interrogation technique. Establish superiority, and don't rush unless you have to.

Heroes. The man on the floor was one. Washington's file listed numerous battlefield citations. His time in-country was spent mostly in the Korengal Valley, a nasty place near the northeast border with Pakistan. Stories coming out of that hell-hole were rife with insanities brought on in wars where captured terrain stayed occupied only during the day. At night, it went back to the locals as if nothing had changed. There was no front. No advances. No storming of the Rhine. When a cave was liberated, the history was written in blood, not freedom. It took a strong commander to keep troops fighting useless battles where there were no friendlies. And Washington was on the fast track to Captain, according to what I'd read in his file.

In one of the ops, his squad had been ambushed by insurgents outside Yaka China. The attackers were mostly from a Wahhibi sect of Islam, fundamentalists nearly as rigid as the Taliban and mostly confined to the tree-lined valley. It was an insertion mission, but it seemed not even Rangers could go undetected. Washington and his wounded radioman called an airstrike on themselves to keep from being butchered in hand-to-hand combat. An AC-130 gunship blew away all the hadjis, leaving Washington with shrapnel cuts and one other squad survivor. His men had nicknamed him Shaq, as in "attack."

The H & Ks leaned against the wall. Not too far to reach at the slightest hint of incursion but not of much use during an interrogation. I took off my helmet and laid it on the dirt floor.

"I figure you get why this is happening, Washington," I said. "Reading your dossier, it's hard to understand why a patriot of your level would go bad. But you did. We can skip the denials. You've already been ratted out by Thorsten and some of the others."

Lies. I lived in a country where truths were as hard to find as beautiful women. They were all hidden. No one but a condemned dope pusher and arms dealer had betrayed Washington. He still had a slim chance to be free if he convinced us he was falsely accused. I didn't think so. And I'd use any tactic necessary to get at the truth.

Washington tried to roll to his side.

"Can I sit?" he asked. "It's getting really uncomfortable." He smiled. "I know, I know. The fun's just gettin' started, and I don't understand what 'uncomfortable' means yet. Ya da, ya da, ya da." No more smile. "Go for it, white bread."

Finnen stepped to Washington and helped him to the chair.

"Sure, laddy," he said. "Can I bring you a spot of tea and some biscuits? We're all civilized here."

Right now, my pattern would normally have been a bullet to the knee. Get his focused attention without letting him bleed out. In the field, there was no time for long-term questioning. Today, it was different. He was one of ours. There was no deadline. The compound was protected, even if I hadn't seen anyone on the way in. And I didn't have another soul on my dance card.

I set the Hush Puppy on the table and pulled the other chair close to Washington.

"Let's start with where the money comes from," I said. "The boys said you were the paymaster." I was just guessing, but Thorsten certainly wasn't the don of this syndicate.

Silence. Washington was thinking. He clearly realized answers were his only salvation. He wasn't trying to protect his country, religion, or loved ones.

Outside, two crows were fighting, their squawks echoing around the courtyard. In the distance, sounds of an AK-47 were answered quickly by semi-automatic fire. The patrol must have made contact nearby. The room was getting stuffier, smoke mixing with the smell of the unwashed. Not fear. It was poker time, and I had placed the first bet.

Washington looked up.

"I'll talk if we can deal," he said. "No excuses. No lies. Even if it means Leavenworth, I don't wanna die in this shithole."

Finnen chuckled.

"That's a fine lad," he said. "And who do you think we are? Emissaries from the Holy Father here to give you dispensation? Remember, a handful of truth is worth more than a bag full of gold."

If Finnen weren't the best cut-out I'd ever worked with, I wouldn't be so patient with his blarney. Behind the façade, he was as tough and mean as they came. Must be his Irish roots and his days in Rwanda and Angola after the massacres, still a time for vengeance. He was nearly as tall as Washington but forty pounds lighter. I wouldn't bet on Washington if it came down to a death match.

Minutes passed. I took out my Ka-Bar and mindlessly rubbed the blade on my thigh, composing an email in my head to my mother back home in the warmth and comfort of low-altitude Kansas, humming as I chose my words.

Hi Mom,

I hope Uncle Phil recovered from his gall-bladder surgery and Dad got the new engine in the Chevy. I sure miss those rhubarb pies you bake this time of year. Did Mrs. Skinner find her lost cat? I was wondering how the high school football team fared and if they're celebrating down at the Tastee Freeze. Bob and Sally must be home from their honeymoon at Disney World. Give them my best. Here, not much. The cherry trees are fading around DC, and my job in the accounting office is kinda slow. Wouldn't mind if I caught a cheater trying to pad his expense vouchers to find a little excitement around this place. Going sailing this weekend. Have taken up golf, too, and might get in a few more rounds before it gets cold. Gotta go. I think I might see a zero out of place. Love you and take care.

P.S. Sorry I haven't been returning your calls. My cell phone has been giving me trouble.

There was no use writing to anyone in Millard about where I was or, especially, what I did. They would look at me like I was from another dimension. Better to keep up the lies from the Fairy Tale Kingdom. Anyway, I'd have to decide who I was before I could tell them.

Washington was about to play the next hand. He scowled at me, used to frightening people with his glare. Not today.

"Maybe we could help each other," he said. "You get me outta here walkin' upright, and I'll try to take you to the real bad guys. But you gotta realize, I don't know much. I picked up the money at a drop. Never saw anybody. Never touched the dope except as delivery boy. Got all my orders from email." He was too proud to beg, even if he was coming close. He would know Finnen and I could shoot him anytime we decided he wasn't of value. Or that he was lying. He'd be reported as another unfortunate casualty of war.

"What about the munitions?" I asked.

"Don't know nuthin' about that," he said.

Finnen laughed.

"Now don't be startin' that," he said. "Those little lies tend to breed more offspring. Like the Papists do back in Kildare."

The Ka-Bar slid easily back into its sheath at my waist.

"We'll make this simple," I said. "Every time I think you're lying, I'll take out my Ka-Bar. That'll be a signal you're about to be cut. I'll start somewhere not so critical and move closer to the meat as the lies continue. If you change your story and tell the truth, I'll put the knife away. That way, me and Finnen don't have to keep insulting you. So, let's begin again. What about the munitions?"

This was the hardest question. Trading money for dope was real bad. Trading guns for smack was pure evil and traitorous. It meant someone Washington knew would most likely be killed by a rifle or explosive he directly provided. He shrugged.

"You can start cuttin'," Washington said. "I wouldn't do that. And if I found out someone was, I'd grease him myself."

No hesitation. I sliced through the leg on his camo fatigues and into his calf muscle. The wound wasn't too deep and might've not even required stitches. He tried to kick the knife away and fell backward, chair and all. Blood immediately began to show on his trouser leg. I stood above him.

"That wasn't for the lie, just principle," I said. "If you give the Taliban money, what do you think they do with it? Buy their sweethearts new dresses? Spend it on spiffing up the cave? A vacation in the south of France? Ordering in pizza? Even if you don't hand over the grenades, somebody we know is gettin' blown away."

Finnen moved beside me.

"Now, now Morgan," he said. "You're not playing fair. Didn't you believe him?"

The good guy. Finnen could play any role demanded. He helped the squirming Washington back into his chair and pulled the bleeding man's pants away from the gash.

"That's a bad cut," Finnen said. "You must have slipped and fell on something sharp." Finnen smiled and patted Washington on the shoulder.

Once, on a mission somewhat similar, involving the need to gather intel and not just garbage take out, Finnen had stuffed his backpack with a pork sausage, wooden prayer beads, a picture of the target's mullah, a copy of the Koran, photos of naked young Arab women, a cartoon drawing of two bearded men having sex labeled "An Afternoon with Mohammed" in Arabic, a bottle of wine, and a snapshot of a recently beheaded US aid worker in Afghanistan that appeared on Al Jazeera. We were in another mud house in Jalalabad next to a mosque. The clay walls were thick enough that the target's screams would only echo in this room, not penetrate outside. Before we started the day's interrogation, Finnen lined up all the items in front of the bound mujahedeen.

"You look hungry," Finnen said. "And parched. I've got a little snack for you. Some premium pork sausage from real corn-fed hogs in Iowa. That's in the U S of A, if you didn't know. Couldn't get any of the Olhausen's Finest Irish Sausage custom-made in Dublin. It's the tangiest. Now, you do know where Dublin is, don't you?"

The man, tied with duct tape to a chair, stared ahead as if he didn't understand a word. We all knew he spoke English, and the dance was just beginning.

"Don't fret, laddy," Finnen said. "I won't hold it against you." He cut off a slice of the sausage with his Ka-Bar and pinched the man's nose. "Here's a wee bite," Finnen said, pushing the sausage into the target's mouth. "Chew it well. My mum always said it's good for the digestion and the taste blossoms like a spring rose." He pushed the man's jaw up and down to make sure he was enjoying the essence of pork. "You do know they add in the hoofs and all that good stuff that grows between the pig's toes. Flavoring tis it."

When Finnen took his hand from the struggling man's nose, the hadji tried to spit the sausage out. Finnen watched, smiling, and cut another slice while the man drooled and choked.

"Now, now," Finnen said. "It might be an acquired taste. It's not that bad, though. I'm insulted." He grabbed the man's nose again, shoving another piece between the man's teeth. "Try some more. This time, I'll let you hold it in 'til you swallow and capture the true zest. You understand, they put all the leftover body parts into sausage, including the pig's ass." Finnen kept his fingers clamped tight on the man's nose and worked his jaw.

The man's name was Jamil Farooq. Assets in the community clearly pointed to Farooq for much of the Taliban resurgence in Jalalabad and spoke of his contact with al-Qaeda. The proximity of his house to the mosque meant he was quite influential in the mullah's latest dictates that no girls or women were allowed outdoors. Several offenders had already been publicly whipped. Farooq was responsible for the beheading in the picture Finnen displayed.

After a minute, Farooq's eyelids were about to disappear into his forehead. He was strangling on pork, but most of the meat had found its way to his stomach. Finnen released his grip and stepped back.

"So, enjoyed that, did ya?" Finnen asked. "Now for a little California Pinot Noir to wash it down. I'll just pop the cork and you can have a few sips. My taste goes more to Guinness, but I hear the 2006 was a very good vintage." He had brought a wine opener and screwed out the cork, making sure there was the right amount of "pop" to keep Farooq's focus.

The picture of the beheaded woman was in his pocket. Finnen took it out and held it in front of Farooq.

"While you're savoring the Pinot," Finnen said, "I'll have you gaze on this. She was a fine, red-haired lass. Bernadette Jenkins. I met her once when she was delivering medicine to the refugee camps. She was a nurse and said she came over to help with the health crisis caused by the Taliban displacing so many of their countrymen. Remember Bernadette, Farooq?"

When Farooq's eyes went to the photo, Finnen jabbed the open end of the bottle into Farooq's mouth and squeezed his nose shut, tipping the bottle so it drained toward the back of his mouth. Red wine spilled from the sides and stained the white tunic covering Farooq's upper body. He gagged, again, but Finnen wasn't about to let Farooq spew the Pinot. He thrashed, and Finnen held tight until the wine was nearly gone. Pulling the bottle away, Finnen moved aside and let him sputter until the hadji's head dropped to his chest.

"That must have quenched your thirst," Finnen said, pulling Farooq up by his beard. "When you were sipping, did you get a chance to recognize Ms. Jenkins? Surely you remember. Or did she look different with her head on her shoulders?" Nothing from the bound hadji. Finnen smashed the Pinot bottle against the side of Farooq's head.

From the back of the darkened room, I watched Finnen and the door, my H & K on full auto. We had indisputable evidence Farooq was guilty of both the beheading and other atrocities committed in Allah's name. Voice recordings, photos, and human intel. The only question was why it had taken so long to dispatch Finnen and me to dump the trash. The choice for Farooq was whether to give us the information we wanted on his associates and receive just a little pain or hold out, knowing the seventy-two *houris* were nearby. Finnen was in the "softening up" phase of the interrogation, with vengeance driving him. He had seen Ms. Jenkins more than once—the grapevine told me it was many times—and their Irish roots had helped them bond. I watched, mostly to make sure Finnen didn't totally lose it before we got what we needed from Farooq. Then we could leave him as an example for his brothers in the mosque.

While Farooq dozed, Finnen arranged the rest of his party favors on the floor, picking up the cartoon of Mohammed and holding it in his left hand. He slapped Farooq with his right until he wakened.

"You don't know the lass?" he asked. He put the cartoon in front of Farooq's face. "I'll bet you know these guys. It's your prophet doing the chocolate jig with one of his followers. Don't get a boner, Jamil. You won't be able to enjoy it."

Finnen took out a knife smaller than his Ka-Bar while he held the cartoon close to Farooq's nose. Then, in a blur, he nailed the comic strip face up to Farooq's thigh using the blade. The hadji started to scream, but Finnen covered the man's mouth with his hand until Farooq calmed. Tears were in the hadji's eyes, and sweat ran down his forehead. Finnen reached into his pocket and took out the photo of the naked Arab girls, shoving the picture in Farooq's face.

"I hear all you Abduls swing both ways," Finnen said. "So maybe you'll like this candid shot better. The one on the left looks a little like Rayan, your daughter. It'll be grand when I meet her. Great tits."

Finnen had no intention of dating Rayan. Just another step in the tango.

This time, he used the Ka-Bar. The bigger knife stabbed deeper into Farooq's other thigh. He held Farooq's mouth again. After the hadji settled, Finnen let him breathe.

"While I'm getting ready for Act Two," Finnen said, "I want you to look at both those pictures. There'll be an exam later. I'll expect you to explain why nobody mentions the twenty-six *houris* boys waiting for you as promised in the Koran. Are you all in the closet?"

The little pile on the floor still held a copy of the Koran and the prayer beads. Finnen bent down and picked the book and the *subha* up, unzipping his fly at the same time. He then pissed on the holy book and the beads.

"In case you forget your scriptures," Finnen said, "I brought one along. Sorry if it's gotten wet. I'll just let you study the verses for a bit." He zipped himself and shoved the book hard into Farooq's balls. Next, he strung the *subha* around Farooq's neck, tightening the beads like a wooden garrote.

Farooq's legs straightened as he tried to get air, and the comic of the butt-fucking prophet fell to the dirt floor. Finnen lightened his hold after a few seconds and picked up the cartoon and the knife.

"Oops," Finnen said. "This wasn't in far enough." He plunged the blade, sinking it deeper into Farooq's thigh. "Don't want you to lose your homework." Farooq began to howl and wiggle. Finnen slapped him until he stopped.

To this point, Finnen hadn't allowed Farooq to talk. Only ten minutes had passed, and I figured fifteen minutes of safety was all we had left. I didn't want Farooq to think we were in any hurry, but I nodded at Finnen, signaling him to move it along. Farooq was mumbling his prayers, eyes closed.

We didn't have the luxury of torture methods used in Gitmo. No electricity for the cattle prod. No buckets for water boarding. No bright lights to flash in the face. No days of sleep deprivation. No Snoop Dog played at full volume. No television to play Meow Mix commercials over and over. No enemas, even though it smelled like Farooq had soiled himself. Finnen had to work with what he had: pain and insults.

"So, Jamil," Finnen said. "You ready for the pop quiz?" He pulled back Farooq's head using a handful of hair. "Did Mohammed practice boy love? Why else would he promise twenty-six virgin lads to martyrs? How 'bout you? You want to *daga me ra wazbaisha?*" Suck my dick, in Pashto. Farooq just stared with the wild look of a cornered hyena.

"Okaaaaaaay," Finnen said. "Pop quiz over. You flunked. At least you got to go to school. Not like your daughter or any of her friends."

Finnen showed Farooq the photo of Mullah Rikiti, the cleric from the mosque next door and Farooq's spiritual guide. First, he spit on the picture, wiping mucous across Rikiti's face.

"Movin' on to the final exam," Finnen said. "I want to know who gives Abdul here his orders. Did he have you slaughter Ms. Jenkins? Who runs this sector for the Taliban? Where are you getting your guns? There aren't multiple-choice answers. You have one minute before I start taking slivers out of you with my knife. We've got lots of class time before the bell rings. While you're thinkin', I'll enjoy the rest of the piggy sausage." Finnen started cutting the sausage, using the wiped-off Ka-Bar he had yanked from Jamil's thigh as both a fork and a knife. He never took his eyes off Farooq.

Ten seconds later.

"Time's up," Finnen said. "Who's the mullah's commander?"

The Company and the world already knew Mullah Mohammed Omar was the head of the Taliban. From his hidey hole in a cave somewhere on the border with Pakistan, the strategy he devised was close to the one used to defeat the Russians. Move his men from rock to rock, and make the infidels chase. Eventually, the expenditure of soldiers and money would cause the Americans to leave. Omar was quoted as saying, "What does the life of one mujahedeen compare to the cost of every plane that leaves the ground? We have thousands willing to be martyrs, and that number grows every day. But the Americans have only a limited number of planes. And we have many landmines to take American legs." Finnen wasn't expecting to uncover Omar, just get a little closer.

Nothing from Farooq but wide-eyed wonder.

It would soon be over. No matter how much Finnen waltzed with Farooq, I knew this was part of our job description neither one of us relished. The torture wouldn't continue. Finnen would shoot him and pose Farooq's body for the best psy-ops effect. One more try.

Finnen took hold of the prayer beads and twisted the subha until Farooq couldn't spread his mouth any wider and his head began to slump. Then Finnen released the pressure slightly and slapped the hadji to keep him awake.

"You're about as much fun as a burning orphanage," Finnen said. "Oh, that's right. You'll remember the scene. If you weren't there with Rikiti's boys, you probably saw the pictures of the shish kabob-ed girls. What on earth would justify firebombing an orphanage? Did one of the poor lasses peek out the window? Did the sight of her dark eyes violate your fucked-up code?"

Finnen quickly pushed the tip of the knife into the hadji's left eye and twisted. Not far enough to go into the brain, but the hadji wouldn't be seeing from that side again.

Farooq began to scream, and Finnen covered his mouth.

"An eye for an eye," Finnen said. "Oh, my mistake. That's the bible. I should have said 'those who reject the teachings should be dragged into the scalding water and burnt in the fire.' Sura 40 from the Koran, if you forgot. You and Rikiti can use that one to do most anything, including barbecuing innocent girls."

When Farooq stopped squirming, Finnen held the end of the Ka-Bar to Farooq's right eye.

"Last chance," Finnen said. "You won't be able to find your way to heaven after I take this one."

No words from Farooq. So far, just groans, screams, and a few "Allah"s. Now, mumbles.

Finnen put his ear close to Farooq's mouth.

"What are you saying, mate?" he asked. "Speak louder." Finnen pressed his body closer.

"Did I hear you right?" Finnen asked. "Was that '*ustaa moor kay mandam*'?" I will fuck your mother. "Gotta give it to you. You're a tough donkey. My mum used to say, 'He is scant of news that speaks ill of your mother.' But, sorry, Mum's dead. Taken to the angels by the cancer."

This time, the Ka-Bar went in deeper, blood squirting onto Finnen's hand. Farooq was too dazed to shriek.

"An old Arabic saying," Finnen said. "'Life without a friend is death without a witness.' You've got neither. Unless you count Morgan and me as witnesses to your death. We're not your friends. Anything more, pray tell?"

Prayers. Sometimes nothing worked. The promise of the *houris* was stronger than any threat. Farooq was still muttering when Finnen plunged the Ka-Bar directly into the Afghan's heart.

Finnen left the knife and arranged the pictures on Farooq's lap.

"God is good, but never dance in a small boat," Finnen said, standing back and looking on the dead hadji's body. "I think your boat just sunk, Farooq."

He put on his backpack and started toward the door, H & K in his hand.

"God made time, but man made haste," Finnen said. "Let's hump, Morgan."

The blood from Washington's wound formed a small pool next to his bush boot. Ants marched in a steady caravan back and forth to a tiny hole in the wall. Finnen sat at the desk, watching.

Washington was no Farooq. Even if he may have behaved in a fashion worthy of a firing squad, at least he hadn't beheaded a woman or roasted an orphanage full of girls. And we weren't absolutely sure of his motives or the payoff. Only the word of a condemned man. I slid the knife back into its home.

"Let's start at the beginning," I said. "How were you contacted?"

Still highly trained, tough, and hopeful, Washington stared as if we were the ones being grilled with our hands behind our heads.

"Email," he said. "A message telling me to go to a pick-up point for further orders. Came through from a secure DOD server. You spooks probably know more about it than me. Felt like it was from the magic kingdom you dudes live in. I thought I was takin' orders. Deleted the message and burned the map and instructions after I read 'em like I was told. You got any water?"

The .22 Hush Puppy was under my camo shirt. I took it out and aimed it at Washington's forehead.

"I won't even bother with the knife signals," I said. "That was such a load of bullshit, I may as well save the energy from cutting and let the pistol take chunks out of you." I pulled the trigger, and a bullet imbedded in the wall behind Washington's head, grazing his ear on the way by.

"Didn't know Rangers took orders off the Internet. Finnen may look stupid," I nodded toward a grinning Finnen, "but I'm not."

"Whoa, brother," Washington said, shaking his head. Drops of blood flew off, staining the tan mud walls with red spots. "The email came from Spookville. You're gonna ask how I knew. If you put that pistol away, I'll tell ya."

The .22 easily went under my fatigue top.

"Okay," I said. "We're listening."

"I'm sure you boys've been to Camp Perry," Washington said. Camp Perry was a CIA training center in the Virginia woods outside Langley. "I was invited there myself for some short-term clandestine ed-u-cation beyond what the Army was givin'. There were even some spooks from the German BND there. With this latest cooperative spirit in Afghanistan, the brass thought some of us should bond. I was given a cipher there that read, if I ever heard or saw the word *zoetrope*, I should follow any orders that were included."

"And you didn't ask anyone about it?"

"Fuck that. I was nervous enough, being in the dark kingdom. I was more worried it was some sort of cult test and wondered if I would pass the initiation with my balls still hangin' low. Didn't drink anything but bottled water I took in with me, afraid somebody would put LSD in my glass and become another lab rat for you spooks."

The story was infamous. In search of truth serum—or TD, truth drug—my namesake for the day, Wild Bill Donovan, had piggy-backed research that came out of Nazi concentration camps. He said development was of the greatest importance to national security. The Company had tried many combinations in the quest for an easily administered chemical interrogator including mescaline, heroin, and cocaine. Nothing in the 1950s worked as well as LSD, but the aftereffects and hallucinations sometimes left the receivers in padded rooms. Ken Kesey had been part of one of these experiments while a grad student at Stanford. He found a better use for it. Parties.

The ants were expanding their sphere of influence. I flicked one off my knee.

"Keep goin'," I said. "At least this fairy tale is interesting."

"My throat's dry as Mother Theresa's crack," he said. "And it seems like some'a the blood from what's left of my ear got in my mouth. How 'bout that water?"

Finnen got a bottle out of his pack and walked over to Washington.

"Here," he said, unscrewing the cap and pouring a small amount into Washington's mouth. "But no more Catholic cracks. You don't want to offend He That Is. The punishment could be as eternal as the Irish love of a fallin' down drunk."

Some of the water spilled out the side of Washington's lips, and he licked it with his tongue, sighing.

"Didn't think much of the message at the time," Washington said. "After I'd been in Korengal a while, I got transferred here. Not something that happens often. Grunts usually stay in one place in this rock pile 'til they go home unless they're injured severely. Or killed. When I got the email, mentioning "zoetrope," I figured out why I was reassigned. I was being drafted onto the spook team." Washington stopped and nodded to Finnen for more water.

If Washington's story was true, it was headed in a direction Finnen and I might not want to hear. Or be safe knowing. I looked up at the ceiling and watched a spider make his way slowly toward the corner.

"Go on," I said.

Washington finished his drink and looked at me.

"I read the email," Washington said. "Went to the drop-off point, and the message told me to go to another area on the base and pick up a pack hidden behind a couple of dead trucks. I was not to open it. The next morning, a Humvee would be waiting for me at the motor pool. I was supposed to deliver the pack to a man in Jalalabad. Close to here, by the way. That was the first time."

"But you didn't follow orders," I said. "You opened the pack."

Washington chuckled.

"Wouldn't you?" Washington asked. "Coulda been some kinda IED. I wanted to know something about what was goin' down. But it was just greenbacks. Hundred dollar bills. Lots of 'em. All in those cute little wrappers you white folk see at the bank."

"How many times did you make deliveries?" I asked

"Twice with the money."

"Did you meet anyone when you dropped off the cash?"

"There wasn't any in-tro-duc-tions, ya know what I mean. Just a hand-off to a different Abdul every time in a different location."

"And you didn't have any idea what it was about?"

"Not for a while. I'd read my email and follow orders. Till things changed."

"How so?"

"By then, I was gettin' jumpy and suspicious. Bein' somebody's boy and not knowin' what I was mixed up in. They sent me to make a pick-up, not a drop-off." Washington tried to move his arms. "Say, now that we's all buddies and I'm spillin' my guts, could you take these cuffs off? My arms're gettin' numb. And heavy. You can still shoot me, but there's no use me dyin' like this."

Finnen and I exchanged glances. I nodded.

"Okay," Finnen said. "But we'll have you sit on the floor with your back against the wall. And we'll both have pistols trained on your head. Don't do anything silly."

"I promise," Washington said.

After Finnen had cut the handcuffs and guided Washington to a seat in the dirt with the barrel of his Hush Puppy, he went to his chair again. The prisoner's back was pressed to the wall. I stood and stepped closer, still out of range for a foot strike. There was no way Washington could get up and reach either of us before his head was in pieces.

"Comfortable?" I asked.

"Just like a sunny day at the beach in my chaise lounge," Washington said.

"So now you're no longer a delivery boy."

"Nope. Moved up. I was told to go into the foothills of the mountains with an empty 6x6. Make a pick-up and deliver it to where they're workin' on the pipeline south and west of here."

"Which mountains? If you haven't noticed, we're surrounded."

"The White Mountains. Sometimes they're called the Spin Mountains. Full of caves and bunkers. Opium fields lower down. Supposedly home of Bin Laden. Those mountains."

Parts of his story were coming together and feeding the paranoia that was growing in my stomach. I leaned against the wall.

"And Thorsten went with you?"

"Yeah, the dumbfuck."

"And you were picking up heroin and taking it for shipment by people on the pipeline?"

"You got it."

"From Sheik Wahidi?"

"Didn't get no names, but I heard whispers. That's the one I heard."

"And you never gave it a thought? Just bought and put into the market tons of heroin? You didn't wonder if it was wrong?"

"Look, spook. I believed I was doin' exactly as ordered. I was told never to speak to anyone about what I was doin'. I didn't even know it was about dope 'til I drove to the mountains. I only did it once. Then, I quit openin' my emails. About a week ago."

"You didn't think about going to your commanding officer?"

Washington laughed.

"And be ambushed by a couple'a dudes like you? Or gain a new hole in my head in the middle'a the night? I know enough there's no runnin' from the Company if there's a contract out. Unless your name is Osama. I decided to lay low. Ya know, do my job pacifyin' the natives. At least 'til somebody showed up asking why I couldn't read no more. Somebody just like you, Donovan, or whatever the fuck your name is."

This was turning into something way beyond a clusterfuck. Washington, if I believed him, was no rogue. He had done pretty much what I would have. And Dunne wouldn't have sent Finnen and me out unless nobody at his level knew either. All of it was based on whether Washington was trustworthy. I looked at Finnen.

"We need to talk," I said. "Cuff his hands and feet," I said, pointing the Hush Puppy at Washington.

Finnen smiled and walked to his pack. He looked like he was enjoying the theatre and not surprised by the melodrama. Over beers, a seemingly endless amount, Finnen had told me how much he loved and hated the intrigues of the game we played. How you never quite knew what the real reasons were. It always seemed we "live in a land of broken mirrors," he often said. Now, Finnen claimed he was just being a "good lad. Followin' orders and doin' the devil's biddin'."

"Lucky I came prepared," Finnen said, taking out a few more sets of the plastic handcuffs. This time, he directed Washington to a water pipe that ran from the ceiling to the wall. He bound Washington's hands behind his back to the pipe and then cuffed the man's feet. Double knots.

"Take your time, guys," Washington said. "I don't have plans for the evening."

Next to the desk, a door led to another small, windowless room. Finnen followed me into the darkness and struck a match. A kerosene lamp hung from the rafters. He pulled up the glass and lit the mantel. I shut the door.

"Not what you were expectin', eh Morgan?" Finnen said. "It's all folly. Gotta have a sense of humor."

"There's only one question," I said. "Make that two. Do we believe him? Or do we kill him?"

"I think there might be details he's leavin' out, but the thread feels exactly like the Company's pulling the strings. We've both been up to our tits in tricks like this. Why would you be surprised? Does the sheer audacity of the evil shock you?"

"I thought this was fairly straightforward. A bad seed buying dope from the Taliban. A simple little conspiracy like so many others. Capitalism at its sinful best. But the Company throws a wicked curve ball. Again."

Finnen just shook his head, smiling.

"Oh, Morgan, my lad," he said. "When will you take your thumb out of your mouth?"

"You suspected? You didn't even know why we were going on this op."

"'Tis easier to be deceived by your wife than your friend. At least you know him. And I've never been married. Certainly not to the Company. I go into these things with my eyes open and my brain closed tight as Margaret O'Halloran's legs. You think people like you and me could ever understand the working of the black fairies in Langley? At the end of the day, I just collect my chit and pray we're on the side of St. Patrick."

"I suppose it takes a certain level of naïveté to sneak up and fire a silencer into somebody sleeping in his bed. But I thought it was for the good of the masses, not advancement of some shady plot. So you think we oughta just let Washington walk?"

"More than that. I think we should recruit him. Let him lead us to Wahidi. And wherever else the stench takes us. I don't believe Dunne knows anything." He turned away and watched the shadows from the burning kerosene obscure everything in the room. Even the truth. "It's miles above Dunne, so we'll have to come up with a good story. I'm in if you are, Morgan."

"I agree. I still don't completely trust Washington, but I didn't get the sense he was lying. We'll go back in and make him a friend for life. There're still some questions I want to ask. Dunne's no icon of virtue either, so we might be runnin' naked for awhile."

Back in the other room, Washington's head was slumped to his chest. He looked up when we came through the door.

"You fellas solve any of your issues?" he asked. "Is it a bullet to the head or a free pass?"

Finnen walked toward Washington, Ka-Bar in his hand. The black Ranger started to wriggle, trying to get as far away as possible. He put an inch more between himself and the blade.

"Whoa," Washington said. "Not a fucking knife. Shoot me."

"Don't get your knickers twisted," Finnen said. "I'm cuttin' you free. You're being invited to join the posse."

Finnen sliced through the handcuffs and helped Washington to his feet, leading him to the chair and handing him a fresh bottle of Dasani. Lemon flavored.

From my chair, I kept the .22 pointed at Washington. He might've harbored some lingering resentment against me for slicing him in the thigh and shooting his ear nearly off. I couldn't figure why, but I still aimed at a spot just above the middle of his eyebrows.

"We'd like a few more details," I said. "I don't think you've told us the whole story, but my sense is you've given us the broad strokes. You do know what you're mixed up in means you're an unallowable and deniable risk. If it wasn't for the timing of my interview with Chinar, the next Company man you saw wouldn't be asking questions."

Washington finished the bottle of water in one long pull and stared at me with something less than love. Not hate, either. He was a hard man, and a few little wounds were a minor distraction.

"Does this mean I'm an honorary white boy?" he asked. "Gee, that'd be swell."

Finnen was at the desk, sipping his own Dasani.

"Can't go that far, Washington," he said. "Not unless you change your name. Never heard of no white Washingtons since the Prez. How 'bout McGuire? A good Irish name."

Maybe premature, but I put the .22 in my lap.

"Let's start with the emails," I said. "Do you remember the addresses they came from?"

Washington rubbed his temples.

"You got any aspirin?" he asked. "For some reason, I have a headache and my thigh is throbbing. Maybe a Band-aid, too."

Finnen stood and went to his pack.

"I always carry one'a these," he said, holding up a first-aid kit. He took out a packet of aspirins, a tube of wound-care ointment, and a sterile wrap.

In a few minutes, he finished his nurse duties. "There we are. Fit as an Irish fiddle. Now, you're ready to dance a reel."

"About those addresses," I said.

"After the first one, they came from different Yahoo accounts," Washington said. "They all had 'zoetrope' in the subject line. I'm no computer geek, but I think you can send those messages from most anywhere."

"You don't recall the first address?" I asked.

"No. Just that it looked like it came from a DOD site."

If I enlisted the Company, it wouldn't matter how secure the sender felt; it would only matter how quick he was. Under the Directorate of Science and Technology, the Company nerds could hack into or trace any computer anywhere in the world. They could launch emails from the Pope's private electronic address. Or the President's. They could retrieve any email ever written no matter how long ago it was sent. Electronic information, just like energy, never leaves the universe. If you had the money, time, and brains, every byte in the ether world was accessible. The Company had all three. Within seconds of a tap on the send icon, the Firm would know exactly where that computer was located. Still, it might not help. From my college computer classes, I knew Yahoo addresses and messages could be traced. Getting to the location if the user was changing his position would take too long. All the sender had to do was go to any Kinko's or library, establish an account, log in, and send Washington a message with "zoetrope" in the subject line. Even the DOD address would be relatively worthless now, since there were thousands of DOD user names. But I wasn't about to openly take advantage of the Company resources. Not until I knew more.

The smoke from the lantern was getting thicker by the minute, only a small metal vent in the ceiling allowing the fumes to escape. I rubbed my nose to try to clear some of the bitter smell.

"The computer angle is a dead end for us," I said. "You better start checking your email again, Washington."

"Yes, sir," he said. He looked like he was about to give me a mock salute. He just grinned, savoring his death-row midnight reprieve.

"I think we eliminated the prime money handler when we aced Chinar," I said. "He'll be replaced if this operation is going to continue. I think it will. Too much to gain, even though I can't see what it is right now from the Company's side and if they're involved. I'm more interested in Wahidi. He's the key. Did you go through the poppy fields? See the refinery?"

"Yes," Washington said. He sat back and began to talk.

The scenes he described were known, but not many outsiders had been allowed to view the Afghan heroin industry in person. Even the *New York Times* had written that this year's crop numbers were a new record, resulting in an industry worth more than $150 billion. Much of that going to the Taliban.

"We drove through a poppy field on the way to the pick-up, and I was given a lecture by one of the few in the tribe who spoke English," Washington said. "His name was Mihad. He was proud and jazzed to show an infidel what his clan was growin'. It was the first time I knew what I had been buyin' back in Jalalabad. Thorsten was with me on the tour, and his eyes were poppin' out of his skull."

The way Washington described it, the land in Afghanistan's southeast was relatively flat, below the towering mountains further toward Pakistan. The area had been under a six-year drought. Opium took little water, much less than other crops. Besides, the harvest produced an immense amount of income and poppy growth was encouraged, if not demanded, by local tribal warlords.

Leaving a river valley and climbing into the rolling hills, Washington viewed fields of white, dotted with red and purple: poppy plants in bloom. His guide explained poppy seeds could be found in any of the thousands of bazaars around the country. The growth occurred in two cycles per year in the lower elevations, and one where the weather was more severe. Crops are planted in March and the harvest began three to four months later. The second planting in July was never as productive as the first, since the late-season yield was more prone to disease and weather extremes.

"It was a sea of white, wavin' in the breeze," Washington said. "Broken up by a few skinny trees and paths. Men were in the fields, milkin' the plants, protected by guards with AKs and RPGs."

I knew poppy plants sprout in fifteen days, and the job is to keep the seedlings from being smothered by weeds. If there's not a storm or disease to slow them, the plants blossom in three months. Inside the bloom, a green seed pouch grows the opium resin. When the pouch gets nearly as big as a baseball, a serrated six-tooth trowel, a *ghoza,* is used to make an incision. The cutting is done in the morning, and the pouch is allowed to leak throughout the day. The sticky white milk turns brown and is collected in the evening and formed into a ball for drying. Each pod can be bled six or seven times before the next planting. The pouch seeds are left to dry and become the source of the new crop. Mothers also use the seeds to get their children to nap, brewing a tea that allows work in the fields to be undisturbed.

"Mihad loved the chance ta' speak English," Washington said. "Of course, his AK was always pointing in our general direction, and we had to pass through a half-dozen Taliban checkpoints. The hadjis had all been told two infidels in a 6x6 were allowed through."

Miles of white blossoms. For every half-acre, a *jerib* in Pashto, the farmer could harvest more than 60 pounds of opium, worth about $5,000. If the grower was to plant wheat instead—which is less drought resistant, harder to grow, and more disease prone—he might net $100.

The farmers, most of whom had gone into debt during the opium-growing ban, were now repaying loans and beginning to get back to a normal life, even if it meant lots of armed men in the neighborhood.

A cough. Finnen was getting anxious. Surprisingly, he hadn't asked any questions.

"Is there an end to this tale?" he asked.

The storytelling made Washington more relaxed. The longer we listened, the more confident he seemed he would see the sky again. He rubbed his scalp and slouched further.

"I'm giving ya'all a primer on the industry," he said. "Background. You might need it to understand what we're up against."

Already part of the team. And he still couldn't be quite sure he'd been drafted.

Fidgety, Finnen cracked his knuckles. Unless he was on stage, singing the songs of Ireland, he was impatient with the world.

"Time and tide awaits no man," Finnen said. "Get on with it, lad."

Washington grinned.

"Keep your kilt on," Washington said. "I'm gettin' to the important stuff."

Finnen jumped to his feet, face turning red to the point his freckles disappeared.

"Kilt?" he screamed. "No good Irishman would wear that faggoty-ass shite. The girly skirts are for Scottish queers. Not men. Don't you ever be sayin' somethin' as distasteful as that again. I'll have to take your other ear."

Turning his head in my direction, Washington winked, making me a co-conspirator.

"No disrespect," Washington said, looking at Finnen. "Jivin' with ya." He turned back to me. "When we got through the fields, we came to a walled complex. Guards and razor wire. Inside, we were told to park next to a covered area where big drums of opium were being brewed into heroin. All it takes is boilin' the opium in water and lye. The test of its purity is done with a pH meter. The Afghans used to send the opium direct to Iran, Turkey, Pakistan, and Kazakhstan for processing. But there's extra money in refinin' it yourself. Plus, you can ship more heroin than opium. Bigger payday. A half-dozen turbaned mujahedeen were stirring with long tree branches over a fire like they were cookin' lamb stew for the troops. After the liquid was burned away, they used a car jack to press the opium into bricks and squeeze the last water out. They did that a few times until it was all bone dry. Another group of beards was wrappin' the heroin in colored paper and stamping it with an old hand press. No women or children around."

Back at the desk, Finnen was tapping his bush boots on the dirt floor.

"So, did you meet the chief?" he asked. "Celebrate a successful deal with a cup of that awful shite they call tea?"

"There was a man in a full white robe and skull cap watchin' from across the courtyard," Washington said. "He was cleaner than the rest of the donkey herders. No one approached him. It was obvious he was the mullah."

"Wahidi?" I asked.

"Don't know, but I did hear that name in the middle of all the Pashto trash the slaves were talkin'."

"Arms?"

"They were as well outfitted as a squad of jar heads. AKs, H & Ks, mortars, RPGs, M240 machine guns. All the gear for a fun day in the rock pile." Washington stretched his legs. "There was a guy in the corner. It looked to me like he had bricks of US-made C-4. He was bein' very careful, sticking it into an old car battery. If somebody would'a turned the key on that one, I wouldn't be here talkin' with you."

"How many men?" I asked.

"At least twenty-five outside. Four or five sentries on the walls. Everyone was within arm's length of a weapon."

"What about Thorsten?"

"Like he was at Hooters. Big dumbfuck eyes wide. Lots of, 'Did you see that?' and 'Holy fuckin' shit.' When we di-di'ed out'a there, he couldn't stop talkin'."

"Any ideas about him?"

"Wouldn't trust him even with a distant cousin. The greed was oozing from him like milk from a poppy pod."

"What next?"

"Didn't take more than an hour. They loaded us up. Used old ammo cans for shippin' the skag. Covered 'em with empty crates of dried milk and food supplies. Lots of bowing and 'Allah' bullshit. Then we hit the dirt road to Zareh Sharan and onto the highway toward Kandahar. Still had to go back through the Taliban checkpoints. No problem. It was scarier gettin' past the allies' guard posts. But someone left all the paperwork we needed in the 6x6's glove box. We were on a mercy mission to a refugee camp south of Qalat, about two hundred miles away. That truck didn't have no springs, either. My back still feels like it got run over by a BV10 Viking tank."

Washington stretched and groaned, the pain of his ear and leg wounds seemingly replaced by the memory of hours in a stiff military vehicle not designed for comfort.

"We got to the rendezvous just before dusk," Washington said. "Met up with a couple'a supposed pipeline workers in brand-new Ford SUVs. Stuffed 'em full of dope and threw the other shit out. Never got their names. It wasn't cordial. If I had to guess, they were Company men. Or contractors. And I think the junk was flyin' out on one of the cargo planes coming in to keep the pipeline construction supplied. Them planes mostly go in and out of Ramstein in Germany. They directed us to a pipeline camp a few klicks away, and we got some grub and a cot. Left in the morning and were back at the base by mid-afternoon."

Not the time and place for a full debriefing. There were lots of details left out. I felt Washington was being truthful. The logistics made sense. Just not who was orchestrating. But the operation likely had the Company's signature at the bottom.

The Asian-Pacific Pipeline plans were on hold, but the Trans-Afghanistan natural gas line was being secretly built, linking the Caspian Sea wells in Turkmenistan to India. A consortium of British and other companies were funding the construction. It was rumored the petroleum-pipeline cartel was considering using some of the same routes, abandoning the more northerly Asian-Pacific routes. Where there was money to be made on this scale, American business interests couldn't be far behind, especially if the word "oil" was even whispered. With Karzai's history in Unocal and the Company, it would be easy to find cooperation; it was simple to fly out dope with no customs checks and the right people waiting on the German end.

Several minutes went by. I stared at the wall where the spider had made it to the corner of the ceiling and was waiting for a meal. I hoped he caught one of the sand flies that circled in the gloom.

"You've never heard any names in all this? Or met anyone but couriers or delivery boys?" I asked.

"No," Washington said.

More time. Whatever happened would take some thought and would certainly be extremely dangerous. The Company didn't like anyone mucking about in their plots. I questioned whether this was a rogue operation or if it was sanctioned at a level many pay grades above mine.

Finnen emptied his Dasani and watched me.

"What do you think, Morgan?" he asked. "If what Washington's sayin' is God's truth, there's nasties out there building a pot'a gold. And sellin' aid to the enemy. I don't believe Dunne is up on the scheme'a things. He wouldn't have sent us to visit Washington if he was. Thorsten might be a problem. He could be plannin' a hijacking."

Too many threads. I scratched my beard.

"Let's get Washington back to base," I said, standing. "Talk it over with Dunne. I think you're right—Dunne's probably not involved." I turned to Washington. "You're now part of this op, Washington. We can try to get you reassigned to the spook team. We've gotta be careful. If too many people know, a wrong one might hear. But we can make sure there are operations where you're requested. In the meantime, you don't talk to anyone about this. Agreed?"

"Agreed." Washington said. "I want to find out what's going on as much as you. Who's been usin' me."

It was still daylight when we walked out the door, rifles in hands and looking as if another patrol was successfully completed with no casualties except Washington's leg and an inability to hear from his left ear. We met up with the Rangers a few blocks away and mounted up for the short trip to Gardez. This time, Finnen came along.

Back at the base outside Jalalabad, Finnen and I were alone with Dunne in spook central. Washington stayed in Gardez, checking his email and anticipating a short-term transfer to Tora Bora. Fully debriefed and cleaned up, we drank cold Buds from the small refrigerator and waited for Dunne's opinion, knowing full well his clearance was higher than ours. He could be aware of some top-secret trickery not worthy of sharing with blue-collar field agents like Finnen and me. If that was so, and we had learned too much, we might be rotated home in a body bag.

Nothing of any consequence had changed in the tent. The laptop still sat in front of Dunne like it was attached to his fingers. No more snapshots of somebody's wife and family. The air hadn't been recycled and smelled of the same sand and sweat as the last time. Outside, Birds came and went, fluttering the tent sides. Only the guards were different, replaced by two helmetless NFL linemen in fatigues without nametags and sporting reflective sunglasses. Bench jockeys, itching to get in the game, but trying to act like they were on the first team. Dunne sat in his folding chair, no smile showing off his years of good dental hygiene.

"This Washington cat," he said. "You believe him?"

The Bud was dry. I crinkled the can and tossed it toward a full wastebasket. Rim shot. It joined the ones Finnen had already drained with a metallic *clang*.

"Yup," I said. "No hesitation in the telling. No false bravado. No darting eyes or sweating. Of course, we didn't take along any babble juice. Didn't bring much pain either, if you call a slice with a Ka-Bar and the loss of a chunk of his ear 'nothin' much.' We could ask him in and dust off the waterboard. Everybody thinks we're experts anyway." I walked over to the fridge for another beer. "Maybe a lie detector. But it wouldn't work. I think Washington has a sphincter of steel. Even I can fool the chickenshit things."

A night class at Camp Perry taught us how to trick a lie detector in case we encountered the machine before somebody beat us to death. It was a short course. The obvious point was the Agency and our country didn't want the hired help to divulge any secrets. Die? Better than the dishonor of blabbing out of school. One of the primary methods in fooling the detector was to tighten the sphincter, along with slightly altering breathing and doing times tables in your head for distraction.

The more I thought about it, the more I believed Washington wasn't lying. Since field agents often had to quickly decide if a blind date was telling the truth, we spent more time at Camp Perry learning how to detect lies than hide them. Washington didn't exhibit the typical stiffness of the deceitful or scratch more than any other unwashed grunt. He made eye contact and showed lots of hand movements, even venturing to flip Finnen the finger a few times after his handcuffs were off. Every emotion was timed with the event and met immediately with a natural response. His whole face, not just his lips, smiled. He never turned away or tried to shrink his body. He didn't repeat our words when responding—"Did you steal any of the money before you delivered it to Chinar?" "No, I didn't steal any of the money before I delivered it to Chinar." He just answered no when I asked him. Not a defensive word. If anything, he went on the attack, like when he threatened he was "gonna fuck up your leprechaun ass" after Finnen joked about Washington's heritage as an Afro-American welfare baby. He contracted his denials. "I didn't smoke none'a that shit," rather than "I did not smoke any of the opium." He did talk more than I sensed was natural for him. But that was at my prodding and to piss off Finnen. Silence is uncomfortable for the liar. It also could have been Washington wanted to eke out a few more minutes breathing the thin air. When I abruptly changed topics by asking him what his golf handicap was, he didn't go along. "Don't be talkin' shit. That's a white-bread thing." He didn't even shove Tiger back in my face.

Filling time with idle chatter or speculation wasn't Dunne's thing. He stood up and went to the map.

"From what he told you," Dunne said, "the pick-up must have been about here." He pointed to a spot southeast of Gardez. Finnen and I walked over and looked past his shoulder. "And the drop-off here." He moved his finger in a fairly straight line to the northeast of Kandahar. "Somebody was well connected on both sides to get him that far without having his ass shot up or meeting a squad of 31 echoes." MPs.

"No doubt," I said. "That's more evidence something bigger and smarter than us is afoot."

Beside me, Finnen grinned.

"Fairies and elves across the land," he said. "And dastardly plots. Who do you think's behind this, Dunne? It's beyond the likes of myself and Morgan."

Dunne just stared at the map as if it held the location of Murphy's Gold between the colored pins. Finnen went for another beer, and I walked back to my chair.

"Before we go much further," I said, "we better do something about Thorsten."

Dunne faced me, tapping a pen on the back of his hand.

"You're right, Morgan," he said. "I don't think Thorsten has any intel of value. He was probably recruited for muscle, not brain matter. I checked him out more thoroughly when you were in Gardez. Don't know how he's stayed out of Leavenworth. They won't be missing him at Harvard."

The beer snapped open, and Finnen raised his can in a salute.

"Cheers, mates," he toasted. "I want to cut in on this jig. You boys call the tune, and I'll dance along. Thorsten sounds like the kinda fella who needs some special attention. The kind I like to give more than Morgan. He's got a terrible case a' the conscience lately."

It wasn't so much conscience as doubt.

In college, I'd taken a poly-sci class from Professor Swartzman, an acknowledged lefty. He often ranted about the evil influence of the Agency on the world and recounted many of the less deadly dirty tricks. Like removing people from the cartoon Hollywood version of Orwell's *Animal Farm* and replacing them with pigs so as not to disturb the public. Or pressuring Hollywood to include more wealthy-looking African Americans in the movies to counter the Communist picture of black degradation and exploitation. Or paying intellectuals out of money stolen from the Marshall Plan to further the Company's agenda. Not to mention the wars started in Nicaragua and other developing countries. And the assassinations. The list of government-sanctioned foul play seemed endless. After a while, we all became shell-shocked rather than outraged. But, recently, many of the stories were blooming again . . . like black poppies.

Back at the computer, Dunne was typing.

"Looks like he's still here," Dunne said. "I can make a few calls, and you and Finnen can team up with him in the morning. What cave would you like to visit?"

Thanks to an earlier hot shower, I was feeling like a newbie. I stroked the thigh of my clean fatigues.

"Don't matter," I said. "You set the itinerary. In the meantime, pull up Thorsten's bio. It might have something we can use."

Dunne typed more keys.

"From California," he said. "Out in the valley. Two brothers and two sisters. Parents both alive. High school grad with no distinctions except the football team. Didn't score high enough on his SATs to further his education other than a few months in a community college. Nothing much here except a couple of investigations for prisoner brutality and disorderly conduct. No convictions."

"Can you hack into his email?" I asked.

Dunne looked up at me, the first crooked smile of the day showing his fangs.

"Now that would be illegal," Dunne said. He returned to the screen and began typing.

Minutes passed. Finnen sipped his beer, slowing down now that he had a few dead soldiers in the wastebasket. Earlier, I sent the message I had composed to my mother and now wondered if Dunne read it. Probably. Being in the Company didn't carry any confidentiality provisions, except from my end. Any snooping in my emails would most likely lead to the conclusion they were written in code and I was a counter-agent. They were too saccharine. I started constructing another in my head.

Hi, Mom. Thanks for the message back. Glad to read Uncle Phil is feeling better. Tell him to quit smoking. Dad must be happy getting the truck running again. And that darn cat should stop running away or Mrs. Skinner will have a stroke. Too bad about the Wildcats. I was hoping they would have a better season. That was quite a tale about Bob and Sally losing each other in Disney World. I'm sure their adventure will only make the marriage stronger. I've been really busy. With the economy going sour, we're having to search for more tax breaks and write-downs. Did get out on the Potomac last weekend. Too windy for an amateur like me. Had to make a dash for shore. Visiting a friend from California tomorrow morning. But, mostly it's work and finding ways to save the company money. Sorry about the cell phone. I'll try to call you next week. Give my love to everyone and tell them how much I miss those Kansas corn fields and the best bacon in the world.

By the time I was done composing, Dunne had filled a pad with notes. He stood, walked around his folding desk, and handed me the sheet of paper.

"He's emailing a couple of women," Dunne said. "And his mother. Like you, Morgan, a good boy."

There it was. Dunne's veiled admission he was monitoring. No use having a shit fit. It wouldn't change a thing, and I already suspected.

After inhaling at least six beers, Finnen was sitting straight in his chair, just a slight weave to his head.

"A man loves his sweetheart the most, his wife the best, but his mother the longest," Finnen said. "Does it seem from his missives he loves her like no other? If so, we can use that."

"In Thorsten's words," Dunne said, "she is 'da man,' whatever the fuck that means. From my reading, she's the woman of his life, not like the bimbos who send him nude pictures of themselves and he writes to as if they were pork loin."

CIA lore was more ingrained among military personnel who worked with or around spooks than the general public. The reputation of success at any cost and failure grounds for immediate sanction with extreme prejudice was nurtured by the Company and taken as a Commandment by all grunts. "Thou Shalt Not Fuck With the Agency. Or Fail" was written in the shortened lives of too many and one of the reasons they avoided our compound like it was radioactive. Stories of a secret coven practicing black arts and sorcery was a hot topic in the chow line—the way targets just disappeared, as if their bodies vaporized in smoke.

One story on the grapevine told of a Ranger who hid with a Company agent all night in the middle of a herd of tethered Taliban goats, waiting for the dawn and serenaded by *baa*-ing and shitting. They were supposedly there only for recon of the small mud house. At sunrise, the agent was missing, his escort swearing the man was beside him, still dressed in camo fatigues. But he wasn't. He stepped out of the hut and into the morning bright wearing man jammies and a turban, a bearded head in his hand. The agent lifted the head, holding it up for the grunt to see, and said, "Abdul had a nightmare," tossing it to the goats. Finnen, Dunne, and I knew tales like this only supported the belief that not even mothers were safe if there was a mission to achieve.

"Did Mom send naked pictures, too?" Finnen asked.

Throwing my empty Bud can at Finnen, I said, "Fuck off, you pervert."

No smile from Dunne. He was already scheming. His brief.

"Which cave do you want to visit?" Dunne asked again.

"Your choice," Finnen said. "They all look the same to me. Just make it close. I hate humpin' up them rocky hills. I don't think Morgan gives a shite. He's in better shape than me."

The nearby cave complexes of Tora Bora, or *Spin Ghar* to the Pashtuns, had been the site of bloody battle for years and were the stronghold of the Taliban. Supposedly, they were the hide-out of Bin Laden. Both Finnen and I had been deep into them before, but our work was mostly done in the cities and lowlands. It was too hard to sneak into the caves at night, impossible during the day. They were also the site of mortar placement for the sporadic attacks on the base. The closest caves were within the vision of artillery spotters and the range of 155mm howitzers. It would make sense to Thorsten that we were going out on a run to one of the Taliban gun placements based on friendly intel. We didn't really have to get far into the mountains—just off the base alone with no witnesses lurking and Thorsten believing he was advancing the cause of Operation Enduring Freedom.

Dunne picked up his encrypted satellite cell phone.

"Be ready at 0700. Report here. I'll have everything arranged. Pack light."

He started to punch in numbers and nodded for us to di di.

Loose rocks made the trek into the foothills nearly as slippery as climbing an ice cliff. Even at this altitude, the morning sun caused us to sweat like we were under a heat lamp. Air came in bursts, and Finnen struggled to keep up with the patrol. He was more used to safe houses in the city, where a long walk was to the door. Dunne had coordinated a platoon of Rangers for escort. They would be leaving us soon, acting as rear guard.

Trying to stay in the shadows of boulders and the few bushes, we carefully made our way up the hardscrabble hill. Remnants of earlier habitation came in the form of empty Corn Nut and Lay's Potato Chip wrappers. And a few rocks stained with blood. There hadn't been any activity from this sector for weeks. We were relatively confident no Taliban were observing our ascent. Still, progress was slow. I was less frightened of snipers than vipers.

Snakes. There are eleven varieties of poisonous snakes in Afghanistan, and seven have no anti-venom. I knew the features of them all. The constant nightmares were filled with the faces of those I had killed. And snakes. Like the Sind Krait. This yellow- and black-banded monster's bite was sixteen times more venomous than a cobra. It lived by eating other snakes and could be two meters long. Or the carpet viper. A white-bellied demon with oversized teeth on a squat body. One bite, and the brain would bleed within hours. It could hang in the limbs of bushes and drop in unexpectedly. Or the Oxus cobra, a fat gray or black fiend common to these foothills. A nibble from its fangs caused a neurotoxic reaction leading to respiratory failure and death. Too many to think about. I trudged ahead, lost in the daymare.

After a few hours of slow scrambling, we reached a rock overhang, perfect for the squad's concealment and giving a panoramic view. I waved the Lieutenant to stop. At my side, I told him to scatter his troops close by and wait for Thorsten, Finnen, and me to make our visit. Everyone should be hidden, in case the intel was true and Taliban mortars with 25 mm shells were delivered soon. On my signal, Thorsten and Finnen followed up the slope. A half-hour later, and we were at the opening of a cave.

One of the myths about Afghanistan was that it was dotted with gigantic caves that were big enough for trucks to drive through and could conceal Bin Laden's entourage. Not true. Most of the caverns were man-made hidey holes dug out of the limestone to protect mortars and snipers. Certainly, huge underground complexes had been discovered with a maze of rooms and corridors, able to withstand even the GBU-28 Bunker Busters and AGM-65 Maverick heat-seeking missiles. These were much higher up in the mountains. The entrance to the cave we approached was about the size of half of a normal door with rotting wooden support beams across the top and on the sides. Rocks were piled in neat stacks in front for more defenses. Nobody expected to discover a duplication of the drawings found in Bamian, northwest of Kabul. These murals were the oldest oil paintings in the world and depicted Buddha smiling in celestial scenes. We'd be lucky if we found "Kilroy was here" in Pashto inked into the walls. I motioned Thorsten to go in first, knowing there could be a nest of vipers waiting. Or a booby trap. He shrugged and followed orders, ducking his head and disappearing into the blackness.

First Washington. Now Thorsten. It would be so much simpler if we could have called in the Rangers for a chat. Or even scheduled an appointment in their barracks or at the command center. But spooks and grunts didn't mix unless they were in the field. Both sides wanted it kept that way. Any deviation was cause for rampant rumors. If it became necessary to use extreme methods to find what we sought or to cauterize the cowboy, it would be difficult to mask on the base. Fortunately, these types of missions were rare. Most of the enlistees in Enduring Freedom were here to do their jobs and go back to The World, not play at espionage or conspiracy.

In the distance, the outline of the base shimmered in the heat waves. Above us, black vultures circled, attracted by human presence, which usually meant a meal was soon to come. Trying hard, I couldn't find the squad of men hidden below. They were experts at melting into the rocks in the 50-degree slope. The sun wasn't yet directly overhead, but rays bounced off the limestone, making the thin air burn when I inhaled. An early morning trip to the Company canteen was already digested, and my stomach growled for attention. Finnen was crouched behind one of the rock piles, scanning above.

"All clear," Thorsten said from the darkness.

I went first, Finnen backing in beside me.

After my eyes adjusted, I could see the cave was about five meters wide and three high. Finnen took off his pack and brought out a flashlight and a sixteen-volt battery-powered lantern. When he flicked on the lantern, I could pick out empty green ammunition cans stamped PROPERTY OF THE US ARMY scattered around. Dirty cloth rags and a decaying cardboard box marked SKIPPY'S PEANUT BUTTER – NOT FOR RE-SALE were in the corner of the packed dirt floor. As suspected, no paintings on the walls. There were lots of chips in the limestone, as though bullets had reached inside. The space smelled like musty shit. And piss. Before Thorsten could get cozy, I kicked him in the back of his knees. His helmet rolled off, and his H & K fell to the dirt. He slumped to his knees, and I shoved his face all the way down. By the time he was ready to scream, I had the Ka-Bar pressed against his ear and my knee pushed hard into his back.

"You knew this was gonna be the outcome, one way or the other," I said. "I'm surprised you came along like such a good little lamb, Thorsten." I nicked his ear with the blade, making sure it drew blood. "Oops. Negative on that. You're so fucking dense I could have emailed you an outline of what was going to happen. You wouldn't have understood unless I illustrated it with pictures. Not even the dumbest grunt is stupid enough to mess with the Company. You must have cheated to pass kindergarten. Or beat somebody up."

Watching the door, Finnen was again playing sentry and listening, knowing I was the conductor.

"Can we get this over soon, mate?" Finnen said. "I've got a date with a case of Guinness my mum shipped over. Cut him quick. No mercy."

From his prone position and with the dirt in his mouth, it was hard to interpret Thorsten's exact words. They were something like, "I'll kill you, motherfucker." But I couldn't tell. It was the thought that counted.

In my right hand, the Hush Puppy was pressed in Thorsten's spine, just above his hips and below the bulletproof vest.

"I've got a gun in your back," I said. "I want you to put your arms slowly behind you."

"Do it," Finnen said. "I'd hate to have to ventilate you with this semi-auto. They make such a loud noise." He wasn't even looking at us.

Thorsten did, and I bound his hands with the plastic handcuffs. I stepped away and kicked him in the ankle.

"Sit up," I said.

This man was no hero. He hadn't spilled his blood in an ambush to save the last man in his squad. Dunne told us this morning that one report in his file was of a female soldier beaten and left behind at an enlisted men's club before Thorsten was shipped to Afghanistan. No charges were pressed, but others had seen Thorsten and the woman leave together, and the initials JT were freshly carved on her chest. She was too terrified to talk. Thorsten's first name was Thomas, but his nickname was "Juice," because he was known to shoot up steroids. He was also investigated for being one of a group of white soldiers who would go into Columbus from Fort Benning and ambush blacks, leaving them bleeding with Coca Cola bottles shoved up their asses. They were called the YCBFs, "You Can't Beat the Feeling" gang. He was clever enough to cover his tracks. Not this time. His life depended on whether he told the truth or could deceive us. At least, I believed that's what he was thinking.

Today, there would be no rapport established. No team building. I didn't want to spend any additional seconds breathing the same moldy air than were needed. Thorsten was the type of soldier the Company often used. Too dumb to ask questions. But it seemed he was still stupid enough to get greedy, even if he was messing with the world's biggest clandestine intelligence service. When we were finished, all we had to do was step out and toss one of the M67 fragmentation grenades Finnen carried into the cave and pity Thorsten's short time on the planet.

"Just a few questions," I said. "I'll use small words so you understand. You know Lieutenant Washington? Just nod your head."

He did.

"You delivered heroin with him. Nod your head again."

He did.

"After you slaughtered all the Afghans in that hovel by calling in the Drones and we were back at the base, you said you had something you wanted my help with. You believed you could blackmail me. Were you planning something that had to do with heroin?"

He couldn't look me in the eye, and he tried to shrink away as much as the handcuffs would let him.

"No, I was not planning anything that had to do with heroin."

"What was it, then?"

"I was getting together a bunch a' fellas for a surprise birthday party for one of my buddies. Thought you might be a great secret guest. I know you guys don't get out mixin' much."

Before he could move his head, I slapped him with the side of the Ka-Bar's blade. The tip still drew blood on his cheek.

"I really don't want to waste any more time, Thorsten," I said. "You know as well as I do that it's up to you whether you walk out of here or they pick up the little pieces left over. There won't be enough of you to fill my backpack."

"How about a drink of water first?"

I shook my head. There was no intention of dancing with this cretin. I went right to the point, knowing Thorsten would know exactly what the finale was going to be.

"No. We're gonna talk about your momma. What's she like?"

Thorsten's hooded eyes opened wide.

"This doesn't have anything to do with her? Why are you askin'?"

"I thought maybe we could make a deal. You stop lying. When you tell me how many others are involved and how far your discussions have gone, I can assure you your mother won't get a night visitor. If you tell the truth and keep your word to stay silent, I can have you rotated out tomorrow. Of course, you'll be watched. If we even suspect you're blabbing, she'll be dead before you get home. Then, just before the funeral, you'll be joining her." I put my face close to his, staring into his eyes. "You believe every word I just said, don't you, Thorsten? You know we'll do it, don't you?"

Thorsten hesitated only for a second. He nodded. I stepped back.

Whether it was fear of what spooks could and would do to his mother or just to save his steroid-stretched skin, I'll never know. He began to talk. In minutes, he gave us the names of the others who knew and what their plan was. It all depended on getting to ride shotgun on another trip with Washington and enough advance notice to highjack the truck. They weren't sure yet how to get the dope out of the country, but they would worry about that later and stash the treasure somewhere in the rocks for now.

When he finished ratting everyone out, I used the butt of my H & K to break his left arm. I didn't fracture his leg because he needed both of them to get off the mountain, and I didn't want to have to carry him. Finnen came in from sentry duty and soothed Thorsten while he shrieked, fixing a sling from one of the rags in the corner. I made sure we had all his weapons.

It took us a while to steer Thorsten down to where the other Rangers waited. He fell a few times, but I had stuffed another rag in his mouth so he couldn't scream; loud noises echoed off the rocks.

The Rangers bought into how Thorsten had slipped exploring the cave. They didn't have any choice, and Thorsten didn't voice any denials. Even if they doubted a Ranger would be so careless as to stumble and break his arm, they all wanted to see their families again. Thorsten would be on a Freedom Bird back to The World tomorrow anyway. And the ones he named would be scattered to the Afghan wind.

The routine didn't change. Dunne was again at his computer in the stuffy operations tent at the base, typing away, a cell phone always within reach. Finnen was trying to single-handedly finish Dunne's supply of cold Bud. I was scratching new sandfly bites and sitting in the same chair. More colored pins had been added to the map of Afghanistan. We weren't the only agents Dunne directed.

"Thorsten's on a transport back to California as of 0600," Dunne said. "They put his arm in a cast, and I made sure they shot him up with Demerol to keep him comfortable. And quiet. The others are separately on their way to different fire bases spread across the rock pile."

Dunne scratched at his lengthening beard. Sometimes, but not often, his brief meant he had to go into the field in disguise. He wanted to be ready to blend with the locals if the situation demanded.

"They had visitors during the wee hours of last night. I was told the messengers wore reflective sunglasses even in the dark. They were informed that people who cared for them knew exactly where they'd be stationed for the rest of their tours. The conversations got quite sociable, bringing up names of wives, siblings, parents, children, and mutual friends back home. It seemed the midnight callers knew a lot about loved ones and their state of health. And prognosis if anything ever came up about the lies Thorsten told them. I think they got the drift. They were assured they'd be monitored and those concerned for their safety had very long memories."

As far as I knew, the Company had never stooped to killing or beating the families of American soldiers or operatives, no matter how renegade or evil. Not that they weren't capable. The myth remained, and the threat was usually enough to achieve its goal of cooperation. I couldn't say the same about associates of foreign enemies. Recently, I had been involved in Operation Family Bond. Dunne came up with the name because the real target had seven brothers. We needed information on the movement of the hadji's Taliban cell. He wasn't talking. Dunne had Finnen and I fetch the brothers and parade them naked in front of the shackled Taliban leader. We did a quasi-lineup, taking turns with a Taser on their balls. They were all Taliban. The prisoner didn't do anything but recite prayers until we brought in his wife and daughter. Then, he talked. The men were all shipped to Guantanamo to enjoy the surf and sand. The Taliban cell was dismantled the next night by a series of fire bombs.

A ruthless enemy. The list of their atrocities included a new twist—torture of infants. Beating them with the butts of AKs, then stomping them to death with sandaled feet in front of their parents. During the Taliban's fourteen-month occupation of Taloqan, a former Allied headquarters, those thought to have conspired with the enemy were treated to the brutal murder of their children. In Kunduz, eight teenage boys who were silly enough to chuckle in the presence of a group of Taliban were shot dead for daring to laugh. Outside a Kabul refugee camp, an entire family was burned alive in their tent after a nearby American bombing. With nowhere else to wreak revenge, the Taliban randomly chose the family to vent their anger. Mass executions of civilians and aid workers were commonplace, approaching the level of Bosnia. The list of killings and mutilations, including castration, grew daily. And this was on their own countrymen.

Captured soldiers were treated differently. Outside Bagram Airbase, the bodies of military personnel were found in burlap bags. They had been skinned alive from the waist up. The skin and head had been knotted into the burlap and the soldiers left to die. Often, captives had their arms and legs amputated. Still screaming, the limbless torsos were placed near an Allied position to tempt their comrades into an ambush. A favored Taliban method was beheading. The heads were left for viewing, either in trees or on poles. Or videotaped for wider distribution. No captured soldier was ever returned alive.

Mind fuck.

The litany of slaughter continued.

And I was getting numb.

That was as scary as kraits. No matter if I thought I might be playing on the good team, the feeling grew that I was enlisted in this insanity with no escape. Or that something I couldn't get my head around was going on behind my back. Finnen just laughed when I brought up my fears. "You weren't drafted, lad," he'd say. "Did you think you'd be goin' to Sunday mass?" Of course, any doubts raging in Finnen's head were silenced by beer and limericks. At least now, some of my turmoil could be directed at finding out if I was truly on the virtuous side, not focused on suspects. There was no R & R for my conscience. I would have to work through it alone while I was still waiting to fire the next bullet in the land of a million donkeys. Washington was the lifeline.

One of my bush boots was untied. I bent to tighten the knot.

"Has Washington got any new emails?" I asked.

Stringing together sentences was foreign to Dunne. The speech about Thorsten and his cronies was the longest I'd ever heard him talk. Now, he was resting and regrouping from the effort. After nearly a minute, he said, "I was about to get to that. The answer is yes."

Finnen was more impatient. After another minute, he wiped foam from his mouth and said, "Don't be a tease, Dunne. You're worse than my beautiful cousin Mary, who likes to push her firm, young tits into my arm, knowin' it's taboo. Is Washington makin' another run soon?"

With a world of information at his fingertips to explore, Dunne was in no hurry. He tapped away.

"Tomorrow morning," he said, not looking up. "I've got Morgan assigned as his escort."

"What about me?" Finnen asked.

"Well, you could go back to your mud hootch in the city. I need the quiet anyway. And I'm runnin' short on Bud."

"Not that cave. Gotta' drink it cold. Too many blackouts. Can't you get both of us onboard? I think Washington and I share a common heritage."

"What might that be?"

"Well, as you know, the filthy, motherless English bastards used to bring the good citizens of Ireland across the channel and force us to clean up their shite. Slaves, we were. Just like Washington and his ancestors."

"That's stretching it a bit."

"Also, I can dance. Just put on a little Irish jig, and watch my feet fly. You'd think I was Michael Flatley himself."

"Flatley was born on the south side of Chicago," I said.

"Now," Finnen said, "don't you be holdin' that against him. His mum was from County Sligo."

"Even with these intimate connections," Dunne said, "I think we'll stick to a two-man op. Morgan and Washington. You can stay on base and practice your step dancing. Somewhere far away from me." Dunne stared at Finnen and nodded his head.

No rebuttal. Finnen tossed another empty toward the eternally over-flowing wastebasket. He sighed and slowly shook his head like a disappointed drill sergeant watching the new recruits fuck up his perception of manhood.

For some reason, I craved a cigarette, but there wasn't a single one in sight. Besides, I'd quit after the first one made me puke. And Dunne would grease me if I dared light up. He was a militant anti-smoker. Unconsciously, I patted my fatigue pockets.

"What's the plan?" I asked.

"I've got a few details to finalize," Dunne said. "Why don't you and Finnen shag your asses into town. You won't find any pubs open, but it'll get you out of my life for a while. Report back here by 1730. There's a jeep waiting in the motor pool."

He held up a small envelope like the ones jewelers use to return repaired watches and rings. "All the same, since you'll be in that fine metropolis of Jalalabad, wasting away another spectacular Afghan day, deliver this to a man named Daoud in the market. Normal precautions. He's in the third butcher shop from the right. You'll know him by his smile. All steel teeth, and he has only one hand."

All this was said and done with Dunne's face staring at the computer screen. I wasn't surprised about the chore. No one worked a forty-hour week in Afghanistan, and afternoons off to stroll through the city were rare. And dangerous. We didn't bother with a "fare thee well."

Jalalabad. Unlike most of Afghanistan, the palm-treed city was dressed in green, broken by the favored pastel walls and storefronts. Everywhere, the squiggly lines of Pashto writing advertised car parts, bulk foods, electronics, and cafés. Not quite as many cars as in Millard, but certainly more camels, bicycles, rickshaws, and mopeds. Curly-haired boys raced through the din, acting like there wasn't a war at their front door. The women were covered head to toe, the dye of their burqas blending with the pinks, light blues, and greens of the shops. Turbaned and skull-capped men, some carrying Kalashnikovs, wore rumpled sport coats or vests. All had beards. Gardens seemed to be around every corner, and there were more smiles here than anywhere else I'd seen in-country.

Not many cars or pickups about, Finnen took his time finding the right spot after a few drive-bys.

"Did this one have your name on it?" I asked. "You've been acting like the lot was full."

"Just bein' careful, mate," Finnen said. "An ounce of plannin' is better than a pound of C-4 under the bonnet."

After parking the jeep by a bicycle shop, Finnen and I headed for the market across the crowded street, our H & Ks at our sides. American GIs weren't uncommon here, but a group of young boys still danced around us, begging for *karez*. Candy. When the kids tired of asking, they shouted "*ghwal ookh-raa*, Amerikaner" and ran away, laughing. Eat shit, Americans.

A man, balancing a pile of firewood that was mostly branches, wobbled past on an old Schwinn. A donkey brayed from somewhere behind us, and the air was filled with the smell of spices and rotting meat. On what passed for a sidewalk, a man had set up one of those ring-toss games common at county fairs. If your ring stayed on the peg, the prize was a pack of matches or a roll of toilet paper. Finnen gave the man a couple Afghanis for a throw. He lost.

This bazaar, unlike the ones dedicated to consumer products, was about food. Outside the warren of tent covers that drooped from crooked poles, farmers displayed produce out of piles of fresh melons, potatoes, radishes, garlic, tomatoes, green onions, and carrots. Huge piles of carrots. If Afghans ate that many carrots, they'd piss orange and wouldn't need glasses. One vendor ran a press powered by a bicycle wheel and pedals. He sold the squeezed-out carrot juice in plastic bags and gave us a toothless smile. Most of the produce was from short-term crops. Afghans didn't have the confidence to count on long-term harvests like fruit. Too many rockets, and the Taliban might call apples an abomination at any moment.

Everywhere, people squatting. They didn't stand around with their hands in their jeans, grab-assing. Most of the conversation seemed to take place at knee level, with a lot of hand gestures and shrieks. Especially the women, who looked as if each transaction would be their last. Serious business. Money was exchanged for food that went into colorful woven bags. No paper.

Finnen stopped in front of a crate of potatoes. He picked one up and inspected it, looking at all sides. "*Alu*," said a man dressed like all the others but with one eye oozing milky pus. I knew he said "potato" in Pashto, but Finnen didn't have a clue. He was familiar only with Pashto swear words and insults. Finnen just nodded his head and said, "Not like a good Irish spud. Too yellow. I like 'em whiter."

This was not a secure place. I never took my eye off the jeep for more than a second or two. We were probably surrounded by walls that hid car-bomb factories. We couldn't stay long. Word had surely gotten out that infidels were around, and the jeep would be an easy target. I nudged Finnen's side.

"I'm going to find Daoud," I said. "I think he's right over there." I pointed toward an area just past the vegetable displays where chicken, pig, and goat carcasses hung from wires strung between poles. "You stay here and watch the jeep. And my back. I'll get this over quick. Then we can have a taste of the lamb curry they're famous for at Sahar's café on the edge of town."

Finnen seemed more concerned with some black pits on the potatoes than me or the jeep.

"Looks like some kinda blight," he said. "Maybe a cousin of the one that caused so many of my distant relatives to starve." He picked up another one. "Right-o, mate. I'll be watchin'." He didn't look up.

As I walked past a few stalls selling dried spices both in bulk, bags, and old jars, the rotten meat smell grew stronger. I was just a few steps away from the first butcher shop, and already it was getting hard to breathe without gagging. The flies here weren't the little ones back at the base or in the mountains. They were big enough that I could hear their buzz over the chatter of the market. No attempt was made to brush them away. One particularly bloody piece of indistinguishable meat was veiled in black and about to become airborne. I moved slowly, already attracting enough attention.

On my left, two men began to argue. One was Daoud. He was easy to spot. As he screamed at the other man, he raised his arms threateningly. One arm was missing a hand. Spit flew out his mouth, and slivers of light reflected off his metal teeth. Daoud kept calling the man a "*kharbachiya.*" Donkey. The man replied with "*da dammay zo,*" son of a whore. Arguments like this in Afghanistan weren't known to end without someone dying. Or becoming crippled.

I stepped forward and said, "Excuse me—do you have any fresh prime rib today?"

They ignored me.

The plan had been to fake that I had tripped, falling down, and slipping the envelope under the sawdust on the ground at Daoud's feet. There was no way I could speak to the asset or pay him any particular attention. His cover would be burnt. Daoud and his rival must have spotted me and were making it easier with their drama. Accomplices. At least I hoped so.

Daoud stepped out from behind the counter. Pushing his bearded face into the other man's, he shouted, "*Ustaa moor kay mandam.*" I'm going to fuck your mother. The man grabbed Daoud's vest and they began to wrestle. The envelope was folded in my left fist, H & K in my right hand. As I grasped Daoud to separate the two men, I slipped the envelope into Daoud's pocket. The tussle broke up immediately, mainly because the barrel of my rifle was pointed at both of them.

People were watching. Much of the market noise had ceased. I separated the two men with the tip of the H & K. I gently pushed the accomplice away and motioned Daoud to go back behind the counter of aging meat. He did, with a final "*khooti me ra wa sata*." Lick my balls. After the disagreement was over, I turned away from Daoud and walked back toward Finnen, stopping only once to sample a piece of goat shish kabob grilling on charcoal. It cost me ten Afghanis.

Standing so he could see both me and the jeep with just a slight twist of his head, Finnen chewed on a carrot.

"Smooth, mate," he said. "By the way, I did see you slide that envelope into Daoud's pocket. I knew what to look for. They call that move a pass, you know. Expert in tradecraft am I, Morgan. I did enjoy the little theatre thrown in. Those blokes were good."

"Anyone approach the jeep?"

"Just the usual tourist types and car bombers."

"Carrot tasty?"

"Better than from Aunt Kathleen's garden. She has a black thumb though, not green."

"Then you might not be hungry for a feast at Sahar's. You can watch me eat."

"Wrongo, laddy. I'm always hungry. I just wish they had some ice-cold brew. I'll survive 'til we get back to Dunne's. I'm sure he'll have the fridge refreshed."

"Let's di di."

Finnen waved goodbye to the carrot vendor, and we walked back to the jeep. Before we could mount up, a beat-up white truck entered the street behind us. Turbaned men sat on the bed rails, AKs pointed to the sky. A loudspeaker was on the top of the cab, blaring out Pashto. From what I could understand, it was a lot of references to Allah, Mohammed, and American infidels mixed with directives. The truck had decals on the side claiming it was an official government-of-Afghanistan vehicle. But these weren't civil-service employees. They were dressed like Taliban, and this was no place to be in an American military uniform.

The driver spotted us, and the truck stopped. The men jumped down. They didn't come closer—just stared in our direction. Finnen and I took up positions behind the jeep, H & Ks on full auto. Sound continued to blast from the speakers. The messages must have been taped because I couldn't see anyone talking from inside the truck. People began to slip away. Within seconds, the street was empty.

"Shoulda taken a squad with us like I told you, Morgan," Finnen said. "Ah, 'tis a fine day to meet the Almighty, though." He didn't seem jumpy—only resigned to the fate.

"They won't do anything but bluster," I said. "There's too many of us in the neighborhood."

"You're sure about that? They don't look like they're thinkin' about invitin' us in for a hit off their hookahs."

"It's the old Mexican stand-off. We gotta make sure we're not the first to blink."

"I'm not worried about blinkin'. I'm more concerned about pissin' myself." Not true. Finnen could be confronted with much worse odds than this and still have the same smile that now curled his Irish lips. And he hated to waste piss when it still contained so much alcohol.

One of the men turned his head toward the wall next to the pickup. Surprisingly, he was wearing a floppy green Afghan military cap rather than a dirty turban. He stepped quickly over to a door and used the butt of his AK and his foot to smash through. The others didn't pay him any attention, their total focus on us. Seconds later, we heard a female scream, and the man came out pulling a young woman by the hair. Her face was uncovered, and she wore a long, light-blue dress that went from her shoulders to her bare feet. The man was shouting in her ear. He pushed the girl toward the front of the truck and knocked her to the ground with his rifle. From what I could hear, she had been peeking out a window. Now, it seemed she was going to be tortured before our eyes.

No hesitation. As the man lifted his weapon to hit the sprawled girl, I raised mine and shot a burst from the H & K into the air, bringing the barrel back down and aiming it at the man. No one moved.

"Fuckin' jaysus, Morgan," Finnen said. "That was dumb."

He moved from behind the jeep and slowly walked toward the Taliban.

"In for a penny, in for a pound," he said. "Follow me, Morgan."

I did.

Our salvation would have to mean friendlies heard the cough of the H & K, a sound distinct from AK rounds. These men were mujahedeen and had probably learned to fight against the Russians. We were just better-equipped invaders. It would take a lot more firepower than Finnen and I carried to make them back down.

The man reached for the girl again. She was sobbing, not facing the men, her nose close to the road. This time it was Finnen who reacted. He was careful to fire straight up like I had. Any hint we were about to unload at the Taliban would have meant we'd soon be bleeding alongside the girl.

The man stood again, and the girl took advantage of the diversion. She stood quickly and ran toward us, falling once but scrambling to her feet. I could see the terror in her eyes.

She surprised me. Instead of disappearing into the market, she ran behind my legs and pushed close to my back. Finnen and I were spread a few yards apart, giving the Taliban two targets rather than one, where a bullet could more easily hit either of us. I could feel her sobs.

In a moment of adrenalin clarity, it made some kind of sense. She was condemned. No place to hide in Afghanistan for a girl on the run. If she fled into the market, she would be an untouchable. Taliban spies would narc her out in minutes. She would be dead by sunrise, having caused the Taliban deep disgrace.

A silly thought. Irrelevant to this drama. But it bore into my mind like a drill. I wondered what the Koran said about where this girl's soul would go if she was filled with bullets alongside two infidels. Her death wouldn't be considered martyrdom for Mohammed.

At least the men were hardened enough to keep their AKs pointed to the bright blue sky. Neither of us wanted the situation to escalate. In another time and place, outside a city crawling with American military and Afghan police patrols, we'd already be dead. A firefight here would most likely conclude with Finnen and me leaking blood on the road. A few of the brothers would also die. Those still standing would have to run. Fast. The girl wasn't worth it.

A man in a black turban sitting in the truck's passenger seat said, "*Talal.*" Go. The men began to back away and climb into the truck. Within seconds, they had reversed out of the street, only one mujahedeen shaking his fist and yelling "*sta plar nikkan sara yo kam.*" I'm going to kill your family.

The quickness of their flight didn't quite make sense, but I was too thankful for being able to continue standing to explore any doubts.

When the truck was gone, I turned to the girl. She was trying to cover her face and head with a blue-sleeved arm. She was still crying and trembling. I knew better than to touch her. Finnen didn't. He reached out his hand.

"Now, now, lassie," he said. "The bad guys are gone."

The girl pulled away, exposing her face. She had those arctic-blue eyes relatively common in Afghans. The OCA2 gene mutation had begun close to here near the Caspian about ten thousand years ago and spread around the globe but was even more astonishing and pure close to its roots. It was like looking through a crystal-blue bowl. They were bottomless and reflective at the same time. I only knew because mine were the same, only slightly darker, a further mutation. Like Dunne's too, even though he was a few thousand years down the evolutionary chain.

Her left cheek was red and swelling. Dirt matted her long, black hair. She was average size for a girl of about eighteen. No one had taught her how to trim her dark eyebrows. They nearly connected. But that was all I could criticize. She was criminally gorgeous.

Even Finnen, not the best judge of female beauty, was shocked. He stepped back and whistled.

"Crikey, mate," he said. "She's a looker." He shook his head from side to side. "But you shoulda let them take her rather than us dyin' in the street on account of your need ta' be a hero."

Normally, I didn't respect Finnen's opinion of women. It was most often influenced by the number of Guinness bottles he'd drained. After a night out on R & R, he would say things like, "I like beer better than women. Ya don't have to wash it so it tastes good. It always goes down easy, and you can share it with a friend."

Today, though, his first impression was spot on. This girl could launch her own jihad.

The more I studied her, the more it became apparent she wasn't a girl—a spectacular-looking young woman was more like it. Finnen and I were already under her spell, and it was eerie. Any moment could mean a fusillade from a dozen AKs or a tossed grenade, but we stood like cattle to slaughter taking in the slight curl of her full lips, the astonishing blue of her eyes, and the smooth darkness of her skin. I was adding to the list of super-latives, and time wasn't going to let me finish now. We needed to get gone.

People were beginning to drift back to the market. One of the old women who had been selling carrots stared at us with a scowl and then spit. At least the hag didn't have her face wrapped; she might have drowned. Clucking, she walked across the deserted street to the girl and wrapped her head in a scarf the crone must have carried for emergency concealment. The girl immediately stood, as if she had lost her top in the pool and someone threw her a towel. She was no longer an infidel—only another homeless, frightened refugee.

The rush of an imminent firefight was gone. Finnen and I were in the presence of someone exquisite, surely a candidate for Young Miss Universe. Neither of us budged, no matter how strongly our training thundered "Move out!" That cry was muffled by those eyes.

Sure, there were women back at the base. Not very many, though, and they tended to say, "yes, please" at every station in the chow line. Besides, we were spooks, and nobody spoke to us. This young lady would soon be more stunning than Lieutenant Colonel Richter, the Army's pin-up girl, if a blond, beautiful forty-year-old woman officer could be called "girl." Rumors were rampant about how Richter had climbed the ladder so quickly, but who could accuse the military of anything as crass as favoritism based on a rack that threatened to pop every metal button on her tunic.

Back at Millard, my high school sweetheart was the baton twirler who led the band out at halftime. She had impossibly long hair that threatened to carry her off in a stiff breeze. Aly's dad was an orthodontic surgeon, and her teeth were in perfect sparkling rows that dominated an ever-present smile. Even without the music, she danced. My teammates constantly wanted to know how a heifer like me could be the boyfriend of this queen. They were jealous. I was lucky. Not even the freckles could mar skin that turned brown at the hint of sun. She was stunning. The last time I had seen Aly was on the cover of *Elle*. Compared to the girl bowed in front of me now, Aly would be confined to the back pages in small print.

Bizarre. We were standing in a city in Afghanistan having just offended a truckload of AK-waving Taliban. Snipers could already have our heads in their sights. A grenade could roll to our feet over one of the nearby walls. Our truck could explode momentarily, killed by an RPG fired from that bearded man up by the corner carrying something that looked like a long tube.

It was time to get out.

"We have to di di, Finnen," I said. But I hadn't moved.

"What about the girl?" he asked. He didn't move, either.

"I don't think we can leave her here," I said. "She's shamed herself and her entire family. And humiliated those mujahedeen. They'll drag her through the streets behind their truck."

"Yes, the bastards will. As I said, you already put us at risk for her when we coulda been eatin' hummus somewhere safe. What's your plan, chief?"

"For now, we have to all get out'a here. Fast."

"Ya think?"

"I don't know how to convince her."

"Give it your natural charm."

"Okay."

Stalling. Dumbstruck. Sick. Twenty-five and an assassin, hypnotized by a teenage girl. Or young woman. A fucking drop-dead gorgeous one, for sure. My feet felt as if they were impaled in a bucket of the breakfast oatmeal back at the base. If we took her along, she would be my responsibility. Again, time to move.

"*Num?*" I asked, looking at the girl. Name.

Still looking down at the road, she said "*Khkulay.*" Beautiful.

Nearly dropping my H & K, I began to laugh.

"Perfect," I said. "Finnen, guess what her name means."

"Oh, I don't know," he said. "Jailbait?"

"Of course not," I said. "There's no translation for that. No such thing here."

By now, the market was back to normal. A few vendors even dared to call out the names of the produce they were hawking, behavior frowned on by the Taliban who believed the voice should only be raised in praise of Allah. Lots of furtive glances in our direction. We were still well-armed, and Americans had a reputation for unpredictability. They were in the kill zone.

For the fourth time, my mind shouted, "Move out!" I pointed toward the truck, any ability to translate lost in the moment.

The girl looked up, those eyes holding too many hardships and years.

"Yes," she said. "We must go."

Another shock. Much more, and the circuits would overload. She spoke English, even if her voice quivered with fright.

Finnen stepped back as if he were in the presence of Ann "Goody" Glover, the famous Irish witch and the last woman hanged in Boston.

"Now there's a miracle," he said. "She speaks."

Turning to Finnen, Khkulay said, "My father was a doctor. He was killed for treating women. He taught me English." She looked back at me. "We must leave. I have no place to go. They will kill me by last prayer." She began to search the market with her blue eyes, as though it hid someone who would soon take down the three of us.

No hesitation this time. I led Finnen and the girl to the jeep, scanning rooftops as we went. Seconds later, we cleared the market street and drove away with a beautiful young woman hiding in the cramped space behind the front seats.

After a few questions, we decided the only safe destination for Khku-lay was the base. No uncles or aunts would bother to take in a girl infected by the hands of an American heathen. She had already whispered she was alone, her mother executed alongside her father because there were books written in English at the house when the raid came. She was a pariah and had been living off leftover vegetables scraped from the ground when the market closed for the night. The little of her story she told made sense. I was hoping I'd get the chance to find out more.

No lunch at Sahar's ka-bob shop. The word would already be out to watch for a jeep with two men and a girl. The roadside bombs were now remote-controlled, and the Taliban had cell phones. I sped as fast as the military vehicles, camels, donkeys, and motorcycles would allow.

Outside the city, the palms were replaced by spindly trees. Close to the Kunar River, crops were harvested by women who looked restricted in full dress. Men sat in front of mud hovels, smoking cigarettes and staring. We were on one of the few paved roads in Afghanistan, black-topped only because it was the main route from Jalalabad to the Tora Bora base.

As we approached the gate, I told Khkulay to sit up. There was no use attempting stealth. The jeep would be thoroughly searched. No wave-throughs in Afghanistan unless you sported general's bars or were part of a convoy. I stopped the jeep, and an MP stepped out of the sand-bagged guard shack. He only glanced at me, all eyes on Khkulay, who was modestly keeping her head down but still undeniably gorgeous.

The MP didn't grin, melt, or go goo-gaw. He stared. Maybe he was a catcher on the Don't Ask Don't Tell team.

To the left, a large gate opened, and an M1 Abrams tank rumbled past, followed by a line of trucks, mobile artillery, and Humvees. The MP waited for the noise to die down.

"Papers," he said, finally taking his eyes off Khkulay. He didn't smile.

Finnen and I didn't carry papers. No wallets, no credit cards, no dogtags. Even the birthmark on my leg had been removed, and new, untraceable dental work had been performed on my teeth. If the Company could have altered our fingerprints and DNA, they would have.

I shook my head.

"No chance, man," I said. "Call oh sixteen forty. Tell 'em we're home."

The MP scowled and walked over to the shack, but he knew the drill. He unhooked a phone mounted to the cement wall and punched in a number. After a few words, he nodded his head and hung up. Walking back to the jeep, he frowned even more deeply.

"Step out, please," he said. "Stand over there." He motioned to a wall of sandbags.

He searched the jeep, even using one of those mirrors on a stick to check underneath for bombs. Finished and feeling safe, he walked over to me.

"What about her?" he asked.

"She's a high-level spy," I said. "She infiltrated the largest Taliban cell in Afghanistan and provided us with top-secret information. Her intel has helped to save hundreds of American lives. We're taking her inside to receive the Congressional Medal of Honor. Okay?"

Another stand-off. Tiring, but I didn't want Khkulay touched. Not out of possessiveness. I knew how much her conditioning would make her loathe the feel of any man's hand other than her husband's. The MP didn't know about her religious beliefs, or care. He had a duty to perform. That included frisking of civilians.

"Not okay," he said. "I don't care if she's Chairwoman of the Joint Chiefs of Staff. I have orders to search all non-combatants, especially if they don't have papers or a pass. Move aside."

"Do you have any idea what my boss will do to you if you keep hassling us?" I asked. "Getting demoted to Private would be a good outcome, though losing your tongue for insubordination is more likely."

Legends. Astounding how everyone at this and other bases across Afghanistan had heard the myths. The Company wasn't into denial, and the underground stories became more gruesome and mysterious on each retelling. No one really knew if we were CIA or from some other alphabet-soup intelligence agency. Spooks were all lumped under the umbrella of the Company. It was easier than trying to sort out if we were DIA, NSA, INR, OICI, or operatives from a department so secret it didn't even have a letter designation. The grunts did notice how we were treated by their own commanders, though. Not used to officers acting edgy in front of lower-grade non-coms and civilians, unless they wore suits or dresses, there was always the suspicion we knew something—unfathomable somethings that could be used to achieve whatever furtive goal we sought, prejudiced or unprejudiced, against good guys as well as bad. Mostly, it was the strange, murky tales whispered in the mess halls and during downtime. Like the oft-told technique of wee-hour interrogations by helicopter. Take a few al-Qaeda suspects up for a ride in a black unmarked Bell chopper. Start throwing the actors out the door one by one until the real target unloaded his burden of guilt. Then, let the last man enlist in the Airborne with his first flying lesson. The helicopters were seen exfiltrating, but seemed to always come back empty. And the attitude. . . . Spooks never, ever, took shit from military personnel. If it happened, the repayment was always more severe than the offense.

The MP in front of me was aware of all this, and I could tell his mind was processing the nuances and potential penalties while I continued to glare at him through reflective sunglasses. He looked down at his spit-shined boots, which weren't allowed to be marred by even a speck of the ever-present dust.

"Listen," he said. "Give me a break. I'll get court martialed if I don't search the lady."

The line of Humvees waiting to pass through the gate was getting longer. Behind us, a group of soldiers was in a buoyant mood, happy to be returning to base not disarticulated. The driver honked his horn and yelled, "Move it along, buddy. There's cold ones waitin'."

In his jolly mood, the lieutenant hadn't paid close enough attention. Finnen didn't raise his weapon or pull out a grenade. He just flashed the lieutenant the finger, unsmiling.

At first, the lieutenant reacted like any Army officer robot. He started to open the door of the Humvee to confront the public disobedience with at least a dressing down. Quickly and firmly, the soldier next to him grabbed his arm and began whispering in his ear. The lieutenant's body deflated like one of the fifty-thousand-gallon collapsible fuel bags that dotted the air field. No more honks. End of party. The riders in the Humvee quieted and stared, some kind of message from their heightened battlefield conscious-ness passing between them. *Don't fuck with the spooks.*

It was enough for the MP. "If you can vouch for her," he said, "I'll let you pass. She's your responsibility. And your ass."

I nodded Khkulay toward the jeep.

"Now that's truly American of you," I said to the MP. "Thank you for your gracious hospitality."

Within minutes, we were back at Spookville, explaining to Dunne why on Earth we hadn't just dumped the girl at the nearest refugee camp.

"It would've been a death sentence," I said. "You know better than me those camps are controlled by the Taliban. She couldn't just vanish into a tent city. The refugees would be talking about her in minutes. She wouldn't have survived 'til nightfall."

For once, Dunne's face wasn't buried in the laptop screen. While he had been blunt in his earlier evaluation of our "fuckin' sorry ass" decision to bring Khkulay into the compound, he still couldn't take his blue eyes off hers. It seemed she was a distraction he didn't want. Nevertheless, a few minutes in the presence of such astounding beauty, and he was beginning to soften. It was easy to tell; he had gone a dozen sentences without using the "f" word.

Khkulay was sitting in my usual chair, her head modestly bowed to her chest. She still wore the scarf, and her knees were tight together, hands folded submissively in her lap. Strands of black hair had escaped from her headdress but only helped make her look more fetching, vulnerable, and exotic.

Finnen was enjoying the show from his designated spot near the refrigerator, not participating in the dialogue other than a few grunts and chuckles. He had no inhibitions about drinking alcohol in front of this Muslim lass. Dunne had cordially filled the fridge with Bud, and Finnen was claiming his part of the treasure.

Being careful to not have any contact, I stood behind Khkulay's chair, making sure Dunne's field of vision would include her when he spoke to me. I hoped her looks would do more to convince him to go along with what I had planned than any argument I could summon.

"We can't just hand her over to any of the NGOs," I said. Non-governmental organizations. "They have no way of protecting her. It's obvious we can't send her home either. She doesn't have one. Or family willing to adopt her. There's surely a *fatwa* on her head."

What Dunne did best was plot. His schemes rarely resulted in anything other than a successful op. But they never included women while he was stationed in Afghanistan, unless it was to list them as collateral damage. There were no "honey traps" being set to gather intel from the Taliban. Dunne was a user, and he probably couldn't fathom how Khkulay could be employed to further the Company's agenda. Therefore, he would believe she was of little value to him. He rubbed the side of his face and thought while I waited for the right moment.

Outside, the clamor of tanks and trucks and the sound of distant artillery. The day had clouded over with the high steel gray common to the region. Every once in a while, the chanting of troops exercising in formation drifted through the canvas. The guards outside were clones of the others. It was no use knowing their names. I called them all Bob.

Inside, Dunne's anal character didn't allow for change to his environment. The same table, laptop, desk lamp, maps, smells, and cell phone. Maybe some of the files held new intel, but they were all stamped with the top-secret red designation and closed. A breeze forced sand in through the flaps of the tent, and Finnen went over and secured the canvas. Otherwise, just a dirt-floored room where I had spent hours outlining mission parameters and objectives. The difference was the energy. Khkulay provided something this tent had never experienced. Femininity. And beauty. Dunne pushed a folder an inch to one side, tidying his universe.

"What do you suggest, Morgan?" he asked. "We enlist her? Train her to be the Mata Hari of the rocks?"

I smiled. Pissing him off with my smart mouth wouldn't achieve my goal, and I needed his cooperation.

"Hardly," I said and came around Khkulay's chair, closer to Dunne.

"Well, not the way you're thinkin'," I said. "You know those unmarked Gulfstreams that fly regularly in and out of Bagram? They usually depart with fewer passengers than when they arrived. If you fixed it, Khkulay could have a seat. She speaks fluent English, Arabic, and Pashto. She's intimately aware of the cultural and religious challenges we face. She knows more about the Taliban mindset than any of the analysts in Langley."

I moved within a handshake of Dunne. "I've already proposed it to Khkulay. She's agreed. Didn't take any convincing. She's extremely intelligent. Certainly smart enough to realize there's absolutely no future for her here. I'm proposing Finnen and I escort her to the Kabul airbase. And that you schedule the transport and further arrangements when she gets stateside."

There it was. Simple. I was more nervous than if I had been personally threatened with being dropped into a pit full of vipers. We were used to an exchange of ideas. But that usually meant discussing the various methods of killing and getting back to base without wearing a body bag. Our plans had certainly never involved saving an Afghan damsel in distress. But I believed her destiny was in my hands, and I couldn't let another innocent girl die. Dunne grinned with a smile that would frighten a great white shark.

Even with all the normal torment dished out by older girls to a younger brother, as I grew, I still felt it was my responsibility to protect my sisters from the demons of Millard, Kansas. If I wasn't big enough to physically threaten a rude quarterback who had called Tracy a skank, leading to tearful hours of sobbing behind her closed bedroom door, I could sneak into the locker room and sprinkle his jock with white pepper. Or drop Ex-Lax into his Gatorade. Or leave forged notes from the town punch in his cheerleader girlfriend's locker, thanking the team captain for a "magical night" on a blanket by the reservoir where he "satisfied" her more than any of the "interior linemen." The message was written on pink paper with lots of Xs and Os and swirly hearts. Somehow, my need to be a protector was born in the corn fields, and now Khkulay needed a guardian. And I needed a grain of redemption.

Surprisingly, Dunne caved with minimal resistance and a wink from Finnen.

"Okay, Morgan," Dunne said. "But you're accountable for anything that happens to her."

I smiled and nodded my head, knowing I couldn't let anything go wrong with this one.

"You're already guilty of kidnapping as I see it." Dunne said, the laugh lines crinkling his face. "I think it's better for everyone you're limited to the field."

He sat back and put his hands behind his head. "And there's a certain MP Captain who wants to have a chat with you. Seems you abused one of his men."

Up 'til now, the only sound out of Finnen had been *slurp* and the crinkling of cans. He sat forward, resting the latest Bud on his knee.

"Malarkey," he said. "That gomer was plannin' ta' cop a feel. I could tell by his beady eyes. Morgan was makin' sure Khkulay's virtue stayed intact, like I used to with the girls at St. Mary Margaret's." He lifted the beer toward his mouth. "Not by choice, mind you."

Motives. I kept telling myself they were pure. Even if the girl had been toothless, crippled, and ugly, I'd convinced myself the outcome would have been no different. The scene at the market was evil and needed to be addressed. And sex—I had the normal hormone level of a healthy twenty-five-year-old male who hadn't touched a woman in months unless I counted magazine pictures. I didn't want to run off with Khkulay to a white-sand beach and lick the sand out of her bikini. The way I saw it, I had treated her like she was the little sister I'd never had, no matter how much my lower regions were starving and in denial. Platonic and protective. And that would be the way it would stay. I would be the older brother, only there to guard her. Maybe a kind of babysitter guide for someone new to the world.

The discourse was over. Dunne was no longer infatuated, and it was time to get back on the job. He began typing, responding to what was probably the thousandth critical email he'd received so far today.

"You're going out in the morning," Dunne said. "We'll talk about this more when you get back. Take the girl over to the women's barracks. Speak to Captain Meredith. She'll give her a bunk. Be back here at 0600. Washington and you are pickin' up a load." He turned to Finnen. "And the leprechaun there. He can stay drunk 'til you get back for all I care." The keystrokes made their little *click* sounds. "Now beat it."

Walking across the base, I tried to prepare Khkulay for what was coming, but I wasn't familiar with all the secrets about what went on inside the women's bivouac. If she would be drowned in deodorant, gagged with hairspray, her face smothered in a mud wrap, fingernails painted in red, and legs shaved. Or taught to fire an H & K and disarm a landmine with the tip of a Ka-Bar. What I did know was the females on the base weren't smiley prom queens from Millard. Even if they didn't go out in combat, they were tough and didn't take a pinch on the butt or a whistle lightly. Or without a karate kick to the nuts. Khkulay understood she had already entered Oz and this was just another chapter. In some small way, I would try to be her mentor.

After passing Khkulay off to the first female soldier I encountered with orders to take her to Captain Meredith, we parted with a bow and "*Inshallah.*" I went back to the compound to shave and get some rest before tomorrow's journey deep into Indian country.

The clouds of yesterday had made their passage into the mountains, not shedding any moisture before they reached the peaks of the Hindu Kush. Refugees, carrying sacks and blankets filled with their every possession, trudged alongside the road, fleeing the latest skirmish. The pavement had long ago ended, and the 6x6 bounced across the ruts and ancient water channels. Since leaving the river, the countryside morphed into brown. Not even a bush broke up the steady horizon of rocks and dirt, except near the occasional mud-walled hut. The last Allied checkpoint was behind us by at least twenty-five klicks. We were deep into Taliban country. Washington was the guide on this trip northwest.

Khkulay had provided a diversion, momentarily taking my thoughts off the bigger questions. I couldn't afford to let my Sir Galahad strategy intrude now. That could mean my head on a pole. This time, Washington was told to bring along a satchel filled with hundred-dollar bills he'd retrieved from a hiding place in the motor pool. No more middle men in Jalalabad. The pace must be accelerated. It was harvest time. No one wanted to keep a cash crop waiting in a place that might suffer a direct hit from an A-10 Thunderbolt. The money was now hidden under the engine hood in a mock ammo can. There were surprises sewn into the bag's lining.

Much of the Company intel on the Taliban came from paid informers. Before US troops landed in Afghanistan, the CIA had already recruited assets on the ground. Now, many more eyes and ears reported on Taliban movement at the rate of about $150 a month per snitch. That made it one of the most lucrative professions in Afghanistan, where the average daily salary, if you could find a job, was less than $2. Paid snitches were the primary sources for intelligence and the reason behind most of my missions. The other means of finding information on Taliban and al-Qaeda activity came from the sky. Predator drones were aloft around the clock, and Signal Intelligence Satellites, Sigints, and Quickbirds never slept, relaying pictures and mobile and cell phone transmissions. A particular focus was the Durand Line, the border between Pakistan and Afghanistan. Crossing over the Line gave the Taliban and al-Qaeda a measure of safety when they were in Pakistan, where the US military presence was minimal and they were protected by tribal warlords and an inefficient and corrupt Pakistani army, as well as terrain as rugged as any on Earth.

One troubling issue was how the insurgents could pass so easily back and forth over the Durand Line when satellites and drones tracked their every move, and spies were in their midst. It was well accepted in the clandestine community that there were only fourteen points along the Pakistan–Afghanistan border where any sizable number of insurgents and vehicles could cross. Even if the boundary was more than 2,400 klicks long, almost every inch was impassable by man or donkey and certainly not trucks. It seemed like a relatively simple task to close the fourteen points. . . .

But I couldn't let this one nag more than the other doubts in my head. I was no policy maker.

Then there was the so-called Afghan Army. Since nearly two-thirds of those who enlisted in this phantom force went AWOL, the Army was composed primarily of supporters of the hundreds of warlords who, for whatever reason, had chosen to fight against the Taliban. Hundreds of millions of dollars had been spent by the warlords arming themselves, mostly with Russian-made munitions bought by proceeds from the poppy fields. It was estimated these supposed anti-Taliban fighters numbered more than 200,000. According to Company intel, one northern warlord, Ahmed Mahim, had recently returned from Moscow having spent more than $100 million on Soviet hardware.

The information and subsequent doubts were personally dangerous; there was too much to sift through when we were on our way to take out a cell. The static was distracting, but I couldn't shake the resonance of one issue: Who were the Taliban?

All Afghan men looked the same. Beards, loose-fitting pajama pants, open-toed sandals, vests or old coats, shawls, turbans. It was just as tough as my ancestors had it in 'Nam, distinguishing a Viet Cong from a Vietnamese civilian. One famous Afghan line was "Everyone is Taliban. No one is Taliban." It was common for men to work their jobs until a cell leader called them to action. When the mission was complete, they melted back into their everyday lives. On any given day, there might be one thousand Taliban fighters active in the sector. The next, ten thousand. They didn't have a fifteen-month assigned tour of duty. The call-ups and stand-downs came at the cell commander's orders. And the only way the commanders could outfit their networks and sustain the opposition to the Coalition was the drug trade. Otherwise, they would not have the resources to counter a multi-billion dollar offensive fought primarily by Americans. Hopefully, I was about to make a small contribution in the ongoing battle against the Taliban and the narco trade.

Washington had been silent most of the journey. I didn't tell him about Khkulay, even though he'd probably already heard there was a stunning Afghan girl in the women's barracks. Rumors like that spread faster than the bouts of dysentery that commonly occurred.

We were starting to climb out of the brown and into the green, having passed through numerous Taliban checkpoints with only a few grunts from the metal-teethed men and waves from AKs. At each stop, one of the men was on a radio. Our passes were solid. There was too much money to be made. The road only got worse, turning into a series of ruts and holes big enough for coffins, Occasionally, I spotted men on rock outcroppings above us, rifles on their hips. Washington didn't need a map. The intersections were few and klicks between. No traffic lights. A small stream was his GPS and the most common sound other than the growl of the diesel engine was a groan caused by another crippling pothole. There was little padding in the seats, and the frame of the 6x6 didn't include shock absorbers. It was like riding a bull sitting on a lawn chair with the webbing missing. We were at the stage where Washington seldom left first gear.

"Just around that bend," he said, nodding ahead. "There'll be at least ten guards up there, and we'll be thoroughly searched. No weapons past the sentries. You're gonna feel naked without the Hush Puppy. And Ka-Bar. I'll feel safer, though."

In front about fifty meters, a man holding an AK stepped from behind a tree. He was the first. Within seconds, more appeared. I put on my helmet.

"Not a very friendly looking greeting party," I said. "Reminds me of when Finnen and me stumbled into an NCO club in our civvies and sunglasses. Even the music stopped. But none'a them had beards."

"They recognized you weren't members," Washington said. "They're kinda exclusive in their entrance criteria. No spooks allowed."

"Well, we were invited to leave. Kindly, I must admit. Even after Finnen insulted them with a few knuckle-dragger comments."

"Sounds like that time I went into Big Frenchie's in the bayou. Thought maybe it coulda been the Yankee hat I was wearin' that caused the reception to deteriorate fast. Like the second they laid eyes on me. I didn't have much time to think about it before the baseball bats came out. In hindsight, I think I shoulda stayed at the juke joint down the road. Or carried a Smith and Wesson. They still would'a had more firepower than me."

Nerves. Ten fierce-looking armed men within a few meters.

While Washington and I told lies, both of us constantly scanned the field of vision, looking for escape routes, choosing spots that might provide cover, deciding which target would go down first, identifying other bad guys, and evaluating the potential success of any unrehearsed plan. It was a response drilled into us through training and many firefights. Neither of us would admit fear. The talk was bullshit. But words didn't keep my blood pressure from rising like the price of oil.

The mujahedeen fanned out across the road, knowing well enough if they bunched closer, a grenade tossed from the truck window would pretty much take out them all. One man spoke into a black handheld walkie-talkie; cell phone coverage this far from Jalalabad was spotty at best. The others held their AKs at their waists, aggression only showing in their bearded faces, not through the barrel of a pointed rifle. None of them looked like they had been feasting on mutton and Naan. I couldn't tell anything about their teeth because they weren't smiling. Dirty tunics stained by the brown of the rocks drooped from thin, nearly caved-in chests. Beyond the men, the first of the poppy fields was close to final harvest, and unarmed milkers were beginning the late afternoon's sap collection. From over the hill, smoke rose in a dark funnel cloud. Probably from the lab where the opium was being boiled.

Stepping forward and separating himself from the rest of the turbaned squad, the man with the radio held his hand up, palm out. The truck was barely moving.

"I don't recognize him or any of the other hadjis," Washington said. "You s'pose I should stop this rig? Or make a run for it at two miles an hour?"

"I think he wants you to pull over," I said. "That's what the hand sign means. I speak Pashto."

"They talk with their hands?"

"Nahh, they don't have to say much. Bullets have a way of speakin' for them."

"Roger that. I'll just ease on over to this designated parking slot."

The washboard dirt road was wide enough for only one vehicle. A 6x6 took up every centimeter. Washington put on the brake. Diesel fumes immediately drifted from the exhaust, stinking up the idyllic mountain landscape.

The leader held up his right hand, thumb and forefinger pressed together. He rotated his hand back and forth, indicating Washington should turn off the truck. He did.

"Man," Washington said. "I'm gettin' the hang'a this Pashto shit. Pretty soon, I won't even need an interpreter."

"You should'a gone to language school," I said. "You would have graduated Phi Beta Krappa."

Directly in front of the truck's ram guard, the man motioned us to get out by waving his right hand.

"There, I get it," Washington said like a teenager discovering how simple it was to unsnap his girlfriend's bra strap with one hand in the dark. "He wants us to dismount."

"Brilliant," I said.

Our H & Ks were stowed behind the seats. Without taking our eyes off the man, we reached back to retrieve the rifles.

The man shook his head and then indicated we should get out, more forcefully this time.

"No guns," Washington said. "And he wants us on the ground. Post haste."

"Fuckin' A, Washington," I said. "You'll be teachin' the classes soon."

We opened the doors and stepped onto the dirt, moving slowly around to the front of the truck. Everyone would be jumpy, and quick movements weren't advisable. Washington even held out his hand when he got close to the man.

"Hey, Abdul," he said, a sparkling grin showing off his white teeth. "How's it goin'?"

Shit. One of the slurs used by US soldiers. All Afghan men were named Abdul. Maybe we'd get lucky and his name would really be Abdul.

The man stepped back, handshakes not in the Taliban etiquette.

Washington continued with the grin.

"Hey," he said. "Why don't you tell them other Abduls to put their rifles down." He nodded toward the men, some of whom had started to walk toward us.

Soon enough, the bullets *thwack*-ing into our bodies would make it painfully obvious if any of these Abduls spoke English.

The man either had a sense of humor, not commonplace in the land of few smiles, or he didn't understand the insult. He waved us to the side of the road. We obeyed.

Four men walked past and searched the truck. They didn't have one of those mirrored things, so one got down on his back and pushed himself beneath the 6x6, pulling on hoses and sticking his hands places I would never know. Another hadji climbed into the cab and collected all the weapons he could find. He rummaged around, and I didn't think, without a thorough search, he would find the camouflaged button. He didn't. They kicked the tires and crawled into the back, not bothering to open the hood. After a few minutes, they finished and came back to the man with the walkie-talkie, carrying our rifles and miscellaneous other goodies, like grenades and spare ammo. No one had said a word.

The mujahedeen spoke briefly. Two separated and came toward us, lifting their arms up from their sides.

"Either the Abduls want us to fly," Washington said, "or we're about to get patted down. They better not touch Mr. Happy."

"Just be cool and cooperate," I said. "And Mr. Happy might get another chance to grin."

We held our arms up and spread our legs. The men confiscated pistols, Ka-Bars, ammo, and cell phones. They missed the knife attached to my forearm. Washington's too. They did find the sissy revolver strapped to my ankle. The men walked back to their group, and we were signaled to move to the side, where Washington and I leaned against a kermes oak tree that looked as old as the hills across the valley to the south. The oak's branches were skinny and gnarled, more like thin, bent arrows with sharp tips and barbs than healthy growth. Someone had carved a few indistinguishable words in Arabic in the tree, behavior I was sure would be punishable by a public amputation. There was a famous picture making the rounds on the internet of a young Taliban carrying severed feet and hands through the streets of Kabul. The greenish-colored limbs supposedly came from convicted shoplifters and were mounted on a line. The boy was smiling and holding them up like he'd just caught a few record-setting bass.

Just behind us, a drainage ditch had been dug, leading to the creek below. A few gooseberry and hawthorn bushes were scattered along the banks. Only a hint of water darkened the bottom of the channel. No rain had fallen in weeks. I scuffed the toe of my boot in the dirt, rolling around a golf ball-sized pebble.

"Are you gonna detonate the Abdul shit?" I asked Washington.

"Just funnin'," Washington said. "I can switch to Mohammed if you think that'd be less edgy. Maybe Mo for short."

"Worse," I said. "How 'bout you don't use any names."

At times, Washington loved the ghetto shtick. But I knew he was a University of Michigan grad with a degree in economics and co-captain of the Wolverine wrestling team that was NCAA champions the year Washington took third in the 197-pound division. He carried less bulk three years ago. He pushed back his helmet and continued watching as the men gathered together in front of the 6x6.

"I do think Mo might be better," he said. "It's the most popular name on Earth. Better chance of gettin' it right."

"I thought it was 'dick head,'" I said. "Maybe you should use that if you feel compelled to name-call. They won't understand."

I was certain none of the men were named Bob. And they weren't intimidated in the presence of a CIA agent. No way could I bluster my way through like back at the base.

During the banter, I knew both of us, no matter how relaxed we might appear, were ready to cross the ditch and try to dissolve into the rocks. Unarmed, our chances were slim to none. Only our lips moved. Not our eyes. Those never strayed from the Abdul conference now taking place within the length of a Humvee stretch limo.

"Dick head. That's a white boy name," Washington said. "Never heard no black man use it. All it would mean is that the brother had a large head anyways."

"Oh, there it is," I said. "It took all these hours for you to finally bring that urban myth up. You just had to get it in before we both died." I crossed my legs, leaning harder into the oak. "Good timing."

"And you should see me jump. I can dunk with the ball between my elbows."

"I suppose you can dance as well as Michael Jackson, too. A true renaissance man."

One mujahedeen broke away from the group and walked quickly in the direction of the smoke. The others either rested the butt of their AKs in the dirt or kept the barrels pointed at us. Several lit up Marlboro cigarettes.

"Sho 'nough, Morgan," Washington said. His eyes tracked the man moving away, while mine stayed on the hadjis gathered by the truck. "Right now, I wish I smoked. Like Sammy Davis Jr. in those old black-and-white photos. He always seemed to have a cigarette in his right hand and the smoke curlin' around him."

"Or Sharon Stone in *Basic Instinct*," I said. "When the police officer tells her not to smoke. She crosses her legs and lights up anyway. Then takes a drag that lasts longer than it took me to unzip my fly."

Overhead, a formation of A-10s appeared with a roar from behind the mountains to the east. The planes dipped into the valley and headed toward us. The Taliban pointed and screamed "*alwateka!*" Airplane. Some of the men ran for cover behind the closest boulders. The others just watched the A-10s close the distance.

If we were going to bolt, now was the time. But I knew there was no escape. If we were the target, the A-10s would reach us in a second. They were armed with a GAU-8/A Avenger 30 mm cannon. It could shoot the 480 explosive rounds in less than five seconds and drop one of its 1,000-pound bombs before we could scramble to safety. The safest place would be more than a hundred yards away; everything else would be vaporized or shredded. I knew Dunne was responsible for this air raid.

The A-10s passed by without even a wave, disappearing over the hills to the west. Seconds later, the first concussions shook the ground and smoke painted the horizon. It was the first time Washington and I had looked away from the Taliban. When we turned back, they were jumping up and down, rifles raised to the sky, cursing the infidel planes, celebrating that they hadn't been in the drop zone.

"Those dick heads need a dancin' lesson," Washington said. "That must be the jihad jig. Never been done in any joint I been in."

"I don't think Arthur Murray's got a franchise in Jalalabad," I said. "And no MTV."

We watched while a few of the Taliban hugged and did the kiss-kiss routine on their bearded cheeks. Their joy would soon turn to anger against America, and we knew we were the nearest representatives.

"Who'd you sign your SGLI over to?" I asked. Servicemen's Group Life Insurance. "Hope it's somebody that appreciates your supreme sacrifice and they spend it on something other than a new Cadillac."

"Yaw'll furgits the bucket'a fried chicken and watermelon, massah," Washington said.

If it weren't for a band of fuming mujahedeen waving their rifles at us, the course of discussion between Washington and me might have been different. As it was, there were no limits. And we both knew it was just a form of macho Hallmark cards and the soldier's inability to say "I love you" before his world incinerated.

"In the almighty words of the Reverend Al Sharpton," I said, "prepare for the end."

Two of the men separated from the group, waving their arms and striding toward us. One was screaming *"zwhan mar shay!"* I think that meant "you will die young and unmarried!" Or it could have been one of the other popular Pashtun insults. "Your grandmother is dead, and her pussy is still moving!" The second furious hadji pulled a knife with a curved blade from his belt. He was within ten feet, waving the dagger at us, still advancing. His eyes were glazed, and he was soon to reach rapture. Washington took one step forward, shaking out his arms and spreading his legs.

"Fuck that candy ass knife shit, Abdul," he said. "Bring it on."

I moved to his side. The man would have two targets, both experienced in disarming a man with a blade. And killing him.

Before the hadji could raise the knife, a shot echoed through the rocks. The bullet whizzed over our heads and embedded in the oak behind us. The man froze, then turned around. It was the mujahedeen with the walkie-talkie. His AK was pointed at the three of us. A faint wisp of smoke drifted from the barrel. No friendly smile. He didn't say a word, just nodded his head to the right, indicating the men should move away. Muttering, they did. Washington and I relaxed.

"I want to comment on that Cadillac slur, honkey," Washington said. "What I wanna know is why white folk think an SUV has more class? Get through all them snow drifts in Florida blockin' the funeral procession?"

The Taliban appeared to be deciding what to do next. And when. We observed, and Washington continued.

"Speakin' about white people and fags, you hear the one about why gay white men use ribbed condoms?" He didn't look at me, and I didn't respond. He would tell me the answer. "Traction in the mud." Washington slapped his thigh and whooped.

In the last gasps of life, nothing was sacred. Dis everyone.

The mujahedeen glared. I smiled and shook my head, pointing to Washington, hoping my gestures let them know the laughter wasn't directed at them.

"Jesus, Washington," I hissed. "These guys don't tell jokes unless they involve donkeys. Or dead infidels. Stow it."

Washington pointed to his chest, grinning, trying to signal it was all about him.

"Gotta wrap it up," Washington said. "At least my people have rhythm. Did you see Cheney dancin' in the video on YouTube? I coulda' looked better if I had rigor mortis."

"All out'a your system now?" I asked. "They're comin' over again. I think it might be time to change the subject and focus on dope."

"There you go. Again," Washington said. "Black men and dope. One and the same to whitey."

"I wasn't the one who recruited you for this deal," I said. "Take it up with your minders. They coulda' chose Thorsten. I've been wonderin' why it was you."

"Like I said, black men and dope. The only reason I can come up with. Make's me hate 'em even more."

The hadji with the walkie-talkie led the way. He pointed to the truck. Washington and I mounted up and were signaled forward, AKs not wavering from our heads. Washington started the truck, and we moved forward at two miles an hour, the mujahedeen walking along beside us as armed escort.

Around the bend and over a slight rise, the poppy meadows opened up. At each one, a guard with an AK protected the perimeter. The plots were broken up by rocks, paths, and a few withered wild privet tress and camel thorn bushes. The bucolic scene was spectacular, right out of *Better Homes and Gardens*. Pretty white blossoms swaying in the breeze with only a few reds and blues giving depth to the carpet of flowers. Harvesters in the field, stooping to tend the crop, all framed in blue sky and snowcapped mountains. A small sparrow hawk rode the wind stream, gliding slowly above. The smell was like someone had just mown wet grass. At the edges of the fields, burlap bags were piled, some already containing the fruits of the day's yield. Washington made a couple of turns, the terrain constantly rising. After a klick, we began to drop toward a small valley and the first signs of habitation.

A few mud-walled houses, the biggest with a wooden porch and an antenna attached to a tile chimney beside a small satellite dish. Pole structures with roofs covered in plastic tarps. A dented and scratched Land Rover parked by the rusting bodies of two old Toyota trucks with the windows blown out and flat tires. Chickens pecking in the dirt and dogs lying in the sun, panting and watching the invaders pull into the courtyard. All around, men at work and the sound of a generator. Some were stirring large cauldrons, while others stacked bricks of heroin or moved bags of opium from place to place. One of the huts held the printing press, and a man was stacking pieces of paper after they were stamped. At every corner of the compound, an armed guard faced outward. On the roofs, more lookouts. Just before the gate, a hadji manned a Russian-made PK 7.62mm machine gun surrounded by sandbags. The man beside him had an M79 bloop gun. Washington stopped the truck. He didn't even need to apply the brakes, and the 6x6 didn't jerk as if we had been speeding. He simply shut down the engine.

"Hey, Morgan," Washington said. "They didn't ask about the money."

"I suppose they think we'd be foolish to come here without it," I said. "Or suicidal." I slowly turned my head, counting the number of men and munitions. "It'd take a battalion of Rangers to root out these bad guys. They probably have underground bunkers, too, so even the GMLRS smart bombs would just be a hiccup."

A hadji in a long, flowing robe stepped out of the door of the largest house and onto the porch. He was unarmed and had a black scarf around his neck, curled below a black turban. Over six feet tall, his beard was untrimmed, touching his chest. The sandals on his feet weren't dust covered like everyone else's, and his robe had been freshly washed. A cigarette was in his right hand. He beckoned us to come inside.

"If there is such an Abdul," Washington said, "that's Sheik Wahidi. He didn't introduce himself last time around."

"You're probably right," I said. "No 'Abdul' shit with this mullah. Lots of them speak English. Learn on the Internet or at foreign schools. Comes in handy when they're trying to intercept our communications. Or torturing prisoners."

We stepped down from the truck and walked across the dirt courtyard, still accompanied by our AK-carrying ushers.

The only sound was the crackling of the fire and the hum of the generator. The chickens hopped away, wings flapping and raising dust. Skinny dogs slunk under the porch. None had barked. The Taliban were known to cut out dogs' tongues for quiet but kept them around to hunt snakes. Smoke from the cooking opium rose to our left. The smell was like cedar burning. No one talked or prayed. It was still too early for *Salatu-I-Asr*. Afternoon prayer.

"Greetings," the man said and went on in perfect lyrical British boarding-school English. "Please come inside. We can speak and have a cup of Tora tea. I'm sure you're tired after your journey." The man turned to the side, careful not to show his back, gesturing us to enter.

No windows in the dark room. Candles burned from the top of a low table sitting on a large rug that reached to the corners. The carpet was decorated in twisting designs of red and green. Several old chairs and foot stools bordered the lacquered table. In the middle, a copy of the Koran was held open by a purple cloth place marker. A door led to what appeared to be a small kitchen, where a silver teapot was hissing, steam drifting toward the ceiling. Nothing on the walls. No pictures of Mohammed, heresy in the Islamic world, or photos of the family.

"Please take a seat," the man said. "I'll attend to the tea." He walked to the open door and began pouring the drinks into clear glasses.

Washington and I moved the chairs so that we faced outside and sat, taking off our helmets. We both wore camo fatigues and bush boots.

Lights blinked from a radio to our right, mounted on a shelf against the wall. Earphones dangled off the side, and the Bose imprint was obvious even in the dim light. A laptop computer sprouted wires that led to a hole in the wall, probably attached to the generator and the satellite dish. The Company knew Iran had launched the Safir 313 satellite years ago, not only to track possible missile attacks, but also to provide communications links for terrorists. A new color printer, scanner, and fax was on the floor next to a shredder. A cell phone sat in a cradle, the green light showing it was fully charged.

"Equipped with everything the successful small-business owner needs," Washington said, nodding toward the devices. "Ya think he dials up porn?"

"More like Mullah Omar," I said.

Omar's titles were Commander of the Faith and Emir of Afghanistan. The reclusive leader had been the Taliban chieftain since 1996 and had not been seen in public for years. Thought to be in his late forties, Omar was born to landless peasants and was a member of the Hotak tribe. He had instituted Sharia in Afghanistan, the strictest interpretation of Islamic law. One of his favorite punishments was to have married adulterers in Kabul beaten, stoned, flogged, and beheaded in the National Soccer Stadium.

Omar also had the giant stone carvings of Buddha in Banyan destroyed, saying the idols were "an offense to the morality of Islam and signified worship of false gods." The man brewing the tea in the other room was certainly in contact with Omar or his ministers. Even from a cave in the Hindu Kush foothills, Omar still needed money. He had instituted a 20 percent tax on opium farmers and the heroin trade. Cash for smack had to come from somewhere, even if it was passed to him from his sworn enemy, America.

The wooden chairs weren't in condition to hold Washington's weight. His shrieked on every inhale, the legs bowing as if they were about to snap.

"Comfy digs," he said. "Centuries better than some'a them caves we sanitized."

"Beats the tents back at the base, too," I said.

"What do you care? Spooks sleep in coffins anyways."

"Now there's another myth. We use body bags."

"Speakin' a your brothers. Did ya hear the one about the spooks that found three IEDs alongside the road? The head spook leans over to pick one'a the IEDs up. The other says, 'Be careful, it might explode.' The head spook continues to reach for the IED and says, 'Quit worryin'. We'll tell 'em there was only two.'"

"What do ya' call two million Americans holding their hands up? The Army."

"Harsh, Morgan," Washington said. "If Abdul wasn't comin' back with that girly tray full'a sissy tea, I'd have to show you what the Modern Army is made of." Washington knew my name wasn't Donovan. No need to hide behind that cover any longer. We were on the same team, even if his tour of the major leagues might only last for a cup of coffee and a donut.

"And if you don't can the 'Abdul' shit," I said, "I'll cut off your arms and legs and throw you in the road. Nobody in the Army will come to your rescue. They're all in line to call home to their mommas anyways. Just be cool."

Without talking it over, one of us was constantly focused on the door facing the courtyard. The other watched the man who was stepping into the room with tea and a plate of cinnamon and honey-covered Naan. He set the tray on the table and handed us the clear glasses now turned a dark green from the tea. He sat in the empty chair.

"Gentlemen," he said. "Please partake of my humble offering of sweet bread and tea. I'm sorry we haven't had time to prepare a feast for your arrival common among my people." He pointed to the plate of Naan with a crooked finger like Moses parting the Red Sea. "Welcome to my house." He bowed. "May Allah bless your hearths and give you many wives to keep you warm."

I expected Washington to say something like, "One would do. As long as she has huge tits." He didn't.

Instead, he blew on his tea, trying to cool it down. He bowed to the man.

"Thank you for your gracious hospitality. We are honored to be here. It is so rare that men from our differing cultures can share a quiet moment." He set the tea on the table. "Let me introduce us. I am Lieutenant Ty Washington." He nodded to me. "This is my escort and personal assistant, Private Frank Morgan."

The man smiled, gently.

"There is no need for names. We are brothers, and will all be Mohammed when we rise to heaven."

It seemed my role was supportive in the bullshit. I kept silent and let these two fence.

"Yes," Washington said. "I believe the Koran says, 'And if ye die, or are slain, Lo, it is unto Allah that ye are brought together.' I trust your intentions are pure in that regard." He smiled.

The man allowed himself to chuckle.

"Don't worry, Lieutenant," he said. "The Koran also says, 'He who crosses your doorstep is like a King.'" He sipped his tea. "It is interesting to speak to an American who has studied the Koran. Where did you learn?"

"There are many Americans versed in the Koran. I am just one."

A single word or gesture from this man and we would be flayed and boiled in one of the cauldrons waiting outside to cook a batch of opium. I was sure he was Sheik Wahidi. If he wasn't, he was a high-level Taliban. The relatively sumptuous quarters, the latest technology, the number of men under his command, and the mass of valuable product outside the door meant he had to be someone Omar and his ministers trusted.

Gray streaked the man's beard, and tinted hair curled at the ends in fine wisps. One eye drooped just enough to notice. His fingers were long, easily wrapping around the tea glass, and his straight white teeth held no steel that I could see. He spoke softly, as if we were delicate treasures he did not want broken. While he was nearly as tall as Washington, he appeared to be fifty pounds lighter. His tanned skin was dotted with moles, and wrinkles creased his forehead. Even with the droop, his eyes were clear and deep and spoke of things divine. He was the incarnation of serene, educated evil.

"I know that to be true," the man said. "There are a number of scholars of the Koran in America. Imam Feisal Abdul Rauf has written many fine treatises on the Holy Book. I believe he lives in New York and has even lectured your FBI."

"Yes," Washington said. "I have read his books and have especially appreciated his interpretation of the verses as they apply to women. That is always a topic Americans want to discuss. Imam Rauf quotes Verse 33 often to explain that the Koran does not value a man more than a woman. 'For men and women who remember God constantly, for all of them has God prepared forgiveness of sins and a mighty reward.'"

Through the door, men were trudging past the gate carrying burlap bags over their shoulders. Guards accompanied them, AKs at their waists and not acting hostile. They took the bags to a shed and threw them in piles already threatening to fall over. The dogs came out and smelled the men's sandaled feet, hoping they might have tracked in a meal on their toes. The men sat and lit cigarettes, talking softly.

After a few more minutes of scholarly discourse and our decline of a second cup of tea, the man said, "I believe we have business to attend to. Please follow me." He rose and waved us past him.

As we stepped onto the porch, another sortie of A-10s appeared on the horizon, streaking in our general direction. The man stopped and shaded his eyes with his hand, staring skyward. The planes roared overhead, leaving a vapor trail and disappearing, followed in seconds by the sound of explosions. The man didn't say a word, just sighed and motioned us to follow.

The truck had been parked out of our sight. Now, I could see men were just finishing loading the back of the 6x6 with heroin packed in used metal ammo boxes. No one appeared relaxed, part of their riches being handed over to infidels.

Our host stopped by the truck. Without looking at either of us, he said, "I believe you have something for me. Please get it now."

Washington nodded to me. I was his boy, and the dirty work would fall into my hands. No offense. For now.

The truck's hood latch was between the struts of the ram guard. I pushed the handle to the side, and the hood popped open. Metal arms held the bonnet so it wouldn't crush someone with their head inside. I secured the supports and stretched to reach over the wheel well, freeing the first ammo can. One was secured to each side. Washington just watched while I struggled with the awkward weight.

Finally, the Taliban leader beckoned one of the dope loaders to help. Together, we freed the cans and set them on the ground. My helper stepped back.

"Please leave them there," the mullah said. "I believe it is time for you to go. You should be far away before nightfall. I hear the roads are extremely dangerous in the dark." He turned to walk away, not bothering to give any orders concerning the millions of dollars in cash inside the duffel bags and ammo cans. It would be foolish to stiff the Taliban while we were still in their sector.

"*Inshallah*," he said.

"*Inshallah*," Washington said. He walked to the driver's side and pulled himself into the truck. I went to the passenger's door and climbed in. All our weapons had been replaced, but twenty rifles were now pointed directly at our heads.

The opium stirrers watched, not taking their hands off the poles. A faint lye smell hung in the air. If there was a time to send us to God, it was now. My hand was on a grenade.

During his interrogation, Washington had forgotten to mention part of the process. The step required after boiling opium was to sift the remaining white material through one of the burlap bags stacked against the side of the shed. The substance that remained was morphine. In another out building, men were drying the bags and straining the morphine, ready to begin adding the chemicals to finally turn it to heroin. Fifty-five gallon drums marked sodium carbonate, ethyl alcohol, ether, and acetone in English were lined up in the shed beside a number of other, unlabeled barrels.

Washington started the truck with the usual cloud of black smoke billowing over the front and the rattling sound of a hundred old men with tuberculosis. He eased the 6x6 around the courtyard so the front faced down the road. No one waved goodbye as we left the compound.

"You're a piece a' fuckin' work, Washington," I said. "What was all that satanic verses gibberish? You a member of the Nation of Islam? A follower of Farrakhan?"

"Nope," Washington said. "Just a student of theology. You know, find out why we're here and where we're goin' in the eyes of different religions. Not just blindly chase the bible according to Langley like you spooks. If you gave it a try, you might find out there's a world of possibility outside a training manual."

His focus never left the road and the sentries we passed at walking speed. He grinned. "Ah, fuck that. Life's too short, and I ain't getting' no seventy-two virgins. Did ya hear about the CIA firing squad that stood in a circle? Or the new CIA secret weapon? A solar-powered flashlight."

As we left the last sentry, Washington sped up as fast as our backs could tolerate. The cans of heroin bounced around the back, causing a vinegar smell to invade the cab. The sun had already dropped behind the closest hills, and we wanted to get as far away as possible before the A-10s arrived.

The two closeby A-10s missions had been diversions to cover what would happen in the next few minutes. Dunne had sewn detonating devices in the bag holding the money. They were remotely wired to ten pounds of C-4 in each can, enough to leave a big hole in the ground where the Taliban compound and dope refinery used to be. A switch below the dash would set off the plastic explosives instantly when I pushed the disguised button. The range was four miles, and we needed to get that far away quickly. Hopefully, the blast would be considered just another bombing raid by other invaders in the vicinity, not linked to us by any of the checkpoint personnel or valley watchers. The crucial part was that all communications equipment from the Taliban opium factory was destroyed. If not, it would be a short ride for me and Washington. An A-10s fly-by was scheduled in five minutes, and we were supposed to match setting off the C-4 with their arrival.

The Company was expert in shape-charging bombs, and the false panel in the ammo cans should conceal the deadly plastic long enough for

Washington and me to be safely down the potholed road. When the bombs went off, each charge held enough C-4 to destroy a twenty-inch steel beam. Or a tank. More than adequate to obliterate pole sheds and mud houses. And people.

The money wasn't an issue. Dunne's slush fund seemed limitless. The cost per head to kill each al-Qaeda or Taliban terrorist was calculated at about $200,000. At least twenty-five would soon be dead. We were saving taxpayer dollars.

All of this could have been done easier if Washington had given us the coordinates of the dope stronghold. He wasn't exactly sure, and the valley was sprinkled with other small factory and living sites like this one. No one really wanted to disintegrate civilians, even if they were dope growers. The decision had been made to make the pickup so that Phase II could become a go. That didn't cancel the need for retribution. As long as we weren't at a checkpoint, our chances of a healthy return to base were at least 50-50. Much less if angry mujahedeens were picking themselves up from the gravel with easy targets available after the A-10s roared past and the ground shook like one of the earthquakes familiar to all Afghans. My hand was close to the button and waited for the appearance of the A-10s.

"So I'm a private," I said.

"Yup," Washington said. I had interrupted his humming of "Sweet Georgia Brown." "You're my boy. Piss you off to have a brother in the power seat for once?" He looked at me, the first time his eyes had been off the rutted road since we left the poppy fields. "Handle it."

Shadows covered the hills surrounding us. Rock outcroppings as big as condominiums towered above us on both sides. The creek we followed was sprinkled with boulders, and saw grass grew between the stones. Rippling brown water cascaded in small rapids and formed eddies close to the banks; there was too much irrigation going on from the plateaus above to keep the water clear. The sky was the nearly transparent blue of Morocco. Chukars rose from the long grasses along the stream bed as we passed, clucking in horror. If we had to make a run for it, this was the only road. And there was no return.

On the hillside, mountain goats picked their way between crevices on the steep slope. The six or seven bearded and horned free-range animals were lucky to be in the wild, not used as the prize in *Buzkashi*, the national sport of Afghanistan. In that game, a dead goat was placed between teams of mounted horseman. The first to drag the carcass across a pre-set goal was the winner. The contests sometimes lasted more than a week and were meant to re-enact ancient mountain goat hunts. Both horses and riders often died, not to mention the already dead goat that was nearly shredded by the time the game ended. I had watched one of these matches outside Jalalabad, pitting two rival villages. Lots of Afghani currency exchanged hands amidst the dust and parked Toyota pickups.

The first A-10 appeared over the hills, followed immediately by a second. They would reach their target in a few heart beats. I waited only long enough to count to five and pushed the detonator switch under the dashboard.

Two explosions, not far apart in distance and within a few klicks of our position. Washington stopped humming and held up his right hand waiting for me to give him some skin. I didn't.

"I'm still pissed at being made your slave," I said. "And a fucking private? You could have at least said I was a sergeant."

"Get over it, white bread," Washington said. "No use carryin' a grudge."

"Okay," I said, and slapped his hand, both of us grinning like the Wolverines had just won the BCS.

Washington turned his grinning face back and concentrated on the obstacle course of road in front of the 6x6, pushing his helmet higher on his head.

"You think any Abduls survived?" he asked.

I took out my Ka-Bar and mindlessly rubbed it on my thigh.

"Not likely," I said. "Dunne treats C-4 like it's Play-Doh and he's makin' little art projects. He's a master of molding the gunk into tight places and packin' enough charge to do the job right. My guess is that hadji factory better have its insurance premium up to date."

"Boys and their toys."

"The man who dies with the biggest bang . . . dies."

"Speakin' a philosophy, did you know what Muslim women use for birth control?"

"Nope."

"Their faces."

Washington hadn't met Khkulay and didn't know anything about her. By now, Finnen, the dog that he was, had probably become acquainted, weaseling his Irish charm into her hijab, but not her knickers. I couldn't wait to get back to the base and defend her honor from an attack by limerick. I put away the knife and stared at a yew tree pocked with bullet holes alongside the road.

"Jesus, Washington," I said. "You're a sexist racist chauvinist religious bigot."

"Born in the land of equal oppor-tun-i-ty."

"Offend everyone."

"Do you know how many Afghans it takes to change a light bulb? None. They sit in the dark and blame the Jews for it."

It was hard to reconcile this man with both his record and the scene of him bleeding and taped to a chair in a Jalalabad safe house, mocking us. Humor of the macabre. I only wished I could enjoy life the way he did in this rock pile stained in crimson. Nevertheless, besides Finnen, I was coming to believe there wasn't a man in Afghanistan or on the planet who I would rather have alongside me to face the beards.

Ahead, two trucks with glaring red letters reading Cowboy painted on the doors were parked nose to nose, blocking the road. One had a light bar on the top for hunting nonbelievers in the dark and smokestack-like air ventilators running up the sides to more efficiently filter the dust. The pickups were in good condition and could be on a poster for the Toyota Motor company. The background was rolling hills, steep mountains, and blue sky. The downside was the AKs pointed in our direction.

It was rumored Mullah Omar preferred Chevy Suburbans with tinted windows, and his ministers were partial to Land Cruisers. But 4x4 pickups were still the most common vehicle in Afghanistan. While the Taliban had waged jihad against technology, publicly hanging televisions, stringing light poles with tape pulled from video cassettes, digging mass graves for cell phones, and putting laptops to death, they were still addicted to trucks. The two Toyotas in front of us were owned by mujahedeen several levels below the elite. Washington shifted into first and slowed.

"Should I stop or go to ram speed?" he asked.

"Ya think?" I asked. It was becoming the standard reply to stupid questions.

"Maybe we could nudge those trucks into the ditch and make a mad dash to safety."

"Ya think?"

"Fuckin' A, Morgan. You sound like a broken record. I'm tryin' my best to come up with a plan to save your poppy-white skin, and you keep actin' like a Valley girl."

Not again. Borrrring.

"Duh," I said.

"Oh, that's awesome. I'm sure that'll like totally work."

Washington braked the truck and stuck his head out the rolled-down window.

"Hey," he said. "You Abduls know the way to Jalalabad? We're kinda lost. Got sidetracked back at the mall."

Two men walked toward us. The other four stayed in the beds of the pickups. All six aimed their rifles at us, and I was sure several more hadjis were hidden in the brush beside the road, our heads in their sights.

The man closest to Washington was the spokesman. He stood far enough from the 6x6 to not be slammed to the dirt if Washington decided to quickly push the door open. He wore a black turban and a dark-green vest with rips across the chest. An ammo belt hung from his waist and held several old Russian-made M76 bottle grenades and 30-caliber bullets. His pajamas didn't reach far below his knees, and dirt colored his ankles and calves the brown of the terrain. One of the fingers on his left hand was missing, but his hands were steady on the AK.

"*Raasem*," he said. Out.

No antennas sprouted from the pickups, and I didn't see anyone with a wireless radio. If they were still enraged about the bombings of the last half-hour, it wasn't obvious. The Taliban always seemed pissed, as if fire ants were eating at their crotches—every breath from a non-Taliban or a woman was deeply offensive.

Washington stepped down, and I climbed out the passenger side to the front of the 6x6. The fingerless hadji waved the barrel of his AK, indicating we should move away. We were unarmed, except for the concealed pistols and knives, not much protection against at least six automatics. Washington joined me, and we patiently watched while the Taliban searched the truck.

"See that Abdul with the limp?" he asked, nodding toward a Taliban on our right. "I think that's not really his foot in the sandal. Maybe stepped on one'a those Russian POMZ mines. They shoulda tried harder to match his skin color to that fake. Looks kinda like they pasted a big Barbie doll's leg below his knee. Don't think the Afghan prosthesis market is up to Western standards."

"Showin' a little compassion, are we now?"

From a Company report, I knew the Russians had left a legacy of nearly ten million landmines scattered across Afghanistan. Usually, the survivors of the blasts were seen begging in the larger cities, rolling around on skateboards or leaning into homemade crutches made from tree limbs. The United Nations had started the Mine Action Program in Afghanistan, MAPA, and had cleared millions of square meters of land. Still, much more of the country was infested with bombs than was bomb free. Only two million landmines had been destroyed, leaving millions more ready to blow off limbs. In bazaars around the country, men in stalls sold artificial feet, legs, and arms from piles that looked like mannequin-stump graveyards.

The hadjis didn't explore too long. It was likely their only assignment was to make sure we hadn't made a detour and sold the heroin someplace else or stashed it in a cave.

Washington had remained relatively silent during the search. Both of us could sense we were closer to slaughter here than back at the refinery. At the moment, these men weren't being directed by a Mullah. One insulting move or word could be our entrance to paradise, no matter what their orders.

After a few minutes, the Taliban with one good foot jabbed the barrel of his AK into my back, then Washington's, prodding us to the truck.

"Ouch," Washington said, turning to face the gimp. "That hurts. You want me to rip off that dummy foot and beat you to death with it?"

I thought Washington understood the danger. Wrong. I was beginning to feel he was suicidal as well as brave and intelligent. Maybe I was misguided about the last one, too.

"Stow it, Washington," I said. "You'll live. But not if you keep jacking your lips around these men."

"There it is," Washington said as we continued to walk to the 6x6. "You whiteys are obsessed with two black male body parts. Dicks and lips. I knew you couldn't last the day without bringin' both a' them up."

"Not guilty, Washington," I said. "It's you with the dick lip fascinations. I haven't been sayin' much. You're the Chatty Cathy. If you don't shut your fat lips now, you won't be able to recite the 'I had a dream' speech like I been expectin'. Get in the truck."

"Fat lips? You can't stop yourself, honkey."

We went to our designated seats. The limping hadji even helped me close the door, while the fingerless man stared at Washington like he was a new species. Not many black men in this valley.

The Toyotas were moved, and Washington drove through, leaving the hadji roadblock with a wave and a "see ya next year in Paris, Abdul" salute.

Within a few hours and another blockade, we were back at the Tora Bora base. Dunne had assured us we had a free pass through the gate and no MPs would hassle us on our return as long as we used the password "Libido," perfect for Washington. It worked.

Washington parked the most valuable truck on base in the CIA compound and returned to his barracks to be debriefed in the morning. He hadn't stopped lecturing the entire way back, trying to convince me of the superior heritage of black culture and the "tiny dick" syndrome that afflicted the white race and adversely impacted so many of the ruling-class decisions. I was impatient to evaluate the damage Finnen had wrought and rushed the goodbyes, leaving it with "We'll finish this tomorrow. Or not."

"Smells like smack," Dunne said from his station at the computer. "I'll have to assign someone to guard the truck who can keep his yap shut while he's standing by millions in dope, dreaming of a villa in the Caribbean." He gave me the only glance since I entered the tent. "Tell me all about it."

For once, Finnen wasn't in the corner, crushing Bud cans and protecting the stash like a junky. I went to the fridge, having a rare hankering for the taste of beer. No moral stance, I had just never gotten used to it except when the purpose was to get wasted. I'd have one later, maybe.

Finnen's absence was cause for suspicion, and I couldn't take my mind off his probable schmoozing of Khkulay to give anything but the barest recap to Dunne. Finnen was a dog of war, and his sniffing needed to be stopped.

I had stowed my H & K against the canvas wall and stripped to a dull gray t-shirt and my camo pants, unlacing my boots and letting fresh air reunite with toes that smelled like wet burlap. The Hush Puppy and Ka-Bar were on the ground next to me.

It didn't take more than one glance to see the only things that changed were the position of a few pins in the map and the number of flies caught in the spider web in the ceiling corner. Dunne's passion for order and sameness overcame any desire for an upgrade to his environment. I scratched the ever-present but intensifying itch around my balls.

"So we left Wahidi, or whatever his name was, with your custom-made gift and di di'ed for the base," I said, summing up the mission. "The last thing out of the refinery was 'boom.'"

Dunne had granted me the courtesy of at least two glances away from his laptop during my five-minute speech and only a couple questions. Now, he honored me with another fleeting look.

"Short on detail," Dunne said. "But we can fully debrief later. For now, get some sleep. You and Washington will be heading south first thing in the morning. You've got a rendezvous tomorrow night at the pipeline."

"Doesn't Washington get the pleasure of unburdening himself to you, too?"

"Not now. You can both fill me in when you get back. There are some fine points we need to address before you leave. Be here at 0530. I've already told Washington's commander. Have a nice night." All this was said to the computer screen.

"Have you seen Finnen?"

"No. I haven't seen Finnen. I assigned him to guard detail just to get him out of here." Dunne's eyes blinked like a strobe light. "Had him keep the perimeter clear and gave him a lunch break myself. I heard he used it sniffin' around the women's barracks."

Fuck. No telling what the degenerate Irish man was up to. But, by the way Dunne responded with a forced frown that threatened to explode in a loud guffaw, I knew he was lying. Must be covering for Finnen's shenanigans.

I picked up my weapons and shirt, with no intention of showering or eating before going on an elf hunt. Not bothering to say "Allah, Allah Akbar," I walked out of the tent. Dunne wouldn't have heard me anyway, lost as he always was in the ether world.

꩜

The women's barracks. A row of tents, walkways swept clean. Sandbags protected the walls. Big numbers sewn in black with a white background on each of the canvas quarters. Orderly, like all the barracks, with the exception of the more relaxed atmosphere inside the Company sector. I half-expected potted plants to be growing in cute harmony with the dust, providing colorful contrast to the faded green, and clothes lines filled with bras and panties. But this would make the females stand out even more in the modern Army, distinctions they were trying to blur. Most wanted to be considered as mean as the male Rangers, but the differences in strength, size, and hormones would always make it impossible except in Super Hero comic books. I approached the first female grunt I saw.

"I'm looking for an Afghan woman who was brought here last night," I said. "Do you know where I might find her?"

The soldier was taller than my six-foot height. She wore a green cloth hat with the bill perfectly pointed and probably starched. Her fatigues were loose, not giving any hint of body type other than the width of her shoulders. They were linebacker sized. No makeup and bushy eyebrows, she was not a candidate for a *Cosmopolitan* cover. She had that uncanny female ability to searchingly look deep into my retinas and convey the wonders of the universe. And to make me aware there was no place to hide. I felt like dropping to my knees and confessing.

"Aren't you a long way from home, spook?" she asked.

No escape. It was always as if I had an "S" tattooed on my forehead. Usually, it served me. The sheep parted like I was the Pope. No one risked asking too many questions in a war zone. I always went to the front of the line. CIA operatives were ghouls and phantoms, ready, after any provocation, to wreak punishment, a reputation we cherished. But that was in the land of men. I almost stammered.

"Just some Company business," I said. "Do you know where she is?"

It wasn't just this instance; women had always intimidated me. Back in The World, my older sisters had treated me like I wasn't in on anything, whispering, giggling, and pointing. There was the constant "Trevor did . . ." or "Sean said . . ." What I never understood was how the boy's behaviors were wrong, but they obviously were by the volume of my sisters' shrieks. I was teased and ridiculed, especially when my parents were out of earshot. Then it became worse. They got the "curse" and tits, and I was no longer worthy of breathing the same estrogen-charged air. Then, real boyfriends came into their lives, and I was told to "ride your teeny balls out of the room and disappear." But that wasn't all.

My mother ruled with kindness and seemed to know my every thought, especially the bad ones, according to her Catholic eyes. She missed nothing.

A witch in an apron, she could detect the smallest fib or even the thought I might be about to tell one. I adored her, even if she scared me. Too much love was a burden I didn't know if I could handle. All of this was fodder for one of the base psychiatrists who were now part of Operation Enduring Freedom. But most of it felt like a bunch of sissy lame nonsense when I was surrounded by so many with real issues. Nevertheless, my mission now was to extract the intel I needed from this Amazon and find Khkulay without running back to the compound and hiding under my cot, sucking my thumb.

The woman in front of me stared like Mom.

"Would that business be social," she asked. "or *business* business?"

I wouldn't be able to withstand the torture much longer. I looked down and watched a green Indian garden lizard crawl under the nearest tent.

"Purely social," I said. "I left my Hush Puppy behind."

Everyone knew about the features of a silenced .22. And what the barrel pushed against a head meant. The Rangers preferred more firepower, while the Hush Puppy was infamous as the spook weapon of choice.

My smile didn't work. She frowned.

"No dogs here for you to practice on," she said.

I grinned with just enough malice to let her question.

"Darn," I said. "I'm getting kind of rusty. Haven't been out since last night."

Programmed. No matter how frightened, training took control. Don't let anyone intimidate. Keep the mystery burning. She took a small unconscious step back and straightened, making her even taller.

"I like cats better," she said. "Not all the leg humping and slobbering." She moved forward. "You don't sacrifice cats, do you?"

"Only on Sundays," I said. My stupid grin was tiring my dimpled cheeks. Just a small-town boy talking to a woman about murdering animals. Happens every day in Millard.

She had a big nose that hooked downward a fraction at the tip and a hint of a mustache. Now, her nostrils flared.

"You spooks are disgusting," she said. "For the life of me, I don't understand why on Earth you are allowed to shit in our nest. Been out waterboarding?"

This was going well. One simple question, and now the situation had deteriorated to a Congressional hearing on torture methods. Time for a veto. I stopped the silly grin.

"Take it up with your Senator, ma'am," I said. "Or you could visit our little chamber of horrors and see for yourself what fun it is on the dark side. Have you seen the girl?"

Now she was ramrod military straight.

"Captain Meredith to you," she said. Conditioning. She was falling back on the old Army officer routine. I should be honored to be in her presence, not an insubordinate low life non-com scum, even if I was from the CIA. She seemed to be getting ready to spit.

Trying to calculate the odds of running into her, the Captain Meredith who Dunne had dispatched me to for Khkulay's safe keeping, I struggled to regroup. Meredith wasn't around yesterday, and I had made the hand off to a Sergeant with fiery red fingernails. Even if this woman standing stiff and tall in front of me wasn't wearing a nametag or stripes, I should have guessed by her bearing she might have been *the* Captain Meredith. It was all about Khkulay and her well-being.

Infatuation. Not with the Captain or Khkulay, but the thought interrupted, and I knew this fascination was a disease my immune system hadn't built antibodies against. The syndrome nearly always resulted in misjudgments and embarrassment. Like the time back at university when I fell for a blond-haired beautiful classmate in Political Science 305, Comparison of Geo-Political Trends in the Muslim World. I believed our relationship was torrid, even though we had only met a few times in the library for study group and one late-night walk back to her dorm afterward. She had been passionate about the ongoing crisis in Palestine and said things like, "The absolute tyranny of the Israeli cabal has caused emotional castration for Palestinian males." What I heard was, "Let's sneak into my dorm room and fuck."

When I answered yes, it was to that fantasy; it wasn't a response to "Do you agree with my hypothesis?" In my lameness, I put my arm around her waist, believing I was starting the foreplay all women craved. She gave a little yelp and pulled away, knocking my books out of my other hand as she twisted. "That is exactly the type of behavior the Islamic world finds appalling and the reason Muslim women wear the hijab," she said loud enough for passing students to hear. "They do *not* want to be preyed upon and disrespected by men." Giggles from the audience. She stomped away, leaving my cheeks on fire and me chasing papers made airborne by the wind blowing across the Quad.

This evening's mission should have been simple. Find Khkulay. Make sure everything was fine and she was adjusting to another reality with a minimum of shock. No one would be dying. Or tortured. This was tougher than sneaking alone into a dark cave in the middle of Taliban country.

Unfortunately, Captain Meredith was still at attention in front of me, working up enough contempt for a real dressing down, something expertly taught at OCS. But it was my turn.

"O-O-7 here," I said.

Cool. She didn't blink.

"I've always heard about Company arrogance and insolence," she said "If I could, I'd have you put in the blockade."

"Yes, ma'am," I said. I gave her a limp-wristed half-ass salute. "And if the Intelligence Committee hadn't voted to limit CIA interrogation methods, I'd have your ass on an operating table with the cattle prods out. There'd only be one question. Where's the girl?"

As always in my interactions with women, things were going well. At least I hadn't put my arm around her and steered her toward the nearest vacant cot. She began to shake her head back and forth.

"Fucking spooks," she said.

It was amazing how many times "fucking" came before "spooks." As if we were really getting any. I was ready for a do-over.

"Let's start again," I said. "Pretend we're just two lonely people in a war zone who meet under the stars on a warm evening cocooned by the gentle breeze and searching for that special person we've always known was out there waiting for us. I whisper softly in your ear." I bent slightly toward her, feigning intimacy. "Where's the fucking girl?"

No slap. That would be too feminine. Meredith just turned and walked away, leaving me with a *humph* to consider. Another notch on my belt.

Now, who to offend next? I wondered.

Not much foot traffic. The scent of perfume. Boom boxes played softly as I strolled down the paths between quarters, headed for the tent near where I'd left Khkulay. Good place to start; I should have planned this strategy earlier before the battle with Meredith.

Murmurs and laughter. No beer-driven guffaws. Even some candles. The women probably were engaged in séances or absorbed in the latest Danielle Steele epic. Filing cuticles and folding fresh laundry while they updated each other on the latest base gossip. What the fuck did I know? It was no longer the Man's Army, and I had no point of reference other than two sisters who ignored me whenever they could. No women in my training group at Langley or Camp Perry. This place was as foreign as a mosque. And I was uncomfortable.

A few female soldiers passed, avoiding eye contact. It wasn't that men weren't allowed in this sector; it was more that male grunts would rather be somewhere else, slugging down beer and swapping stories about stupid or dead hadjis unless one of the tents held a sure thing. No time and no place for romance.

Finally, a cheery-faced woman with a bath towel over her shoulder gave me directions without even whispering "fuckin' spook." Maybe I had shape-shifted.

Outside the tent labeled 12W, I wondered about the protocol. Was I supposed to knock on one of the metal support poles? Scratch on the canvas? Clear my throat loudly a few times? Barge in and startle women in bras and panties? Send them a text message saying I was outside and would like a word?

Standing with arms tight to my sides in the dim light of the overheads, I felt absurd. I was a trained assassin. A college graduate with, oh, three or four close physical relationships with women behind me. (No use lying to myself. Make that two, counting the one I paid for on a drunken Saturday night I don't even remember. Anyway, Finnen told me I did the deed, so I gotta count it.) A man highly skilled at the twelve ways to conduct an unarmed kill in two seconds, and a practitioner versed in making instant life-changing decisions. In this moment, I was childishly frozen to the dirt, the internal conflict threatening to cause me to weep or spew the last meal of shit on a shingle.

"Fed Ex," I said loudly.

After shaking the tent flap, I stepped back and waited for a signature. Or for someone to rescue me from hell.

The angel appeared in rumpled fatigues and freshly applied ruby lipstick. Her brown hair was pulled back in a ponytail and tied with a rubber band. Margolis was printed on her sewn nametag, and the ID was slanted thirty degrees above parallel, riding the crest of an awesome tit. Behind her, a lamp covered with a dark-red shade sat on an ammo box provided back lighting to her tanned features. A small cleft in her chin was the only blemish on a smooth face. She smiled, displaying straight white teeth, the orthodontics well above military competence.

"Tooth fairy," she said. Perfect.

The smile vanished. She stepped back with a little gasp.

Time to reconsider. The shape-shifting hadn't worked its magic this time. It could be the short growth of an unshaven jaw, not the "S" imprinted on my forehead. And the not quite strack fatigues. Or just my aura. I raised both hands so she could see I wasn't holding any weapons.

"Be cool, and nobody will get hurt," I said. I laughed. It was a line I loved to use just before the garrote tightened around a target's neck. This soldier didn't know that, but from the look of her now wide eyes, she suspected.

Margolis jumped, moving farther away.

"Don't take me seriously," I said. "It's just my infantile attempt at gallows humor."

Behind the soldier and sitting on her cot, the woman with the red fingernails from yesterday was watching. She began to giggle.

"Oh, don't let him bother you, Amber," she said. "He's harmless."

Sure. I was a non-toxic blend of wit and good cheer. Except when I wasn't.

I stepped past the flap and moved inside the tent.

"Sorry to interrupt," I said. "I'm looking for Khkulay. Do you know where she is? The way I'm treated around here, it seems the intel is 'Top Secret.'"

The first soldier had moved closer to her H & K. The one with the bright-colored finger tips stood and walked toward me.

"That girl's a doll," the second woman said. "She's somethin' else. So fresh and innocent." She put her clenched fists on her hips. "And what might be your intentions toward her, spook?"

This female grunt came from a somewhat different mold. Broad at the beam, she barely made the woman's Army height minimum of four-foot-ten. She certainly was pushing the supposed weight maximum of 121 pounds, but I didn't think there were too many scales around. Her eyes were spread far apart, and her brows had been trimmed to a fine line. Curly hair in a buzzed Afro, this woman wouldn't take shit from me or no man. Still, I tried to loosen things up.

"Well, thought I'd take her for a candlelit dinner at Chez Mess Hall," I said. "I've booked a table by the window. I prefer the Prix Fixe menu. Or the chef's recommendation."

"And I 'spose you forgot the flowers?"

"Sorry. The florist was closed. I returned too late from protecting the free world."

"Figures."

"I'll make it up to her with a bottle of the best Pinot Noir."

"So, what you really want, spook?"

"Just a brief conversation. That's all. You know, make sure she's adjusting."

"You come walkin' in here like some horny teenager. I can see whats you wants."

"I assure you, I have the highest regards for Khkulay and am only concerned for her well-being."

"Yaa. That's exacly what Leroy said 'bout me. I was three months pregnant 'fore he snuck out the door." She turned and pointed to a photo of a girl in braids and a high-collared white blouse sitting on the ammo can. "That's what becum'a that night. Laqeesha." She smiled and then looked back. "Ain't she the cutest little thang."

I grinned what I thought would be confirmation of her opinion.

"Don't you be smilin' at me, spook. That strategy's workin' 'bout as well as what we're doin' here. You better come up with a better plan."

Short of going back for my assault rifle and a few grenades, it was seemingly impossible to pry out information from anyone around here. I'd had an easier time with targets when all I had to do was pull out a pair of pliers.

No time for surrender, I forged ahead. Maybe honesty would work. It did with Mom. I cleared my throat and shrunk my body.

"I apologize," I said. "It seems crossing to the women's side of the barracks makes me lose track of who I am. I start sweating and forgetting there are real people here who care about the plight of humanity and the destiny of our great nation. My mother used to say, 'Son, there are times when a soft voice spoken with a pure heart is louder than the harshest cry.' She always treated us and Dad in the same gentle way. I'm proud to be her son and am sorry if I have let her and you down."

There. Mom, Dad, and apple pie. Mixed with doses of humility, contriteness, and submission. Oughta work.

"Now that's the biggest crocka shit I heard since Rufus told me he wasn't married and never been ta jail," she said. "Why don't you slink back inta the hole you crawled outta, spook?"

Re-deployment. I turned to leave. I'd just been handed my head unlike any bad guy had been able to do since I'd arrived in this rock pile. And there was nobody I could waste to vent my frustration.

As I opened the tent flap, I almost ran into Khkulay. She was obviously returning from the shower. Her long black hair was still wet and hung straight below her shoulders. A pair of oversized fatigues had replaced the robe. Even in the dimness, muted light from the overheads reflected off those glacial blue eyes. Someone had painted her fingernails pink. When she saw me, a faint blush appeared on her cheeks, making her look fourteen. She smiled and quickly moved past, tying a scarf over her hair. She walked to the back of the tent and didn't turn around until she had adjusted the headdress to cover all her hair except the strands on her forehead.

"*Salam Aleikum*, Khkulay," I said. Peace be with you.

"*Wa Aleikum as salam,* Mr. Morgan," she said. And peace be with you, too. She sat on the furthest cot and folded her hands in her lap.

I took a few small steps into the tent, knowing full well the gatekeepers wouldn't let me get closer.

"Are you being treated well?" I asked.

"Of course," Khkulay said. "Did you expect I would be flogged?" She laughed.

"Have you had enough to eat?" I asked.

"Yes," she said. "I especially liked the fresh fruits. We don't get that many here."

"And you have a comfortable place to sleep?"

"Yes. It is much softer than the floor."

"Did Mr. Finnen visit?"

"Yes. For a short time. He said he had duties to attend to. We had a nice talk. He is a good man."

Fuckin' Irish imp. Dunne was right. He must have snuck away unseen like the spook he was; it wasn't a false rumor.

The other two women in the tent were grinning, listening to my loser attempt at small talk. Their eyes went back and forth between Khkulay and me like they were watching a video game. I was the carrion feed for those two vultures.

What I wanted to do was extract Khkulay from the perimeter secured by the two harpies, but I believed she wouldn't be relaxed alone with a man other than her husband for quite some time.

The woman with the red fingernails went to her cot and yawned.

"Lights out in a few minutes, spook," she said. "I do hate ta miss your skill in lady killin'. You're almost makin' me swoon. Toddle on." She waved a limp wrist.

"Spook?" Khkulay said. "Why do you call him *spook*? What does that word mean?"

"You better ask him," the curly-haired woman said, nodding in my direction. "What you gots to say for yourself, spook?"

Unraveled by women again. There was no way I could tell Khkulay the truth. That I was paid to sneak up on her countrymen and put a knife into their spines or crush their balls until they gave me the names of anyone, even people they didn't know or had never heard of. I looked at my boots.

"Accounting," I said. "My job is to make sure everything and everyone is paid on time and all the columns are balanced." I wiped my hand across my brow and *shush*-ed like it was exhausting work and I carried the burden of so many. "It's an important part of how things get done around here. Some people resent my position, and they've taken to calling those of us in the accounting department spooks, because they think money just supernaturally appears in our hands. The word *spook* is similar to *ghost*. It's like some of the fine women around here are called *dykes*. Named for the famous little Dutch boy who saved his city from flooding by sticking his finger in the dike. These ladies are the kind who stick their fingers in places most women don't want to go, solving lots of individual issues and lending a gentle touch. American military personnel enjoy giving things and people nicknames."

I turned my head to the two other women who were now sitting close on their cots, mouths open wide in awe of my learned and articulate explanation. "Don't you ladies agree?"

"Who you be callin' dyke, spook? I ain't no dyke. Laqeesha's my proof. Amber sure ain't neither. She runs from her own voice."

The other soldier, Amber, hadn't said a word since she told me she was the tooth fairy. She had been staring for the last few minutes, inspecting me like I was on the morgue table. She continued her postmortem in silence.

Diversion. Get them away from the real concern. Focused on their sexuality rather than my job description. It almost worked.

"I still don't understand," Khkulay said. But she didn't look confused.

"Listen up, girl," the red finger-nailed soldier said, facing Khkulay. "Don't you be lettin' no man tell you lies. You got plenty a time for that. They all can't stop theyselves." She turned back to me. "As for you, spook, get yo'self on outta here. You been doin' too much insultin'. Ain't no bulldaggers in this tent."

I started to leave, opening the flap by reaching behind with my left hand.

"It was great getting to see you again, Khkulay," I said. "I'll check in tomorrow or as soon as I get can get away from keeping all the numbers in the right place. I'm glad these ladies are taking such good care of you." I looked at Amber, obviously the less aggressive of the two soldiers. "And I trust you two will fill in Khkulay with all the correct information on my MOS and the heavy responsibilities of the accounting branch. Anything else might be considered a violation of US Criminal Code 18." Treason. I smiled and waved. "Good night, ladies."

Walking back to the compound, I marveled at the way I could make women nearly black out with my charm. What I really wanted to do was put Finnen under six feet of shamrock, but I'd done too much of that lately. We'd just have a heart to heart.

The next time I saw Finnen was at the morning's pre-skag-delivery planning session. Washington and Dunne were there, and I didn't want to conduct an interrogation of him with those two in earshot. If only the elf were going with me on the trek to drop off the smack, I could have arranged an accident. Not fatal. Only have him listed as another casualty of Enduring Freedom with a ticket back to The World. Finnen was staying on base, helping Dunne sift through intel on the mission and tracking its tentacles through whatever covert operation was in play. That meant every coffee break would find Finnen sniveling around in the women's sector until Dunne's promise to ship her to Kabul and on to the United States was met.

The tent seemed to be carved in marble and unable to change in any way. I could only imagine what Dunne's house outside Reston, Virginia, was like. If a coaster was moved, he'd notice and put it back in its rightful place with a stern warning to whoever had offended his sense of order. This morning, his fingers were frantic on the laptop keyboard, and the view hadn't altered by even a pin placement, but Washington's presence added something to the atmosphere. He stood in the corner, claiming his ass would be "numb as a whitey's nuts" from hours bouncing in the 6x6 and he needed to give his "cheeks some fresh air" while he could. I watched Finnen fidget at his station next to the fridge. He looked back and forth between the beer stash and his watch, obviously using all his will power to keep from popping a can at 0530.

"How did it go for you yesterday?" I asked Finnen.

He looked up from the fridge.

"Boring as watching clover grow," he said. "My orders were to keep any busybodies from gettin' within ten meters of the tent without an invite. Nobody did."

"How was lunch?"

"Ahhh, Morgan," Finnen said, smiling. "Could ya be more oblique, matey? I've already heard how impressive you were with your looks and charm. The lasses are wet dreamin' about ya. Pinin' away, breathlessly awaiting another visit from yourself."

In the clandestine world, there was no way to keep secrets when it came to the battlefield of the sexes, even if it was platonic. While it was crucial to find out what the Taliban's next move might be to stay alive and plan accordingly, what most of the personnel on the base wanted to know was who was fucking who. Or about to. Or wanted to. Or even fantasized about. The base was probably filled with titters about the "dumbass spook" that got his "pecker in a ringer" in pursuit of "raghead pussy." That would be from the men. The women would be whispering, "Last night, there was this yummy spook who tried to put a move on the cute Afghan girl staying in that tent with the pink geraniums outside. She's so vulnerable. It was just adorable the way he tried to win her heart. He was soooo . . . sweet. Acted like Billy in the fifth grade, sweatin' and stammerin' and sayin' silly things. Did everything but bring a box of See's chocolates. I sure hope she gives the relationship a chance to grow and he's all for commitment. From what I hear, he didn't get close to first base." And all I was trying to do was be a big brother.

"By the by," Finnen said. "Did she give you a taste of the chocolates I bought for her?"

No beaming leprechaun smile from me.

"Just remember," I said. "She's vulnerable." I almost gagged on the word and knew it was a mistake as soon as it left my lips. The word I can't repeat is never used by assassins unless in reference to a target's position—rarely then, either. Too much baggage with the V-word, and Finnen would jump on it like a rusting beer can.

"It's about empowerment," Finnen said. "Giving her the freedom for self-actualization so she can discover a meaningful relationship without the boundaries of male dominance. Connecting with her inner goddess and redefining the self."

Washington slapped his thigh.

"Ain't heard none'a that shit since I was datin' Ms. Frigid," he said. "Like ta' talked me inta the grave 'fore she gave it up."

Dunne hadn't stopped his keyboarding.

"Fellas," he said. "Can we get down to business? You can get closure later."

My face was turning the color of Laqeesha's mom's fingernails.

"Yes," I said, glancing at Finnen. "Later."

"A little background on the day's operation," Dunne said. It would be the Cliff's Notes version. Dunne was a man of only few words when he typed. "The trans-Afghanistan pipeline is part of a broader geo-strategic program put in place by the United States in partnership with the petroleum and natural gas industries. The intent is to supply the West's need for oil and enhance the quality of life in the countries crossed by the pipeline. Helped by Saudi Prince Abdullah, first Unocal, together with a consortium of other multi-nationals, began talks with Afghan and Turkmenistan government officials and war lords. In 1995, the Unocal syndicate was granted the rights to build the line with the assistance of the current President of Afghanistan, Hamid Karzai, and the then-president Rabbani. Pre-1995, the United States had supported the Taliban in their war with the Russians. When that conflict ended, and the Taliban took control of Afghanistan, the contract with Unocal was no longer valid. But the goal remained and a new group, led by Amoco, later to be acquired by British Petroleum, resurfaced the project. Since Afghanistan was not recognized by the Clinton administration and the UN, negotiations stalled. With the election of President Bush, and our campaign against terrorism, the oil companies and governments feel the necessary protection provided by Coalition forces allows the beginning of the pipeline. For security reasons, the 1,780 kilometers of pipes will be buried three meters underground and cross Afghanistan and into the Baluchistan area of Pakistan. At the moment, an Argentinean company, Bridas, is spearheading the construction, through a new company called CentGas, with the covert help of US and British commercial interests and the protection of US military forces.

Most of the construction is being done by a division of a German company, Wintershall. They have a significant stake in the expense and profit."

Ten times more than I'd ever heard Dunne speak, even in other briefings or over a rare beer. He appeared exhausted and pushed away from the computer screen.

"What's that got to do with a plot to buy Afghan white from the Taliban?" Finnen asked. "Sounds like business as usual to me."

"I'm getting there," Dunne said. "I don't think you have much pressing in your daybook, Finnen. Just give me a second to check for messages." He moved forward to his laptop.

Finnen couldn't control himself. He reached for a Bud and snapped open the top, licking the bubbles from the sides. "Aaaahhh," he groaned. "Irish honey."

The smile had never left Washington's face. He was a newby in Spookville, getting a taste of the Earth-changing discussions that took place within the inner sanctum.

"Breakfast?" Washington asked, watching Finnen chug the beer.

"It's a staple of the Irish and spooks," Finnen said. "Beer will always have a place as its own essential food group in our diet. It feeds the demand for maudlin conversation and the singin' of 'Danny Boy.'" Finnen began to hum along to his own inner voice.

"At least I don't have a detail as critical as staring at a canvas tent on your dance card today, Finnen," Dunne said. "You'll be in the bag by noon."

"Well before that, if the sweet nectar has its way with me," Finnen said, opening another.

Thoughts of Finnen using his often-bragged-of magnetism on Khkulay made my skin itch with hate. I couldn't fathom why the skirts didn't terrorize him like they did me. His lilting voice and sonnets got him fumbling with panties quicker than I could unsheathe my Ka-Bar. He talked of female conquest like it came easier than shooting dogs. I couldn't let it happen with Khkulay. He was a player, and I hadn't even been drafted. Even if I had come to love Finnen as a brother, the way only comrades-in-arms in wartime did (something unspoken and never to leave my lips), Finnen and me were on opposing sides in this battle. I watched him throw an empty at the trash can.

"I love you like a brother, Finnen," I said. "Nobody, with the exception of maybe Washington, who's still on a yet-to-be-determined basis, would I rather have in a firefight beside me. But I don't want to hear later you stumbled into the women's barracks today after I leave. Khkulay needs time to adjust and rest. Not be dogged by an Irish drunk."

"Your fine words remind me of last night," Finnen said. "I was staggerin' to my bunk, blessed after many cans of Bud, and I felt somethin' runnin' down my leg. All I could think ta do was stop and pray ta the Lord. What I said to Himself was, 'Please, Lord, let it be blood.'"

Washington was enjoying the show. His belief system must have been in shambles. None of the rumored human sacrifices, spell-casting rituals, acts of bestiality, global intrigues, blood drinking, or extraordinary rendition were taking place. Nothing but the ramblings of a computer-obsessed spy, a slobbering drunk, and a star-crossed wannabe savior. We were human, not vampires, after all. He snickered.

"Y'all is certainly fucked up," he said. "Thought I needed to go the circus to see clowns. But it ain't been in town 'til now."

As though he hadn't heard a word, Dunne was recharged after his email fix and continued without missing a beat.

"Now we get to the murky part," Dunne said. "Much of what I said was summed up in the Michael Moore movie, *Fahrenheit 9/11*, as a conspiracy by President Bush, Hamid Karzai, the Taliban, Haliburton, and big oil to get the pipeline built with security supplied by the Coalition in case a local warlord isn't getting a big enough cut. Moore's theory has been debunked by numerous experts paid for by Republicans, and no Western oil company has claimed any interest in proceeding. Nonetheless, transports filled with steel piping are landing every day on a new runway built by Army engineers south of Qalat. Under the guise of 'road construction,' shovels and earth movers are digging a three-meter-deep trench that's already fifty klicks long. The pipe-laying crews are right behind. Not many journalists are visiting the area, except a recent feature article writer from the *Washington Post* who is now working in Missoula, Montana. And the one that got smoked by an RPG. The sector's been designated 'off limits' for being too dangerous for tourists. And Michael Moore. Of course, the Company is fully aware of the project."

He sat back and put his hands behind his head. "I'm trying to decipher how heroin fits in. It's no black op that I'm aware of." The blinking started again. "Could be way above my pay-grade level, but I don't think so. I can understand the logistics. Those transports deadheading to Germany have more than enough room for the whole year's poppy crop from the entire country. Lots of people would have to be getting paid off. It's giving me a headache. I think Morgan and Washington are my only aspirin. All the right passes are in the 6x6's glove box. I'll expect answers when you two get back," Dunne said, looking at me and then at Washington. "I'll do as much research as I can here without getting anyone suspicious, while Finnen can give me a hand if he doesn't drown himself in Bud. He's gonna be busy later."

We were his 0530. The next appointment was waiting. He sat up, shook out his hands, and started typing again.

"Take off," he said. "I've got work to do and people to see. Finnen, go get some chow."

Dismissed. The three of us walked out of the tent and headed in different directions. Before Finnen could get too far away, I said, "Remember what I said, Finnen. Give Khkulay some space."

Finnen continued on his way to the mess tent, looking over his shoulder.

"Been thinkin' about that," he said. "You're right. She needs to find her true path. Just get home safely, lad." He waved. "Cheers."

He couldn't have surprised me more if he spontaneously combusted.

The road to Qalat was the main north-south highway from Kabul to Kandahar, turning west, then north, and ending in Herat. We didn't want to travel through Kabul's traffic and hordes of watchers, so we used the only shortcut available that would connect us to pavement without being exposed in the country's capital. Driving out of the base just after daybreak, Washington steered us down the Valley of the Kunar on a surface that would be marked 4 Wheel Drive Only in the states, but a vast improvement over yesterday's trail into the foothills. On our left, the Khyber Pass to Pakistan through the Himalayas. On the right, the Hindu Kush.

Leaving the relative green of Jalalabad, we were soon in the tan of the valley, the vista broken by scrub trees, bushes, and piles of jagged stone. White-capped peaks towered on both sides across the uneven plains. Thirty kilometers southeast, and we would stop this back-crippling leg and be on asphalt.

Within a few klicks of Jalalabad, vehicles and people disappeared, leaving mostly goats and a few mud huts. Men seemed to be on the porch, smoking cigarettes at every hovel, not waving a greeting and glaring at us with chalky eyes. Jeeps and Army trucks passed occasionally in a veil of dust, soldiers unsmiling and staring at the sides of the road, trying to spot any hint of IEDs. A few burned out pickup hulks tried to sprout weeds, but there wasn't enough water beyond a few meters from the trickle in the river bed. It was another crackling-clear day in Afghanistan and, this low, it was easier to breathe. We were at five thousand feet and would soon drop below three thousand.

Washington concentrated on driving, after a while giving up swerving to avoid bumps. It was all one big pothole. He was reciting his continuous mantra of "fuckin' shit, man" every time a hole caused our backs to fuse with our heads. If we took our helmets off, we'd certainly leave brain matter on the roof of the cab. While Washington swore, I thought.

Too many intangibles. My usual brief was to follow orders and a defined operational plan. The variables were accounted for and alternatives available in case of a glitch. Or disaster. This mission almost felt rogue, believing it was only Dunne and Finnen who really knew what we were up to. No communiqués to Langley or Northern Alliance headquarters that I knew about. No request for more intel from CIA Southwest Asia analysts admitted to by Dunne. And certainly no chance this time to call in the Drones. We were flying bare, and our targets weren't Taliban.

Washington had described them as "white-bread civilians with no social skills" and that even Thorsten's feeble attempts at conversation had met with silence, making me believe they might be from the Firm. Or some other intelligence agency, foreign most likely. Special Ops for sure. Then there was the Taliban. But there was a puppet master in play with deep pockets and a long reach to organize something as delicate and complex as this operation. When there was hundreds of millions to be made, there were lots of possibilities, and the worst case was that it involved my employers. As Finnen would say, "Ahh laddy, it's all just melodrama. Ya can't take it serious."

It took nearly two hours to reach pavement. If it was Afghan Highway 1, there was no American point of reference. I'd been on better roads in the Kansas back country, and not ones requiring detours around camels, donkeys, and turbaned or veiled people clutching blankets on their heads stuffed with all their possessions. The military vehicles didn't stop for anything in Indian country, leading to lots of animal corpses alongside the road. The humans had been buried or hauled off by wailing women.

When the ride smoothed, I took off my helmet and stroked the bumps on my head.

"What do you think we're gettin' into?" I asked Washington. He set his helmet in the space between the seats next to our H & Ks.

"Don't rightly know, massuh," he said. "I's just the driver."

"Detonate that shit, Washington. You're a college graduate, and you never set foot in a ghetto. You played that card too many times. You're not gonna get any white man's guilt out of me."

"In terms of the geo-political ramifications of our highly secretive mission and the controlling assets directing our movements, it is difficult for me to object-i-fy. I can speculate, but that and two bucks won't get me a latte. All pays the same. And I ain't got nowheres to cash the check."

"If that means you're not gonna guess, try anyway. Where do you think the men in the SUVs came from? You saw them."

"As I said back in Gardez, when we was having such a friendly happy time, don't really know."

"Hypothesize."

"They wasn't wearin' those mirrored shades you spooks like. You know, just like the ones you got on now. They weren't talkin', so it was tough to hear any accent unless I could pick it up from hand signs and grunts. They were dressed in zipped-up black leather coats and jeans. It was chilly in the night. Easy to spot the pistols bulgin' under their arms. The license plates on the vehicles were Afghan, and I didn't see no reason to remember 'em. They were in good shape. Probably some kind of ex-Special Forces. But that wasn't a surprise. Real business-like. I figured them to be mercenaries." He paused and scratched his ear. "Funny, now that I think of it. Their shoes. Clunky black mothers. Almost like they had steel toes. Not even Company spooks would be sportin' things that ugly. My sense now, they were German. Kinda Doc Marten-ish, but with less style." He rubbed his chin. "That's all I gots."

Something had been niggling at me about the possibility of a German connection. Just because I was only a low E-grade assassin didn't mean I was a zombie. Dunne had helped plant the Kraut seed. We were trained to think and act, picking up signals from our environment and trusting our senses. There would be no way to know 'til tonight. But it was one of the first things I wanted clarified if I could somehow escape the Khkulay cloud and think with anything but the salvation hormone. I watched Washington's huge hands guide the steering wheel.

"Good stuff," I said. "I knew you could do it. Maybe you can join NYPD or CID when your tour's up."

"Sure," Washington said. "Arrest crack heads and crackers. Not my thing."

"Well, you look like a cop."

❧

Disguises of Company agents were wide-ranging, responding to whatever was demanded to blend. Could be a tuxedo or a turban. In Afghanistan, I might as well have enlisted in the Army. The only variation was a sometimes-beard, pajamas, vest, and head covering. Otherwise, fatigues. With my ability to say *sodar,* rather than *pig* when someone slighted me, a few days without shaving, and the boring off-white Afghan male dress code easily copied even without a Salvation Army nearby, I could pass for a local if no one got too inquisitive. The Taliban couldn't tell I was in the CIA. I looked like any of the other thousands of GIs fighting terrorism. It was only the American side that was rarely fooled.

Once, a few months ago and not long after my arrival on Afghan dirt, I was dispatched to Kabul. I'd put in a search on hotel.com. As was always the case, the message came up "No Rooms Available." Or in any city in Afghanistan. I could get a cot at the CIA Hilton. Kabul was a lower circle of hell. Polluted, noisy, and high enough in altitude, it was impossible to get a breath of clean air. It was all filthy. The smell was donkey and human shit, mixed with truck exhaust. It seemed like every other building was a victim of a mortar round or under construction, with the workers scrambling on wooden or bamboo scaffolding. The colors, when there were any, were the nancy pastels like the pictures of houses in the Caribbean. Pinks and mauves. Otherwise, a uniform brown. Too many children begging, often with stumps for hands or legs, balls of pus in the corners of their eyes. Suicidal motorcyclists dodged in and out of the perpetually stalled traffic, barely missing carts and trucks decorated in psychedelic drawings.

There was nothing exotic about Kabul, unless you liked the sight of men carrying semi-automatic rifles on the street like they were briefcases in Manhattan. For this earlier mission, I came into town from the base before curfew in an old Citroen cab, wearing man jammies, beard, and green fez, Hush Puppy hidden under my vest and Ka-Bar strapped to my thigh. Not much night life. Most of the stores had rolled up and locked their metal doors. A few cafes and tea rooms were open, and the streets were much quieter than when I had come through in daylight. I was supposed to kill a man who had given us false intel, resulting in an ambush costing five American lives.

The driver was a part-time employee of the Company, and he was to drop me in a quiet part of the city, a few blocks from the commercial streets. No lamp posts glowed, and only the moon would light the way. This was a city where the streets had no names. The fire trucks had to wait for the smoke to find the address with the flames. Turning out his headlights before he entered the neighborhood, the man left me at a designated spot near the Mullah Mamood Mosque. I knew the way from there. The taxi would be back in two hours.

Passing unnumbered wooden doors that fronted directly on the street, I stayed on the shadowed side. No pedestrians about for now and the only sound dogs barking. The line of mud-and-stucco walls was a continuous, pitted roughness when I touched the surface. Within minutes, I was in sight of the door I needed to breach, identified from pictures I'd been shown before I left the Kabul CIA compound. The man, Fahim Nabil, was not a suspect. He had supplied mostly useless intel up to the time he sent a patrol to die. For his day job, he ran one of the hundreds of shops that sold pirated video and audio cassettes, something the Taliban had been unable to stop again in Kabul, unlike most everywhere else in the country. Nabil was guilty.

At least he lived in a standalone house, not one of the many apartment buildings in the city—high-rise housing was tough, not knowing when someone would step out a hallway door—or in the surrounding hills, where the homes blended into the rocks like windowed boulders. Whatever Nabil did, his lifestyle took more to support than he could make selling illegally copied tapes.

Standing in the shadows, I had been approached by two men. There was nowhere to hide. If my costume wasn't Afghan enough, I'd have to shoot them. But I was dressed like the two making their way toward me and I hadn't washed these clothes since I'd been in Jalalabad. Any scent of underarm deodorant or cologne would expose me as a foreigner, too. No bother—I wasn't wearing any and couldn't remember the last time I had. There wasn't a spot closeby to hide the bodies. Murdering these two would be considered a glitch. They were probably already wondering what a lone man was doing lurking in the dark. They passed without even an "Allah Allah Akbar." Spoken late-night conversation could be deadly in Afghanistan.

There was a chance Nabil had been important enough to the Taliban or al-Qaeda to warrant guards, but my minders didn't think so, or I would have brought along backup. This way was simpler. I was an expert in silent entry. And just as quiet slipping out. The disguise would get me in. It was up to me what happened next. Afghan locks were not a challenge, and I had learned to scale walls even if there was razor wire or embedded glass on the top. I didn't need to jump. The door opened soundlessly with a few twists of a Home Depot credit card.

The biggest challenges were finding the targets. No map of the bedroom assignments. And the dogs. They didn't care about disguises or even my scent. There would never be a time in Afghanistan when I was someone the dogs recognized by sight or smell, so the costume wasn't for them. I had already tossed a ball of hamburger laced with tranqs over the wall, keeping my oath I wasn't gonna kill any more canines. I had waited a few minutes 'til the whimpering stopped. If the hounds weren't sleeping, the Company nerds had produced an aerosol spray that, when inhaled, led to a restful nap. Better than the Hush Puppy—that was only a last resort. I had a container of the spray disguised as a lighter in my pocket. The spook techno-wizards called it Doggy Get Down, DGD for short.

Inside the dirt courtyard, the dog lay on his side next to a rattan bench, breathing rhythmically. Nothing much around but a few flower pots without flowers. The usual concrete fountain sans water in the middle of the space. Internal porch roofs around the sides, shading doors, and a tiled walkway. A couple windows looking into the courtyard. What I most focused on was identifying anything moving, which seemed to be only the dog's ribs.

A sound. Snoring. Not the dog, it was coming from a small, dark alcove in the far corner. I edged my way along the wall in the darkness toward whomever or whatever was making the noise. A man, AK-47 on his lap, sitting on a folding chair, asleep. The wheezing was rough, as if he had phlegm in his throat. I could have been dressed for a hectic trading session on Wall Street in my Brooks Brothers and bathed in Dior fragrance, and he wouldn't have known. A relatively short beard rested on his chest, and his turban was crooked. No sandals. He was barefooted and was surely mixed up with Nabil—definitely not a professional in the sense of being a member of a highly trained security outfit. If so, he wouldn't be asleep, and I would be dead. No innocent, but undeserving of execution tonight.

Slowly, I moved behind him. No need for the DGD. I used pressure at the base of the man's neck where it met his right shoulder. Squeezing hard with my hand in just the right spot, he wouldn't wake up before I was out in the street again. I grabbed the AK before he fell over and his rifle could clatter to the tile in the alcove. After emptying the ammunition, I put the rifle deeper into the recess and the bullet clip into my pocket.

I saw a door was at the end of the niche. The man was probably in this spot to protect this way in and to stay hidden in the shadows, and he had most likely depended on the dog to sound an intruder alert. I went to the door; the handle was curlicued wrought iron, and I softly pushed down on the lever and slid inside, leaving the door partly open.

The smell of tea and curry—common smells in Afghan living quarters. No lights or candles. Shapes hanging on the walls. Chairs in each corner and a mirror reflecting what little moonlight penetrated the dimness from the curtained window. I didn't need to check the knot on my tie; I didn't own one, and there was no one to impress or fool. A low table holding cups and glasses. Rugs on the floor and two people sleeping on big pillows. I moved to the gently breathing bodies. One was bigger than the other and had a beard. Nabil. Beside him, it was either a boy or a woman. Much smaller and no beard. The task now was to kill Nabil with as little disturbance as possible to the target's sleep mate. Even a silenced bullet makes enough of a *phuppp* sound to waken someone cuddled beside the condemned.

I had bent down, Hush Puppy in one hand. The tip of the barrel was an inch away from Nabil's head and aimed between his eyes with a slight upward angle so the subsonic hollow-point .22 round would bounce around in his brain and scrub it clean. The other hand was poised over Nabil's partner's mouth. No movement beyond breathing. I pulled the trigger on the Hush Puppy. Nabil's head bounced on the pillow, and I clamped down hard on the innocent's lips. No blood spurt. No thrashing. No protest. Beside Nabil, the young boy's eyes snapped open, and he tried to sit up. I pushed him back down and showed him the silenced pistol, shaking my head back and forth and gently hissing *ssshhh* for him to stay quiet. No telling if there were more guards about or others sleeping in different rooms. The boy strained to turn his head toward Nabil. I didn't let him. He jerked, kicked his legs, tried to get up. I applied more pressure to his face and put a knee on his thigh. "No *zharra*," I whispered. No crying. I wanted to calm him without shooting. The boy settled and stared. I took my hand off his mouth and used the sleeper hold that had carried the guard to dream land. In minutes, I was down the street, waiting for the taxi.

The Afghan costume hadn't mattered with the guard, Nabil, and the boy. Without it, I would have had to abort or grease two pedestrians. It didn't really take a master of disguise to fool anyone here, in a land united in its sameness; it only took the willingness to wear man jammies and smell like a homeless man living under a Manhattan bridge.

The documents Dunne provided got us through two Coalition checkpoints with only a few shakes of the head and "fuckin' spook" comments. Just beyond the second barricade, Humvees blocked the road. Beside the trucks, five Deltas were watching a Toyota pickup burn while scanning the flat horizon. We were on an open plain, and there was little place for snipers to hide. Still, the Rangers were grouped so the entire field of vision was covered.

The truck was overturned, black smoke funneling from the tires. Orange flames waved in the firestorm and crackled like crushing tin foil. An occasional *pop* as something overheated and exploded from the pressure. The smell of a barbecue. Washington stopped the 6x6, unable to cross the ditches on each side of the road. We dismounted and walked closer to the scene.

"What happened?" Washington asked the first soldier we approached.

The shredded bodies of two men lay in the dirt several yards apart, surrounded by the Rangers. Smoke drifted from the part of the carcasses still intact. One man was missing most of his head, and the other had no arms. No turbans. No hair, even. Skulls and no eyebrows. Blackened blood sizzled on burnt skin like bubbling Vaseline turned the color of simmering charcoal.

"Tried a detour," the first soldier said with only a glance at us then focused back on the bodies. "Wasted 'em with an XM25 grenade launcher. Nowhere ta run, nowhere ta hide."

The soldier was just a boy. Younger than me and not long out of high school. He was slender and tall. Green eyes that danced in the reflection of the flames and a pimple on his cheek that needed to be squeezed. His camouflaged helmet was tight enough on his head that it looked like it was super-glued on.

"You got any marshmallows?" another soldier asked. This one was about the same age, but stockier. Grease streaked his camo pants as if he'd been crawling under a Humvee. He poked the barrel of his H & K at the body below him, prodding it gently, like he was rearranging ashes.

"Raghead rag-oo," the Ranger beside him said.

"Muj mush." And the chorus began, while we all looked down at the burning remains.

"Taliban tar-tar."

"Hadji burger."

"Mohammed mayonnaise."

"Al-Qaeda quesadilla."

"Bin Laden bagel."

"Turban toasties."

"Pashto pasta."

"Abdul Alfredo," Washington chimed in.

"Enough," a soldier who must have been their lieutenant said. He was the oldest, but not the most hardened looking. "Bag 'em and tag 'em."

"What do we write on the tags. sir?" the pimpled one asked. "S'mores? Crispy critters?" He pointed to one of the dead hadji's bare feet. "And they ain't got no toes left to attach the tags on. I'm afraid if we try ta pin 'em to their chests, their lungs'll cave in like a burnt chicken's. No flesh left worth pokin'."

"Just toss 'em in the bags," the lieutenant said. "It'll get sorted later." He turned away and walked back to the Humvees.

The Rangers continued to stare down.

"Broiled bad guys."

"Grilled gomers."

"Fire-roasted Fedayeen."

"Porkless barbecue."

"Jelly donuts."

"I said stow that shit," the lieutenant said over his shoulder. "Move out. Now."

The Rangers dispersed, turning their heads away from the still-smoldering bodies. One headed to the Humvees, I presumed, to fetch the body bags.

Washington and I went to the 6x6 and waited for them to clear the road. Inside the truck, I took off my helmet and tried to wipe the smoke from bloodshot eyes.

"Do you think any one of those Rangers except the lieutenant was older than twenty?" I asked.

"Maybe in dog years," Washington said. "In terms of experience, they were old ones." He stared straight ahead, a frown on his face. No more jokes.

"The lieutenant didn't look any older than you or me," I said.

"Probably a fresh cherry outta West Point. Had that stick-up-your-ass disease."

Men in suits and gray hair sending boys, and now girls, out to die. Kids who hadn't seen much worse than a skinned knee from a bicycle accident watching while jelly-covered bodies disintegrated before their eyes. Buddies sent home legless from IEDs. Teenage medics crawling toward injured soldiers, holding intestines from falling out with their hands. The screams of wounded squad members pinned down by a sniper, helpless while they listened to someone they knew—a friend—slowly bleed to death in loud agony. The litany of monstrosities never seemed to slow. Boys and girls from cities and farms who were growing up on the horror, while the puppet masters called the cadence.

In 'Nam, the anthem was "don't mean nuthin'." The phrase wasn't used much in the rock pile, though. It was not up to date and didn't capture the nuance of fighting terrorism—9/11 meant something to us. Chasing VC into tunnels didn't, nor did the Domino Theory or Henry Kissinger's lies. 'Nam vets used the words as a catch all, like when they witnessed a medic jam a fountain pen into a buddy's neck to open a breathing channel from a sucking chest wound. There wasn't much else to say to contain the insanity. What the 'Nam grunts really were trying to convey by saying "don't mean nuthin'" was this: "It means everything. But I can't express it in words that make any sense of the situation or describe the true horror." Today, it was just a different place. But the story stayed the same.

In both cases, we were eating the young. I was older than the Rangers at the cookout. And Washington. I cared, as did they, about protecting the nation and the world from radical Islam and suicide bombers. But . . . none of us knew if we were really doing that. Or if the CIA really did rule the world.

Sometimes it felt like a video game and we had reached the deadly final level. There was no reason to doubt the commitment and patriotism of the Rangers or any other soldier in Afghanistan. No draft had forced them here. Still, I wondered if there were enough psychiatrists to treat soldiers who got their last growth spurt amid the blood and carnage of Afghanistan.

Moving south again on Afghan Highway 1, Washington remained silent. We were losing altitude, and the plains were expanding, the mountains distant on both sides and lost in the haze. Even less to view here except camels carrying bundles of wood and the occasional Afghan or US Army patrol. We passed through a few small villages, not much more than mud huts, chickens, dogs, and Coca Cola signs. The river was long past, and the background was nearly a total brown.

The truck held MREs and bottles of Dasani water. Neither of us had eaten. I opened a water and offered it to Washington.

"You've been awfully quiet," I said. "Would you like to talk? Share your innermost feelings?"

"No," Washington said. "And I'm not feelin' vulnerable either."

"Okay," I said. "But if you change your mind, I'm here for you."

"Dolly Parton?"

"Wynona, I think."

"Speakin' a Dolly. Did you hear she was havin' back problems and had to cancel a few concerts? When she was asked about it, she said, pointin' to her chest, 'You'd have a back ache too if you had to carry around these puppies all day.' Fine woman she is."

"No, I didn't hear that. I was thinkin' more about that wienie roast we witnessed. How those boys could look at all that seared flesh and sleep at night."

Washington sat straighter in his seat and finished the water, handing the empty back to me.

"Once, in the Korengal, my squad was sent out to a village to deliver food supplies to a house that had become kind of an orphanage. At least that was what we were told. Before, every time we passed, doin' our hearts and minds thing, little girls would look out the windows and door. Not wave. Not smile. Just stare. Too many for even a Catholic family. I asked around and they said one a the warlords, Ahmad Shah, the dude who controlled the place, had set it up for girls who had their families wiped out by the fightin'. Some a the money we were handin' out was supposedly helpin' feed them."

He clenched both hands on the steering wheel hard enough for me to see the veins on his wrists become black worms.

"We came in slow and unannounced. There'd been an ambush the day before a klick up the mountain. When we got there and went inside, two hadjis ran out the back door. We had a 'no fire' order in effect, so we couldn't shoot 'em. Wish we would'a." He shook his head. "Shit."

Washington's eyes went down, and he closed them for a second before he looked back to the pavement. "The girls were naked and lined up against the wall. Not one of 'em could'a been over twelve, the marryin' age in those parts. Two a the girls, neither of 'em older than eight, were on their backs on a filthy rug in the corner. Both were bleedin' from their hairless privates and had fresh bruises on their faces and chests. We called for a medic and gave 'em the shirts off our backs to cover up."

He spit out the window and then turned his face forward to the road.

"Most of my men couldn't stay inside. After the first few minutes, Withers, a young grunt from Arkansas, said, 'Looks like the hadjis got loose in the chicken coop.' I hit him in the jaw with the butt of my H & K and knocked him clean out the door."

He wiped his forehead with his sleeve and sighed.

"Ya' know, Morgan, Withers was one a my best men. Fearless, even the few times we were pinned down. Always carried hard candy in his pocket to give to the kids. Helped old hajib'ed women with their loads. Even worked with some of 'em plantin' a rock flower garden. He didn't mean nuthin'. He was hurtin' bad and just trying ta cope with it all, like the rest of us. I was too angry at the time. Wanted to hit someone, and I thought Withers gave me the excuse. We all get carried away by words. They're just words, not what's in your heart." Washington blinked twice rapidly and then closed his eyes again for a few seconds. "Withers got killed by a sniper couple'a weeks later. First one shot in the ambush. Only two of us made it."

Nothing to say. I was quiet and didn't do anything stupid like pat him soothingly on the thigh. I'd asked for it, and now I had another atrocity story to file away for the darkness.

Silence again. I decided to pass the time by mentally drafting another message to Mom.

Hi, Mom. Only have a few minutes. Your last email sounded like everyone was doing well. That's great. Here, still stuck in my calculator. I even see numbers in my dreams. Funny how the number two has been in the picture so often recently. I've been kind of self-absorbed lately so yesterday I visited an orphanage for Afghan war victims who've been shipped over here for rehabilitation. Made friends with two of the cutest little girls. They're both around eight and still don't smile much. I can't get them off my mind. I hope it's better for them in America. The only weird thing was the two Afghan men who were talking to the girls when I got there. They literally ran out like there was a fox in the hen house or a fire. Strange. Well, gotta get back to work. Two important projects to finish. Give my love to everyone.

⚜

The sun was dropping behind the southernmost part of the Hindu Kush. We were within a few klicks of Qalat, around one hundred miles northeast of Kandahar, close to the rendezvous point. C-130J transport planes rumbled overhead, dropping to the airbase from the flights out of Kabul to the north or circling to unload steel and construction supplies for the pipeline from Europe. Busy time just before dark, when flying became much more dangerous. In flat terrain, the night offered more places to hide with one of the remaining CIA-supplied Strela 2 surface-to-air rockets or the Stingers used to shoot down the Russian Hind helicopter gunships, weapons that had almost defeated the Afghans by themselves in the 1980s.

Since we were on the main north-south thoroughfare in Afghanistan, the highway had been comparatively safe, and we had passed our last Coalition checkpoint a half-hour ago. Safety didn't mean Washington hadn't taken note of any object or broken down pickup on the side of the road. We were in a country where the IED technology perfected in Iran and field trialed in Iraq was used more frequently. The new shape-charged copper filled IEDs could penetrate a tank like a surgeon's scalpel on flesh. No need for the old ball-bearing type, the latest technology provided a more focused stream of armor-piercing hot metal, able to break through the strongest layers of steel. Bodies were a barrier as meaningless as the wind.

Washington pulled the 6x6 over and applied the parking brake, leaving the diesel engine rattling.

"Need ta piss," he said. "And we got a few hours to wait. Made good time."

I opened my door and followed him ditchside.

"We can't hang around here too long," Washington said, shaking himself dry. "A lone 6x6'll draw attention from hadji eyes we can't see."

Beside him, but trying not to glance and confirm Washington's whiteman's paranoia, I zipped up my camos.

Just over a small rise in the dirt, the burnt-out, blackened hulk of a truck was growing rocks. Washington nodded toward it.

"That's what's left of the *Wall Street Journal* reporter out here to investigate the new construction," Washington said. "Somebody hit his truck with an RPG. Thorsten knew about it and laughed. We stopped in the same spot last time. Thorsten said it served the guy right for interfering with America's dependency on oil. Didn't believe that cracker could use words with more than two syllables, but he might'a been right."

"Not many hostiles out here," I said. It had all the signs of a search-and-destroy mission with a specific target. Like anyone on the scent of the truth.

"Let's get closer to the pipeline," I said. "The warlords've probably made it a 'no fire' zone. Don't want to threaten their income."

"There's a turn-off a few klicks away," Washington said. "I'll head to it, and we can park on the new road they punched in for construction. The rendezvous point isn't far from there."

"You know how things'll go down better than me," I said. "Any new insights?"

Washington went around the ram guard to his side of the truck, and I got in the passenger seat.

"Now that the main objective is intel," Washington said, taking off the parking brake, "I'll follow your lead in the gathering end. My course on torture wasn't nearly as long as yours, and I don't have the hands-on experience. We just gotta make sure there's no watchers and no screamin'. I'd hate to wake up the snakes."

"Remember, I'm just the slave. You're the boss man. We'll make the play on your signal."

"Keep that Hush Puppy oiled. Thanks for lendin' me one. Don't wanna use the H & Ks. Too messy. I'm feelin' like a real spook now. No dog's safe around me."

🐾

At the dirt road junction, we turned east. By now, the stars and a rising moon were the only illumination other than the truck's headlights. We parked and I broke out the MREs. Washington liked the beef jerky, and I preferred the lasagna and apple sauce. We both were sure to eat the "specially designed for the military" power bars. It was going to be a long night, and we would need the energy. Just in case, I handed Washington a couple of the white pills Dunne made sure I carried every time I went out on a scavenger hunt. We chewed the caffeine-laced gum from the MREs after washing down the Dexedrine with Dasani. Finished, our eyes were open wide enough that the dim light was almost painful. Fully chemically activated, there was no way either of us would be able to take a nap.

Sitting back in the 6x6 seat, trying not to jiggle too much, I thought about what Dunne had told us in the context of what I already knew. On a trip to Washington, DC, Hamid Karzai had been quoted recently as saying, "The rules are simple. Just come in and look for oil, and then we'll see what we can do for you." No doubt Karzai was in bed with the cartels and the US government. That meant the Company, even with Dunne's denials and nervous tic. Exploiting land and people for oil was nothing new to the conglomerates, and they had always had allies in the White House and Pentagon under the guise of "national interest." It was the drug part and my involvement that was puzzling.

The Company had shown its skills as a major player in the export of both cocaine and smack. None of my instructors at Langley had bothered to deny the history, sidestepping the issue with the old and tired "operational goals were achieved in order to advance and protect national security" line.

From the early days in Southeast Asia, the CIA had flown opium in its own planes operated by Tiger and Evergreen Airlines, helping to make the Burmese General, Khun Sa, one of the world's richest men from his roost in the Golden Triangle. The excuse was eliciting the support of the Hmong and other hill tribes in the fight against North Vietnam through trade of their main money crop, opium. In Nicaragua, the justification was propping up the Contra rebels and overthrowing the government of its neighboring country, El Salvador, while the cocaine imported through Oliver North and his cronies became the basis for the crack epidemic still raging in the streets of America. Columbian narco-trafficers were protected to strengthen US mineral and oil rights in that South American country, even to the extent of shielding Pablo Escobar from capture until his behavior became too much of a media burden.

Now, Afghanistan. Old generalities and stories that everybody knew and the Company called scurrilous lies. Their truth wasn't the concern—if the Firm was involved, why did Dunne let Washington, Finnen, and I continue to breathe? Dunne was either out of the "need to know" circle, had a conscience, or was in it up to his sparkling blue eyes. Or . . . the CIA wasn't involved, and he was carefully trying to find out who the real bad guys were without raising the alert level to red in Langley. Maybe get a major promotion and a leather chair outside of the rock pile if he reported back with a resolution.

It was nearing midnight, and we could have another piece of the puzzle solved in a few minutes if everything went according to plan.

D esolation. The moon was higher and provided us with a view across the empty dirt plain. The only relief was the outline of the high mountains to the east and west and a few masses of sandstone. It was somewhat like the flat landscape of the Kansas cornfields minus the corn. No people or huts, but there was evidence of a major digging project. The road we were parked on came into existence only to help in building the pipeline. The camels and goats didn't need it. Beside the 6x6, a pump station surrounded by a chain link fence had been erected. No sign of the buried pipes other than a wide disturbance in the soil. The smell of motor oil, lubricant, and grease still lingered in the air. Washington and I stood next to the truck, no firearms visible.

Five minutes after our arrival and right on time, two sets of headlights appeared on the western horizon, the direction of the air strip outside Qalat. Beams bounced up and down from the ruts in the dirt. Dust separated the two vehicles. Washington and I were silent, and I assumed both of us were trying to anticipate surprises. The men in the SUVs would be highly trained and most likely had killed. And would be willing to do so again.

They parked with the rear ends of the Ford Expedition SUVs pointed to the back of the 6x6. All the seats, other than the driver's, had been removed, including the passenger-side front. I still wasn't sure that all the ammo cans would fit inside. Two men got out, the overhead cab lights disconnected and dark. They were dressed exactly as Washington had described. Black coats, shirts, pants, and ugly thick shoes. No handshakes. No greetings. They went directly to the back of the 6x6 and threw open the flap above the tailgate.

"How ya'all doin'?" Washington asked.

No response.

"Well, I'm just fine, if I do say so myself," Washington said as they walked by without acknowledgment of any kind.

The two men went to the SUVs and reached to open the doors at the rear. A nod from Washington, and, a second later, we were poking our Hush Puppies against their spines. "What you got in here?" Washington asked, patting the side of the man in front of him and taking out a Sig Sauer P226 pistol from underneath the man's coat. I did the same with my captive.

"On your ass, kraut," Washington said, making an assumption. He pulled the man back and tripped him at the same time, following him to the ground with the barrel of the Hush Puppy, never losing contact with the .22 and the man's body. It was all orchestrated. I did the same within a heartbeat. Now, we were both crouched above our prey with Hush Puppies pressed to their temples.

The pattern was the same. Get their attention first, and show it was serious merciless drama. Before the man below me could try some Special Forces escape trick, I lifted the pistol and shot him in the knee, immediately bringing the barrel back to his face and standing up. The man started to reach for his wounded leg, and I shouted, "No! Don't move!" He lay back down and started to groan, eyes closed.

"Harsh," Washington said. While the man below him watched his partner writhe in anguish like a wounded twin, Washington followed my lead.

After patting down the man underneath him, Washington walked over and stood beside me. I had already frisked mine. No additional guns or knives.

"So far, a good night's work, my man," Washington said. "Let's skin 'em while they're still alive and then smother 'em with their own pelts. Just like we did the last ones. That was pure joy."

It was probable at least one of the men spoke English. Violence was its own language, but we needed to ask questions and get reliable answers before we killed them. That was the verdict. They were dead men, but we wanted to give them hope. On our side, it helped that these two were most likely mercenaries. There was no country but greed for them to defend. No wife and children to shield. No conscience. Nothing to betray.

I kicked the closest man in the bleeding knee. He jumped but didn't howl—only a curse and tightening of lips.

"Okay, Adolph," I said, "you've got one slim chance. You tell us who you're working for, and we'll let you limp home to Berlin. Don't act like you don't understand. I heard you say 'shit,' not 'scheise.'" I kicked him again in the same spot. "You can start now by giving me your name."

The man was planning his strategy. With a crippled knee, he would be sure it was impossible to get up and take the pistols from our hands. The real question was how much he could get away with not telling us and still get back to the beer garden. I had been in the game too often. Washington was learning.

I waited a few seconds and shot him in the other knee. It would be counterproductive to let him analyze too long. Once he started talking, I knew it was an open faucet.

"Cruel," Washington said. He shot the other man in the knee.

"I hope you missed an artery," I said. "A few inches off and these two will bleed to death before we get the information we need."

"I'll have you know I took first place at sniper school," Washington said. "Weren't no man—white, black, brown, or yellow—who was more accurate." He raised his pistol and shot the man in the toe of his ugly shoe. "If ya'all wants ta check it out, you'll find he's missin' his little pinky."

"Klaus," one man grunted.

Washington looked at me and nodded.

We weren't psychopaths. It was all part of the movie. These two had to understand it wasn't a comedy and believe we were bloodthirsty, pitiless madmen. Americans.

"Pleasure to meet ya, Klaus," I said. "No use lyin'. My name's Morgan, and this joker beside me is Washington. Hope that little taste of truthfulness sets a good precedent for the proceedings." I kicked him again in the wound. "Now who sent you out here in the middle of the night to pick up millions of dollars worth of smack?"

Scheise. He was still thinking. At this rate, we'd have to whittle them down to talking heads.

Washington was the good guy.

"Joker?" he asked. "Reminds me, did you hear about Hitler's new microwave? It seats five hundred."

Klaus groaned, and I didn't think it was about the lame joke.

"Wintershall," Klaus said.

If it was German, of course, it would be. Wintershall had signed an oil-extraction and oil-export agreement with the Turkmenistan President. That Southwest Asian country was the source of much of the oil that would be flowing through the pipeline, and Wintershall was the major funding source. Wintershall was the largest oil company in Germany and one of the biggest in the world, its roots beginning about the time of the rise of the Nazis. At least some of Dunne's intel was real.

"Who do you report to at Wintershall?"

"We are in security. We do what we are told."

"Who gives the orders? I need a name."

"Heinrich Schultz. He is the head of security."

"And Schultz reports to the Wintershall President."

"Of course."

"Who trained you?"

"KSK."

"Kommando Spezialkräefte," Washington said. "The German Special Forces commandos. Very elite group of krauts. Met some at Camp Perry. Tough as year-old bratwurst." He smiled down at Klaus. "Not as tough as Rangers, now, wouldn't ya say, Klaus?"

"What do you do with the dope?" I asked.

"Take it to the plane and load it," Klaus said.

"Okay. Where does this plane depart and arrive?"

"The pipeline air field. About twenty klicks west of here."

"And it goes to?"

"Frankfurt."

Some good news. It wasn't Ramstein. Less of a chance of US military collusion. At least at that end. Someone was still sending Washington emails and pulling strings to allow him to deliver money and dope from inside a base in a warzone. Something not easy to arrange or disguise.

"When the heroin gets to Frankfurt," I said, "where do you take it?"

"Kassel. About one hundred kilometers north. It is the head office of Wintershall."

"And you deliver the dope to Schultz."

"No. We take it to a warehouse, and it is left there. I don't know what happens next. I don't know the men who receive the heroin. We use a Wintershall van. That is the end of our duties."

"Do you bring money with you when you come back?"

"Yes."

"Who gives it to you?"

"Are you going to kill us?"

"Yet to be determined. If you keep answering, you might get to see your Fräulein again. If not, the vultures will, be peckin' at you by daybreak."

Klaus turned to the man beside him who was groaning and muttering.

"What's his name?" I asked.

"Werner," Klaus said.

"Since you're doin' all the talkin', we'll shoot Werner first. Or use a Ka-Bar on his balls." I took my Ka-Bar from the sheath at my thigh and exposed the blade to the moon rays, holding the knife close to Washington's face. "I think Kathy here is gettin' hungry. Needs a taste of sauerkraut. What do you think, Washington?"

"She's been fasting," Washington said. "It's been a day or two since she last castrated anyone. She's gotta be jonesin' for nutsack."

Insane. Klaus had to confirm for himself his wavering opinion that we were two wack-job soldiers out for a night of zany murder and mayhem. I sensed he was beginning to digress. I couldn't let him before he went into shock. I bent down and put the tip of the Ka-Bar on his pant-covered dick.

"I repeat," I said, "who gives you the money?"

Klaus tried to turn away. Pressure from the knife on his crotch wouldn't let him.

"Herr Schultz," he said.

"How does it get to Gardez?"

"I don't know. Our responsibility is only to bring it to Qalat."

"And then you, what, just leave it lyin' around? Who do you deliver it to?"

Klaus went on the babble, telling us how he would guard the money until an unnamed American soldier made the pick-up, using different passwords, claiming no recognition of the grunt or where the money went. Usually, it would be divided, and different men, one American and one Afghan, would do the fetching. After releasing the cash, Klaus and Werner returned to Kassel and resumed their normal leg-breaking duties until it was time to meet Washington or whoever made the heroin drop on the next visit. There had been several other dope drivers besides Washington, and Klaus didn't know names or what happened to them. Klaus and Werner were "couriers only," he said.

"You had no idea why the men who brought the heroin were changed?"

"No."

"But they were always US soldiers?"

"Yes."

"You didn't kill them, did you Klaus? Take the dope and destroy the trucks? Make it look like another successful Taliban hunting party?"

In the last few klicks before we got to the pumping station, we had seen the burnt-out shells of three trucks. Nothing remarkable here, where they grew like the occasional mulberry tree and AAA wasn't around to tow them to the garage.

Klaus hesitated. Confessing to being players in an international drug cartel was bad but not nearly as evil and dangerous as admitting murder of US soldiers while two of their countrymen and brothers listened. I pulled the trigger on the Hush Puppy, and the bullet passed close enough to his head that he surely felt the breeze and the chunks of dirt that zapped into the side of his skull.

"Yes. We were ordered to kill them after the second delivery."

"And you never heard a single name or saw any on uniforms?"

"*Nein.*"

Beside me, Washington had been scuffing his boot on the ground as if he was getting impatient. And angry.

"This is *scheiße*," Washington said. Bullshit. "They're just good Nazis who fly in with millions of dollars in cash and fly back with a ton of dope after executing US military personnel. And zay know nuzzing." He squatted and put the tip of his Hush Puppy on the end of Klaus's nose. "*Gib mir einen Namen oder ich schiesse Ihre Nase.*" Give me a name or I will shoot off your nose.

"*Ich habe noch nie jemand gesehen. Ich habe nie gehört, keine Namen,*" Klaus said. I never met anyone. I never heard any names.

The Hush Puppy made its patented *phuuppp* sound. Klaus tried to grab what was left of his nose, and Washington pushed his arm down.

"Abernathy," Klaus said, before blood filled his mouth. He began to spit so he could breathe. Gasping for air, he said "*Er kam, um uns zu sehen.*" He came to see us.

This was too important. I kicked him in the wounded knee for the third time and let him splutter.

"English, Klaus," I said. "We're in Afghanistan." Washington hadn't told me he spoke German. I wanted to follow along with the plot, too, and continued to marvel at Washington's depth.

Klaus was losing it fast. Blood was flowing freely from the stump of his nose into his mouth. I used the sleeve of my camo to wipe his lips.

"Speak to me, Klaus," I said.

His eyes were closed and jaws open wide. He was wheezing.

"Abernathy was talking to us. Another man, a sergeant, came into the hangar and said 'Captain Abernathy, sir. The convoy is leaving.' Abernathy was very upset." All of this was mumbled slowly and between Klaus's gasps. "Abernathy said, 'Forget what you heard' to us and left. He had already told us the money would be transferred the next day instead of that day. We were to use the same password. 'Discotheque.'" He looked at Washington for the first time. "Do not kill me. *Bitte.*"

"Okay," I said. "You've cooperated. Only a few more easy questions. Did you know what you were buying?"

"*Ja,*" Klaus said. "Heroin."

"And you knew you were buying it from the Taliban?"

"*Ja.*"

"And they were using the money to buy arms to kill Coalition forces, including your KSP brothers?"

Klaus paused. He looked away.

"*Ja.*"

"And the heroin you delivered, you had to know it was going into the arms of junkies all over the world, probably a lot in Deutschland."

"It wasn't what I wanted. I was only taking orders."

"Did you ever see any other Americans around who might have been involved?"

"Once, a few months ago, a man in civilian clothes watched us unload the truck. I didn't know who he was and told him to leave. He just smiled and walked away."

"No name?"

"*Nein.*"

"What did he look like?"

"Older. In shape. Blue eyes and good teeth."

A sigh from Washington. In the dark plain, it was easy to see for miles. Headlights appeared in the south from a place where no road was supposed to exist. The bouncing of the beams told us it probably didn't. The vehicle wouldn't be close for at least a half-hour. Washington and I looked at each other and nodded. He shot Klaus. I shot Werner. Both in the head.

Quickly, we arranged the Germans' bodies in the front seats of the SUVs. I took the RPG out of the back, and Washington pulled the 6x6 about twenty-five meters away. I aimed at a fuel tank, and the SUVs went up in one fireball and a very loud *boom!*

Within seconds, I was in the 6x6, and we were driving back toward the highway with our headlights off. The tail lights had been smashed out with the butt of the RPG, and it was easy to follow the dirt road in the moonbeams. We were on our way back to Jalalabad with a truck bearing fifty ammo cans filled with sand. Finnen had made the switch during the night, and I had no idea where the heroin was now but was confident it wasn't ever going into anyone's vein unless the CIA gained an advantage.

Nothing much to say until we reached the pavement. The trip out seemed smoother than the way in. Washington had no trouble staying on the dirt track. I assumed both of us were processing what we had just done. And what we had learned.

There was no traffic on the highway. The moon was lower and no longer blocked the stars with its brightness. This high, the galaxies were easy to distinguish in the blackness. Rocks and dirt made up the view—no cityscapes or passing lanes to interrupt the unlined road. Carcasses of torched vehicles were the only dots on the horizon, along with sporadic abandoned huts. The night air was clean and smelled of dirt. Beginning to climb as we drove north, breathing would become increasingly difficult, having adjusted to the lower elevation of the kill zone. Our eyes were as wide open as the tops of Bud cans. We were nowhere near the end of the Dexedrine high, not even starting to come down. Little in the way of conversation other than the passing of water bottles. I fidgeted and tried to focus on anything that might be hiding a roadside bomb.

"Did you believe Klaus?" I asked Washington.

Washington didn't take his eyes off the pavement—just shook his head up and down.

"Nothing to be gained from lying," he said. "I don't think he was protectin' the Rise of the Third Reich."

"I know you were only at Gardez for a few wake-ups, but ever heard of Abernathy?"

"I've been thinkin' that over. There was talk of a Captain who was losin' more men than anyone else. The grunts nicknamed him Captain Auschwitz. If you went out, you didn't return. I think it was Abernathy." Washington shook his right hand and put it on his thigh, steering with the fingers of his left. "There was some vague link with Kabul and the Afghan National Army. Captain Auschwitz was said to have spent time there training officers before he was deployed to Gardez. Liaisoned with Generals Khan and Dostum. The more I think about it, the more sure I am Abernathy is Captain Auschwitz. Never met the man, but his name was whispered. You know, in case you might get sent to his squad and fall victim to the spell. Nobody wanted the duty or to bring on attention from the evil spirits. Kinda like with spooks."

Better to be talking than lost in my own ugly fantasies. I moved the Hush Puppy at my waist an inch. It was jabbing me in the side.

"I heard you sigh when Klaus described the mystery man," I said. "What was that about?"

"You know the reputation of spooks," Washington said. "If it don't smell fishy, it's not them. The complexities escape ordinary grunts like me. But it sure seemed like he was talkin' about Dunne. If you were gonna describe him, what would be the first things you'd say?"

"Exactly what Klaus did. There're lots of other men here who fit the bill, but not many running around in civvies who'd have access to the pipeline hangars."

"So, what do ya think it means?"

"Could be we're gonna have to find out. We'll have to watch our backs if the Company is conducting the symphony. I always thought it was a possibility and Dunne is only playing dumb. Wouldn't be the first time assets were sent to the field with misinformation. I can't grasp what is to be gained from selling dope so the Taliban can buy guns. And having Klaus and Werner execute American soldiers."

"You're makin' my skull throb. Too many gy-rations for me."

"You've been initiated now, Washington," I said. "Once you're in the cult, no escape."

"Should I be honored? Or shittin' in my camos?"

"Both."

"Gonna be kinda hard to get back to my squad now. They're civilized."

"No worries there. Dunne already has you on temporary detail to him. Easy enough to make it permanent. Besides, you've heard too much."

"Fuck all, Morgan. Don't know if I want to make a career move like that. Shootin' off toes isn't part of my job experience. Or ambition."

"A classic, Washington. That one will become part of spook lore for sure. Recounted for decades at the annual Company wienie roasts."

"Didn't do it to make the Hall of Infamy. Those were two bad dudes."

"Drug runners and murderers, not to mention supplying the cash to fund terrorists. The kind of enemy I like to introduce to Ms. Hush Puppy. You'll get used to it. Not enjoy it, unless you're a sociopath. I gotta remind myself every day we're fightin' the good fight, even if I can't see through the mirrors."

"I'm square with that. Been thinkin' about it. It's not much different from using a .50 cal machine gun on a bunker of al-Qaeda. Dead's dead. They won't remember the pain."

"It's a fine line we tread. I came over to help lower the chances there'll be another 9/11. What I've learned is how to get information, like I'm Google on Dexedrine carrying a silenced pistol. And to kill. Not the bodies stuffed with foam back at Camp Perry. Real people. Most, thank God, are surely guilty. But the ones that haunt are the maybe innocents. And the women and kids. I won't do it anymore, no matter what Dunne or Langley order. No more fire fights in villages or huts where there's civilians around. Those krauts deserved to die, no question. Doesn't mean I enjoyed it. I'd do it again. What it does mean is that I'm committed to making Kansas a safer place."

"You Republican?"

I slapped him on the arm.

"If I tell you, I gotta kill ya."

"You worship Dick Cheney? Sounded just like one a his speeches. Or maybe it was the O'Reilly factor."

"Blue blood democrat."

"I knew you had a brain, not just a blind believer."

"Don't forget a conscience. If I didn't, I'd just be another serial killer."

"No more preachin'. I gotta get to where you are on my own if I'm gonna have any sleep for the rest of my life." Washington put two hands back on the wheel after he rubbed his jaw. "What we gonna do about Abernathy?"

"Our job is to bring back the intel. Doesn't mean we have to tell all. People like Dunne and higher are making the decisions. This one could be special, since Dunne says he's gotta dance around Langley while he's makin' sure he's not shittin' in one a their dirty nests. For now, we just ride along and try to keep our scalps."

"All fine by me, unless I conclude I'd rather be doin' easy stuff like huntin' down Taliban and al-Qaeda and blowin' 'em up. I'm just a simple soldier, not inclined toward all the scheming. Makes my head explode."

"You no longer have a choice, Washington. Not that I'll put a bullet between your eyes in the dark if you try to run. Since we've gotten to be such great buddies, that'll be Finnen's job. You're already part of the secret sect, and you know too much. No threats. Just the facts."

"And if I was to make an appointment with that Anderson Cooper CNN dude who's always lookin' for something beyond the normal carnage? Fill him in on how the spooks aren't exactly followin' the Geneva Convention or even the prohibitions of Section 18 of the US code."

"Since we've been denyin' it for over fifty years, why would your story make cable TV in the day of Gitmo? We'd just have to drag out all the proof of how mentally unstable you are."

"What proof?"

"Well, the Company writers do fiction really well. I'm sure they could invent your history, and it would be really sad. They're experts at legends. It'd make it really tough for you to get a job when you rotate out."

"You'd do that?"

"Not me. I'm only called for pest control."

Washington chuckled, the laugh showing sparkling white teeth in the dim light of the dashboard.

"Ya know, Morgan," he said. "A guy's gotta like you. You don't fuck around with small talk. You're true to your convictions. Tell it like it is, even if it's bullshit. Don't see you bein' the life of anyone's party, though. You're too ugly."

"I find that comment intrusive and offensive," I said. "And you think you're Denzel?"

"Naw, nothin' like that girlie boy."

Ahead, the lights of the first road block. Washington began to slow the 6x6 and we cruised to a stop. Lots of H & Ks pointed in our direction. There'd been a shift change since we came through earlier and no one was familiar. The sentries didn't have the luxury of a gate; they'd just pulled Humvees across the road. And a tank. Two soldiers walked to the truck, signaling us to get out. Until they were sure we were friendlies, there was a need to keep their rifles trained at our heads. It was too dark and there had been too much bloodshed to take risks.

"Papers," the first soldier said.

"And a fine evening to you too," Washington said. "Do you know the way to the beach?"

"Stand over there," the soldier said, pointing with the H & K barrel to the side of the road.

"Sure," Washington said, stepping toward the ditch. "My girlfriend and me were just out for a midnight swim. Must a taken a wrong turn at Kandahar."

I handed over the documents from the glove box. The second soldier took them and examined the papers using a flashlight. Nobody but Washington smiled.

"You guys in any need of dope?" he asked. "We got a shit load in back. If you play nicey-nice, we'll share."

They hadn't really inspected me, but they would know soon enough. Washington had yet to refine the look, so he was just another jive ass breakin' their balls.

There was only one important piece of paper in the envelope. It was on top and displayed the logo of the CIA, an eagle, looking constipated and roosting on a bunch of pointed spikes. It was a free pass anywhere in the world ruled by America. The soldier handed the envelope back.

"Fuckin' spooks," he said. He turned to the soldiers behind the Humvees, still pointing their weapons at our heads. "Let 'em through." The two grunts walked away.

"Say, is this the way to San Jose?" Washington asked. "Ya'll forgot ta give me directions."

"Get in the truck," I said. "Before they decide that pass must be as phony as you."

"You just wanna get back and see the girl. Finnen might already have his hand in the jelly by the time you ever get a lick."

"I really don't want to shoot you. Maybe I'll just leave you here with your buddies. You can hitchhike."

The sun was rising by the time we made it to Jalalabad. Washington drove the entire trip. Once he got going, his mouth ran as fast as the 6x6 engine's injectors. I tried to ignore him and concentrate on Dunne and the next steps, battling thoughts of Khkulay and Finnen like they were traitors.

A terminal case of the dry heaves. Run over by a Humvee. Too many hours hugging a latrine slit hole. The death of his best friend Bud. Who could tell what made Finnen look like he'd been ridden hard and put away dry. In the chair, he held his head in his hands, elbows on his knees, and moaned. Dunne's tent smelled like someone had drained a brewery while spewing. And it all came from Finnen's corner. He shook his head and started his mantra again.

"I before E except in Budweiser." He gulped for air. "I before D except in Budweiser." Another gulp. "Keep goin'. You'll get it lad. I before E except in Budweiser."

Surprisingly, Dunne was at the map, not embedded in his laptop.

"Shut up, Finnen," he said. "And you owe me for the beer. It had to have been two cases." Dunne turned and faced Finnen, pointing at the waste basket that used to be next to the fridge. It was impossible to tell now, buried as it was, in a pile of empty Bud cans. "And clean up that mess. It's the maid's day off."

Finnen groaned more and looked down, his pupils hidden somewhere behind the red.

"At least my bladder's still workin'," he said. "My feet are warm and dry."

Another spectacle for Washington to enjoy. After hours in the driver's seat, he chose again to stand close to the door flap as if fairies were about to invade and he wanted to be first out.

"I certainly appreciate the professionalism I've observed around here," Washington said. "Makes me feel confident the world is secure from the terrorist threat."

"Could ya please stop yellin'," Finnen said, rubbing his temples. "My head feels like someone hit me with a full can of beer right between these very eyes."

"Did it yourself a few minutes ago," Dunne said. "It was an empty. You fell over anyway."

"As I was sayin'," Washington said, "I'm honored to be part of an organization that sets the standard for truth and personal hygiene."

"What's that god-awful smell?" Finnen asked, sniffing like he was a bird dog.

"Check your blouse, Finnen," Dunne said.

Finnen looked down and gasped.

"Jaysus," he said. "Now that's a waste of God's own." It looked like he was about to start lapping at his shirt as he held it in front of his face.

"Don't you even think about it," Dunne said. "I'm about to have you court martialed for showing up in this condition. You don't need to add disgusting behavior to the list."

"First, I didn't just show up, I never left. Second," Finnen held up three fingers, "the Company doesn't do court martials."

From my assigned chair, I wasn't enjoying the display. At least it appeared Finnen's night involved more important activities than smoothing his way into Khkulay's hijab. I cleared my throat.

"If everyone is ready," I said, "it's time to convene the meeting."

We didn't have any rules. There was a certain hierarchy Finnen despised and I followed. Dunne was our minder, but it wasn't the same as the officer-to-enlisted man protocol of the Army. Dunne liked to stress the need for "team play." Finnen liked to push the boundaries. But Dunne still called the shots, knowing full well he couldn't squash our creative talents by coming down too hard.

Dunne sat back at his computer, this time not disappearing into the blinking cursor. He looked at Washington.

"From the little bit Morgan's told me," Dunne said, "I think you could be a valuable member of the team."

Washington scratched his butt.

"As long as you're not pitchin' and me catchin'," Washington said.

Dunne didn't smile.

"No matter what they say out there," Dunne said, waving his hand to encompass the universe, "we don't play in that league. Unless we do." He dropped his hand and sat straighter in his chair. "So you think Abernathy could be mixed up in this story?"

Washington put his hands in his pockets and leaned against a tent pole, still looking like he wasn't sure if he wanted to fill any position on this team.

"Seems so," Washington said. "I can't be certain, but, with your powers, you could find out. Maybe look in some chicken guts or ask the Oujia board."

"In this country, we use goats," Dunne said. "Rest assured, I'll know more by the time you get back from morning chow."

No one was paying me any attention. It seemed like I was a prisoner in the asylum. It always did in Afghanistan. I crossed my legs and tried to look solemn, even though I could see Finnen faced toward the corner, standing up, wavering, and reaching for his fly. It was a brief window to get in a few words before the explosion.

"I think we should visit Abernathy," I said. "Of course, that would be after you've confirmed what Washington and I suspect is true. The dicey part is that he's a US Army officer. We might have to use different techniques."

Finnen had thought better of it and was sitting back down, mumbling, "Not another waste. Can't be givin' it away."

Dunne was focused on me while I spoke; then, he turned toward Finnen.

"Good try, but the diversion didn't work, Morgan." Dunne said. "If Finnen would'a unzipped his pants, I'd have nailed his dick to the tent pole with my Ka-Bar." He looked back at me. "He's in no shape for anything but rehab. It'll be you and Washington. I'm gonna give Finnen a day to dry out, even if I have to tie him to the chair."

In some ways, we were a brotherhood. I hated to use the description but knew it to be accurate. Finnen had been in-country longer than the combined time of Dunne, Washington, and me. Often, he'd been my cut-out and done everything possible in a supportive role to make sure I returned uninjured with mission accomplished. Much of his last year had been spent holed up in the Jalalabad safe house with no beer and no one to talk to. Time spent here was a vacation, and Dunne wasn't going to piss on it. Or waste Finnen's merciless talents for strategizing. The Company shrinks had suggested the Firm become more warm and friendly to its assets before they all began to rave and write their memoirs.

The siren's call of the laptop was too much for Dunne, and he couldn't resist the "You've Got Mail" tease that sounded without the words. He reached for his mouse. "We already know the Generals Khan and Dostum both have villas in Tuscany," Dunne said while he looked at the screen and hit a few keys. He was an expert multi-tasker. "As well as castles here. Off shore bank accounts totaling in the hundreds of millions. Mistresses, Mercedes, Rolexes, all the trappings not easily affordable on a general's salary. The Company has been more focused on any links to the Taliban or al-Qaeda. No one gives a shit about money. Seems like everybody's got more than they can spend. Or you and I will ever see unless we steal from the drug runners. It's what they do with it to support terrorism."

Something earth-shaking must have been delivered to his inbox. He sat forward and read the message, leaning back after a few seconds and sighing. "As long as they support what we're doing here, there's no pressure to have them removed. They know life can be precarious if they change sides and act accordingly. But this drug, oil, and Taliban scenario is pushing the envelope. They must be getting greedy."

Dunne was morphing. In the last few days, more words had come from his mouth than even my Aunt Jane used—the same woman who wouldn't stop talking even if her bra came unsnapped. Now, Dunne needed to rest his lungs. And stop the eye twitch. He watched the rippling of the tent roof and put his hands behind his head.

"Go eat," he said. "The oatmeal is particularly tender this morning. I'll have things more thought out when you get back." He bobbed his head at Finnen. "Take him with you. Throw him in the shower first thing or you won't enjoy breakfast."

I stood and went to help the staggering Finnen.

"We need to make a decision about Khkulay," I said. "She can't stay here forever."

"Right now," Dunne said, "we've got a conspiracy on our plate. One that could be the source of the bullets that fly at your head. And we haven't even spoken in depth about the German end of things. When there's closure, we'll take care of Khkulay. For now, she can stay where she is."

"Ooh, ooh," Washington said. "Loves that 'closure' shit. You boys talk like you do astral projections. Wanna read my chart?"

"I told you before," Dunne said, "we use entrails." He motioned toward the tent flap. "Off you go."

Finnen wasn't nearly as heavy as I anticipated, even with a few gallons of Bud in his belly and on his shirt. Draped over my shoulder, the biggest weight was carrying the stink. It was like back in grade school when most of the fifth grade got food poisoning from bad sloppy joes, and we were all lined up to toss our chocolate chip cookies at the same time in the restroom. Most of us couldn't wait, and we slid around in puke before our turn came for the toilet stall. Finnen rested his head on my shoulder, mumbling, "Oh, the yuck of the Irish."

Showered and fed, we were back in Dunne's lair, having administered a half-dozen aspirins to Finnen, burning his clothes, and borrowing clean ones from another agent who was in the field. Washington and I wore fresh fatigues and were clean shaven, knowing we would have to pass as soldiers . . . if that was possible.

Someone had sprayed lavender room deodorizer in the space, but there was still a lingering urp smell. The tent flap was open—an unsuccessful attempt to vent the fumes. Dunne was riffling through files, organizing his life.

Finnen made a direct line toward the fridge.

"If you so much as lick the door," Dunne said, "I'll put you on the A list." The A list contained the real bad guys who were to be shot on sight if capture wasn't absolutely assured. People like Bin Laden and Zawahiri. "I want you sitting in Morgan's chair."

Finnen gave a puppy-dog look and slunk toward my usual spot.

"At least I'll die in the best of health," Finnen said.

Washington and I pulled folding chairs beside Finnen, surrounding him in case of a collapse caused by an earthquake or the more likely Bud vertigo.

Dunne folded his arms on his chest. He always wore either a white collared shirt and black slacks or fatigues. Today he was in his "go to the office not the bush" outfit.

"Abernathy," Dunne said. He paused to give just the perfect amount of weight to the name. Finnen burped.

"Excuse me," Finnen said. "Must'a been the oatmeal."

Dunne wasn't humored. He glared but continued.

"Seems the Captain has been building for his retirement," Dunne said. "I traced nearly a million dollars to an account in the Grand Caymans under the name Williamson. It's Abernathy, though. His wife's maiden name is Kathleen Williamson."

Finnen grinned.

"A fine Irish lass she must be with that name. Do ya know if she has big tits? She could be a widow soon."

Dunne ignored him and uncrossed his arms, reaching for a file.

"Funny how dumb West Point grads can be," Dunne said. "Did he really think he could hide the blood money by using his wife's name? Stupid. Makes me wonder if it's just more diversion."

Washington was smoothing out the wrinkles in his camo fatigues. He looked at Dunne.

"Naw," Washington said. "Most a them Pointy grads have bodies by the Army and brains by Mattel."

"Okay," Dunne said. "I'm leanin' that way too. There's a straight trail from Kabul to Gardez. Abernathy's time with the Afghanistan General Staff was spent in close contact with Khan and Dostum. Actually, I ran into him a few times when I was there. He was the direct onsite link to Northern Command and the pipeline construction. Before he came to Afghanistan, he was stationed at Anderson Barracks in Dexheim, Germany. Speaks kraut. No ties with the Company. I don't think this is a rogue CIA operation or Abernathy's being run by us. But I'm not positive enough yet to assume it isn't something out of Langley."

He looked back and forth between Washington and me but couldn't hold our eyes.

"You two are going to have to have a frank talk with him. Today. You're going to Gardez. I checked. He's on the base. I've arranged for the three of you to have some quiet time just outside of town. Your cover will be you're meeting with a German military contingent in order to look at preparations for a temporary billet in the sector. Abernathy was requested because of his language skills. You're both Captains for the day, so dress and act accordingly. Pick him up at 1330. The passes are in the Humvee outside. We probably want to keep him in place and turn him. And sorta healthy, though a little persuasion can be used. Not on his face. Get humpin'."

Circles within circles. Or in the case of the Company, mirrors reflecting mirrors. Dunne wasn't telling the whole truth, but I didn't know what he and his masters had devised and if it was all coming apart. I wasn't about to leak what Klaus had said about the blue-eyed man, but I sure as hell was going to try to step around the landmines.

Washington and I stood to leave. Dunne stared at Finnen, who appeared to be sleeping, his chin to his chest and drool leaking out the corner of his mouth.

"Finnen," Dunne barked.

The Irishman jumped to his feet and reached for the pistol that wasn't at his waist. He looked quickly around the tent and then back at Dunne.

"Jaysus gawd," he said. "You like ta stop the sweetness flowin' in my veins. Worse than a banshee's shriek."

"You're staying with me," Dunne said. "And keeping sober. If you haven't noticed, I put a lock on the fridge."

Finnen turned to the refrigerator, panic on his face.

"Prison is no place for the guiltless," he said. "Those Buds did nothing to deserve such punishment."

"You did," Dunne said. "Now sit down, and give me some peace."

Washington and I left before the wailing could begin.

Khkulay would have to wait until later. It was a sadness only Finnen understood. But she was my responsibility, not Finnen's, even if I suspected he might disagree.

A few klicks outside Gardez, Washington stopped the Humvee beside an abandoned complex of unroofed buildings. An Afghan developer must have gone bust. There was no sign of habitation. Not far behind the mud-brick construction, the foothills of the Himalayas began and the nearest snow was an easy walk to the east. Overhead, the sun was sending its rays through clear sky, warming the endless brown-rock terrain, broken only by a few clumps of grass trying to exist on water left over from last year's blizzards. No tire tracks in the pebbles. The ground was too hard and windblown.

Abernathy had been quiet during the drive from the Gardez base, sitting in the back seat. There was no trouble finding him in the command tent and no one had asked us for papers, even at the road block. It was getting late and would soon turn cold.

All of us carried H & K semi-automatics as we walked to the nearest ruin. Washington went inside the door-less entry first, followed by Abernathy, then me. I turned back to make sure we were out of sight of any watchers and slammed Abernathy in the back of the knees with the butt of my H & K, grabbing his as he fell. I stood over him, with my rifle touching the back of his head.

"Welcome to the confessional, traitor," I said.

Washington went out the far side to inspect the other empty buildings. If we had neighbors, they would soon be relocating.

"Crawl over there and sit against the wall," I said to Abernathy, pointing with the muzzle of the rifle.

He did and was facing me within seconds, his camo boots pointed toward the non-existent ceiling. There was no shock or anger on his face. In my experience, the guilty are often waiting for payback to come, and they see me as the errand boy. It was my first clue that Abernathy was mixed up in something well above his performance rating.

Average height and weight and buzz-cut hair, Abernathy was indistinguishable from the thousands of other grunts in Afghanistan, except for the space between his eyes. The top of his nose flattened into a gap as wide as a baseball bat and looked as if someone had hit him with it. He didn't tremble or yell in protest of his unfair treatment. He did wipe his nose with his sleeve, but he had been coughing on the ride out, and I assumed he was fighting one of the lingering flus afflicting so many grunts in Afghanistan, not beginning the session crying.

Kicking a rock in front of him, Washington returned through the far entrance.

"Clear," he said.

Abernathy watched him, a puzzled look on his face like he recognized Washington.

I leaned the two rifles against the wall, and Washington went behind me to take up a sentry position. The Ka-Bar came easily out of its sheath, and I held it at my side. The normal etiquette wasn't appropriate today. I wouldn't begin by shooting Abernathy in the knee.

"Start with Khan and Dostum," I said, watching Abernathy for tells. "Which one are you helping trade dope for money to buy weapons for the Taliban?"

Abernathy didn't cringe or weep. He didn't even start to blink rapidly.

"I don't know what you're talking about," Abernathy said. "And what you're doing is worth a life sentence at Leavenworth."

I just shook my head. More for me than him. He was going to make it hard, and I was tired of blowing off knee caps and ears. But I took out the Hush Puppy anyway.

"The story of my life," I said. "I get some bad guy alone and ask a few simple questions. They always start with the 'I don't know what you're talking about' routine. Then, after I shoot off some flesh, lo' and behold, they were lying." I pointed the pistol at Abernathy's knees. "Which one do you want me to start with?"

Reflexively, Abernathy drew his knees to his chest.

"Mistake," I said. "If I miss by even a centimeter, you and Kathleen won't be able to share anymore fudge. You'll be spendin' that million stashed in the Caymans on a dick transplant."

The first sign he knew it wasn't going to go easy. His eyelids opened wide, and his jaw dropped.

"This doesn't have anything to do with her," he said.

I crouched low to the ground and looked back at Washington, turning again to Abernathy, as if I was going to impart a deep secret.

"Listen," I said softly. "Don't tell anyone else. We already have Kathleen locked up with a bunch of black dykes and junkies at the Fairfield County Jail. We're not supposed to be operating on American soil, but you know how it is. At least we kept her close to Bridgeport so the kids can come visit if anyone ever finds out where she's being held. She's not scheduled to see the judge for a couple weeks. Or we might let Homeland Security have her for an indefinite stay. The courts are backed up months. Paperwork and all." I took out a cell phone and held it toward Abernathy. "Here, wanna call Trevor and Holly? I hear they miss their dad. And mom."

Abernathy's eyes flared. He'd already reached the anger level of grieving for his wasted life.

"You can't do that," he said.

I stood up and yawned, putting the cell phone in my pocket. Not much sleep after the chemically charged night before.

"You've already guessed who we work for," I said. "The Army wouldn't handle you this way. They'd probably follow all those silly laws and such. Put you on trial. Embarrass everyone who's ever known you, including them. Then stand you up in front of the firing squad. Play it by the book."

I stretched and yawned again, straightening after I finished, glaring at Abernathy.

"We don't have rules. The law is to get the job done. If it means leavin' your big-titted wife to marry one a those strap-on queens and your kids to be farmed out to an orphanage for troubled psychopathic children because no one they know will ever be found fit enough to be responsible parents after we smear them, hell, that's just the way it's gotta be. Makes me queasy ta think about it. But, hey, it's your choice."

Washington could hear everything but my little secret chat with Abernathy. He turned his head and spoke over his shoulder.

"You need any help in there?" he asked. "I could start shooting off his toes. I haven't done any a that since last night, and it'd be cool to have more target practice."

The Hush Puppy was getting heavy. I put it to my side.

"Naw," I said. "You keep watchin' for the rescue party that's not coming. I think Abernathy's about to spill it all. He knows I'd like nothing better than to start on his knees and work my way up. I think he's more concerned about himself than the little ones or his wife becoming a bean flicker."

I raised the pistol and shot, aimed just to the left of Abernathy's head. Chunks of dried mud flew into his cheeks, and red marks swelled below his eye.

"Gettin' close to chow time, Abernathy. We wanna get back before it's all inhaled by the knuckle draggers. We can leave you here for the snakes to crawl into the holes I put in your belly, or you can start talking. I'm gonna count to ten and then start puncturing your stomach. Even if you're dead, it won't save your wife. We know she's in on it." We didn't, but it was no time for the truth.

As usual, once they started, they gushed. Abernathy leaned forward and put his head in his hands.

"It's Dostum," Abernathy said. "He set it all up. My job was to make sure everything ran smoothly. Dostum got me transferred to Gardez to be closer. The money was picked up and turned over for the dope. I was the monitor."

General Abdul Rashid Dostum. There was a character not even the Company could make up. I had read his file; it was lengthy and vile. During the war with the Russians, he fought with them, not against. At least not until he saw the Soviets were going to be evicted. Then, as a leader of the Northern Alliance, he recaptured Mazar-i-Sharif from the Taliban, the town he once controlled. Atrocities were heavily reported. For a short period, he joined forces with the Islamist leader Gulbuddin Hekmatyar, a close cousin to the Taliban. Later, he turned against Hekmatyar and battled him throughout the north. Dostum was nicknamed Pasha because he lived and ruled like a sultan while he ruled over his kingdom in northern Afghanistan, which comprised six provinces and five million people. The Taliban forced him into exile in 1998, but the appointment of one of Dostum's cronies, General Fahim, led to his being invited back. Recently his house had been raided in an attempt to free a kidnapped former ally of Dostum's. Akbar Bai was a government official who had supposedly betrayed or slighted Dostum. Bai and three others were released before the shooting began after an agreement by Dostum to help in the inquiry of the kidnapping he had conducted himself. Afghan follies. The Company believed, if Dostum was removed, the entire north would break out in civil war. Collusion by the Company in this drugs-for-guns conspiracy wouldn't be the first time a bloodthirsty megalomaniac was kept in power, even if Langley knew.

Now came the pleading. Abernathy looked at me with beagle eyes.

"I had no choice," Abernathy said. "They threatened me like you just did. Except they said they would kill her. And the children. There was nothing else I could do to protect them."

The usual excuse. Tired and untrue. I smiled.

"And you never thought about reporting it to the brass?" I asked. "Do you seriously think anyone would let your family be killed? They would have been moved and under surveillance the same day you reported the threat."

"Dostum told me he would find out," Abernathy said. "He had ears inside the Army and the CIA, and he'd be informed immediately. He said my family was already being watched."

The second usual excuse. Even more tiresome and false. I shook my head and made a *tsk tsk tsk* sound.

"And the money in the Caymans?" I asked. "I suppose that was a gesture of good faith."

"No," Abernathy said. "They put it in my wife Kathleen's name, knowing it would be easily discovered if anybody looked. It was a guarantee. They said if I didn't follow orders, they'd leak the news I was working with the Taliban. Money means little to them. They showed pictures they'd faked of me shaking hands with a Taliban Sheik named Wahidi. I never touched the money."

"So you just went along with this scheme. Didn't tell anybody and helped fund the IEDs that mangle US soldiers. If I believed you, I'd be as pathetic as you are."

I walked over to Washington.

"What do you think of this traitor?" I asked him.

Washington pivoted and stepped into the open-air room.

"I've got some questions for the Captain," Washington said. "I'll delay my answer until we have a few moments to chat. You guard the door. Or what's supposed to be one."

We exchanged positions, and Washington stood over Abernathy, not bothering to display his Hush Puppy. He was always the good guy. He started with a smile.

"Why me?" he asked. "You know what I'm askin'? Why'd you pick me to be your boy?"

"Who are you?" Abernathy said. "I thought you were a spook."

I laughed.

"Just a wannabe," I said.

"My ass," Washington said over his shoulder. He swung his head slowly back to Abernathy, "I'm Lieutenant Tyrone Laverne Washington. Delta. Out of the Korengal to Gardez."

"Tyrone Laverne?" I asked. "Perfect. Did your momma name you after somebody on *The Redd Foxx Show*?"

"We'll discuss my heritage at a later time," Washington said to me. "Maybe just a second before I toss a frag into your bunk."

Abernathy was surprised again. This time he must have known it was more personal.

"You're *that* Washington?" Abernathy asked. "I thought I recognized you."

"That be me," Washington said.

"I was told to make it random. I closed my eyes and let the curser scroll though the Gardez deployment list. When I stopped, whatever name it was blinking on was chosen."

"And here I thought I was special."

"No, Lieutenant, you weren't."

"How many men did you pick?"

"At least six, mostly from my own sphere of command. I did bias the selection process some."

"And you know why you had to keep picking more?"

Abernathy slumped. He knew. Not even an attempt at denial.

"Yes," he said without looking up.

"What did they tell you?" Washington asked.

"That the men were ambushed. That the heroin delivery was done in a hostile country. That one of the southern warlords was getting greedy. That the men tried to steal the merchandise. A roadside bomb. A different reason or two every time I had to find someone else."

"And it didn't occur to you it was always on the second trip?"

"Yes. It did. But I was in too deep."

"Okay, now that we've established you took money for feeding the Taliban weapons and shipping drugs, and you also colluded in the murder of US soldiers, I want to know about the German connection. What's all this got to do with oil and your stationing in Germany?"

Abernathy was beginning to come apart. I didn't sense he was an evil man from birth. It came to him later in life. He wouldn't look at us and continued to stare at his knees.

"When I was in Germany," Abernathy said, "I was on a team who cooperated with a company called Wintershall on questions concerning the security of the oil pipeline. This is my second deployment to Afghanistan. Someone arranged to have me sent back after my time with Wintershall and moved to Kabul, where I met Dostum. It must have all been planned. But I knew nothing about heroin and the Taliban ties before I got to Kabul."

It could have happened that way. None of the signs Abernathy was lying anymore. Maybe by omission. Dostum was influential with both the Company and the US military. He could have specifically requested Abernathy because of his familiarity with the German language and pipeline experience. No one would have suspected. They would be too concerned with keeping Dostum fighting the good fight to ask any questions. If not, Abernathy had been part of the plot from the beginning. And probably someone even higher was involved. Or the Company. More mirrors.

"Who was your contact at Wintershall?" Washington asked.

"A man named Schultz," Abernathy said. "Dostum and him told me what to do. I met Schultz when I was in Germany and later, here. At Qalat. He came out for a progress inspection."

"How did you communicate?"

"Always by satellite phone. They used the Eutelsat. Encrypted."

"Back to me. And the others. How did you get into DOD email?"

"I didn't. The techies in Kassel figured out how to send the first message to each of you looking like it came from someone in DOD. After that, they gave me Yahoo addresses. I just had to keep track of the passwords. They were clever enough to make it seem as if the soldiers were doing something secret and important. And valuable, rather than sanitizing another cave."

"And you did all the logistics?"

"No. It was Dostum and Schultz. I just had to arrange for the couriers and keep an eye on them. I had authority in the motor pool. It was easy to get a truck and have the men dispatched."

"No one wondered why the grunts you were sending out didn't come back?"

"You've been in a command center. They're too frantic. No one said anything."

Washington had heard enough. He walked over to me.

"He's a douche bag," Washington said. "He's guilty of enough crimes to hang him twenty times. The kinda guy you like to hire."

"Like you," I said.

Washington hadn't gotten pissed at me for all the snide comments or anything else. Now, he was. He tensed, and I could see it was time for an apology before we had to race to see whose Ka-Bar came out first.

"Sorry," I said. "No excuse for that. It was the kind of silly remark that seems to get me in trouble way too often. I gotta learn to think before I open my mouth. You're a good man and absolutely no similarity to that piece of shit. Like jokin' about cancer. I apologize."

Washington relaxed and patted me on the back, but the intensity of his eyes didn't go down a degree.

"Ain't we all just the best of buddies around here," Washington said. "I can feel the love. Should we kill him now? Or have a little fun with the Ka-Bar first?"

"The Ka-Bar is a terrific idea," I said, walking toward Abernathy and taking out my knife. "Let's start with his nuts. We should be boogyin' down the road, so we'll begin with the jewels and not save them for dessert."

Before, Abernathy was close to six-feet tall. Now, he shrunk to much less in the fetal position.

"Don't," he said.

"Afraid to die?" I asked. "What could you have possibly been thinking would be the outcome? You'd fly home to Kathleen and the kids and retire on a tropical island? From the time I kicked you to the ground, you should have known there was just one ending to this disgusting story. It's only a matter of how you go. But it's going to be painful either way."

"Please don't," Abernathy begged.

"Oh," I said. "I forgot to mention Kathleen. Since she is such a fine-looking woman, we'll make sure she's only lickin' the prettiest snatch in the federal penitentiary. And the kids. They're not ever going to Harvard. You'll be the lucky one. Dead."

The tough ones spit in my face. The cowards groveled. Abernathy didn't have any virgins to look forward to. I was convinced his religion was greed. And stupidity. Perfect. We could still use him.

"Stand up," I said.

"What?" Abernathy asked.

"Stand up."

Slowly, he did, his eyes bouncing around, trying to anticipate what was coming next.

"Unbutton your fly," I said.

In the shadows of the roofless building, his eyes were a dark green. They opened wide enough to drive the Humvee through.

"You can't," he said.

"I can," I said. "And I will. Unbutton your fly. Take it out." I jabbed the tip of the Ka-Bar into his thigh just deep enough to feel flesh.

Looking down, sobs shook his body and Abernathy did as he was ordered.

"Put it in your left hand," I said.

He did.

From behind me, Washington started to chuckle.

"It's damn straight true," Washington said. "You white boys are hung like minnows. He's gotta fish just ta get it out."

No eye contact. Abernathy stared at the ground below his dick.

"Now put your right hand over your heart," I said.

Tears began to drop in the dirt. Abernathy was turning to green-eyed Jell-O.

"Now repeat after me," I said. "Look me in the eye when you're doin' it."

Abernathy raised his head.

"I hereby swear," I said.

"I hereby swear," Abernathy said.

"That by the power invested in this worthless tool."

"That by the power invested in this worthless tool."

"And the fine odor of Kathleen's quim."

"And the fine odor of Kathleen's quim."

"I will forever follow the orders given to me by any representative of the CIA."

"I will forever follow the orders given to me by any representative of the CIA."

"I pledge allegiance and faithfulness to the United States of America and all its subsidiaries."

"I pledge allegiance and faithfulness to the United States of America and all its subsidiaries."

"And if I violate my oath, my dick will be sliced from me and stuffed in my traitorous bung hole."

"And if I violate my oath, my dick will be sliced from me and stuffed in my traitorous bung hole."

"By the powers vested in me as Emperor of the Warlocks, I hereby anoint you a Knight of the Darkness. You don't have to repeat that."

I slapped him on the back.

"Congratulations, you slimy bastard," I said. "You're part of the greatest organization the world has ever known. The Central Intelligence Agency."

Washington stepped over, a grin on his face.

"Welcome aboard, numb nuts," he said. "I'd shake your hand, but anything that's touched that thing," he nodded down, "must have gangrene by now."

Abernathy fainted and slid to the dirt floor. I reached down and slapped him until he awakened.

"Not a good way to start your first day as a double agent," I said. "That's one of the rules. No sleeping on the job." I lifted him to his feet.

"What we're gonna do," I said, "is drop you off in Gardez. You're gonna act like you completed successful negotiations with the krauts and carry on with your everyday life. You know, the life of a snake and a traitor. Not even a breath about today. If Dostum or Schultz calls, you'll answer the phone. Situation normal, all fucked up. We'll do lunch later and tell you what we want."

I pulled his nose to my nose by his fatigue top and stared into his eyes, giving him a serious, intense "I'll kill you if you betray me" look.

"We'll know your every move and word. If we even get a glimmer that you're tripling on us, you'll be left dickless in a cave, and Kathleen will be pullin' trains for the guards *and* the dykes."

Next to me, Washington was giving Abernathy the same passionate stare.

"Ah shit," he said, "can't we just cut a little off him? You know, he got injured when he slipped gettin' out of the Humvee and gouged himself in the thigh on something sharp. He'll only need a few stitches." Washington looked at me. "He owes me."

Releasing the hold on Abernathy's coat, I stepped back.

"Have at him," I said.

It was hard even for me to see the strike. Washington's Ka-Bar went into Abernathy's thigh just below the groin so fast it was nearly invisible. Abernathy started to slump, and I held him up. Blood showed through the tan of his pants.

The wound wouldn't be fatal or even that deep. Washington was too well trained. But it would hurt. And if there was any chance Abernathy had fooled himself into believing we weren't prepared to be pitiless, he'd remember every time he looked at the scar. No forgetting his balls were ours. *We* were the good guys.

"You might want to have that looked at when you get back to the base," I said, pushing him toward the non-door. "Washington used it last night on somebody else, and you might get infected. Ask for an HIV test, too, even if it won't show up for at least six weeks."

On the short trip to the base, Washington sat in the back, rifle trained on Abernathy's head. We gave the turncoat his H & K when we dropped him in the barracks.

"Keep the faith," Washington said as he waved goodbye.

We were in Jalalabad before midnight and spent only minutes giving Dunne a bullet-point debriefing. It was late, and Washington and I needed sleep or more chemicals. Rumor had it that too many hours awake on Dexedrine led to paranoia and hallucinations. Nothing new. We chose sleep and the red pills Dunne offered, promising to rest and be back at 0700.

Khkulay would have to wait again.

Y ou boys have your passports up to date?" Dunne asked as we
entered his tent office in the morning. He didn't turn away from his
computer.

Finnen looked as spiffy as I'd ever seen him, and he was seated as far
away as he could get from the fridge.

"Didn't need it when I boarded the plane at Fort Lewis," Washington
said, taking a chair. "It seemed my uniform was enough."

"Are you talking about the one of mine that reads 'Morgan'?" I asked
before I reached my assigned space. "Or one of the others?"

Dunne flipped Washington and me an envelope each.

"Doesn't matter," he said. "You're new men now. Those'll work. You'll
only be in Germany for a short time anyway. And it won't be R & R." He
went back to his laptop. "Finnen already has his."

The Irishman was no longer drooling, and he smelled of Right Guard
deodorant, as if he'd smeared his body in the gel. His eyes had reverted to
an approximation of white around the pupils. He was wearing jeans and a
Guinness is God's Blood green sweatshirt. He shook his head and looked at
Dunne.

"How could ya be so insensitive?" Finnen said. "Crompton. It sounds
like I'm in the fookin' House of Lords."

Dunne tapped away on the keyboard.

"Ask me if I give a shite," Dunne said. "I don't. You'll be back before
you start bending over for the Queen." He took his hands away from the

computer and crossed his arms on his chest, the signal he was about to be solemn. "Those passports are for 'just in case.' Shouldn't need 'em. You three are going to Frankfurt via Qalat. Then on to Kassel to visit Schultz. The meeting's set. You'll be met by one a their choppers and flown to the Wintershall complex. You're a high-level contingent with 'ears only' information for Schultz concerning the future of the pipeline and the projected pullout of US troops, if there were such a thing. I'll fill you in later. Now, I want to hear more about Abernathy."

Washington looked fresh today, too. Clean fatigues and a shave. He seemed to like the scent of the Good Life by Davidoff. Or he stole it from my foot locker, as Finnen liked to do. It wafted off Washington's bald skull. He was grinning, apparently overjoyed at another sunny day not having to chase Taliban through the rocks.

"Abernathy's duly sworn in," Washington said. "How come I didn't get no ceremony? Is it a racial thing?"

Clean as well, I felt more rested than I had in the last few weeks. No cologne or sweatshirt, I had come to the gathering in a bath robe, having been yanked out of my cot by Washington just a few minutes ago. I crossed my legs to make sure too much wasn't on display. I slept naked.

"It's not always about you, Washington," I said. "And I told you that you've played all the cards in the race deck. We're the same color here. Red, white, and blue."

Washington stood and saluted. Finnen took the cue and did the same, but his hand was limp and his body was more hunched, not the military strack of Washington's.

"Sit down," Dunne said. "Can we get on with it?"

Two sharp "yes, sirs," and Finnen and Washington sat.

Over the next hour, Washington and I recounted our conversation with Abernathy. Dunne took some notes and Finnen listened, every few minutes looking around the tent and asking, "Anything to drink in this cesspit? And what's that smell?"

Only once did I bother to tell him it was his lunch from yesterday.

"I don't remember eatin' yesterday," he said, shaking his head back and forth in concern for his memory loss.

After we wound down and Dunne's questions were answered, he sat back and put his hands behind his head. This pose indicated he was about to speculate.

"I think your analysis is correct, Morgan," he said. "We can use Abernathy 'til we can't. Then we'll call the disposal unit. He got put in the major leagues when he wasn't good enough for the minors. Sure, he shoulda informed somebody other than his wife. I know Kathleen's a ball-breakin' money grabber and would have pushed him to get more cash. That's the profile I've read."

There was a chill in the early morning Afghan air. The breeze tickled parts of my body I thought were covered, and I adjusted my robe.

"What good will it be for us to fly to Germany?" I asked. "I'm sure there're other assets stationed there who could have a chat with Herr Schultz."

Dunne sat up and didn't respond to the spell of his laptop. His face was more stern than usual. No teeth showed, and his brows were squeezed together in concentration as he scanned the tent flap instead of his three attentive agents.

"I've got enough information now to almost believe there's no Company involvement," Dunne said. "Your visit with Schultz will nail it down. In the meantime, I want the intel restricted to the four of us."

Again, the whole story wasn't coming out. Dunne was blurring the full picture. I couldn't believe he was a cowboy in an operation this big. Too many logistical issues to be solo with threads that would surely reach clear to the NSC. However it unraveled, American soldiers were dying or being sacrificed to further some agenda I didn't comprehend. If the scheme was being run by a cartel composed of big oil, Afghan government officials, and Taliban chiefs, with rogue US military assistance, there was little chance the Company didn't know. Too much history with oil and drugs, and too many spies in Kabul. Besides, Klaus had already identified someone who sounded like Dunne.

But nothing in my brief gave me permission to question anything. Decisions were out of my sphere of influence, but there was no way I would cooperate in the killing of blameless US soldiers. I needed to find out more, if only to help protect the grunts and tame the growing Dunne suspicions.

The temperature in the tent hadn't risen even with the morning sun now overhead. I looked through the flaps and was again amazed at the clarity of the blue sky and cinched up the neck of my robe like a suburban housewife.

"Even if we find out something valuable in Germany," I said, watching Dunne, "there's Dostum. Didn't you know him from your time in Kabul?"

As far as I knew, Dunne had only lied to me by omission or if it was more advantageous to achieving the goal. He had never seemed nervous, nor had he developed a tic, even if eye contact was rare. Now, his face twitched slightly, and I was afraid of what that meant.

"If I could," Dunne said, "I'd let you use one of your refined intel-collecting techniques on Dostum when you get back. I'll work on that while you're enjoying the German countryside."

He leaned forward like what was coming was too secret for the canvas walls to hear. "This is what you're gonna do."

We bent toward him and listened, part of the coven.

At least the transport had enough seats for each of us to sleep. No stewardesses to ply Finnen with drinks. The Boeing C-17A Globemaster III didn't have a first-class compartment, but we weren't forced to lean against the metal walls in the back, strapped to rails like human cargo. With a range of 5,412 miles empty like we were, the Globemaster easily made it to Frankfurt in seven hours without refueling.

I wished I could have glimpsed something of Germany, but the non-existent windows didn't allow for a view. It was my first visit, and I wouldn't be here long. The flight wasn't smooth like a commercial trip. It seemed neither of the pilots was concerned about comfort or avoiding air pockets. They must have flown through every windstorm they could find, based on the bucking we encountered.

Even with the buffeting, my head was back at Jalalabad. I'd been able to speak briefly to Khkulay. She was becoming a star in the women's compound. She looked good in fatigues. The soldiers were giving her lessons on makeup and hair styles, not how to fire an RPG. No one seemed in any hurry to send her packing to a refugee camp or anywhere else for now. Dunne had worked his magic. I was glad for the distraction; it kept me away from the maudlin.

The Globemaster landed in Frankfurt and taxied to the cargo terminal in a heavy drizzle. We all shivered in a cold that absorbed through the skin and froze the bones. Nothing like the piercing chill of Afghanistan. It was honest and didn't sneak up on you, forcing you to hide under a sissy umbrella. All three of us huddled under one supplied by the Globemaster pilot. We crossed the tarmac, dodging Zamboni-looking trucks, forklifts with piles of steel pipe, and other planes. No gateway to walk through in warmth and cover. No passport control or security. If this was the level of customs, every plane could be jammed with smack. We made our way to where a twin-engine Bell 430 helicopter was parked, with "Wintershall" painted in red on the side. Two unsmiling men in long, black overcoats waved us aboard, and we were immediately on our way to Kassel.

In civilization, Finnen, Washington, and I were out of our element. There was a society here, not dinosaurs. Trying to look the part of US military officers, we were outfitted in starched dress uniforms with bars and braids. Dunne had neglected to give us raincoats, and we shivered before the Bell's heating system could overcome the opening of the door. Worse, no one wore a turban or a hijab. No one yelled "*Khootey me ookhra*" at us. Eat my balls. Or pointed an AK47 at our heads. All of this was done behind our backs.

It didn't take us long to fly the one hundred and fifty klicks, and we were treated to a panorama of modern Germany. Mostly countryside after we left metropolitan Frankfurt, flying over smaller towns, villages, islands of forest, flocks of Mercedes, and farms. None of us had been here before, and we tried to look like sophisticates but couldn't help being tourists. Every time Finnen made a silly observation like "Look, it's the remains of a concentration camp. That smokestack must be the crematorium," I nudged him hard in the ribs. Washington was silent, seemingly uncomfortable in his stiff shirt. His comments were more in the vein of "Move over, motherfucker, and quit leanin' on me"—hissed to Finnen, who was in the middle. I didn't know if I was Larry, Moe, or Curly in this movie.

At the Wintershall headquarters, we buzzed the complex and landed in the big circle marked with a huge capital H painted in blue for *Hubschrauber*. Helicopter.

The building wasn't impressive: fourteen windowed stories of flesh-colored stucco. It did have its own tram stop, and four people hovered under umbrellas waiting for the next trolley to appear. We had passed over a city with several large parks and one main boulevard that ended at a columned structure that looked like a miniature Reichstag. The streets would be lined with green at another time of year, but now the trees were drooping skeletons like the ones that surrounded the Wintershall offices. One of the two escorts jumped out of the Bell first and held the door open. We did the useless reflexive stooping routine and hurried toward the building entrance, as if walking straight and tall would mean decapitation by the still-spinning rotor blades. Finnen skipped ahead, a small child in Euro Disney.

Inside, we shook ourselves like drenched Dobermans. A Fräulein, resembling Marlene Dietrich in a tight skirt, met us with barely a smile.

"*Willkomen*, gentlemen," she said.

Too much red lipstick. But, if they promoted here based on breast size, she would be CEO. Her white blouse was razor pressed and about to detonate with the pressure coming from under her bra.

"Lordy me," Finnen croaked, not able to drag his eyes away from our greeter's chest.

This was Germany, and she wasn't amused. She turned a perfectly rounded firm rear end to us and said, "Please follow me."

No stopping now, Finnen whistled under his breath and whispered, "I'm gettin' a woody." He put his officer's cap over his crotch and followed, about to break out in a goosestep if I hadn't stopped him with another shot to the ribs.

Washington was a different story. He squirmed in his uniform and constantly brushed his creased pants, ignoring Finnen. More often than not, he was scowling when I looked at him. A man that big and unhappy was scary. I had no idea what had gotten up his rectum, but didn't want to be in Schultz's brogues.

All three of us carried briefcases. It wasn't to look efficient or officious. The false bottoms in each hid a Hush Puppy and Ka-Bar, de rigueur for

Company assassins. I also had a garrote in my pocket disguised as a lighter. Flick the switch, and out came the monofilament line that could, with a twist and a giggle, cut through neck bone like it was vanilla ice cream.

The Dietrich lookalike led us to an elevator marked *Exekutiven Nur.* Executives Only. She pushed a button and stepped aside, ushering us in first. There was only one choice labeled 14 on the control panel. She touched the number, and we rose.

On the way up, I reviewed Dunne's contingency plan. If we had to shoot our way out of the building, there would be a black-windowed Mercedes 600 sedan idling at the corner of Schumacher and Weserstrasse, a few blocks west. I hoped that didn't happen and we would be returning in the Bell; it would be too messy, and there were no rocks to hide behind. I wanted to find the *Notfall* exit stairways. Emergency. They would be marked by that stickman walking down a staircase symbol I'd seen in a summer university break trip to London and Pairs made in another life. I didn't have to worry about translating with Washington playing the grump.

At the top level, Marlene stepped out first and waved her hand. "On your left, *bitte*," she said.

It was a long, carpeted hallway, the walls covered in dark cherry-colored wood, lit by muted sconces on the sides. No stickman icon. I looked in the opposite direction. It was there, the green image framed in a white background. I turned back after giving our escort a smile and followed Finnen and Washington toward the only door. It was at the end and a masterpiece of cedar carving, displaying curlicues, gargoyles, flower buds, and swirls. No tag announcing "Bad Guy." If there were legions of assistants typing madly to keep up with the heavy business demands of a multi-national petroleum giant, none were in evidence. Washington didn't even bother to knock on the door. He put his hand on the burnished ornate handle and engaged the lever, walking straight into the room. The woman let out a small gasp, obviously exclaiming on the rudeness. I trailed after Washington and Finnen, ushering Marlene in first. She refused with a stern shake of her head.

The far wall was blinding. Floor-to-ceiling windows giving a view onto a park I could barely make out in the glare, my eyes having adjusted to the dimness of the hallway. A space the size of a ballroom and way too big and plush for the Head of Security. Ornate carpets covered much of the stained wood floor and broke the expanse into separate areas with overstuffed chairs and polished oak tables. Lamps and sconces lit the parts of the room that needed more illumination. The same thick wood paneling as in the hall, only darker. Paintings of Teutonic Generals on horses leading their men into battle and portraits of unyielding men in nineteenth-century suits. Hounds on the chase. No flowers or knickknacks. Nothing to dilute the sense of pompous heaviness except the brightness from the windows. The smell was expensive cigars and money.

The woman walked around us as we gawked and said, "Your American ten o'clock, Herr Schultz," she said.

From in front of the dazzling view, a tall, silver-haired man stood from behind a mahogany desk the size of two billiard tables. He walked around the side toward us.

"*Ja*, Helga." he said. "*Danke.*"

Schultz was taller than Washington and ten kilos lighter. His suit must have been tailored while it was still on his body, the fit was so precise. When he strode toward us with a slight limp, it was as if he had brown pin-striped Burmese silk skin. His shoes appeared to have been cut from the finest Italian leather and polished with hundred-dollar bills. Gold and diamond rings on his left hand reflected the window light as he moved across a carpet, which probably cost a dozen Afghan women ten years of their lives to weave. His bearing was regimental and stiff, presenting the aura of a graduate of the Prussian Military Academy. He held out his right arm stiffly, and I could immediately see, by the color and texture of his hand, it was a prosthetic. But it was his face that was the most remarkable.

A map of Berlin etched in scars. One hairless eyelid sagging to almost hide its vision. A nose with the right nostril closed by skin melted into the cartilage. Unframed glasses. The lips on the right side of his mouth turned down in a perpetual frown. Only half a chin. It looked as if he had tried to eat a grenade, except for the perfect teeth. He spoke clearly and in fluent English.

"Gentlemen," he said. "Dieter Schultz." His smile could cause a room full of kindergartners to become hysterical in fright. His face was terrifying—but with not a hint of evil. It was right there to see.

He shook our hands individually as we introduced ourselves.

"I apologize for the rain," he said. "Or maybe it's a good change from where you've been. I know there's very little precipitation there." He turned toward an alcove away from the window with a sofa and chairs. "Please, we'll sit over here. Would you like Helga to bring us some hot coffee or tea?"

The three of us declined and followed him to the leather seats.

"Helga," Schultz said. "Make sure we are not disturbed, *bitte*."

Helga bowed and left, softly closing the door behind her.

Finished with my scan of the room, I hadn't detected any cameras. I was confident the room would be bugged, if only to record the high-level business deals and intrigues that took place.

They sat, Schultz taking the largest chair in front of a massive unlit stone fireplace. He crossed his legs and folded his hands on his lap. I remained standing.

"How shall we begin?" he asked.

No feeble jokes from Finnen or comment from Washington. I placed my briefcase on the rug beside me after taking a seat in a high-backed armchair.

"First," I said, "I must request that any cameras or audio recording devices be turned off. Our discussions are considered private by the United States government, and any taping whatsoever is strictly prohibited."

An attempt at a smile through crooked, mangled lips and straight teeth.

"I assure you there is no such equipment in operation," Schultz said.

Finnen nodded faintly in agreement. The surveillance detector in his pocket must have given an "all clear" vibration. I had already decided the windows were thick enough to prevent penetration by parabolics.

Not taking chances, I said, "I see you have a fine Berendsen stereo system." I pointed toward a cabinet next to the fireplace. It was glass enclosed and held hardback books with mostly German titles. On the bottom shelf, a high-wattage Berendsen tuner and amplifier. "It would be nice to listen to a Brahms concerto, don't you think?"

Schultz knew as well as everyone else in the cavernous room that my request was really a demand to veil our conversation as much as possible.

Schultz uncrossed his legs and stood.

"I don't have Brahms," Schultz said. "I tend to enjoy Mozart more. His Sonata Number 4 in E flat would do nicely. Will that be satisfactory?"

"Yes," I said. "That will be fine."

As he walked to the dark-grained unit and opened the cabinet doors that held rows of CDs, I stood and went to the fireplace, acting like I was inspecting the rock pattern.

The piano solo came on, and Schultz returned to his throne.

When he sat and was apparently comfortable, I stepped in back of him and strung the garrote around his neck, applying only enough pressure to prevent him from crying out, not to make him bleed or leave his head rolling on the expensive rug like a well-used and scarred soccer ball.

At the same time, Finnen and Washington reached for their briefcases and took out the hidden pistols and Ka-Bars. Washington went to the door and Finnen to the windows, staying concealed behind the heavy open drapes. When they were in position, I let Herr Schultz breathe a little easier.

"Before we start the real questions," I said, "how does a Head of Security get an office like this? It should be reserved for the conglomerate King."

Knowing the smallest movement would cause the garrote to sink into his skin, Schultz barely opened his mouth.

"Herr Zwitserloot is rarely here," Schultz said. "He's in Ludwigshafen, the BASF headquarters. We are a subsidiary. I use his office when he is away."

"Does he know you are buying heroin and shipping it to Germany on company planes?" I asked.

"I do not understand. Nothing like that is occurring. He cannot know about something that does not exist."

It was always, always the same. No one could skip past the denial phase. At least we weren't in a cave or an abandoned mud house. The view of the park out the window was spectacular.

"Tsk, tsk, tsk, Dieter, Dieter, Dieter," I said, shaking my head and scowling. "I can tell by your bearing you have a military background. And certainly, you weren't a private. You're keenly aware I've been dispatched to get information and that the methods I employ are up to me. I'm sure you've used some of those techniques yourself. But I might have a few new kinks you haven't seen."

I tightened the wire enough that his head jerked back. "We can start by making a deal. If you tell the truth, there's a chance we can turn you to get the others we want. Otherwise, your death will be mourned as just another Nazi gaining his reward." I loosened the garrote again. "Talk to me, Dieter."

Schultz gasped, trying to fill his lungs in one breath. A few seconds, and he was ready to talk.

"Why do you people insist on calling all Germans Nazis?" he asked. "I have served the Fatherland. Now, I work for Wintershall. I am not a Nazi and do not follow their beliefs. Nor have I ever."

"One point for the bad guy," I said. "I apologize for my callous ethno-centricity." I leaned closer to his ear. "But that's irrelevant. What you do follow is the god of money. And that has led to the worship and support of the Taliban and al-Qaeda. The result is friends of mine dying from bullets and bombs you helped pay for."

This time, the garrote went deep enough to cut into the skin. Blood seeped around the wire and began to drip on his white collar.

"Enough lectures. We don't have time for you to get a doctorate in geo-politics. I want names. Who are you working with in Afghanistan?" His legs stopped flopping when I released the pressure and let him catch his breath.

"How do you know my orders, if there were any, don't come from Washington?" Schultz asked. "And you are making a rather big mistake."

Washington and Finnen both looked at me, eyebrows raised in wonder. Or maybe glee from Finnen.

The one strategy Schultz could use to stall. He would be aware we were serious and not the least shy about strangling him. Bringing the US government into the picture was his only card. No question he was highly intelligent and a trained warrior. No question he had thought about the possibility of a visit like this. I had to find out if his reference to Washington was synonymous with Langley. Or Dunne. Finding out if the Company was involved was hypothetically the main purpose for the trip anyway. We already knew his man in Afghanistan was Dostum.

"Okay," I said, "we'll skip ahead. Who in Washington is your contact?"

He tried to wipe away some of the blood on his neck, managing only to smear it like red finger paints.

"If I told you now," Schultz said, "it would just be a short while longer before I was killed."

"No," I said. "You could go to *Bild* or the *New York Times*. Put your own twist on things before the garbage collectors were dispatched. I'm sure you've thought this through."

"It would only delay the inevitable. A horrible accident."

This man had lived with pain. He would not grovel like Abernathy. Death was familiar, and he had obviously stared it down in the past and arranged it for others. His pride would keep from begging, puking, or wetting himself, telling the truth only if it served him. I didn't sense saving his own life was of that much significance. Pain and threatened death would not be motivators. Money wouldn't either, unless he needed to buy a small country.

Loosening the wire until it hung slack around Schultz's neck, I let the spring pull the garrote into its fake lighter home and walked around in front of him. There would be no run for the door or attempt to take me hostage. He was too smart, knowing he couldn't escape the other weapons in the room. Even if he yelled, I would be on him before the words got out. Just in case, Washington walked over to me and handed me a Hush Puppy, replacing his with the one in my briefcase. He went back to the door.

Beside the book and stereo cabinet, a picture hung on the wall showing five uniformed soldiers standing in front of a Leopard 2 German tank. Schultz was in the middle and barely recognizable without the scars. The men were smiling. Schultz wore a beaked campaign hat and appeared to be the one in charge. The background was unrecognizable and could have been in Vermont but probably was a training exercise in Bavaria. The others were shorter and less distinguished. Schultz had once been a handsome man. No more. He watched me, preparing for the next round.

The Hush Puppy felt better than the garrote and was more familiar. I rested it on my thigh, barrel pointed at Schultz.

"Worse than death or torture to you would be exposing your evil and Wintershall's," I said. "We have enough proof for you to be hung and the company disbanded. Your legacy would be traitor. Every history book would put you just below Himmler." I nodded toward the picture. "I notice the only photo you have displayed in this office that isn't your office is one of you in German military uniform. I assume you may have commanded a Panzer Division. Is that right?"

"*Ja*," Schultz said.

"I'll make some more assumptions," I said. "You don't really care about or need the money. Wintershall has overextended itself on the pipeline project, and you came up with a solution for the crisis. You're conditioned to serve your masters and, now that you're retired from the army, you have new commandments to follow. You're being a good Wintershall German. You don't take your marching orders from Washington or anyone outside the Rhineland. You are too nationalistic and arrogant for that. Right so far?"

The blood was already coagulated, leaving a stripe with bubbles around his neck. Schultz crossed his legs as if we were having a friendly discussion on the superiority of the Aryan race.

"Proceed," he said.

"I'm willing to trade truth for truth, not lies," I said. "As you probably suspect, we are from one of the intelligence services of the United States government. We know there is no connection between you and anyone in power in Washington." No rapid blinking or tic on my face. "We are not on a social visit, only to get information. I wrote the book on modern torture, and you wouldn't be a successful candidate. What I will do, now that I've been honest and cutting your balls off won't work, is tell you what is going to happen if you don't cooperate."

I leaned forward and took the Hush Puppy off my thigh, still pointing the barrel at Schultz's damaged face.

"My organization will present undeniable proof that Wintershall, directly through your personal management and coordination, has been buying heroin from the Taliban and selling it to drug lords to distribute throughout the country and the world. The money delivered to the Taliban has been used to buy weapons that have killed Coalition forces, including German. The profit made in marketing the heroin has kept Wintershall operating and allowed the pipeline construction to continue. It is about greed. And treason. Every one of those is a statement of fact. Correct?"

No smirk. No protest. Just a stare as if Schultz believed his eyes could blow me away like a frag.

"And if there is involvement by an intelligence organization inside the United States government?" Schultz asked.

"We both know there is not," I said, even if I didn't. "If there were, it is too heinous to believe, and it could be denied with incontrovertible proof, all focused back at you and Wintershall. You must know how it works. Germans have never been as good at spin and public relations as American intelligence branches. In the US, it's called CYA. Cover Your Ass. And spy agencies are the experts."

The time for Schultz's next meeting might be approaching. I had no idea how long his ten o'clock was scheduled to last. But I didn't want to stay much longer.

Rubbing one of his scars, Schultz was in no rush, considering his options. I looked at my watch and whispered, "Tick tock, tick tock." After nearly a minute, Schultz put his good hand down.

"I will give you answers under one condition," Schultz said. "None of this must ever come out. I understand the project has been terminated on your end. We will act as if none of this happened, including today. Agreed?"

"Agreed," I said, wondering how he knew so quickly. His couriers could have experienced an unfortunate rocket attack in a land known for such incidents. I didn't believe Abernathy would be stupid enough to inform him. "But I have one more condition. We know your contact in Afghanistan is General Dostum. We do not want him to hear the news that anything has changed. Clear?"

"Ja."

"You have not spoken to him in the last few days and he doesn't realize the project is compromised?"

"I have not, and I just found out myself a few minutes before your arrival. There has been no communication with General Dostum."

"Who else knew about this at Wintershall?"

"No one above me. I brought in the money, and it was deposited in a special fund that was not questioned. No one wanted to know."

"Who did you sell the heroin to?"

"The Russian Mafia."

"There are American oil companies supporting the pipeline. Was anyone from any of those in on the scheme?"

"No."

"Was Karzai involved?"

"I do not know. General Dostum has a Swiss account where his percentage is deposited. I am unaware of how he distributes the money."

"There is an American soldier named Captain Abernathy who was monitoring things in Afghanistan. Was there anyone else?"

"He was the only one we used. More people would have brought unacceptable risk."

"No other Americans were involved in any capacity."

"None."

"You didn't meet anyone from the US Government when you were in Qalat?"

"Yes, I did."

"Name."

"I wasn't given one."

"What did he look like?"

"Average height. Good condition. Short brown hair."

"Blue eyes?"

"Yes."

"What did you discuss?"

"Some of the American couriers had died. He was concerned about that and other logistics."

"Did he tell you to stop the killing?"

"Yes."

"And you didn't?"

"*Nein.* I left it up to Klaus to decide if the couriers were trustworthy. He claimed they were not and needed to be eliminated."

It was just a slap. But it was with the barrel of the Hush Puppy across Schultz's ugly scar. He pulled his head back, not crying out. At best, I should have knee-capped him. No time and the wound would surely lead to a red alert from Helga or whoever entered the room next.

From his position by the window, and having been unbelievably silent for longer than I'd ever seen except when he was passed out, Finnen said, "Boss, there's a limo that just pulled up. Four very well dressed men got out and are headed for the lobby. I think they could be Schultzy boy's eleven o'clock."

"Final questions," I said, making sure Schultz could see the pistol pointed at his head. "You have no connections to any intelligence agencies of the United States?"

"I do not," Schultz said.

"But you believe they are aware of this conspiracy?"

"I do."

"This is what's going to happen," I said. "We will walk out of here having completed a successful and productive meeting. We will not be needing transportation to the airport or anywhere else. You will clean yourself up in the executive bathroom I'm pretty sure is through the door at the far end and carry on with your day. You will not put out an alarm to detain us. You will assume further instructions from anyone using the password "Gertrude" came from us and will be strictly followed. That includes answering any questions. If you do not, our contacts within the BND go to the very top, and there are publications around the globe that would just die for this story. You will be under surveillance, and any deviations will be immediately noticed and punished. If you are a good boy, your stellar reputation as a patriot will remain intact. So will Wintershall's. Agreed?"

No hesitation.

"Agreed," Schultz said.

"There's another American saying you should get to know. You're my bitch."

"I don't understand."

"Yes, you do. Close your eyes," I said, lifting the pistol and standing.

"What?"

"Close your eyes. Now."

He did.

"Turn your head and press your face hard against the back of the chair." Awkwardly, he did.

I stepped to him and jammed the tip of the Hush Puppy into his right ear and covered his left with my other hand.

I nodded at Finnen.

Soundlessly, the Irishman walked to his open briefcase. Dunne had sent us with other surprises, including a package of shaped C-4, a remote detonator, and a roll of duct tape. There wasn't enough plastic explosive to demolish the entire building, but, if the right button was pushed, the structure would no longer have a fourteenth floor.

First, Finnen sliced off a few lengths of tape with his Ka-Bar. Then, he picked up the C-4 that had been molded like a flat cutting board and the detonator. He quietly walked to a portrait of a man with a silver beard, gold-buttoned tunic, and unframed glasses like Schultz's. He could have been a long-dead Kaiser or Schultz's great grandfather. The painting was at the far end of the room, away from the windows. Within seconds, Finnen had attached the bomb and the detonator behind the artwork and gave Washington and me a bow just like Helga's. He went to the briefcases and closed them, taking both and joining Washington by the door.

Pulling the pistol out of Herr Schultz's ear and my other hand away, I stepped back.

"Turn around," I said.

He did.

"In case you were thinking of disrupting our departure," I said, "there is a bomb hidden in the room. It will kill anyone on this floor if it explodes and probably those a few floors down. If we are prevented in any way from leaving, it will be detonated. You will find it soon enough, but not before we are far away from the blast area. We have also concealed a listening device. If you give orders to evacuate, leave the room, or make any move to have us stopped, the bomb will explode. The range of the detonator and the bug is several miles, so don't think about intercepting us after we are off the premises. Thank you for your time. I believe your eleven o'clock is waiting."

We stuffed our guns and Ka-Bars under our uniform tops and went out the door.

Outside, there was no sign of Helga. She was probably greeting the new arrivals. Not wanting to chance that Schultz would trap us in the elevator, we took the stairs. In the lobby, Helga and the eleven o'clock were just entering the lift.

Finnen couldn't resist. This time his wolf whistle was piercing.

The rain hadn't stopped. We bypassed the chopper and walked to Schumacher. In two minutes, we were at the corner of the boulevard where it intersected with Weserstrasse. The car was exactly where it was supposed to be.

No Globemaster. A company Gulfstream was waiting for us at the private-jet section of the Frankfurt airport. Again, no passport or customs control. We boarded and were on our way to Afghanistan within two hours of leaving the Wintershall headquarters. This time, there was an open bar.

F innen went straight for the hard stuff, forsaking his darling Guiness. The bottle of Bushmills was half empty before the jet could reach cruising altitude. There was even ice in a silver canister, but Finnen drank whiskey neat, claiming if he wanted "piss in it, I'd do it meself." Washington had a vodka tonic with a slice of fresh lemon, while I nursed a chilled Diet Coke. Not a righteous abolitionist, I wanted to think without dissolving into the plush leather seats like Finnen was about to do.

If the Globemaster was utilitarian, the Gulfstream was decadent. The cabin would luxuriously house two Afghan families. No pissing in a slit in the floor, either. The restroom was equipped with soft cloth towels, designer colognes, hair spray, shaving gear, tooth paste, Burt's Bees soap, and more rich-people consumables than most residents of Kabul would see in their lives. When it was sleep time, the soft chairs reclined to flat, and feather pillows were available on a wooden cabinet at the front below copies of the most important daily newspapers and a sprinkling of magazines like *The Economist* and *US News and World Report*. No glaring overhead lights. The cabin was muted, and the Monet print on the front wall was barely visible. Finger-food platters were set out on the bar and provided for anyone with a vegetarian taste or enough meat to fill a lioness. Finnen was drinking his supper.

"Say Finnen," I said, "Did you think your covert skills mean you have super powers? The Invisible Spook?"

"What do ya mean, lad?" Finnen asked. He was sprawled in his seat as if his bones were liquid, taking care not to spill a drop of his whiskey. That would be considered heresy.

The ice and Diet Coke–filled glass was getting low. I poured in more and tossed the empty into a bronzed waste basket.

"I suppose you wouldn't believe I saw you carving on those very expensive and classy cherry wood walls at Dieter's office," I said.

"Saw it, too," Washington said. He was now holding a Grolsch in his hand, the vodka drained, and the cold not yet evaporated on the green glass. He smiled. It was his first since we touched down on German soil hours ago.

"'Twas nothin'," Finnen said, adding another splash of Bushmill's to his tumbler.

"So what does P.O. stand for?" I asked. "I know who Helga is. But you carved 'P.O. loves Helga' inside a heart with an arrow through it." I took a sip of my non-alcoholic drink. "Are P.O. the initials of your real name?" I put the glass down on a pewter coaster engraved with the logo of the Central Intelligence Agency. Finnen had already snuck two into his pocket.

"If I told you, you'd just call me a poofter," he said.

"You know, of course," I said, "that was childish and unprofessional. Like the time you shit on the rug in that hadji's apartment in Jalalabad. I half-expected you to smear it on the wall with a note that read 'Finnen was here.'"

"I always want to leave 'em with somethin' to remember me by," Finnen said. "Besides, my stomach was actin' up from that lamb kebab we had for lunch."

Washington was staring at his beer, not really engaged in the conversation until this point.

"Fuckin' krauts," he said. "Hate them people. Egotistical, self-righteous bastards. The whole damn country is nuthin' but neo-Nazis."

Turning to his now scowling face, I asked, "Do I sense some inner turmoil? A hidden agenda buried deep in your psyche?"

"You ain't no shrink," Washington said, his eyes on me. "And I wasn't molested as a child. My momma breast fed me, and Daddy didn't abandon us to live in no crack house. So, fuck off, Morgan."

The back of the leather seat sighed in pleasure when I sat up straight.

"I detect a level of anger that's not healthy to keep bottled up, Washington," I said. "Would you care to expand on your feelings?"

"Yes, Washington," Finnen said. "Who pissed in your suds?"

"Don't wanna talk about nuthin'," Washington said. "Just leave me the fuck alone."

"It's a long flight to Kabul," Finnen said. "And we don't charge by the hour."

"At least talking it through might shed light on some of the issues that are holding you back from your true essence," I said.

"If I needed to have this conversation," Washington said, "it wouldn't be with you two freaks. I'd go have a chat with a bartender. One of ya shits on the rug, and the other shoots people in the nuts."

"I only did that once," Finnen said. "Usually I just piss." He rubbed his stomach. "Tummy problems."

"Can't say it was only the one time for me," I said. "But they all were bad guys."

The ride was smooth and felt like we were skiing in the Alps, not even enough turbulence to make waves in my drink. I waited for Washington to say more, but he was lost in the cloth-covered ceiling.

"Since the moment you heard we were going to Germany," I said, "you've been as grumpy as my grandfather after his chemo treatment. We're just trying to help. Give the assassin's perspective."

Washington slumped. Maybe it was the impact of the Grolsch bottles he'd chugged to chase the vodka. Or it was my skills at interrogation even without a Ka-Bar pressed to his balls. For whatever reason, he looked at me with his eyes nearly closed.

"In the Korengal," he said, "we were training a squad of Germans from the Coalition forces in pacification procedures. Trying to get the fuckin' pig-headed pricks to understand killin' every man, woman, or child wasn't the key to winning hearts and minds and only led to more slaughter."

He slid up, his massive back flush against the leather.

"We used to argue policy at night. Sometimes even on patrol. That's where I improved my German. Our orders were not to fire unless fired upon. Made everyone jumpy. The Kraut Captain, Schramm was his name, spit every time an Afghan walked by. And they weren't Taliban or al-Qaeda.

Without using the words, it was obvious he believed Germans were the superior race, certainly better than any black mongrel like me. The men in his squad weren't much better. I'd catch them makin' monkey grunts when they thought I couldn't hear. Laughin' and slappin' each other on the back."

He stared at the thick carpet on the floor.

"After a few weeks and against my recommendation, the Germans were sent out alone. It was supposed to be an easy sweep. Just check in on a nearby village where there hadn't been any trouble in months. The place was Laniyal, a group of wooden huts on the valley slope. Lots of kids and women in shawls. A few dogs, chickens, and goats. Old men smokin' on the porch. Nothin' much in the way of conveniences. People trying to scratch a living outta the rocks in a war zone."

He looked up, and I might have imagined a tear in his eye.

"We came in behind the Germans. By the time we got there, fifteen villagers were dead. No German wounded. They claimed someone fired on them from the mosque. No weapons were found or anyone to back up their story. Only bodies. Mostly women and children."

Washington finished his Grolsch and opened another, stalling before he told the worst part.

"There was this one girl. *Sandara.* Her name meant 'song.' She was ten, and I got to know her when we helped her mother plant some carrots. I used ta' bring her candy and little trinkets I found in the Korengal markets. Like her name, she was always singing. I couldn't understand the words, but the spirit was there. One of the Germans, Corporal Koch, was draggin' her body into the street. Her mother, *Nazo,* was cryin' and pullin' on Koch's arm. Sandara had been hit in the throat. Koch kept pushin' Nazo away, and she fell to the dirt and sobbed. I fired over his head. He stopped and let her go. Captain Schramm saw what I did and ordered his squad to make an arrest. My men surrounded me and there was a standoff, rifles on auto and leveled at each other. Schramm kept yelling *'Ficken schwarzer affe!'* Fuckin' black monkey. It all ended fairly quickly, and Schramm reported it as an ambush. No matter what I said, that's the way it went down. On the march back to base, Schramm's squad started singin' *'Deutschland Uber Alles.'* That night, I made sure he wouldn't be leading men into battle against kids again."

Washington closed his eyes and sunk into his chair.

No jokes. Nothing for Finnen or me to say. Another insanity. We were quiet, trying to let the roar of the twin jet engines drown the noise in our heads.

The bar held only the world's best liquors. I stood and took the few steps to the metal racks, upgrading to fifteen-year-old vintage Laphroaig scotch. Neat.

Maybe Finnen had the key. Whiskey and beer. Or anything strong enough to reach oblivion. I rarely ragged on Finnen about his pranks, drinking, or infantile jokes. Neither did Dunne. Finnen had seen more than either of us and chosen his path for fending off the visions.

During an all-nighter at the Jalalabad base, Finnen told a story from his days in Kosovo. The CIA had ties with the KLA, Kosovo Liberation Army, a group formed to militarily defend the lives of Albania Serbs who were being ethnically cleansed by the Yugoslavian government. The Company's goal was to gain information on the country's president, the butcher Slobodan Milošević, and the movement of his troops. An asset inside the KLA provided Finnen with intel that two of Milošević's primary underground agents responsible for the massacre in Racak were living closeby in a house outside Prizren. The couple was married and had been trained by Milošević's brutal secret service division, the YPA. Finnen was given an assassination order.

In the post-midnight darkness, he slipped into their house only to find the two had separate bedrooms. After using a Hush Puppy on the husband, he crept into the wife's quarters and held his hand over her mouth. Finnen knew she spoke English. "I just killed your mate, lassy," he hissed in her ear. "After he was dead, but before he stopped kickin', I fucked him up the ass. You know, the special place where courageous people go to celebrate. But don't you worry your sweet self, I used a condom. Here it is."

Finnen took out a rubber smeared with his spit and wiped it on her face. "Smell good? Personally, I think it stinks like shite. But who's to question matters of taste."

He pulled the woman out of bed and dragged her into the husband's room. The dead man was naked and lying on his stomach. Finnen had stuck little Irish drink flags mounted on toothpicks in the man's anus. He turned on his flashlight and showed the women his patriotic display.

"Now, you might be thinkin' I shot him in the hole. Not true, unless you count this fine specimen of manhood between my legs. It was the head. See that spot a blood on the pillow? Anyway, I just have ta leave ya with a wee bit of advice, darlin'. Some day you'll look back on this night and laugh nervously from your grave. A cold one it'll be, too. Just remember the fine Irish spunk on your face and how I left your husband salutin' ya from his best side."

Finnen left her staring. He had finished his tale by saying, "I never shoot women. Unless I do."

Afghanistan, the rock Land of Oz, was turning the three of us into people we didn't recognize. I had seen Finnen weep, and it wasn't caused by the threat of an empty bottle. Washington told stories no one should hear. And I had my own fears; women topped the list.

What bothered me most—what I had grown to fear the most—was that we all had such little remorse for the recent killings and torture. They were bad guys, period. I still believed we were fighting on the right side. No difference from when I first signed on. The change was the innocents. Collateral damage came easily off the lips and was simply passed over as just another statistic. Like spending three trillion dollars on the war in Iraq. No one has any idea what a trillion is. It's just a big number. If I said, "If you spread dollar bills end to end, three trillion of them would reach the moon and back," people would kind of understand and exclaim "Wow, that's huge!" Looking at 3,000,000,000,000 was just a lot of zeros. "Two suspected Taliban insurgents were killed today in an airstrike that also claimed the lives of fifteen civilian bystanders" wasn't even news—except if you were related. The important part was the "two" and the belief there was still a possibility of winning a war with no defined front in a land where no one but politicians wanted us to be. The dollars were being well spent in protecting the world from terrorism. There was no value in reading further unless you were the one who called in the strike. I had done that too often and wouldn't do it again.

The macabre attempt at jokes was an escape from madness. Operation Enduring Freedom wasn't another Vietnam War just because we weren't killing Vietnamese; Vietnam was a conflict. Afghanistan was an operation. The time zones in Afghanistan are better suited to network primetime news than Vietnam's. Britney Spears will never displace The Doors for emotional background music. Some smart Americans actually believed we were defending a democracy in Vietnam. Oil is always more important than rice. Conical bamboo hats hold out more rain than turbans. The list Finnen and I made comparing incursions came during another binge and was to avoid the day's horror. On the way back to base, we had passed an M-1 Abrams tank that had been the victim of the new type of IEDs. When the gunners tried to get out of the burning tank, the hadjis hit them with an RPG. Bodies littered the highway, and grunts stood beside the corpses, helmets off and crying. Stupid gags and infantile inane attempts at humor were a deflection of the fright and revulsion. Beyond alcohol and pills, making wisecracks was one of the few tools available. Patriotism could no longer drown the visions of burning and bleeding flesh.

Washington and Finnen were asleep. I was trying, but too much had happened in the last few days. Questions remained, and I wondered if Herr Schultz was telling the truth. We didn't have the time, and I believed we had been there only to make a preliminary evaluation. Or add weight to the message that the guns, dope, and oil play was finished. If Schultz kept his word, he would be a significant asset in further ops. Abernathy was of no more use and would have his life course soon altered. Sheik Wahidi was dead. The wild card was Dostum and how high the plot reached. If it was all the way to Karzai, it wouldn't be my decision.

As I nodded off thinking of Khkulay, I knew Dunne would, one way or the other, provide some of the answers when we returned to Jalalabad.

The Gulfstream landed at Bagram airbase in Kabul, and we were met by a driver from the Company's local station—an air-conditioned Chevy Tahoe, black, the CIA's color. At least we would avoid a ride to Jalalabad in a stripped-down military hummer, and we would have no problem with the MPs at the gates. Bagram was its usual snake pit of activity with newbies arriving but very few bloodied vets returning. At least twenty-five models of planes crisscrossed runways in patterns that had to be hair raising and confusing. Avoiding the hundreds of vehicles dodging in and out would be a challenge. I watched in awe as a Globemaster barely missed squishing a 6x6. Washington seemed bored, and Finnen couldn't have cared less about the bedlam out the windows. He held his head in his hands, eyes closed, and whined.

"Turn down the noise," he said. "And stop makin' fun of my condition. It's the natural way of things where I come from, painful though it is."

"No one said a word," Washington said.

Finnen opened his eyes and quickly glanced up.

"Are you sure?" Finnen asked. "I coulda sworn somebody remarked on the way my skull feels like I got hit by a shillelagh."

"No one said a word," Washington said again. "And I don't even know what a shillelagh is."

"Those damn voices," Finnen said, putting his head back in his hands. "Bushmills always brings the banshees out."

"Did you take your medication?" Washington asked.

"I did," Finnen said. "Came in a brown bottle and went down smooth as Maggie McGuire's fine Irish ass."

"I meant your lithium," Washington said, a seemingly harmless attempt at humor. "For your schizophrenia."

"Speakin' of fun," Finnen said, ignoring the jibe about his mental health, "is there a pub in this direction?"

At least another hour of the bickering before we were in Jalalabad, and all I could think about was Khkulay. Maybe it was just the longing for a gentle conversation that wasn't filled with "fuckin' spook" references. Or compensation for the absence of two sisters. Most likely, she was a life raft in a sea of blood. Whatever.

Finnen and Washington could start the debriefing. I was headed straight for the women's compound.

꙳

Jeans and a white sweater. Freshly showered, black hair to her shoulders, peeking out the sides of her scarf and drying in the crisp Afghan air. Bush boots and a touch of lipstick. A smile so beautiful it could erase every other thought about treating her like a sister. A cheerleader lost in Oz. I stood in front of Khkulay with a million things to say. Nothing came out.

"How have you been, Mr. Morgan?" she asked.

Maybe next she would start calling me "sir." I brushed my hand through my hair, knowing from the mirror that even with the premature graying, I still didn't look a day over thirty. At least I thought so.

"Fine," I said. "Been busy. Nuthin' special. Just the usual business."

I wondered if I sounded as much like an imbecile as I felt. We were in the realm of innocent small talk.

Khkulay continued to smile.

"Have you been back to the city?" she asked.

Now, which city would that be? Gardez? Jalalabad? Qalat? Kabul? Frankfurt? Kassel? I cleared my throat, hoping it was just phlegm that caused the blockage.

"No," I said. "Stayed close to base." Comforting. Lying helped. "Lots of responsibilities to take care of here."

Her eyes went down, and the smile vanished.

"Yes," she said. "The women here have been telling me you have a very busy schedule. Something about people on your dance card who don't do the tango anymore." She looked up. "Often, I don't understand what they are saying. Is that a dance? Are you an instructor?"

In my limited experience and observation, the other evolutionary step women had taken was they couldn't keep quiet about any male–female interaction, no matter how childlike. At least that was my history, albeit a possible overgeneralization. But female Company agents were the same, and I had witnessed their gossip sessions. They could be trusted with the most highly Top Secret information, but when they got together outside the office, the whispering was about who was dorking who. Or who might be. The female soldiers in Khkulay's tent couldn't overcome their DNA, and I must have appeared too transparent. The relationship, even if I was trying to be more of a chaperone than a beau, just had to be dissected. I scuffed my boot in the dirt and watched a rock roll away, not looking anything like a tango teacher.

"No," I said. "They were making a joke. I think it had to do with people who aren't responsible enough to watch their accounts. Offenders sometimes have to be called in and given a stern lecture."

The smile. Just a hint of the sorrow. Sadness was as much a part of her as the hijab covering most of her head.

"Yes," she said, "now I understand. Would you like a cup of tea?"

If she was inviting me into the tent, it was a major breakthrough. In her culture, it would be impossible and extremely risky for any man to be alone with her other than a brother, husband, mullah, or father. Dangerous for her, not the man. His actions were normal, and any blasphemous behavior was purely the result of irresistible feminine temptation and women's ability to cast spells on naive men. If the tent was empty of others, it seemed the soldier sisterhood was already having a positive impact in giving Khkulay another perspective. I nodded my freshly shorn head.

"Yes," I said. "I would enjoy that."

Following her into the tent, I was amazed at the orderliness. I shouldn't have been. It was the Army. Even though attempts had been made to make the space homey, everything seemed to be in a designated station. Uniforms folded or hanging from rope clotheslines in makeshift closets. No underwear showing, probably pressed and residing in footlockers. Candles hidden. Pictures stowed. Cots made. The differences were subtle and glaring at the same time. A small vase filled with fake roses. A mirror outlined with pink ribbon. A lampshade with a red veil. A Buddha statue connected to an incense holder. Small touches that softened the area and made it unlike the bare masculinity of a male soldier's tent.

As I passed a small end table, I was surprised to see a book sitting on top titled *A Treatise on the Virtues of Jihad*. The name was written in Pashto, and no one else who came into the tent would have been able to translate the label. I had read the manuscript. It was a terrorist and insurgent textbook written by Sheik Abdulla Makdum, one of the supposed intellectual apologists for the slaughter of infidels. The thesis was a nonsensical justification for holy war and the killing of anyone who paid taxes to an enemy of Islam. Or anyone who drove a truck delivering food to anyone who might possibly be involved in anti-Muslim activity. If civilians supported a government like the United States, viewed as the devil's own, they could be put to death by whatever means possible. Just for breathing. One of the most startling quotes was, "In Islam, there is only death or Jihad. There is no other way." Fundamentally, everyone who was not a believer was an enemy, and holy war was demanded against them. It was all insane bullshit but also the most popular book in the insurgent community and required reading. It could have just as well been titled *A Validation for Murdering Everyone Who Does Not Think Like Me. Then Dying.* I turned the book over and inspected the blank back cover, putting it back as if it were a grenade with the pin out.

"Doing some reading in your free time?" I asked, pointing to the book.

Khkulay turned around from where she was lighting a small, single-burner cook stove.

"Yes," she said. "Captain Meredith gave it to me. One of the soldiers found it in an empty building in Jalalabad. I have never read it. My father would not allow such a book in our house."

Standing straight, I wondered if the gulf was too wide and it was already time to kill the fantasies.

"What do you think?" I asked.

She smiled but with her forehead furrowed, as if she were concentrating.

"It is always worthwhile to try to comprehend what your countrymen believe," she said. "I think I am much closer to the situation than you. I do understand how the humiliating condition of most Muslim men has led to an inferiority complex that they feel can only be fought through the end of a gun or a bomb strapped to the chest. I do not agree in any way but have sadly witnessed the result of the beliefs. The attitude has also dramatically and harmfully affected women in the Muslim world."

Fuckin' A. A brain, too.

It was my turn to raise my eyebrows.

"You could be lecturing tomorrow at the State Department," I said. "Your direct experiences and insights would be extremely helpful. You continue to amaze me."

We both blushed. I tried to recover from being so rudely forward.

"You must have had many books at your house," I said. "And many discussions."

Khkulay looked down, sadness dampening her eyes. Another blunder; I attempted to make amends.

"Sorry," I said. "I didn't mean to remind you about what you've lost. I really came to talk about the future."

The water was beginning to steam. She dropped tea bags into cups and poured.

"Don't apologize," she said, without turning. "I do wish I could get some of my books, but I'm afraid they may have been Yabba Dabba Doo'ed by now."

A frown. This time it was me who had no idea what she was talking about.

"What do you mean?" I asked. "That sounds like Fred Flintstone. Is he popular here?"

A smile and a soft laugh.

"Yes," she said. "Very. But what it has meant is that many of Mr. Flintstone's words have become part of our culture. First, Yabba Dabba Doo was a way to describe US soldiers. Then, because of the air drops of crates and supplies into Afghan villages and the way they sometimes caused huts to be destroyed, it took on a bigger meaning: the ruin of personal possessions by soldiers or fighters. On either side, even if the intention was humanitarian." She laughed again. "Some of the people who received the aid thought the meatballs in the cans of spaghetti came from horse droppings."

She walked over and handed me a cup of tea. It smelled like jasmine.

"I'm sorry we only have cots for chairs," she said. "Please take a seat while we enjoy our tea." We sat two cots apart.

"I mentioned it before," I said. "Are you still interested in coming to America? I've spoken to my commander, and I think it can be arranged. A job. Housing. Everything you need. I could accompany you and help you get settled."

She sipped and studied me. This kind of conversation would be totally off limits for her and filled with innuendo.

"I don't have other choices," she said. "If I stay, I die. There is no one here who will miss me." She held the cup in both hands and rested it on her lap. "We spoke of this before, and I still feel the same. I've considered every alternative and am convinced I would like to come to your country." She let her head fall to her breast. "It is not easy."

Leaving a land where she couldn't go outside and was jeopardizing her life by reading a book. A country at war with no end in sight. Didn't seem like a tough decision. But no one was asking me to defect, and my need to comfort and protect her clouded rational judgment.

Having finished my tea, I rested the empty cup on my thigh.

"That's terrific," I said. "I think we could be leaving in a day or two. There're a few more projects to be completed, but they shouldn't take long."

She smiled, and I hoped it was from the happiness of getting to go on a journey.

"Will I be working in accounting like you?" she asked.

Not likely.

I shook my head.

"Maybe with the same department in the government," I said. "But in another office."

"Thank you," she said. "I've never been strong with numbers. Like the women say here, I'm more of a people person. They said you had a difficult job because people often got real sick around you." She looked at me with wide-open eyes. Concentrating. "Why would they say that?"

To be a successful spook, lying had to be quick and easy and have something of the truth included. I shook my head again and grinned.

"They're joking," I said. "I don't carry any disease. Everybody is afraid I might make them explain what they've been doing and keep all the receipts. Keeping close watch on the numbers gives most of them a headache, and that means I do, too."

No way she believed me, but Khkulay didn't know what else to think. I could tell by the puzzled look.

"Good," she said. "I didn't want to catch the spook flu they talked about. They said it could be pretty bad."

"Ignore them. They're just jealous."

We chatted superficially for the next few minutes, and I thanked her for the tea, saying I had to get back to work and would stop by when I could.

No handshake before I left. Still, it was another few minutes I could feed on to get me through the time until we were on the way to The World.

Arms crossed and glowering, Dunne was pissed.

"No need to lie, Morgan," he said. "I know exactly where you were. If I wasn't such an enabler myself, you'd be grounded."

Finnen was back by the fridge, no brewskie in his hand.

Washington had a new station and wasn't standing at the door looking like he wanted to be the first one out when the frag was tossed in. He was sitting in a chair next to my designated spot, again, enjoying his introductions to the heady world of spookdom.

"Yes, sir," Washington said. "That's why you were watchin' the hardcore action on the Russian Love Slaves website when Finnen and me came in. Looked like you was romancin' somethin' alright."

Finnen belched, not a sneaky one, with enough pressure to bulge the canvas sides of the tent and be heard easily over the noise of the choppers. He didn't bother to excuse himself—just wiped his mouth with a fatigue sleeve.

Oh, my buddies. Doing the best they could to deflect Dunne.

"Won't work," Dunne said, not taking his eyes off me. "You can't protect him by questioning my love life or making animal sounds. If this were the Army, I'd have you thrown in the blockade, Morgan. You should be concerned with the national interest and your tenuous career. Not moping around the women's compound like somebody killed your pet gerbil."

"Speakin' of gerbils," Washington said. "Did you hear Richard Gere had ta go to the emergency room with one up his ass? Maybe he could make a new movie. *Romancing the Rodent*."

This time it was a fart. The smell immediately overwhelmed the odor of paperwork and used Kleenex. Shockwaves trembled Finnen's pants and he lifted his leg, scratching his right cheek, not once looking up.

Dunne ignored the sound and the smell.

"Morgan," he said. "Sit down."

My regular chair was on station. I sat, feeling like an assassin caught losing track of his target by stopping for a latte at Starbucks. Whatever that felt like. Dunne wasn't going to intimidate me or pour water on the innocent flame that was Khkulay. There wasn't much he could do other than send her back to Jalalabad and me out to an ambush, both certain death. I straightened up and tried to focus on something other than a smile.

"First," Dunne said, "you're restricted to your quarters or here until this operation is completed." He put his arms to his sides and bent forward. "Second, if you want the girl to see the shores of America, you will stay away from her until I say the restriction is lifted."

It wasn't even worth laughing. That would only make him angrier. He couldn't really be serious. Part of my training came from Dunne. Just a little slice. In the other sessions and years, I learned how to go pretty much wherever I wanted whenever I chose without anyone knowing. I was no swashbuckling movie secret agent, but there wasn't a chance Dunne could prevent me from seeing Khkulay if I was anywhere within a hundred klicks.

Finnen came alive.

"What is it, April Fool's Day?" he asked. "Better check the calendar, 'cause I can't believe what I'm hearin'."

Finnen looked down at his watch and thumped it with his finger, then put the Timex up to his ear. "Damn thing must a stopped when Morgan and I were out doing the dirty jobs for our country that no one wants on their résumé. Defendin' freedom and risking our lives." He brought the watch away from his ear, shaking it like it was a mischievous school boy and not looking at anyone in the tent.

"Stayin' up for days and nights because our employer has filled us with little white pills. Committing acts banned by international treaties and punishable as war crimes, as well as bein' completely illegal by the laws of our own country. And all on the salary of a mid-level secretary."

He thumped the Timex again. "Fuck all, gonna have ta go Swiss next time, but I don't think I can afford it. Maybe one a the dead hadjis we run across'll have a spare Rolex I can borrow. Would that be called the spoils of war?" He smiled for the first time but kept his focus on the watch. "Oops, better not. That might be against the law."

At least now Dunne was watching Finnen, listening to his patriotic reverie, and not me.

"Finished?" Dunne asked. His arms were crossed again, the sign of maximum seriousness.

"Not quite," Finnen said. "The world ain't gonna end because Morgan was a coupla hours late coming home to see daddy. You gotta give him a shot at savin' the skirt of his life, not spank him like a kid who didn't put away his toys. Man, I hated that." Finally, he looked at Dunne. "You been grumblin' ever since me and Washington strolled in here, and I ain't even touched the fridge. There's something eatin' at you besides Morgan."

Dunne turned his attention to Washington.

"You got anything more to add before we get to work?" Dunne asked.

In the last few days, it had always been kind of fun, planning the torture and death of bad guys. Washington looked somewhat shell shocked, but he still smiled.

"That about sums it up," he said. "Am I grounded, too?"

"Oh, please, please," Finnen said. "Ground me, too. I can't bear the thought of being away from my fridge again. I missed her so." Finnen dropped to his knees and began rubbing and kissing the small refrigerator.

It took mounting a major campaign, but Dunne grinned. Granted, a crooked, sardonic one, but it was still progress. He glanced at me before he swung to the laptop.

"Forget everything I said," Dunne said. "For once, Finnen made sense." He checked his messages. It was the closest thing to an apology I'd ever heard Dunne make, and I had yet to say a word. I wondered what the whole "restriction" ploy was about and couldn't figure out the reason.

Dunne went on. "We are under a time constraint. Dostum is leaving for Germany in two days under the pretext of negotiations with the German high command about reported upcoming troop movements. From what I've heard from Finnen and Washington, without the input of you, Morgan," he frowned at me, "Dostum will probably make a side trip to Kassel."

Nothing of earth-shaking import on the screen, Dunne sat back. "Karzai is going for a State visit to Paris on the same schedule. I want to at least get to Dostum before he leaves and has time to make plans with Herr Schultz."

Being an observer was something new. It was more normal that Dunne and I did the talking and strategizing, while Finnen drank and burped. Washington was a cherry and had little input, not familiar with spook deceptions. Now that the mood had calmed and Finnen was occupied with caressing his blinking girlfriend, I rubbed my thighs and sat up.

"Have you been able to verify that none of this is being orchestrated by the Company?" I asked.

"I haven't been able to find any slug trails," Dunne said, not looking at me. "From what I've been told, Schultz and Wintershall were on their own. Is that your opinion?"

"Not necessarily."

While Washington wasn't as much of a long-term investment as me, in private, we had agreed to not discuss with anyone the Klaus and Schultz descriptions of a man who sounded a lot like Dunne. I wanted to know what kind of tricks we were into, and Washington didn't fancy thinking about any of the intrigue, saying, "I gotta see their eyeballs or tracers before I fire, not a mind fuck. Thought the migraines were cured, but you spooks bring 'em back like dick warts."

Finnen hadn't expressed the least bit of concern over Schultz's American contact in Qalat, and I hadn't brought it up during the flight back from Frankfurt.

Turning from his laptop screen, Dunne finally looked at me, his blue eyes searching.

"What do you mean, Morgan?" Dunne asked.

Even a short tour of Afghanistan and many months of training with the Company meant I was aware of what lengths Langley would go to achieve success. Sacrificing an agent to attain a higher goal was normal policy, even though it might be considered unfortunate when discussed over a cup of cappuccino. I still needed more confirmation before blabbing to Dunne what I suspected. I leaned forward—our signal it was serious time.

"Just a hunch," I said. "I think we should have more intel."

"I don't know what's cooking in your brain, Morgan," Dunne said. "The Taliban will deal with anyone who'll get them guns, so it doesn't have to involve the Company. Big oil plays their own game with their own armies, and dope is too much a hot ticket for Langley to make that mistake again."

"What about Dostum?"

"He's got history. He uses us when it's of value. The opposite's true."

"Do you know him?"

"Met him during a stint in Kabul."

"Ever been to Qalat?"

"Sure. It's part of my territory."

"Frankfurt?"

"What are you getting at, Morgan? Why the interrogation?"

Vast quantities of early-morning, afternoon, or evening beer would never keep Finnen from paying attention. Most of his slobbering was a ruse like good-old-boy Georgia lawyers who relished using dumb, cracker accents to conceal their Harvard education and intelligence. Little escaped him, no matter how much alcohol flowed through his blood stream or onto his shirt. He was back at his post in the chair, having finished caressing his true love, the refrigerator.

"I think Morgan's just practicin' his tradecraft," Finnen said. "But I don't believe he's ready to stick his Ka-Bar in your nuts. Yet." Finnen yawned. "Let's get on with it. I feel an urge to go to Kabul and visit the tittie bars."

Dunne continued to glare at me, and I could almost hear the silicon chips in his brain processing new information. I had wanted to plant the seed of doubt, but I may have gone too far. I sat back and folded my arms on my chest.

"Kabul and Dostum could be the keys," I said. "Are we gonna open him up?"

Decisions. I had only a small taste of the choices that confronted Dunne every minute. Factoring in the requirements of his masters while dancing with his agents and the realities of Afghanistan. Assuring actions were deniable. He had to make a decision now, and I watched as he stared at me, sifting through fact and suspicion. After nearly a minute, he gave me a slight nod.

Getting ready for the briefing, Dunne got comfortable in his chair. He pushed away from the laptop and rested his hands on his knees.

"Dostum is a true nasty," Dunne said. "One time, outside Mazar-i Sharif, he put four hundred Taliban in a container until they suffocated. When the doors were opened, a witness said it smelled like a boatload of dead fish. At the Qila Jangi, prisoners he hadn't been able to starve to death were handcuffed and brought to the courtyard. They were forced to kneel and shot in the head. Those starved or executed were buried in a mass grave just outside the walls. The list of atrocities against Dostum's own people and foreign insurgents is too lengthy to detail, but the victims total in the tens of thousands."

Dunne was about to switch gears and cleared his throat, looking at the map of Afghanistan. "As for the Taliban and al-Qaeda, it's much like Dostum's on-again, off-again relationship with the Company. If it furthers his agenda of power and money, he goes along. If not, Dostum's capable of anything. This heroin triangle couldn't exist without someone in a high position clearing the decks. There're a lot of people in Karzai's circle who could or would be involved, but the information you've gathered and I've been able to track all points to Dostum."

No matter how distracted by the siren call of Budweiser Finnen looked, I knew he was listening. Washington had sat back and inhaled the lecture, nodding his head every now and then. He was content with his new permanent transfer to the Company and appeared oblivious to the undercurrents. Dunne swiveled back to me from his study of the map.

"Now to heroin," Dunne said. "Dostum is very likely the biggest supplier of heroin in the history of the planet, making Khun Sa look like a bit player. With the cooperation of the Taliban, he controls the opium fields and refineries almost completely down to southern Afghanistan, where he still is active. The warlords there have established their own shipment routes through Iran and into Turkey. Even though Dostum has murdered thousands of Taliban, his logistical talent and marketing connections give him a pass. The Friendship Bridge from northern Afghanistan, Dostum's kingdom, to Uzbekistan is the most active heroin border crossing in the world. SUVs crammed with smack, supposedly camouflaged with tar-papered windows, cross in convoys on a regular basis. Lately, the price for cooperation by the Uzbek customs and border agents has increased, as has the cost of protection Dostum has received from the Uzbekistan government in Tashkent. I believe the recent joint project with Wintershall is a response to the escalating price of collaboration and the threatened safety of the transit routes. Also, since Herr Schultz was likely a neophyte in the drug world, it is probable Dostum got a higher price and was able to involve himself more deeply in the oil game as well."

A moan came from Finnen's corner. He was nearly slumped to the floor and struggled to look in our direction.

"If I don't get a beer soon," he said, "this headache is gonna break through the skin." Finnen tried to stand with the help of the fridge girl. "All this talkin' isn't helpin' either. Can't you just get to the point? When are we gonna kill him?"

Washington was cleaned up and smelled like he'd borrowed some of the cologne Finnen stole from me. He seemed more comfortable in loose fatigues than the dress uniform he wore to Kassel. He stuck his legs out in front of his body and leaned back.

"Doesn't seem like Dostum is contributing much to the well-being of the planet," Washington said. "I'd sure like to go along when he gets shot in the head. Or do it myself."

"Make that three," I said. "It's too bad you're so rusty, Dunne, or we could play a foursome."

"There's a problem," Dunne said. "Not with my abilities in the field. As I told you before, Dostum has been on the Company payroll on and off for years. He knows lots of skeletons. If you don't think people at Langley knew Dostum is mixed up in the dope-for-money-and-guns business, you're naïve. That's what's bothered me from the beginning. When you toss in the oil factor, the picture becomes even murkier." Dunne had moved from the lecturing pose to the more focused here's-what-we-need-to-do posture, bending forward to bring us into the conspiracy.

Chameleon. A lizard that can change colors and appearance. It was necessary that field agents be able to morph to someone else in seconds. If for no other reason, it kept the target off balance. Dunne had been a successful CIA operative in many places around the world. Distraction was a tool he found valuable. From the earlier denials of Company involvement, he was now hinting Langley was at least aware of the plot and he would become a co-conspirator in uncovering the truth. Just like a broken mirror, I knew the reflection could be skewed, but I would go along with Dunne's transformation until I understood what the real agenda was.

Dunne was almost whispering, having beckoned Finnen closer. The four of us were clumped together, listening like gossiping schoolgirls.

"I'm not that far from my twenty years, and I don't want to go out being called rogue," Dunne said. "On the other hand, I've been given lots of freedom to act against the Taliban while I'm here. Kind of a blank check. Doing something to slow the Taliban and al-Qaeda's ability to buy weapons would be an operation I could remember, even if someone will be along to fill Dostum's shoes before the poppies sprout on his grave. I know you boys have been thinking about this, too, and probably have come to the same conclusions."

The fridge was rattling. Finnen turned and watched, a look of terror on his face.

"Sure have," Finnen said, still checking out the status of his treasure. "It's right up there on the list with how big my hemorrhoid's gettin' sitting here listening to you guys yak. Let's just blow on outta this tent and waste the lad. If the Company can't handle killin' someone who's responsible for supplying the arms that are sending our soldiers home in body bags, fook 'em."

"Well, I'm the cherry," Washington said. "And I ain't up on all the geopolitical ramifications, but Finnen's got my vote."

"Mine, too," I said. "The question is, do we kill him or figure out how to turn him while we do some damage to the smack market? And find out who's running him and for what purpose?"

"Kill him," Finnen said.

"Yup," Washington said. "And make it slow and painful."

"You know, of course," Dunne said, "we'll be flying naked. I can't tell Langley, and they would probably reassign me to Anchorage watching Russian fishing trawlers if I even suggested it. If we present them with a fait accompli, we might even live."

The Company would look more than amateurish if they didn't know the biggest dope dealer in the world was from a country that supplied 90 percent of the globe's heroin. The Agency's excuses would be wide ranging. Reasons like, how can we stop it? If we spray Agent Orange on the poppy crops, there will be civil war and instability beyond what already exists. If we close the major border crossings, they'll find other ways to export. If we kill all the high-ranking officials involved, we'll just have to groom new contacts. Better the devil you know. If we let the Generals and politicians make lots of money, it motivates them to help us. If the Taliban don't have cash for carbines, then Iran will become even more involved. At least this way, we're keeping somewhat of a handle on an explosive situation. Opium is the biggest component of the Afghan gross national product. Well above camel trading and goat herding. People have to eat even if the fruit of their labor blossoms on the graves of dead Americans. Status quo was better than chaos quo. Geo-political reasoning well beyond me. And Dunne was still suspect even with his selfless gesture.

The real question was how—and why—I was being used and only fed enough intel to keep me in the game. The growing concern was the old Company policy of deniability. If things went sideways, Washington, Finnen, and I would take the fall. We were hands-on agents, not diplomats or strategists. And there was at least one person, Dostum, who needed to die for more than just drug running. He was a mass murderer. The Company would have to recruit a new Afghan military asset. In the immortal words of Finnen, "fook' em."

Three more wild cards beyond my doubts. Khkulay, Karzai, and oil.

The dirt floor was pebbled with smalls clods that made it look like brown, pimpled skin. I hoped the bumps weren't really alive and moving around the way they seemed to be as I stared down.

"We're all seeing it the same," I said. "The Company has a history of supporting dictators and murderers. It always seems to backfire, but the policy of expedience continues. This time, we can do something about it and probably help the Company even if they'll shit when they find out, if they don't already know. And we can rid the human race of another mutant killer."

"Ya think?" Finnen asked. He was approximately sitting up, slouched in his chair like he was liquid. "Ya think I like all this drinking? Ya think I enjoy spendin' fifty hours awake, hunkered down and waiting to grease someone who'll be replaced in minutes with all the applicants on the list? Ya think I like the stink of goats and unwashed pajamas? Ya think the limericks and Irish routine are real? Or just somethin' to make me forget what I'm doin' and fly away, even for a moment?"

"As to the first one," I said. "Yes." I realized then that it was going to be a while before I could steer things around to Khkulay.

"And yes to all the rest," Washington said.

"Ditto," Dunne said.

Finnen's head lolled to his shoulder, eyes closed. But his lips still moved like he was among the talking dead.

"You grab ass and 'ooh and aah' like you just found the Holy fookin' Grail," Finnen said. "I been in this shit hole rock pile longer than all of ya together. I grasp the fact there's a steep learning curve. You fellas, with all the evidence in front of your eejit faces, are just gettin' to the top. It's a long ride down, boy'os, and my skids have been oiled with God's blood. Maybe you oughta join me."

Finnen opened his eyes.

"Yum, that sounds like first call." He walked across the tent and reached for the fridge door. "Ya know, before I came here, I wasn't such a cheerful drunk. Just a drunk. It's either laugh or eat a Hush Puppy."

The Bud foamed at the top, and Finnen lapped up the bubbles before he tipped the can. He sank back, head facing the ceiling.

"When you decide what time we're leavin' for Kabul, call my personal assistant. Bud will put it down in my day book."

"Did you just call me an eejit?" Washington asked. He was watching Finnen empty the can and start the crushing ritual. "Is that like an elf?"

"No," Finnen said. "It's a fairy that slapped you and whispered, 'Stop bein' so fuckin' stupid, eejit.'"

Once it started, the mocking could go on for a very long time. I needed to change the direction. Dunne was the driver, and I focused on him.

"Khkulay," I said. "I think we should finish our business in Kabul and fly that Gulfstream out of Bagram right after, non-stop to Andrews. Khkulay can be waiting on the plane. I assume you've already cleared her visa?"

"Of course," Dunne said. "Anything else I can do to assist in your life?"

"Thank you," I said. "Are we paying a visit to Karzai while we're near the palace?"

"That would be truly suicidal," Dunne said. "He's really not such a bad guy, and he's very well protected. Word is he's the only official around here who hasn't had anybody killed or murdered anyone himself. An angel coated in oil."

Dunne smiled. Twice in two days.

"But if we exterminated everyone who stands to make money from burning the remaining fossil fuel, we'd have to train a legion of assassins. He's the elected president of a sovereign nation. We don't assassinate leaders of democratic countries." A pause. "Besides, it'd be almost impossible to get near Karzai. He's guarded not only by his people but Dynacorp agents. They're as tough as anyone in the Agency. And just as smart. If we get anywhere close to Karzai, the Company will know, and there won't be a Gulfstream waiting for us at Bagram. It'll be a firing squad."

Okay, so we weren't going to quench the planet's thirst for oil. That wouldn't have been achieved even if we wasted Karzai. But we could save Khkulay and rid the earth of a genocidal maniac. And, hopefully, I could cover my ass and the others', too.

"We flyin' or drivin'?" Finnen asked. He popped a third can. "If you fellas are gonna jack your lips all day, I gotta pace myself for the ride."

Again, Dunne motioned us all closer. Even Finnen staggered over.

It was "here's what we're gonna do" time. After he checked all corners of the tent, Dunne leaned back over, like someone might be listening and everything was still strictly classified "ears only."

"As much as I'd like to tag along," Dunne said, "it's better if I manage things from here." No surprise. "You boys take out Dostum and get on the flight. I've already got the three of you scheduled for some stateside R & R. When the shit hits, I'll do my best to keep you from getting splattered." He looked at me. "And yes, Morgan, she'll be on board. Gives you an incentive to get out alive."

"What's my incentive?" Finnen asked.

We all chuckled and shook our heads.

"What's so funny?" Finnen asked.

"Another chance to visit the Emerald Isle?" I asked.

"Another chance to drink it dry?" Washington asked.

"Can't be done," Finnen said. "Tried that."

"Another shot at a world record skid mark on your shorts?" Dunne asked, for the first time joining the fun. The lizard was putting on new skin.

"Another opportunity to blow out your eardrums belching?" Washington asked.

"More time to reach the high notes in 'Danny Boy'?" I asked.

"I can take all the shite you hand out about drinkin', fartin', and belchin'," Finnen said "But I won't tolerate any raggin' on my fine tenor." He started to hum, tuning up for a repeat stanza.

"That's enough," Dunne said. "Here's what we're going to do."

It would be a nighttime op, the way we liked it.

K abul. Twelve hours later.
       We decided it was better to drive than fly. The traffic wasn't an issue, and there were no frequent-flyer miles for a chopper ride. Parked in a vintage King Cab Toyota pickup a few blocks from Dostum's sentried castle, Washington and I checked our arsenals and high-tech gadgets while Finnen continued his nap.

A vehicle in the best neighborhood of Kabul late at night was still like a flying saucer in Manhattan. Dunne had enlisted a driver, and the three assassins would soon have to leave the truck to start our recon and assault. We would be extracted in less than two hours, well before dawn.

The most popular building material in the city was canvas, and the Toyota had driven through miles of makeshift tents and mud walls. Hills could be found on the fringes of Kabul, climbing swiftly to the lower mountains and soon into the Himalayas. In the dark, clear sky, we could see the outlines of the peaks and the snow glistening in the moonlight. The color here was brown, not the pastels of Jalalabad. Normally, non-natives would be surrounded by beggars and amputees, but it was well into the hours of shadow. The time of the Taliban.

Bearded and unsmiling, the turbaned driver pulled as close as he could get to a tarped overhang and waited for our final preparations. Not even a grunt had escaped his throat during the ride, and he avoided our eyes as if he didn't want to remember. No street lights, and, if there were, they would most likely be unlit in a city where the flow of electricity was rarer than the sight of a camel spitting. I swiveled to Finnen snoring in the back, while making the third Hush Puppy ammo check.

"Killing time, Finnen," I whispered. "Wake up, sleepy spook." Washington shook Finnen's arm at the same time.

Finnen's eyes snapped open, and he twisted his head in panic.

"My sweet Jaysus," he said. "Where am I?"

"Close to the gates of paradise if you don't get ready," I said.

Finnen sat up and began patting the pockets in his black pants and thin jacket.

"And here I thought I was on my two-hundred-foot yacht in Monaco harbor," he said. "Enjoyin' a chilled bottle of Canard-Duchêne champagne, served on a gold platter by two topless *Vogue* models." He looked around, examining the scene outside the truck windows. He frowned. "Have ta wait until tomorrow."

If Finnen had been asleep, he was probably dreaming of dead hadjis, not nearly naked women or luxurious yachts. It was more likely he was visualizing the op in his mind, rehearsing every step. Behind all the jesting, he was keenly aware of the intricacies and fall-backs of an operation and knew what a poor outcome meant. There was nobody better to have along, except maybe Washington.

All three of us were cloaked in black from head to toe. Black crepe-soled shoes, loose black jeans, black spandex turtleneck shirts, black buckle-less belts, black wool stocking caps, black windbreakers with lots of pockets, and black charcoal smeared on our faces—except for Washington. Cat burglars on the way to the ball. Or assassins.

It wasn't a movie, and there was no "let's go through this one more time." No communal hug or hand slap. We got out of the truck and silently waited in the gloom for ten minutes after the Toyota left, scanning every inch of the surroundings. I was the team leader, and, after making sure no eyes were watching, we began the assault, staying in the shadows as much as possible.

Anything that would clank was taped to our bodies—knives, pistols, grenades of different flavors, climbing gear, and some of the latest Company wizardry. No rifles. If we had to lug H & Ks around and use them, we were dead. The only chance for survival was stealth.

Jay Leno wasn't playing on TVs as we passed boarded-up windows or closed flaps. It seemed as if we were slinking through an endless construction site. What passed for porch overhangs were canvas or plastic coverings draped over variations of scaffolding. No dogs, thank goodness. It took us half an hour to cover two blocks of sleeping neighborhood. Then the first challenge.

Back at base, Dunne had displayed aerial photos of Dostum's heavily guarded compound. Either bulldozers or nature had cleared the hundred yards surrounding the castle. It was most likely a combination, and the only path providing cover was still open and surely mined as well as planted with sensors. Lookouts would be stationed on the turrets. Not the kind who would light up a cigarette or fall asleep, either. These were highly motivated army professionals who knew if there was any kind of breach, they would be killed even if they survived the attack.

Nothing we could do about the mines in the dark except pray we didn't encounter any. It would take days to do a sweep, and little more than an hour remained before our ride to Bagram returned. We'd be crawling anyway, and I would be on point, Finnen and Washington following my exact path.

A few boulders and scraggly bushes were on the chosen route, and I didn't hesitate or give a final "good luck, fellas" when we reached the last building. I dropped to my knees and started to inch toward the walls, night-vision goggles over my eyes. A few minutes before, Finnen had used a small black box the size of a pack of Camels and pushed a button. If it worked, all the sensors and movement detectors would still be on green, sending the "all clear" to whoever was monitoring even when we broke the laser beams. The Company nerds had just introduced the device—the XX Beamer 1. If it didn't work, the bullets whumping into our bodies would let the techies know further updates were required.

Communication was made through hand signs. Any noise would be easily heard across the empty expanse as well as picked up by the listening equipment, which we didn't know if the XX Beamer 1 had correctly jammed. It took us fifteen minutes to crawl and duck our way to the base of the wall.

Washington's turn. He took out a titanium line wound around a graphite spool with padded hooks attached at the end and mounted on an air gun. The whole package was smaller than a softball. By the photos Dunne had shown us, we were in the best spot for scaling the twenty-five-foot high walls, farthest away from guard towers. Washington aimed toward the moonlit sky and pulled the trigger. A gentle *whumpf,* and the line sped toward the top of the mud and stones. If he had to do this more than once, it would heighten the risk of being heard many times over. Nothing fell back, though, and Washington put all his weight on the line and yanked down a few times. He nodded his head and began to climb, using his black-gloved hands to keep the sharp wire from slicing into flesh. Above, there was a narrow walkway just over the top that would give him a place to wait and motion the "clear" signal.

Besides snakes, mines, and women, what scared me the most were heights. Planes and choppers didn't count. But rappelling was something I had to force myself to do, and I followed the instruction of "don't look down" by the letter. Washington was watching, bent over the edge and waving me up. I took a deep breath and started the scramble, nowhere as fluid as he had been.

At the top, Washington helped me over, and I crouched with my back to the stone, scanning for anyone who might have detected our presence. Washington beckoned Finnen, and the Irishman squatted beside me in seconds. We left the line in place, knowing if we used it again, we weren't dead.

A lit courtyard was below with a least five new black SUVs parked in a straight line. A marble statue of an olive tree spouting water out of the branches took up the middle of the cobblestones. This time, it was turned on. A castle, not out of place in the Rhineland, filled most of the compound. Dostum must have more in common with Schultz than I thought. Five stories, topped with an Afghan flag blowing in the mountain breeze. Turrets and carved frescoes. Arched leaded windows. Smoke billowing from rocked chimneys. I half-expected knights on horses to appear from behind the wooden gates.

The walkway only allowed us to move toward the castle in single file. There was no railing, and I kept my focus on the nearest guard tower, not daring any more glances below, or I might faint. I took out the air-powered ID 12 dart gun, and we duck-walked forward, me in the lead. Anyone hit with a treated projectile would instantly be asleep from the mixture of barbiturates and polymers strong enough to drop a charging lion. There would not be time to rub the sting.

No door on the first guard tower. A bearded, uniformed man was intent on the scene below, resting his AK47 on the jutted stones, his back to us and his head slightly turned to the left. The sentry was blowing on a hot cup of tea, a Thermos at his feet. I stepped into the small covered room and shot him in the neck. Washington helped ease him to the rock floor and kept the rifle and cup from clattering when they fell. He would be dozing for at least three hours.

Twenty yards ahead, a thick wooden door led inside the castle. If it had been locked, it wouldn't have mattered; we carried the tools to get in anyway. But it was unlocked, doubtless to let more men through without delay. I gently swung the door open, and we stepped inside; Finnen closed it behind him.

Always with helpful answers, Dunne had informed us the guards didn't change hourly. Late-night shifts were all graveyard. Only daylight brought fresh troops. Dostum was under constant surveillance wherever he was, and the job of observing him helped a number of Afghan CIA assets earn a living. We also knew there were inside patrols and that Dostum's bedroom was on the corner of the fifth floor. We were on the third.

The low, muted rumble of generators. Bronzed, serpentined wall lamps dimmed by brown shades. Tiled floor with long rugs running down the hallway. The smell of kerosene and rock dust. A high ceiling, crisscrossed with wooden beams. Dark-colored tapestries without human figures. Heavy doors on both sides. Beyond, a staircase as wide as an Abrams tank. I moved slowly forward, knowing Finnen was on trace, his back to Washington.

We had to get past the stairwell, climb two floors higher and down the hall on the right to the far corner. If anyone came out of their room or a patrol appeared, we would have to take them out silently, or the shooting would start. There was no way we could stay alive in a firefight.

The first obstacle was the stairs. The banister was carved wood. Again, with swirling designs. No animals or people allowed to falsely worship Allah. The floor changed from local stone to what must have been Italian marble covered in thick woven Afghan carpet. I looked down and saw a guard with an AK climbing the stairs toward us. Stepping back into a shadow, I pressed against the rough stone wall. Washington did the same, while Finnen froze and continued to watch behind us.

From the braids on his shoulders, I could tell the man must have been the chief of security, not just the average guard. He was definitely an officer in the Army of Afghanistan. His mustache curled around the edges of his mouth, and he wore a red beret. His black boots had been laced nearly to his knees, and his pants bagged out at his thighs. He was looking down at his feet as he came up.

When the man rounded the corner, I walked soundlessly to him and pressed the tip of the dart gun to the skin above his collar. Again, Washington helped ease the man to the rug, and we carried him to the side of the stairwell, doing our best to stuff his body behind a large vase holding dried elephant grass.

No more distractions. We made it up the stairs to the top level and down the dimly lit hall in a few minutes.

Doors could be dangerous, as they were always unpredictable. The slightest squeak, and whoever was inside would grab for their handgun and scream for the guards. No need to fret this time, though. This one was heavy wood, and the hinges were strong enough to hold the weight without squealing when the door opened.

Washington stayed outside, while Finnen and I crept into Dostum's bedroom.

Candles. A bottle of wine and two crystal glasses on a bulky end table next to a Beretta Px4 Storm pistol. An open copy of the Koran and a pair of reading glasses. A canopied bed large enough to sleep my infiltration squad without touching even if we were blanket carnivores. Original oils on the walls, one surely a Chagall. A large window curtained in flowing crimson to the right of the bed. Passionflower incense still burning in a pewter holder beside a bottle of KY jelly. Silk sheets and two people, one a balding, middle-aged, mustachioed man. The other, a black-haired girl about twelve years old. She was awake and appeared to be crying. At least the tears and her quivering flat chest made it look that way. She was naked. I held my index finger to my lips in the universal sign to be quiet. Her eyes couldn't open any wider, but she looked down and pulled a sheet over her legs and boyish breasts. Finnen went to her and shot his dart gun into her arm. Now, she would sleep.

Complications. If the girl was found in bed with a dead general, no pleas of innocence would be accepted. Summary execution. This was a land of disposables. Finnen swiveled to me and nodded. We were thinking the same, and the girl would be coming with us on the exfiltration even if we had to carry her.

Dostum's lips were flapping on each exhale. A bottle with an Ambien label sitting on the end table might have been the source of his heavy breathing. The room had been warmed by a fireplace against the far wall. Dostum had pushed the thick blankets to his feet and was covered only by a sheet to the armpits. He was one of those hairy Neanderthal gorillas with kinky curls growing to his chin. His back was probably Velcro, too, but I wasn't going to see it. I walked to his side of the bed and took out the Hush Puppy, since there would not be a need for tranquilizing darts. His would be the long sleep, and he'd already had one of his promised virgins tonight.

Just a few questions before I sent him on his journey. Not bothering to slap him awake, I used standard procedure and shot him in the thigh. A flesh wound, but enough that I had to cover his mouth as his eyes snapped open, and he tried to lift his head. The other hand held the Hush Puppy to his temple.

"If you scream," I said, "it will be the last sound you ever make. Nod your head if you agree."

He did.

The blood was seeping through the gold silk. His leg was trembling, and Dostum made no attempt to reach the wound while he stared at me. I took my hand away from his mouth, leaving the silenced pistol on station at the side of his head.

Time. In 'Nam, they called them mad minutes. When a firefight erupted, the insanity seemed never-ending as tracers crossed paths, and the world exploded in a fireball. Screams of the injured and dying. Flames and smoke. Deafening noise. Blood haze in the air. A coppery dirt-and-fear odor. But, mostly, the sounds of my mad minutes were soft voices and the *phuuup* of the Hush Puppy. The smell was always shit as the target did the death void. We had only a few minutes and no time for a lengthy interrogation, certainly no chance to survive a true mad minute.

Dostum's head sank deeper into his feather pillow as I pushed harder.

"Is Karzai involved in the heroin business?" I asked.

Even if we couldn't kill the president, at least it might be good intel to trade with the Company for our lives. An awful big *might*. The Agency probably already knew when Karzai blinked.

"What heroin?" Dostum asked.

The never-ending pattern. I slumped involuntarily.

"Just shoot the bastard," Finnen hissed. "I got a fresh bottle of Bushmills reserved on the jet."

The Ka-Bar in its sheath at my waist came out faster than a Dostum heartbeat. I nailed his bicep to the mattress. If he was planning to jump at me, he would have to chew off his arm. For the first time, Dostum began to struggle, and I immediately clamped down on his mouth.

"Last lie," I said. "Is Karzai part of the heroin trade?"

Dostum nodded his head.

"Was he mixed up with Wintershall and Schultz?" I asked

Not a tough General, Dostum began to sniffle. He shook his head no. This was a complete role reversal. He was the one always doing the torturing. He wouldn't last long, and I sensed Dostum would give up his entire family and Allah to save him more pain. Genocidal cowards were that way. This one hadn't even begun reciting his Koranic verses.

Finnen was searching the room for the girl's clothes. He found them draped over an overstuffed chair in the corner. They were only a set of pajamas and a robe, a pair of slippers below on the rug. He came over to the bed and began gently dressing the girl.

"Is Karzai helping arm the Taliban like you?" I asked Dostum.

Hesitation. Always a sign a lie was coming. A new wound, and he might bleed out. I twisted the knife and then slapped Dostum before he could scream.

"Is he?" I hissed.

"Yes," he said.

"Why?" I asked.

Dostum's eyes began to flutter. I slapped him again.

"Why?" I asked again.

"No one wants the Americans to leave. There is too much money to be made. Where will it come from if you go home?" He stopped and gasped. "The war must continue. The Taliban will kill the poppies if they take control again. The aid money cannot stop, or the government will fall."

"Oil?"

"No. It is not our oil. We charge only for the pipeline to cross our country."

"Did you suffocate prisoners in sealed containers?"

No reply.

Finnen was finished dressing the girl and lifted her to his chest.

"Fuckin' shoot him," Finnen said. "Or I will. Quit playin' with the right and wrong of it, and kill him." He started toward the door.

For the first time, Dostum seemed to notice Finnen was in the room. He looked at him, and his eyes opened wide.

"Why don't you ask the Irishman these questions?" Dostum asked.

As he neared the end of the bed, Finnen stopped and stared down at Dostum.

"Just kill him," Finnen said. "Or I will." He started to lay the girl down.

I looked back and forth between Finnen and Dostum.

"You know each other?" I asked.

A last chance for Dostum. Divide and conquer. Make the cancer grow.

"Of course," Dostum said, nodding feebly toward Finnen. "He helped set everything up. Him and his bosses at the CIA."

The girl was asleep at Dostum's feet, and a Hush Puppy was now in Finnen's hand.

"No time for his lyin'," Finnen said.

The predictable bounce of the head when Finnen shot Dostum between the eyes. The impact of the hollow-nosed bullet crashing into the skull always caused the little jump as the lead began to rattle around in the target's brain, scrubbing away all the evil inside.

Dostum had already pissed on the plush sheets. Now, the urine smell was joined by the odor of diarrhea. I breathed through the mouth, cursing myself for forgetting the Vicks. All I could do was gape at the lifeless body and wondered if Finnen would shoot me next.

He was waiting with the girl by the door.

"You go first," he whispered. "I've got the suitcase. We'll talk later. Now, we gotta di di."

I followed him into the hallway, making sure I stayed behind him.

Outside, Washington signaled there was no danger, only glancing at Finnen's luggage before he moved off down the corridor in the lead.

Nothing slowed the short walk back to the still-attached line on the castle wall. No alarms or guards. Sloppy, but these weren't Dynacorp or Special Forces guards. Their incentive was to stay alive and collect the few Afghanis Dostum doled out. With his death, the morning would mean neither had been accomplished.

When we reached the exit point, I moved into the lead and motioned Finnen and Washington to stay still. The only other sentry capable of viewing our run across the open space below to the truck was in his room twenty yards away. The other one was still snoring. I crept to the guard and shot him with a dart, letting him slide to the stone floor.

Washington was the strongest and most experienced at rappelling. He took the girl from Finnen and went down first, while Finnen and I scanned the castle and the courtyard. I tried to make sure Finnen's weapon was never pointed at me. All of us were on the ground and moving across the empty terrain within a minute, not nearly as worried about snipers as mines. I tried to lead us in the same path.

The Toyota pickup chugged to a stop just as we got to the rendezvous point, and we headed for the waiting Gulfstream warming its engines at Bagram. And Khkulay. Now she had a new little sister. And I had apparently lost a friend.

Since leaving Kansas and joining the Company, religion was something I had only thought about. And not that often. My career led to being introduced to a level of bad people lightyears beyond the average criminal. Most of them were either mass murderers or involved with mass murder. At times like now, I often wondered if the angels Finnen spoke of protected us. Or made us invisible to evildoers. Sure, we were skilled assassins, but being on the right side must help. The real challenge was understanding what the right side was and believing we weren't the bad guys.

The girl slept all the way to the airstrip. Engines already warm, the ultra long-range Gulfstream V waited exactly where it was promised to be. Washington carried the girl and began to climb the steps to the cabin. The Toyota driver didn't bother to wave before he sped off.

Finnen and I had unloaded the truck and were standing at the bottom of the stairs. I pressed my Hush Puppy into Finnen's side and yelled to Washington. "We'll be up in a minute," I said. "There're a few things left to clean up." Washington nodded and disappeared through the door.

The fucking grin. Finnen was almost laughing, but I kept the pressure from the barrel pushing into his side.

"Shocked, are we?" Finnen asked. "I've been warnin' ya you gotta lose that Kansas trust in the way the world works. There's witches and goblins out there. And now, I'm thinkin', you believe I'm one."

"Are you?" I asked. "Or did you and Dunne figure me and Washington for the fall guys? I wondered why Dunne kept sending me out with Washington and keeping you at the base. Gave you two the time to figure who to blame if things went bad."

"Maybe you oughta ask Khkulay. Let's go upstairs and talk ta her."

A gasp. It could have been the altitude sickness again. Or a hint the woman I had obsessed over was something other than the icon I had designed.

"What are you up to, Finnen? Khkulay doesn't know anything." I twisted the Hush Puppy and pushed harder.

"Is everyone in Kansas as stupid as you, Morgan? Now why would Dunne have allowed her on the base? Because he's a big-hearted soul and gives a shite about one Afghan woman? Or maybe she was a good distraction, especially in light of your teenage sense of heroism. Setting up that fake Taliban scene took a lot of work. Didn't you notice there was an Afghan government seal on the door of the truck? And one of the fake Taliban didn't take off his army hat. You gotta watch every step with those eejits." Finnen shook his head in disgust. "Now let's get outta the cold and closer to the nectar. Dunne'll tell all."

He started toward the stairs, whistling the first bars of "Cockles and Mussels."

I could shoot him now. It would surely be easy to escape from one of the most highly guarded and reinforced spots on the planet. I could jump the fence and disappear into the Hindu Kush to live the rest of a short life out as a . . . what?

I followed Finnen into the Gulfstream.

Khkulay. And Dunne. They were sitting across the aisle from each other. Khkulay held a glass of fresh-squeezed orange juice, and Dunne had something amber-colored in his crystal glass. Neat.

"I hope that's not my Bushmills," Finnen said as he gazed down at the sleeping girl Washington had laid down in an empty seat.

Dunne frowned, and I glanced at Khkulay. No greetings. Washington went straight to the head, not bothering with the social niceties.

"A regular refugee camp this is becoming," Dunne said. "Don't tell me, 'She would have been killed if you left her.'"

"Just as you will be if there's no Bushmills left," Finnen said, moving the few steps to the desk at the front of the passenger cabin.

Khkulay's jaw dropped, and her eyebrows rose into her forehead as she took in the sight of our outfits, blackened faces, and weapons.

"Is this what accountants do?" she asked.

Laughter from everyone but Khkulay and me.

Finnen began to take the tape off his weapons and set them on the small writing desk at the front.

"Let's see," he said. "This one shot off all those naughty zeros," putting the Hush Puppy down. Releasing his Ka-Bar and the Sig Sauer strapped to his ankle next, he placed them beside the Hush Puppy. "And these two helped us solve the mystery of the missing receipts for dinner at Chez Jalalabad." Last, besides his jacket stuffed with the high-tech equipment and tools, he took out the grenades. "And these beauties were just in case anybody lied about their expense accounts."

He finished by dropping his wind breaker on top of the pile. "There we go. Must of misplaced my adding machine." He stepped to the bar, grinning and delighted at the still-unopened bottle of Bushmills. "I'll drink to that," he said and twisted his hand to break the seal.

Washington came out of the head, fluffing the front of his pants, a small dark spot forming below his crotch.

"Almost didn't make it," Washington said. "Abdul the driver couldn't miss a pothole." He looked at Khkulay. "Pardon me, ma'am. I'm not used to having ladies around." Washington began to unload his arsenal.

Dunne looked at Khkulay.

"Could you please step into the rest room for a few minutes?" he said. "The flight will be leaving soon, and I need to speak with these gentlemen in private."

Speechless and dizzy. Too much information. Too many tricks. I stood close to the door, feeling like the jet was already airborne and swaying in the high-altitude currents.

Khkulay stood, and the girl from Dostum's bed continued to sleep.

"Certainly," Khkulay said.

Finnen began to laugh, slapping his free hand on his thigh.

"Give it up, Dunne," Finnen said. "Morgan knows. But I think you owe him a wee bit of explanation." Finnen turned to Khkulay. "Ms. Masari, you can sit back down, too. I'm sure there're parts of this you weren't made aware of and might find enchanting." Finnen nodded to Washington. "And I think he'd love to hear about how low his new employers will stoop."

We all sat, Finnen with a glass of scotch, Washington a predictable cold Grolsch, Dunne sipping something brown, and Ms. Masari tasting her orange juice. Nothing yet for me. My head was already spinning like the turbines in the Gulfstream's engine that was now warming up for takeoff.

The co-pilot came out of the flight deck and closed the jet's outside door. He was wearing a starched white shirt, dark tie, and those phony pilot-striped shoulder pads. He couldn't have been more than thirty, barely older than me or Washington. But not Finnen or Dunne. The co-pilot's black trousers were creased sharp enough to cut a grapefruit, and he still didn't need to shave.

"Gentlemen and ladies," he said, "our flight plan takes us over the Himalayas, across northern India and through cleared Chinese air space . . ."

"Stow it," Finnen said. "Get this baby crankin'. I have a date tonight. Or is it tomorrow?" He looked at his watch and slapped the face. "Darn thing." There was a lady present.

"We'll have lift off in just a few minutes," the co-pilot said. "Please fasten your seat belts."

"What about the weapons?" Washington asked, motioning toward the pile on the desk and taking out his Sig Sauer. "They didn't find them at security. Aren't you worried about a highjacking?"

"I'm sure you gentlemen can protect us," the co-pilot said. "Have a good flight." He pivoted and walked to the pilot's cabin, ignoring the rest.

"Darn straight," Washington said. "If either of these spooks tries anything, I'll throw them out the door. They need to know what it means to be in the Airborne."

"You and how many divisions of your Army?" Finnen asked.

"Wouldn't take even half a me," Washington said.

"Which half would that be?" Finnen asked. "It wouldn't be the part that holds your brain. You ain't got one."

Not now. Not with the noise in my head.

"Shut the fuck up!" I yelled, angry at everyone, including Khkulay—or whatever her name was. "Tell me what's been happening." I looked at Ms. Masari. "Especially with her."

Dunne was in the front row of seats, not enjoying the show.

"First," Dunne said. "I want to know what went down with Dostum. That'll have a bearing on what I tell you."

"Had ta shoot him meself," Finnen said. "Double-oh-seven there was actin' like Father Murphy in the confessional."

Dunne paid no attention to Finnen, continuing to stare at me.

"What did Dostum say?" Dunne asked.

"Not Hail Marys or Our Fathers," Finnen said. "Personally, I wasn't payin' too much attention since I was takin' care of the little lass the bastard had just raped." He lifted his glass toward the nearly comatose girl. "At least that was until Dostum said I was his mate."

Washington's mouth opened and immediately curled into an "I'll be goddamned" smile. He was getting confirmation in his belief of native spook sleaze. I just turned my head to the ceiling, afraid I might shoot someone if I looked him—or her—in the eye.

"Dostum told us Karzai knows about the dope but no direct participation," Finnen said. "Karzai isn't acquainted with Wintershall or Schultz. Dostum claimed nobody in power wants us to leave. Too much money to be made. Nothing about oil, since the Afghans don't have any except to allow transport. Dostum was thick with the Taliban, making sure they're strong enough to continue the war and keep the aid dollars flowing. That's what he said before I shot him right after he blabbed to Morgan about me. Nothing we didn't already know."

Dunne looked at Washington. "What did you hear?"

Surprised by the switch of focus, Washington almost choked on his beer.

"Nuthin'," Washington spluttered. "They made me stay outside and guard the door. I think they were afraid I might see some of the spook voodoo. I missed the party. Of course, they made the house darky carry the girl. That be me." He took another long drink and let out a long "aaah," mimicking Finnen's best.

"Before we go any further," Dunne said, "I want you all to know something. About the Russian Girl's web page." He was talking about the "gotcha" back on the base. "That's an encrypted Top Secret site. You shouldn't be talking about it to anyone around Langley."

Finnen and Washington couldn't stop the grins from wrinkling their faces.

"Oh, the one that comes with the wet Kleenex?" Finnen asked.

"Does the laundry service include stain removal?" Washington asked.

"If we call, will you answer on the bone-a-phone?" Finnen asked. The litany began.

"Is it assault with a friendly weapon?"

"Burpin' the worm?"

"Shakin' hands with the guvnor?"

"Custard's Last Stand?"

"Enough," I said. "I don't give a shit about Dunne's sexual orientation. Or porn-site preferences. I want to know the whole story. And if you were willing to sacrifice Washington and me. And who is she?" I said, pointing at Ms. Masari.

Silence.

Khkulay, aka Ms. Masari, stood and stepped to the bar. She went back to her seat after refreshing her orange juice. She was stunning in tight jeans and a white blouse that highlighted her dark, smooth skin. On the way, she had bent over to check on the girl, putting a blanket from the overhead on top of the young one's pajamas and adjusting her seat belt.

The plane began to taxi. Everyone but Khkulay disregarded the instruction to fasten their seat belts.

"How long has Ms. Masari been working for you?" I asked, watching Dunne finish whatever it was he was drinking.

The only thing missing in Dunne's appearance was the laptop appendage. He looked more comfortable than usual, sprawled in the leather chair with his shirt unbuttoned down to the middle of his chest. But he was watching me, taking note that I still hadn't unloaded my weapons.

"Not long," Dunne said. "Never, in fact. She was on a death list we found on a Taliban cell leader. The story she told you was true. Her parents were killed by the Taliban. A few weeks ago in Jalalabad. One of our assets found her in the market and told me she might be valuable in providing background and analysis. It took us a while to check on her. Finnen knew most of the plan, but not her. She didn't even know your real MOS. Of course, Ms. Masari understands the Taliban better than any of us. We had her stay at her house until it was safe to get her out and she was cleared. The scene at the market gave me the chance to do that. And to get the savior fluids running in you so we'd have lots of opportunity to explain how you messed up the mission. If you did."

There was no way I could bring myself to thinking of Khkulay as new Agent Masari. She was still the girl Finnen and I had rescued. She wasn't smiling or smirking when I looked at her.

"Is that right?" I asked Khkulay.

She bowed her head and said, "Yes, Morgan."

"And did you know I wasn't an accountant?"

"No. I'm still not really sure, but I have seen what you *can* do. No one would tell me anything about you except in whispers."

"There was a need for all the drama?" I asked.

It was Dunne's turn. He bent forward in his seat.

"Distraction," Dunne said. "We wanted to make sure you had something else to think about when you were out hunting intel and targets. You've been getting a little confused lately about your job, and this operation was too important for you to have doubts. I knew you would want the mission over so you could get back to being Prince Valiant."

Dunne shook his head from side to side, while I marveled at the complexity the Company could design.

"You proved it," Dunne said. "You're getting sloppy. The men we hired to act like Taliban took the wrong truck. You should have noticed the government decal and been suspicious. And the man with the floppy army hat? No Taliban would ride around in a pickup designated like that or wear part of an Afghan army uniform. It just showed me you were diverted by a helpless, beautiful face and would go along with things just so you could see her again."

"Sounds like a lot of work to me," I said. "And it was all to keep me from asking questions? You're full of shit, Dunne. There was more to it than that."

That ugly white-toothed smile. Dunne looked like Ted Bundy when he grinned.

"Good news and bad," Dunne said. "If you'll just sit down after you stow your gear, I'll tell all. The plane's about to lift off, and I don't want you to hurt yourself if you fall."

The plane was turning, about to reach the end of the runway. Overhead lights flickered as the pilot completed his pre-flight check.

Massacre them all. Purge the demons, and replace the memory with the bodies of bleeding Company assets. And innocents like Khkulay and Washington. A certain death sentence for me.

Then, it clicked. I had been used and deceived. Exactly what I signed on for and nothing less than I should expect. Maybe there'd come a time for settlement, but it wasn't now. I quickly unpacked and took a seat as the Gulfstream began to speed toward the dark sky. Dunne's distraction was still working, and I was sitting right across the aisle from her.

With our backs pressed against leather, we didn't speak. Inside my head, I was slapping myself. Whether Khkulay was involved didn't mean she had betrayed me. It was all my fantasy. Not hers. The Company had never been shy about using women to achieve their goals. Finnen had told me about one of the strategies he had developed while he was in Bosnia. He was trying to find a Serbian genocidal monster named Azbelnek. Intel said Azbelnek and his men liked young girls. The city was full of orphans, and Finnen had no trouble recruiting actors for his plan. He only had to offer the girls a hot meal and a safe place to sleep. The orphanage was raided every few weeks, and many of the hungry children disappeared. Azbelnek was supposedly holed up in a bombed-out apartment complex in Sarajevo. The operation was a variation on the "honey trap" plots. Finnen called it a "kiddy trap." From his hidden position across the street in another crumbling building, Finnen and his Croatian squad watched the shawled girls stumble down the cratered street in front of Azbelnek's hideout. He had instructed the children to act disoriented and lost. He gave them Mars bars to seal the deal, promising more if they did what he asked. Slowly, the girls moved across the open space. Within minutes, three armed men came out of the collapsing apartment. They were dead before they reached the girls, who hid behind a crumbling wall as Finnen had told them to do. Azbelnek took longer to die, and the Croats hung his body from what was left of the third-floor wall with a sign that read "Baby Raper" in Bosnian. As far as I could tell, nothing like that had been done with or to Khkulay by the Company. And it wasn't her fault whatever tricks had been used and the reasons why.

Eyes raised to the cloth-covered ceiling, Finnen appeared to have found Shangri-La. He was slouched in his unbuckled seat and wasn't any longer confining himself by the use of one of the crystal glasses. The bottle of Bushmills was in his hand and a leprechaun smile on his face.

During the months of my tour, Finnen was the closest thing to a friend I had made. Dunne was all business, and Washington was only just found. I knew Finnen hated the Taliban, and his opinion wasn't based on Company policy. While he may have helped Dunne devise the scheme, I would still trust Finnen with my life. If we had been discovered inside Dostum's castle, Finnen would have died, too. The rest of the tricks were just noise.

The question remained why Dunne felt the need for "distraction" and if he was setting me up to take the responsibility for any failure. I believed I knew the answer, but I wanted Dunne's confession.

The plane was reaching cruising altitude, and everyone seemed lost in their visions of the rock pile we had just left. Or dreams of other times and places. I cleared my throat and watched Dunne sip from his drink.

"What's the good news?" I asked Dunne.

Dunne looked at me and raised his glass.

"You're the best field agent I've ever met," Dunne said.

Finnen gagged.

"And meself?" Finnen asked. "I suppose I'm just a lump'a Newcastle coal?'

"It's not always just about you, Finnen," Dunne said. "You're good, too, but you're a drunk and a philanderer."

"Cheers, mate," Finnen said, toasting Dunne with his drink, a huge grin on his face. "I accept the compliment."

"Morgan has shown his expertise in interrogation, disinformation, and combat. He's never failed one mission," Dunne said, glaring at Finnen.

"The bad news, Morgan, is you're developing a conscience," Dunne said. "That's a dangerous load to carry in your job. And you have this romantic view of the world. The mission was too important for guilt or self-examination to slow you down. I figured with your mind set on saving the girl, you'd do most anything it took to see her again. And if you blundered, I had two excuses. Salvation and an unpatriotic morality."

"And what was the mission?" I asked.

"Exactly what I told you," Dunne said. "The only disinformation was the level of Company involvement. And, of course, Ms. Masari, in a small way. We knew Dostum was a drug lord, but he was keeping the North relatively peaceful and under his control. He was giving us enough intel that we were stopping most of the arms deliveries to the Taliban. And the money was traceable to the weapons dealers who were permanently sanctioned when we could get to them. It was 'need to know' and I felt, with Khkulay in the mix and your suspicions about CIA connections, you'd have to follow it out. Meant the same result for me."

"And if we failed?" I asked.

Something new. Dunne actually turned away, his teeth covered in a grimace.

"There was a stringer from the *Financial Times* snooping around Qalat," Dunne said. "He was hot on the oil trail after the reporter from the *Wall Street Journal* was killed. We had the story ready to feed him. You were a pissed-off soldier who was getting revenge for a drug deal gone wrong. All the legend was in place. We'd just have to show him your body. That would be the public story. The Company would have its own. But I knew it wouldn't ever get that far. As I said, you're too good. If you got caught somewhere along the line before the hit on Dostum, both you and Washington, you wouldn't know much."

"You were gonna have us killed?"

"If you failed, we wouldn't have had to. You'd be dead already."

"Why now? If Dostum was so valuable, why kill him?"

"Dostum and Schultz were murdering innocent soldiers. It was just a few days 'til the stringer found out and connected the dots. And the Company has a conscience too. Sometimes. Dostum was losing control of the North and acting crazier. He was a psychopath and becoming uncooperative."

"Wintershall?"

"The Trans-Afghan pipeline is important to stability in the region. A benefit for all concerned and meets many of the United States's strategic objectives. Wintershall was willing to take the gamble on building it. No one else was. Wintershall over-extended themselves, and Dostum knew it. He contacted Schultz, not us. We didn't stop them."

"Were you running Abernathy?"

"No. He was Dostum's man."

"What's going to happen with Abernathy?"

"He'll be dishonorably discharged soon, and he'll find the Cayman account empty. His wife will be a single mom soon, after she's seen the pictures Langley's sending her. Abernathy's gonna find it rough to get a job."

"You're letting him off easy."

"You know we don't shoot American citizens. We'll just ruin his life."

Everyone in the cabin seemed to be quietly processing what Dunne had revealed. Washington couldn't stop shaking his head and beaming.

"Did you create Washington, too?"

"No. He only knows what you do now."

A laugh. Washington sat up and pounded the arm of his seat.

"There it is," Washington said. "Can't trust the black man. I was waitin' for that. Shoulda never saved your honkey white ass."

"Me, too," Finnen said. "Morgan doesn't think much of the Irish either."

The plane made a slight dip, and the rolling in my stomach increased further. I looked at Khkulay.

"Why is she here?" I asked.

"During the time you were in the field," Dunne said, "I questioned her. It quickly became obvious she would be a great asset for analysis. With her language skills and history, Langley agreed. She won't have any trouble getting a green card. Afghans with her background are hard to find."

"She didn't know anything about this?" I asked.

"Not most of it," Dunne said. "Not until now. She had no reason to believe you were anything but a knight in shining armor. All she knew was that we'd be coming to extract her at the time we did and to look out the window when she heard the Taliban loudspeaker. I had a rough time explaining to my Afghan Army contacts how to do it and why to go to the trouble of saving a girl. They almost got it right."

Wheels within wheels. So many tricks, the Company continued to deceive even itself in the confusion and get lost in the mirrors.

Surrender. I wasn't going to change the way the world worked. Or the Company. I sighed and sat back in my seat.

It would take a long time to digest everything we had done. I couldn't change anything now, and it was another step away from Kansas. But there was still Khkulay.

On the plane, there were two young females I had helped set free, even if one had been orchestrated by Dunne. Nobody else knew about the third: that girl's eyes were what drove me to Khkulay, and I couldn't block the scene, no matter how hard I tried to keep the vision of her face away or redeem myself. I never knew her name, but his was Kazim Allmahar. He was a captain in the Afghan intelligence service and a double agent for the Taliban. Allmahar had leaked information to the Taliban about Mehtar Lam, the secret control for many of the operations taking place in the North. Lam had been beheaded and his skull paraded through Jalalabad on the end of a sharpened shovel with a sign dangling below that read "American Puppet." My assignment was to kill Allmahar while he slept in his fourth-floor condo and leave no traces that would disturb the delicate relationship between the Afghan intelligence branch and the CIA. I had been dressed as an Afghan in sandals, turban, loose tunic, vest, and beard. If I was seen, no one would recognize me as anything other than a local.

Apartment buildings were one of my toughest challenges. Too many people and the constant threat of an insomniac roaming the corridors or stairwells. Few escape routes and no place to hide in narrow hallways. Even at 4:00 a.m., the assassin's hour, the wrong door could open. But I had made it inside Allmahar's apartment without being seen.

The smell of laundry, cigarettes, and the evening's curry. Rugs on the walls in the dim light seeping from the small-balcony glass door. A tiny living room with a passageway leading down a hall. Dishes drying in a sink to the left next to a humming refrigerator. No toys or crayoned pictures. Nothing to indicate the presence of children. My eyes were adjusted to the darkness, even though it was still hard to see through the blackness of the hallway. Halfway in, a door creaked and a figure the size of a man with two heads stepped out. As soon as he looked in my direction, I would be spotted. I fired the silenced Hush Puppy. Something fell to the floor, but it wasn't the man. As I moved forward, my target looked toward the floor, and his mouth opened, prepared to scream. I shot him in the heart. When I checked his body, I found her beneath him. Dead. A hole between her blue eyes. Eyes I could never forget. She couldn't have been older than five. In seconds, a woman rushed out of the bedroom and wailed; she slumped on top of the bodies and never even looked at me. I stood and ran out.

No one asked about collateral damage. No one cared but me. Not even Finnen had heard the story. It was my private nightmare. Allmahar was permanently benched from the war on terrorism, and that was all that mattered to my masters. At night, I justified the murders by reviewing the picture of Lam's head paraded through Jalalabad and tried to excuse my mistake with that image. And the burning Towers. The guiltless had died there, too. A second meant eternity, especially when I hadn't waited one more to make sure I wasn't shooting an innocent just to save my life. Back in

Langley, my scars would be fodder for the Company shrinks, but the second I saw her, I knew nothing would keep me from saving Khkulay.

For now, this was all too much to digest. I'd have to push it to the back of my head and wait for a calmer moment to decipher everything I'd learned. I couldn't go pointing fingers now; not without truly understanding what had happened and why I was part of it. An hour later, resigned to history, I decided to distract myself and find out more about the woman who had so obviously steered my thoughts over the last few days.

The leather chairs swiveled to the aisle. I turned toward Khkulay across the narrow space, doing my best to drown out the bickering of Washington and Finnen.

No matter how much I craved to talk and get to know more about her, I understood she was in a completely alien universe, even if she was now Company talent. While she tried to listen to the banter, she was also inspecting the cabin. It was likely the plushest room she'd ever been in or seen outside television.

To me, it was a replica of the one we'd flown from Frankfurt. Only the color scheme had changed. This Gulfstream was darker and had more wood wainscoting. The passenger cabin was bigger, and so was the bar, to Finnen's delight. The seats were fractionally softer and were heated. As we cruised over the mountains, I asked Khkulay if I could get her a blanket. She shook her head no and tried to look out the window. Dawn was just breaking over the Himalayas, and the hills were spectacular in the orange glow.

Finnen and Washington had changed topics from macho threats to the blues. Dunne was asleep.

"If you don't think Van Morrison can out sing, out play, and out write any of those boys from the Delta, you haven't listened," Finnen said.

"I admit, for a white boy born in Belfast," Washington said, "he sure learned well. But where'd he get his style? Blind Willie Johnson? Howlin' Wolf? You name 'em, and Van stole somethin' from each of 'em."

"Now, now, Washington," Finnen said. "Don't be blasphemin' my God Van. I'll have to break this bottle of Jameson's over your thick skull. The waste of good whiskey would truly take me to the depths of despair."

Khkulay had a puzzled look on her face.

"I truly don't understand those two," she said. "They switch from one thing to the next and are always threatening to kill each other."

"Male bonding," I said. "Maybe, in your country, the men share a hookah and reminisce about throwing out the Russians. With American men, there's always a need to posture."

"Posture? What does that mean?"

Finnen turned toward us, his third glass nearly dry.

"I heard that, Morgan," Finnen said. "I'm choosin' to ignore it because there're more important things to talk about than doubts of your masculinity. Who's the better blues man? Robert Johnson or Van Morrison?"

Words unspoken. None of the four men in the cabin would directly admit how sharing the immediate threat of death forged remarkably strong ties and feelings. It also meant we broadcast on the same wavelength. Another old cliché: the best friend you'll ever have is the one next to you in the foxhole. Soldiers talked about it all the time. And mourned the loss. The haunting scenes of horror weren't the only ones that brought tremors at the Vietnam Memorial. It was the memory of comrades who walked the same bush patrols and manned the firebases together. Washington and Finnen had gone through the fire beside each other. No insult would ever let them lose sight of the journey.

Not bothering to answer Finnen's question, I watched Khkulay shift in her chair, placing her hands in her lap.

"Don't mean nuthin'," I said. "If the American culture allowed them to hug, they would. They were born to the belief the toughest and meanest win. Then trained to be killers. Any sign of weakness is considered dangerous. Love is a mine field they're not prepared to cross, and they're not equipped to show it to each other."

"There's a song runnin' through my head," Finnen said. "Can't get it out."

"What might that be?" Washington asked, taking the cue.

"Something like this," Finnen said, humming to get the right note so he could begin. "From my man Van. It's all about 'warm love.'"

"Stop," I said.

He stopped, winding down by humming a few more bars.

"Couldn't help it," Finnen said. "I can feel the love flowin' through the plane, and I just get carried away."

"Barry White for me," Washington said. He cleared his throat and started the words to "Can't Get Enough of Your Love." His voice was much better than Finnen's, a deep bass almost matching White's. This time I let the whole first verse finish before I told him to halt.

"I think you three like to tease more than anything," Khkulay said. "I don't understand most of it, but that seems to be what you're doing. Do you ever get serious?"

Silence. I knew what was going through all our heads. To us, serious was the same as dead. Better to go there only when necessary.

Finnen stood and walked to the bar. Washington watched Kashmir pass out the window. Khkulay quietly scanned our faces, probably sensing she had thrown a grenade into the nest.

I leaned toward her and touched her arm.

"Khkulay," I said. "All of us work for the United States Central Intelligence Agency. It's where I hope your job will be. Washington is a new recruit, but Finnen, Dunne, and I have been in the field for the Agency for what feels like forever. I can't tell you exactly what we do, but you've heard much of it. Now, you're an agent too."

She smiled and reached to touch my arm.

"Every American in my country is a spy," Khkulay said. "The Taliban tell us that every day. Do you think I'm getting cold feet, as you say in America?"

Finnen was back to his chair, his glass refilled.

"Jaysus, Morgan," Finnen said. "Now we have to kill her."

Khkulay's eyes popped open wide, and she studied Finnen as he laughed.

"Sorry, mum," he said. "Just tryin' to get serious. Didn't mean it."

I put my hand on Khkulay's armrest.

"We have many hours left before we reach the States," I said. "Why don't you get some rest? When you wake up, you can ask me anything you want to know about your new country."

"Do you think I will ever lead a normal life?" Khkulay asked.

"Of course," I said. I leaned forward and whispered. "But stay away from the Finnen's of the world. They're poison."

She nodded and laid her head back, closing her eyes. I did the same. Finnen and Washington resumed their grousing, but more quietly, while the young girl continued to sleep and dream like Dunne.

I had spent more than a year in Afghanistan. This trip back to the States wasn't just about leaving with Khkulay; it was time to go home before I completely morphed into someone I didn't know. Although still a patriot, the more I experienced here, the less I was a believer in the potential success of Operation Enduring Freedom. Unfortunately, I hadn't been a normal soldier taking orders and doing mostly the same boring thing every day, spiced with a few moments of terror. Employment with the Company meant fresh adventures all the time. Deadly ones, always with the potential for betrayal. I wasn't the beat cop who never fired his gun. Mine was in use most days. Even if I had resolved not to assassinate any more innocents or dogs, there was the continual risk of collateral damage. We had saved the girl from Dostum and rescued Khkulay. The heroin, oil, and Taliban matrix was well beyond my comprehension. The global answers eluded me. What I did know was that some extremely bad guys had been terminally sanctioned by my hands. Many more than the guiltless. The several thousand dollars waiting for me at Kansas National Bank had nothing to do with anything except a few nights out in nice restaurants. Or a trip to Disney World. I wasn't a bounty hunter. I was a paid CIA assassin and, one way or the other, I had to live with it, putting all the brain chatter to sleep. Trust was not something remaining in my genetic code. It had been purged by years of Company propaganda. Now, I no longer even trusted my minders. Too much treachery seeped from the halls of Langley and spread its stench around the globe. I hoped things would change when we touched down in The World. And I could simply breathe.

Washington was the first to notice, Finnen and me realizing the change a heartbeat later. Just a subtle shift in the plane's course. A long lazy turn that meant we were now flying toward the sun, opposite of where it had been when I closed my eyes. Khkulay softly snored, a contented smile curving her lips, apparently comfortable being anywhere on the planet other than Kabul. Her contentment was far from the dread swiftly invading my skull. Dunne hadn't budged. The battle camaraderie between Finnen, Washington, and me had given us a group consciousness and singularity that now translated into alarm bells that tolled as one.

"What the fook is happenin', pogues?" Finnen asked, concerned enough to set his glass of single malt on the armrest.

"Seems like we're going back east," Washington said. "Reminds me of that Insane Clown Posse ditty." He lacked only the *chunka, chunka* of a Snoop Dog tune, as he rhymed the words. Washington grinned, his huge set of long white teeth reflecting the light from the windows, and nodded around the cabin. "There are five of us. The pilots gotta be in on the gig, whatever it is."

"Jaysus," Finnen said, "is everything in your noggin a rap song? It seems we're bein' highjacked, and you quote fookin' clowns." He shook his head and picked up the tumbler, draining what was left in one slug.

Surprisingly, Dunne continued to snooze. After a few seconds of watching his chest heave in and out much too quickly for REM sleep, I began to understand. There was no way we were traveling to the USA. The destination was unclear, most likely highly classified, but it was probable Dunne knew something. His brief was to be a shape-shifter, and I could only guess at his motives, knowing full well "Deceit" should have been the "D" of his middle name. Years of my believing he truly cared, freshly supported by his latest actions, now proved the old Company axiom true—"Don't trust anyone, especially another agent."

A Gulfstream in the air wasn't the place for a shootout. If I was quiet and the .22 bullet from my Hush Puppy lodged in Dunne's brain, we might not decompress. A hollow-point slug would undoubtedly expand throughout his brain cavity, bouncing around like a Mexican jumping bean and ruining any chance for his further intellectual growth. It would also likely stay confined in his lying skull, saving us from an airless freefall. I stood swiftly and had the barrel of the pistol on Dunne's earhole before he could open his eyes.

"Only the truth will set you free," I hissed, pressing the Hush Puppy hard into Dunne's ear flap.

Once I'd heard that Viet Cong prisoners often smiled before a grunt lit up the VC's gas-soaked pajamas with a Zippo. The myth was that this portrayed relief over escaping the drudgery and terror of days living underground in rat-, spider-, and snake-infested tunnels that stank of human misery. Awake now, Dunne's smirk must have come from seeing his game was nearly up too. No more lies. No more sending innocents out to die. Peace and eternal rest. I wasn't going to make it a pain-free release. I shoved and twisted the tip of the barrel harder into his lobe, forcing his head against the back of the seat rest.

"Not gonna make it easy for you to join all the others you've had murdered," I said. "At least not with two working legs. I'll start with your knees." I twisted the pistol more firmly, pushing it nearly inside his head. "Where are we going?"

Finnen had taken out his Ka-Bar and was rubbing it on his thigh, a behavior I'd seen countless times when he was bored, anxious, or ready to slice someone from ear to jaw.

"Give this bloke the honor of carvin' him," Finnen said, pointing the knife at his own chest.

"Somebody do it real soon like," Washington said, sitting back and relaxing. "Haven't heard a man scream in, oh, a couple hours."

"Games up, eh, boys?" Dunne said. "I told them you wouldn't go down easy. But you know the cretins back at Langley won't listen. Especially when it means no more promotions." He tried to move his head away from the Hush Puppy that was nearly embedded in his auditory lobe. I didn't let that happen.

"Answer the question now," I said. "None of us cares about the silly intrigues your kind plays at. Unless it concerns our futures."

Dunne only grinned wider.

Never big on patience, even with a bottle of Jameson's circulating in his bloodstream, Finnen bent forward and cut a straight line across Dunne's knee, the blood immediately soaking through his trousers. That brought a quick end to Dunne's arrogance. He tried to reach down and stanch the flow.

"Let it bleed," I said, forcing him against the seat. "You won't die from that wound. The next one, maybe."

"Loved that one," Finnen said. "The Beatles?"

"That was 'Let It Be,' bleedin' eedjit," Washington said, in perfect Belfastese.

Khkulay was watching, not even blinking her dark eyes. I didn't know how long she'd been awake, but she was no stranger to violence. She knew it was dangerous to make any movement or even to hint she objected. The Taliban wrath easily turned to girls just for being there. She'd witnessed their cruelty many times. We weren't part of that stone-age tribe. Still, a knife to the knee might convince her we were descended from Azrael, the Islamic Angel of Death. Maybe one of my endearing smiles would break the mood.

"We're trying to get information," I said, grinning. "And we don't have much time. He's working for men more immoral than the Taliban. The Great Satan, the American government." It wouldn't have surprised me if Khkulay had begun to scream a "Death to the Yankees" slogan. She didn't, continuing to stare at Dunne's seeping wound.

"Sorry, lass," Finnen said, "You can close those eyes. We've got to loosen his tongue." He nodded at Dunne and put the knife on the spook's other knee.

The scent of lavender and expensive leather that had floated through the jet was now replaced by the copper smell of blood and the sour aroma of fear. Dunne wasn't as tough as he required his field operatives to be, and he was sweating through his fatigue shirt, the glistening beads covering his forehead.

Torture. Not a favorite sport. I had often been the perpetrator. And the witness. Too many times to keep my dreams peaceful. Never once did I believe it was unnecessary. We were fighting battles that meant failure equated to death—ours and others. No one I'd tormented was guiltless, usually deserving harsher treatment than I was willing to give. Finnen didn't have quite the same boundaries, having grown up surrounded by The Troubles and its daily cruelties usually made available for the public view. He and his neighbors learned about torture, including hooding and forcing prisoners to stand against a wall in the "search position" for hours, soaked in ice water, until their muscles cramped into one never-ending spasm. And that was the least agonizing.

On this Gulfstream, there wasn't much of a political agenda among the unshackled passengers. We were battling terror, greed, fanaticism, and betrayal. Mostly, it was now about survival. Ours. The Company had passed the limit of allowable tricks and was threatening our existence. Wherever the plane was headed, it wasn't going to be a vacation for us.

Finnen sliced Dunne's other knee.

"Those were baby cuts, sleeveen," Finnen said, obviously unaware of *all* the deceits Dunne had crafted. "Those tendons on the back will be next. A little nip, and you'll not be walking upright agin'."

A gasp, and Dunne's face wrinkled in a grimace.

"Jaslyk," he whispered.

"Shit," Washington said. "No escape from that hell. Besides, they've never seen a black man there except in cartoons." He stretched out his oak-barrel legs. "Oh, I think they may have one darky in the Tashkent zoo."

We'd all heard the rumors. In our business, the destination of renditioned prisoners was top secret. Nonetheless, the myths buzzed through the camps like an electrical storm. Guantanamo was a paradise compared to the bleak evil of this site in a country ruled by a madman, Islam Karimov, a buffoon who forced all citizens to memorize books written by him describing his super-human talents. Jaslyk prison was located in Karakalpakstan, an area of northwestern Uzbekistan and often called The World's Worst Place. Jaslyk was modified to address the growing terrorist threat to the Uzbeks in the late 1990s, mostly holding religious prisoners from the Islamic Movement of Uzbekistan and carried the codename UY 64/71. Remnants of Russian experiments to use and contain chemical warfare weapons could still be seen around the facility. Entrance to Jaslyk was by rail only, and no roads led to the camp through the empty steppe. The most notorious punishment there was boiling prisoners to death, usually after burning over 70 percent of their bodies. No one had been known to survive confinement at Jaslyk. We couldn't let the jet land.

It only took Dunne a few seconds to recover. Finnen hadn't cut him deeply, or the blood would have been seeping into the carpet and Dunne gone into shock. Instead, Dunne tried his best to look unfazed.

"One way or another," Dunne said, "you boys are doomed. I don't know about the girl, but witnesses aren't too popular in the Firm. Make it easy on yourselves, and let us get to Jaslyk. They only want to ask a few simple questions."

"About oil, drugs, terrorism, and murder," I said, "all orchestrated by the CIA? A laid-back interrogation? Just as surely as there really were WMDs in Iraq."

"Where you gonna go?" Dunne asked. "You know they'll find you. No hidey hole will be safe."

"At least it won't be Uzbekistan," Washington said. He looked at me. "We have to make a plan and turn this plane in a new direction. Soon."

"Anybody got a big Band-Aid?" Dunne asked, somehow feeling he had the upper hand.

Finnen slapped Dunne on the thigh and laughed.

"Good one, you rotter," Finnen said. "Don't much care if you bleed out. Now shut your trap."

Outside the window, I could see we were again over the Hindu Kush, this time headed west rather than northeast and toward the shores of America. A few minutes earlier, we'd been above the vast Gobi Desert of Mongolia. In better times, we would be taking in the magic of jagged, seemingly endless peaks. What we saw now meant Dunne was probably telling the truth about our target destination. We had to figure out an alternate and then convince the pilots it was in their best interest to cooperate.

"We have to be conscious of Chinese and Russian air space," Finnen said. "Going south is about the only way to get around a new flight plan. And clearances we won't have, even if the Queen said so."

"Can we make it to Thailand?" Washington asked.

"All the Company jets are ultra-long range," Finnen said. "Gotta be able to skip about without refueling and letting the wrong people know where the passengers will be going for their final holiday. Somewhere around ten thousand kilos."

"Speak English," Washington said. "Not that pansy Brit kilo shit. Miles."

"Oh, I'd reckon about seven thousand in Yank terms."

"That'll get us to Chiang Rai Province," Washington said. "I have connections there and know where there are private landing strips we could use."

"You sure they're trustworthy?"

"Well, I had great faith in my first wife," Washington said, "that was until I caught her with a Colonel who just happened to be my CO. I didn't come to attention like he was, if you know what I mean."

Finnen and I glanced at each other and nodded agreement.

"Now," I said, "it's just a matter of persuading the crew the congee at Cabbages and Condoms in Chiang Rai is worth a side trip."

"They've been listening to every word," Dunne said. "And broadcasting it to one of the ALSAT satellites with a real-time link to Langley." He smirked. "You really think you can get away with it?"

There was a small satchel on the floor, and Finnen had explored the contents earlier. He bent down and took out a roll of gray duct tape, holding it in front of Dunne's face.

"Seems some yob left their tools," Finnen said. "All the gear a professional torturer might be needin', including needle-nose pliers, scalpels, torches, clamps, and syringes, along with other miscellaneous treats. All I need is this," he jiggled the tape by Dunne's head. "To shut that big yap a' yours." He ripped off a piece of the tape and pushed it hard over Dunne's mouth.

"No way those boys up front heard anything," Washington said. "Too much classified bullshit going on back here to allow lowly pilots to listen to secret plans to save the world."

"Yes," I agreed. "We've gotta figure out how to turn them to the good side without the plane exploding in midair. Or arrange a greeting party of Seals on the ground."

Patience wasn't in Washington's nature. He stood and strode to the door of the flight deck. The entry was covered in mahogany wood, and the paneling was polished to a glossy red-brown shine. He didn't bother knocking and kicked directly on the handle—hard. The door flew open, banging against something on the side of the narrow opening.

The doorway's small size prevented us from seeing what Washington did next. His bulk barely allowed him to squeeze through, and his wide load blocked light from the windshield. Within seconds, the Gulfstream lurched, meaning Washington had at least a single pilot in his fielder's glove–proportioned hands. Maybe one flyer in each. He wasn't dumb or wicked enough to kill them. Certainly, he would be explaining the advantages of flying under the radar screens to Chiang Rai. And the disadvantages of taking an alternate course from that designated by Langley. There would be no communication with the ALSAT onto any of the demons at the Firm.

A minute later, the jet slowly altered its path southward. I watched the mountains begin to fade on the horizon and checked that Khkulay was alright. She was and was looking forward to the pilot's cabin, finally showing some emotion, her mouth wide seeing what she could of Washington.

Finnen, Washington, and I spent too much time in each other's heads. Without a vote, we had unanimously decided Washington's plan was the best among few choices, and we had nominated him unsaid to carry out the details, while Finnen and I continued our one-sided chat with Dunne. Questions like radio silence, violating airspace, and keeping from getting shot down would be resolved between Washington and the pilots. I turned my attention back to Dunne just as Finnen hoisted a newly poured glass full of Jameson's to his lips.

"Sooo, we still haven't resolved why we were being escorted to Jaslyk," I said. "Because we made a side trip to Germany and put together a plot that included corruption, heroin, and petroleum? That shouldn't be of much importance to the minders in Virginia. Everyday behavior. What kind of snake pit did we uncover?"

"That reminds me of the old Emerald Isle one," Finnen said. "Why'd St. Pat drive all the snakes out of Ireland?" He looked at Dunne and me, a smile already curling his mouth. "No answers? Well, boy'os, because he couldn't afford airfare."

Absurd. We were on a Company jet trying to flee from the most powerful malevolent entity on the planet. The CIA. Even more depraved than the Papacy. And Finnen was telling nauseating juvenile jokes. Could be his brain was stewed in Scotch, and the wiring was shorting out. He was a realist about douche bags like Dunne and saw the world differently than most warriors. Nothing seemed to shock or surprise him. Finnen believed "the blood of the wicked would flow like a river" if he had a role in the play. It wasn't geopolitics or patriotism that motivated him. It was ridding the land of monsters and villains. As long as he felt his quest was just, and he had enough fuel in his flask, he would continue the good fight, telling his silly gags along the road. A man like Dunne, who had proven he was from the dark side, got little sympathy or compassion from Finnen. He would rather make the CIA officer a paraplegic than let Dunne carry on being a devil if he hadn't been ordered to—and if his whiskey ration hadn't been threatened.

"Don't make Morgan ask again," Finnen said. "This knife does magic on legs."

Finnen ripped the tape off Dunne's face, making our former boss frown with the pain. He spit out a few gummy strands and tried to move forward.

"You already have guessed." Dunne said. "You got a little too close for some people to tolerate. They want to keep their pensions, as well as retire with the suitcases full of cash they've already stowed."

"Names," I said.

"Won't do you any good," Dunne said. "You can't get anywhere close. You'll be hunted down and slaughtered well before you can make it back to Virginia. Or the Hamptons."

"So it's simple," I said. "No intrigue. We were just unfortunate to stumble onto something outside our brief. And now we've been slated for extermination."

"That's about it," Dunne said. "If you would have just done strictly as you were told, you'd still be in the rock pile shooting bad guys and eating Big Macs in the PX."

Ambition. It wasn't what drove me, Washington, or Finnen. Ambition was the siren song of the CIA lifers. I had joined to do something that would make me feel proud, useful, and inspired. The longer I stayed with the Company, the more I realized everyone's personal agenda wasn't the same. I had no thoughts of buying an island and retiring on drug, oil, or arms money. I was an adrenaline junky who believed in angels and fought the eternal battle. Greed wasn't in my portfolio, unlike so many others I met, even though they were often my superiors. I wasn't quite sure if we would throw Dunne out the cabin door over the Bay of Bengal. Or turn him loose to chase us around with the help of unlimited funding and technology. We probably needed to vote on this one. I already knew Finnen's choice. Slow, agonizing death. Washington was a wild card.

The young girl from Dostum's bed still slept in the land of narcotic dreams, but there was the problem of Khkulay. She was taking it all in, her body remaining tight and tense. Whether she could understand was another issue. I would find a safe haven for her, in Thailand or somewhere else. She was not going back to Afghanistan to be blinded and raped by the Taliban. I had never been married or had children, but I felt as responsible for Khkulay as any parent.

It was quiet in the cockpit. Washington must have been his most convincing. If he was hovering over me with those bowling-ball biceps and chilling smile, I'd do what he said too, if only on the off chance he might spare me from being crushed in his grip.

The atmosphere in back had become less stressed. While I thought of possible futures, Finnen was off dreaming of swimming in casks of fourteen-year-old Scotch, the Jameson's warming in his fist. Dunne grimaced, the bleeding now over and the pain overcoming shock. Khkulay gaped around the cabin, mostly watching Dunne squirm. I decided to go forward and check on Washington to hear what plans he'd made to get us to Chiang Rai. It was almost two thousand miles on a deadhead from where we were now to northern Thailand. And we would have to stay out of Chinese airspace, filing phony flight plans with other governments if needed, all the time trying to avoid CIA detection. There wouldn't be any orthodox path for this journey, since we'd be ducking several air forces on route. From looking out the windows, I could see we were barely past the Hindu Kush and flying at low elevation to stay off the screens. It was forest and rivers below, splendors I couldn't appreciate in the moment.

"Keep an eye on the prisoner," I said. "We wouldn't want him to escape."

"I hope he tries," Finnen said. "We're short parachutes."

Washington was standing behind the pilots, a hand on the back of each man's chair, his feet braced against the side compartments. He was monitoring the instrument panels and listening to the radio on the co-pilot's headphones. No one was speaking.

"Got it all figured?" I asked.

Without turning, Washington said, "If we make it past the 'stan countries, through Pakistan, across India, and then over Burma and a few other dots on the map, we could just squeak into Thailand. We're trying." He patted each pilot's shoulder. "These boys know if we get shot down, they're as cooked as the rest of us. I think they'll do their darnedest. If not, I told them the story of how I strangled those hadjis outside Jalalabad."

The next few hours were spent watching out the wind screen and listening to Washington hum Al Green tunes in his deep bass voice. He seemed to be having fun, especially when he purred "How Can You Mend a Broken Heart." Earlier, I'd brought him a crate from the back to sit on. The wooden box previously held a supply of Heckler and Koch G3 5.56mm semi-auto rifles and clips of ammunition. There was more to the arsenal in the pantry, including pistols, grenades, helmets, and flak jackets. It appeared the CIA was ready for a shootout no matter whether they landed in the Korengal or San Francisco.

Eventually, I tired of Al Green and went back to the main cabin, where Finnen was totally polluted and serenading Dunne with quotes from William Butler Yeats, the famous fellow Irishman. Now, it was "The Drinking Song," Finnen's favorite. He was reciting in his sing-song voice full of blarney—

"WINE comes in at the mouth
And love comes in at the eye;
That's all we shall know for truth
Before we grow old and die.
I lift the glass to my mouth,
I look at you, and I sigh."

Dunne wasn't impressed, but the melody and words made Khkulay beam.

We'd been flying for several hours at just above the jungle canopy, skirting restricted areas as best as the pilots could manage. With radio silence now in effect, we had no idea if the plane was being tracked. It would be surprising if it wasn't. There was no need to descend more than a few hundred feet for landing, and I guessed we were getting close to the private Thai airfield Washington had suggested.

After giving Finnen a moment to recover from his moving delivery by draining the Jameson's, I motioned him to the pantry. We organized the weapons as logically as possible, aware that, if we were attacked, we'd be completely outnumbered and under-equipped. And probably dead. I stuck the Hush Puppy under my belt, ammo clips and grenades in my pockets, shouldering the H & K, and took a rifle and Sig Sauer P226 to Washington, setting them down just behind him. I returned to my seat, not bothering to buckle up.

As the Gulfstream got closer to the jungle floor, the plane started to sharply plunge and turn. Washington had warned me we would be taking evasive actions, even if we weren't being tailed by anything specific.

"Wooo . . ." Finnen moaned, grabbing the armrest of his padded chair. "Feels like that night I spent in the Guinness Brewery after I got locked in. It was an accident, surely." He groaned louder. "Found meself on the floor, but I thought I was in the middle of the ocean in a typhoon."

Khkulay was losing color in her face, turning the white of Taliban turbans in her province. The dipping of the jet must have felt like riding an angry donkey with a fire ant in its ear.

From the cockpit, Washington shouted, "Hold tight, amigos! We're landing shortly, and it could be a rough one."

Now that he'd quit losing blood, Dunne was more relaxed, except when the Gulfstream lurched hard and the pain made him scowl. I figured he believed there would be a rescue squad of Special Ops soldiers waiting. Could be, but he wasn't going to survive the attack if they were our greeting party.

The cabin began to smell more of sweat and fear. There was even a hint of sick drifting from Finnen. It seemed the turbulence had broken through the Jameson's haze and caused his stomach to spasm and release toxins.

Jungle green gleamed and sparkled out the window, the result of an afternoon monsoon that had dropped its daily torrent of rain. The sky was the dull gray of Southeast Asia, unbroken by any blue, a few dark clouds on the horizon. Below, we passed over a river, and I knew we were in the Golden Triangle, home to some of the fiercest drug dealers and warlords in the world outside of Afghanistan or Mexico. Here, the soldiers didn't stop at decapitation. They cut enemies into little pieces and fed them to the crocs. Or just threw the whole living body into the pen and laughed as the beasts thrashed around, eating.

Recent events had made us hunted men by powerful foes with unlimited budgets. I wasn't too naïve to grasp that evil infected every level of the human species, particularly heinous among those who purported to be our political and moral leaders. For a period a few years back, I'd been mesmerized studying the depth of lies and ruthless depravity that had surrounded decision-making old men during the Vietnam War and had paid great interest in the fiend Henry Kissinger, a man who didn't deserve to still walk the earth with his slicked-back greasy hair. It was decrepit old villains who couldn't fight their way out of a wet paper bag who sent healthy innocent young men out to die for the sake of ego and dollars, all in the bogus claim of patriotism. And Finnen, Washington, and I were, again, part of some veiled conspiracy that would only mean our bloody demise. Too many times I'd excused my behavior with the misguided justification I was "just following orders." Not again. Not when we were being trailed and slated for extermination and had done nothing worse than uncover a nest of snakes. I held tightly to the seat, wondering if this would be my last landing.

The plane bounced hard, and the pilot hit the brakes, not allowing much of a roll-out. A few feet away, the jungle seemed to be about to start devouring us. No buildings or people were in sight. The engines quieted, and Finnen pushed open the cabin door, letting in the sound of an angry jungle. Rotting vegetation stench and the ever-present smoky smell of the third world drifted into the room, almost making me retch. Khkulay put her hand over her mouth, and her eyes became watery. Dunne was on high alert, his injured legs bouncing in expectation of imminent freedom.

From the cockpit, Washington shoved the two pilots into the main cabin and told them to sit in the seats vacated by Finnen and me. He quickly tied them down with plastic restraints and joined us by the door. All of us had our rifles pointed out. We scanned the runway and dense canopy for armed men.

Nothing. No SEALs, monkeys, elephants, or rice farmers. Too quiet. The jungle noise had ceased, and the only sound was rainwater dripping onto the decaying ground. Something was making the insects and animals hush. There was no way we could see into the thick forest. A battalion might be out there, and we wouldn't see them. Quite different from Afghanistan, where the bleak, empty landscape and crystalline sky usually allowed a few klicks of clear, unobstructed vision.

From behind, Dunne began to laugh.

"Gonna shit yourselves?" he asked. "That's good. Then you won't do it in your death rattle. I always thought that was disgusting. And unmanly."

Without a sound and a movement too quick to register, Finnen threw his knife, the blade settling deep into Dunne's upper arm.

"If you say a word or make any noise, arsehole," Finnen hissed, "I'll pull out that knife and stick it between your legs where your tiny willy hangs."

Dunne slumped back, no longer so enthusiastic.

Not bothering to put down the staircase, Washington jumped and rolled when he hit the dirt, never taking his eyes off the bush. Finnen followed, while I stayed onboard, searching for bogies in the tree line. There was no strategizing. We were highly trained and had been in enough firefights together and individually. We knew what to do. If there were bad guys, we'd find out soon enough and take whatever cover we could.

The plane may have had GPS tracking installed. In fact, it surely did. Taking the evasive route we flew meant it would take a little time to scramble troops to annihilate us if they knew our present location, and even the CIA would be reluctant to enter friendly airspace with Predator Drones to blow us into rice kernels. I motioned for Khkulay to follow me, glancing briefly at Dunne and the pilots who were all snugged tight to their seats.

A slight tremor vibrated from Khkulay's hand when she touched my back to keep from fainting, and her black eyes bulged like she had Graves Disease. The young girl didn't notice, drool leaking from her mouth, her eyes closed, and her drugged stupor still evident.

"Stay behind me," I said. "We're gonna jump. I'll help you from the ground."

No more than ten feet to soft soil. Not a problem for a young woman like Khkulay, and I'd done a lot of these kinds of leaps at Camp Peary, aka, The Farm. I went first, immediately turning to Khkulay and motioning her down. No hesitation. She tucked and rolled as if she'd been a combat classmate back in The World.

The firing started seconds after impact. From the sound, the bullets came from AK47s with their muffled, dull *rat-a-tat*. We could see the riflemen behind several banyan trees, and it didn't look as though there were more than a few. By the way the slugs missed us, it was apparent these were not coming from America's strong and brave. More likely, they were a band of hastily assembled locals who had little experience other than murdering unarmed peasants. We took our time and picked them off one by one, a couple survivors disappearing into the bush, one helping a wounded buddy who'd been shot in the leg.

As usual, the mad minute lasted about that long, though it felt like hours and was nothing anyone really got comfortable with. A few seconds of insanity, noise, and terror, followed by almost unbearable silence. I grabbed Khkulay and pushed her toward a small hut I'd noticed a hundred yards away. Finnen and Washington followed, walking backward and protecting the flanks.

There was no discussion about what to do with Dunne and the pilots. Or the blacked-out girl. We weren't murderers and had never intended to kill any of them unless that was the only option. Finnen did shoot out the Gulfstream's tires, though. And Washington had disabled the radios earlier. The worst for the prisoners would be a few mosquito bites until someone came to the rescue. I didn't care if that was drug thugs who might slaughter them for sport or CIA agents ordered to quiet the man. I was admittedly worried about the girl, but didn't believe she would come to any harm worse than what she faced with Dostum—though I did hope a fate better than that was in store for her.

In the thatched hut, I stood next to Washington. The only things in the space were a few rickety chairs, empty Chang beer bottles, and pictures of topless white women on the walls. It was stuffy and airless, smelling of grease and shit. The thin walls wouldn't provide any barrier to rifle shots. Or even blowguns. We had to get out soon.

"Where's the liberating army?" I asked. "Is this another SNAFU? Or did you forget to make the call?"

Washington grinned, never taking his eyes off the surrounding jungle.

"Don't piss yourself, Morgan," he said. "It already stinks in here."

"Then what's next, genius?"

"I'll just bet you the next sound heard will be a Huey. One of those left behind when the Army scampered out of 'Nam."

"The next sound I hear will be a runny fart," Finnen said from the other side of Washington. "I'm still sufferin' from that landing and some bad whiskey. If there ever was such a thing."

Washington ignored Finnen for probably the thousandth time. Today.

"Those old helicopters are popular with the Chin Haw gangs who now dominate the Triangle," Washington said. "Their clan is of Chinese descent and has taken over much of the opium trade coming out of Burma, Laos, and Thailand. I've had some small history with Ma Hseuh-fu, the billionaire lord."

"How'd you contact them?" I asked. "And how do you know the Fu guy?"

"Ever heard of a cell phone?" Washington said, taking his phone out of his pocket and holding it up. "You push this little button here. Then this one. And, shockingly, I've got Fu on the line." He put the phone away. "As for how I found his number, that's for another time. Unless you want to beat me again, I'm not telling. And probably not then, either."

Washington was spot on, as Finnen would say. The chopper landed, and we raced outside. Two fearsome Chinese men dressed in black helped us inside. The Huey lifted off straight away, and we headed north toward Burma.

The flight wasn't very long, and, in a darkening sky, we landed in a jungle fortress complete with enough generators to light a small city. Our hosts were there to welcome us, and we were ushered inside a luxurious teak house with decks completely encircling the building and massive thatch roof. We were made comfortable and given ice-cold mango juice and cold washcloths to refresh. It must have been Washington's past that was providing the luxury. Another mystery I couldn't grasp, though I hoped it wasn't a CIA intrigue, one among many that would keep me awake in the next few months.

Over the following two days, we tried to plan the next moves, knowing full well there would be a bounty on our heads and an international manhunt orchestrated by the Company. The search would be kept out of the eye of the media, publicity always the enemy of the Company.

Eventually, we agreed there was no way we could hide from the CIA. None of us were the kind of agents who had false identities and money stashed around the world. We'd been soldiers in war zones, not spies. But we also couldn't stand and fight. That was ludicrous. One sortie from a Drone, and we were charcoal. We would have to use the intel we already possessed to broker a deal. And no one was better at tough negotiations than a Chinese drug lord. Fu would be our advocate. It came with a price. And her name was Khkulay.

The Chin Haws were Muslims and Fu was a fanatic. He'd been surprised and upset when we arrived with a girl. There was no way he wanted her to stay with infidels unescorted. If we didn't make the deal, he'd likely take her from us anyway. Fu promised to protect Khkulay and raise her like she was another daughter. It took hours of argument, primarily from me, but it was finally settled we would leave Khkulay with Fu. While she eventually agreed, it was difficult for Khkulay to envision a future here, even if it meant she might still, someday, arrive inAmerica.

And then there was the past. The CIA had been in bed with Southeast Asian warlords for decades. Much money had been made through the relationship, both for the Company and the heroin traffickers. And the men in Langley who supervised. Fu doubtless had the number of the director of the Central Intelligence Agency on his speed dial.

When our bickering stopped, I was able to spend a few moments alone with Khkulay. She was understandably reluctant to stay with men she didn't know in a green tropical land that was the complete opposite of the dry rockpile of her ancestry. But she knew she had escaped certain death and was thankful for the rescue. Against all her upbringing, we briefly hugged, and I felt like a father sending a daughter off to be married, with promises we would meet again.

Since I'd had the chance to say goodbye to Khkulay, we told Fu to go ahead. My mind still rattled with questions, mostly about Washington. Finnen's brain, on the other hand, fast became seeped in gallons of yadong, the local home brewed alcohol. "Delicious," he would repeat about fifty times an hour, licking his lips.

For now, we were all safe—including Khkulay, as a guest of the why and whatever Washington's influence had produced. We knew the CIA wouldn't bomb their most profitable partner outside of Afghanistan. And we had names and information that could initiate a Congressional investigation leading to imprisonment of many of the top bureaucrats in the Firm.

And so, we would wait.